The House Rules

We Were at War, and At-War with Ourselves
What To Live and Die For Were Fading

*...but the fastest youth in America
showed us Hope...*

Based on the True Story
of Terry Householter, U.S.M.C.

AN HISTORICAL NOVEL
By
CHRIS HAMILTON

THE HOUSE RULES

Dedication		iii
Contents		v
Introduction		vii
Chapter 1	The House Rules	1
Chapter 2	Ageless, Out Here	7
Chapter 3	Against the Storm	11
Chapter 4	Terry, Dog Days, and a Little Revolution	11
Chapter 5	Searchers, Rebels, and Night Skies	35
Chapter 6	Iron Men, the Fabulous Flippers, and Autumn Saturday Nights	47
Chapter 7	Night Moves, Liberation and Mysteries	63
Chapter 8	A Shift in the Winds	81
Chapter 9	The Wheel Spins	91
Chapter 10	Cold Winds Rising	107
Chapter 11	Per Aspera	117
Chapter 12	The Sifter of Souls	129
Chapter 13	A Thousand Years Deep	137
Chapter 14	Long and Winding Roads	149
Chapter 15	Ad Astra Late January, 1967	163
Chapter 16	A Time for Every Purpose	175
Chapter 17	Red Silk Rising…April 1967	185
Chapter 18	Fire and Rain…Two Years Later, April 1969, Vietnam	203
Chapter 19	Miracles in May…Two Years Back, May in Kansas, 1967	217
Chapter 20	Days of Blood and Gold…May 20, 1967, The State Meet, Salina, Kansas	235
Chapter 21	Days of Blood and Bronze…Two Years Later, May & June, 1969, Vietnam	241
Chapter 22	The Sunsets Beyond	251
Epilogue	2008 KU Relays, University of Kansas, Lawrence	257

INTRODUCTION

Some tales tell themselves, and I am lucky this is one of them. The Kansans and high plains people, I am sure, will read this tale with a song that sings "Yes!" in their heart. Others, I trust, will find they are quickly surprised and intrigued.

It is the remarkable, true, two-world story of small-town Kansas Terry Householter, who was America's fastest high school sprinter in 1967, and who served as a decorated Marine hero, fighting in Vietnam alongside his Marine brothers in horrendous battles. It is equally the story of the soul of Kansas, the wonders of the high plains and its peoples, the life found in great dreams and sacrifice, and the valor of Marines in these most trying times.

Perhaps most people know those times burned with painful social revolutions against stark oppressions and lost opportunities, the grave danger of nuclear world annihilation, and America's most agonizing, deadly and controversial modern war. The struggles and carnage of those years gave birth to a new reality of decency and fairness, and yet they left the nation severely torn, even down to today. The novel's true stories and plots always develop these themes, often with humor. But the novel also shows some of the suffering, sacrifice, and courage in those times, of which current generations are too much unaware. The novel seeks to bring those days alive.

Make no mistake, most of those days in Kansas were suffused with beauty, challenge, meaning and amity. But the times were scarred by some old brutal ways, and by terrifying realities coming at us in the gravest dangers of war that can possibly be imagined. A gritty revolution was on, to change some of the worst brutalities and stifled opportunities (especially for girls). Terry, and other valiant souls, played their role in these unseen battles at home, and "over there", to make things better. The changes to our world, relentlessly descending, altered everything. In the despair of those days, Terry showed us hope, and even things greater than that.

This historical novel is based firmly in true stories. All facts and events presented here about track performances and Vietnam are true and accurate. All the accounts of races, times and records set by Terry in his performances on the track in 1967 are accurate, based on participant and eyewitness interviews, newspaper and meet reports. This includes the accounts of the remarkable middle distance athlete Jim Niehouse of Salina, and others in the truly amazing 1967 Kansas High School State Track meet in Salina. Terry was an incredible sprinter, one of the very greatest, and his feats speak for themselves. But Terry was much more than a sprinter.

I interviewed many dozens of people who knew Terry from boyhood to his Marine days. It is their memories which fill in the details of Terry in this novel. It is not an easy thing to faithfully convey the memories and experiences of others. I will save a few of their quotations for the end of this tale.

Grady Rainbow U.S.M.C. of Oklahoma City was a close friend of Terry. Grady's memoirs of the Mike Company of the 5th Marines Regiment/First Marines Division and of the Vietnam War offer great details about their battles and events, and what Terry and his Marine brothers experienced in the winter and spring of 1969. These details were unknown to us back home, for forty long years. The accounts given in this historical novel are drawn and adapted from Grady's unpublished memoirs, and from his gracious personal interviews, and from on-line histories of Mike Company's Marines, from Terry's letters written to home, and on-line official service branch histories of the Vietnam War. The conversations of the Marines may not be exact, but are true to the events that took place, or are direct or approximate quotations, based directly on interview accounts or documentary sources. The events described about Vietnam are accurate as far as I could follow these sources. There can never be enough thanks to you, Grady, for letting us know much of what happened.

The great majority of individuals in the story are their real selves. About seventy percent of the events which are not track performances, describing Concordia, Kansas and its people, and of school-mates and track team-mates are portrayed accurately.

The rest of the events, not about track, which are perhaps thirty percent of the Concordia events or tales in the novel, are closely true to reality, or the character of actual events. These half dozen or so of the stories and figures presented are more fictionalized for good reasons. For instance, in these tales are several composite characters, who are created to represent similar actions of *groups* of people, and do not portray *any* real individuals. These scenes are similar to actual events, but they are altered or entirely invented to tell a story line in a more coherent way, or at the specific request of individuals, or to protect both the mostly innocent and the not quite as innocent.

The experience of track at Concordia High School, and the witnessing of the incredible performances of Terry on the track, and of the teams of Coach Herschel Betts and Bob Baumann, were among the greatest teachers of my life and of countless others. If this story helps pass on the lessons of character and learning to today's young people from the Kansas ways of life, and from the great tradition of Concordia Track, then a small part of the debt owed to those who have come before, especially Terry, will be paid back.

The War in Vietnam and its issues push into the center of our story. I will let this story of a remarkable Marine Company and of Terry speak for itself. I will only say that the Vietnam War and its political and moral issues are complex from a million angles. I believe the Vietnam Generation, those who fought for it, and against it, actually understand the war and each other better than do the generations before, or after. Our understandings for each other are more sympathetic and realistic in ways which the pundits and partisans of today fail to grasp. I have deep admiration for the Marines of Terry's Company and Regiment, their character, and service. I hope the novel somehow reaches true to their days.

Two helpful hints to the reader. This historical novel is written with a voice that spans several periods of life, but is mainly rooted in "those difficult years" of the late 1960s. Its central story is of the progress and fates of young people in very tough times, and the difference Terry made for us. Unfortunately, today in 2009, our society faces severe challenges again. This story has some things to say about living through tough times, from then, which are relevant to now. This is a tale of courage and ethics that demands remembrance, if we are to retrieve the hard-won lessons of those days to help us through the disturbing threats of today.

The viewpoint in the novel is mainly that of young people facing very difficult trials in a revolutionary, conflict and war-torn age. It is good to remember that most teenagers experience people and events very intensely, and teenagers tend to see others and the world in "black and white", exaggerated contrasts. My youthful reactions (and probably those of others) to the grave and difficult events in those days were marked by these teenage traits. Even so, the trials of those times were dire and very real. Most of our novel's Concordia "antagonists, anti-heroes or nice guys", including the multiple persons or groups behind a composite fictional character, were always more complex than simple. We had no real saints, nor bad-guys. Most have become remarkable civic, business, social and spiritual leaders. If we are gracious and wise, as writers or readers, we would do well to learn not only from the extraordinary life of Terry, but from our better selves.

Now is the time for thanks. It took me months after the novel was essentially finished to sort out where to start. Thanks to Terry, and Kansas who helped me and many of us learn how to see beauty and live meaningfully in spite of any odds stacked against us. Thanks to all my friends and classmates from different years from Concordia High School, many of whom appear in the tale. You, and your memories put flesh on the stories. Thanks especially to coaches Herschel Betts and Bob Baumann; the two of you I will never be able to re-pay. Thanks to Mom and Uncle Norman Mann, who saw far and clearly. They made everyone they ever met feel welcomed and unique. I wish I were more like them. Thanks to Esther Luttrell, a terrific screenwriter and creative author who taught me how to refine my writing, and write from the heart. Thanks to Dad, dear wife Katie, and children Shawn, Noah and Tahira who had to put up with my endless stories for years, and who taught me how to be a better soul. Special thanks to Grady Rainbow, Charlie Switzer, Alan Luecke, Wendell Ganstrom, Louis Hanson, Charlie Dixon, Jack Kasl, Greg Bryant, Gary Diebel, Lyle Pounds, Tom Clark, Marsha Doyenne, Jerry Jones, Peter Foster, John Luecke, Terry's family especially Skip Householter, Lou Frohardt and the rest of you who helped tell the tale, and inspired me to try. Thanks to sister Sue for teaching me real things about how it was for girls. Thanks to Roger, for all the trouble you and Tim got into, and all the laughs.

Ad Astra Per Aspera
West Topeka, Kansas, the beginning of the West
July 16, 2008   Chris Hamilton

The Question:

*What do you need to hold on to
in the bright, and the darkest hours?*

Chapter 1
THE HOUSE RULES

Lighting the Fire

"You're sure...twenty one years since we last saw each other?" Gary Diebel's voice hadn't changed. His hair had no gray in it, a mystery.

"Yeah. It was Christmas 1984, and we were back home from Georgia. We met down at your house, the day after Christmas. First time I got to meet Marcia, and your son. My daughter was just two years, my son just ten, and Mom was still alive."

A vicious ice storm clobbered us the next two days. Forty mile an hour blizzard, ten below, typical Kansas. We got to stay in town longer, and go sledding with the kids on the country club golf course, just like the old days.

But tonight was a hot, breezy evening in July. It was our class re-union.

"Let's step out on the veranda with our drinks. We can hear better out there." Gary led the way. We had a large turnout this year. Not really a surprise, everybody knew everybody in our town and schools, especially from those deeply troubled years.

We talked for awhile of those times, weaving in the stories of our children, schools, first and second spouses, and the war. Inevitably, Gary brought it up. I knew it had to be coming, *the* conversation.

"I've still got the Pumas," said Gary. Nice way to bring it up. Gary wasn't talking about owning a breeding litter of large South American carnivores. I had to shake my head, the memories flooding me. Guys were gathering in with us. Gary took the chance to ask the unique question: "You ever wonder where Terry's gold track shoes ended up?" That hushed us. We talked over this curiosity for a minute, until Gary posed the next question in faltering phrases.

"When do you guys remember...when it all...when people first took notice?" Now we were all fully engaged in *the* conversation, offering different views, when Gary popped up with the one answer we could agree on: "It was a few years before, and we skipped out of the last hour of school," Gary pointed to me, smiling from those pearly whites, "because your renegade brother offered to drive us over there in his old wacked-out '57 Chevy with all those big antennas sticking out of it."

"What do you remember about that?"

"It was at Beloit, no, Marysville. Your brother's car radio with 'Surfer Girl' blaring, and he and Tim Brady joking about the 'ice' they had stored in the trunk...and pulling into the stadium, and smelling corn dogs and roasted peanuts..." With my eyes closed, I shook my head, spilling a little of my iced tea. We were all ears, as Gary unreeled the events of that afternoon, which sealed themselves into the memories of thousands of people, a day *nobody* forgot. What began on a junior high football field would come to change our lives and the lives of the Marines of Company M, 3rd Battalion, 5th Marine Regiment, 1st Marine Division.

* * *

We were scrambling out of Roger's car in the parking lot, and heard the plaintive wail of the coal train. It was huffing its way north through the nearby oak and cottonwood lined park, as the lonesome whistles broke through the conversation of two teenage boys in football uniforms, marching next to us. Here in Kansas, the cottonwoods were yellowing, like their more graceful birch brethren out on the slopes of the Colorado Front Range. The leaves piled up into burnt-yellow mounds, too-little rain, too much heat. Too much August.

We followed behind the athletes, looking them over. One youth, the tall, skinny quarterback, had a blonde slash of hair dangling over green and sharp eyes. The other was a receiver, even taller, with large hands. Both young men stepped carefully down over the limestone curb, both wore the shiny red silk uniforms. The shoulder pads hung loosely on the skinny one, despite the bands pulled up tight, as he punched his words loudly over the deep "thrum, thrum" of the diesel engines behind them on the far edge of the city park. The park held WPA-built dressing rooms of dark limestone, stained from the diesel clouds puffed out by the frequently passing coal trains. Marysville, home of the Bulldogs.

Both young men skittered across the red brick roads like waterbugs, their cleats making that biting "click, click" noise, as yellow-haired quarterback Tom Clark spoke out, "I kind of get the creeps over here with all this black and gold". In this tough town, Marysville's football field crammed itself into the side of a steep hill east of the high school, which crouched high and dark atop the big hill, overlooking the park. The stadium, the school, the limestone in the park all had that "toughened dark" look, coming from diesel and coal, which now fought a subtle war with that special deep cream-and-gold color of sunlight in the September Kansas late afternoon. The streamy wisps of ultra high clouds spread thin, like wisps of cotton. The clouds were picking out their evening dress, a million shadings of pink, turquoise and purple. The kaleidoscoping sunset flowed out from the west. Sunsets, the crown of the Great Plains.

The deep golds of the sunlight and cottonwoods, the paint-shop sky, were unsettled by the black in the rail-town, the stadium, and in the Bulldogs uniforms. Marysville, and Concordia, the great rival to the west, shared a fate in being rail towns, and county-seats. In townfolk imaginations, the similarities ended most bitterly on the football field, especially for teenagers. In the stories, Marysville bore the image of a tough and stained Anglo-Saxon and German Catholic rail town. Concordia wore the cape of the stately Brown Grand theatre, and took pride in the noble French Catholic Cathedral and hospital. The town was a diverse nest of self-conscious European immigrants with more ethnic and religious names than Webster's had terms.

It was the second game of the season, Friday Sept 6, 1963. Both teams gathered for the rituals of strange-looking calisthenics. The Concordia Panthers warmed up in the south part of the Marysville field near the red brick road, with the Bulldogs in the north end, where wheat-stubble fields stretched out beyond and east. The smell of extreme buttery popcorn, cotton candy and slight-burnt corn dogs spread in ribbons across the gathering home and visitors crowds. Soon, after the flip of the coin, and the hand-shake rituals, the too-skinny quarterback, Tom, got to call out after winning the toss, "We'll receive."

Eighth grade football is a coming out party, a sort of Western "bar mitzvah". Families gather to watch hopeful sprouting athletes, or not-completely tuned but proud marching bands. Hormones of young teens are ablaze, as chronic-attention deficit behaviors mark the age: young teens eye each other, their friends, class enemies, sometimes the cheerleaders, and yes even once in awhile, the football team itself. For the parents and adults, however, these are scenes of past wars, of glory days gone by, re-enacted before their eyes. For the junior high coaches, it is survival time. For the visiting dignitaries...the high school coaches, it is recruitment time. Time to size-up the new crop that will land on their door step next year.

The Great Plains just isn't the "midwest". It is the west, with trails and tail winds to the Rocky Mountains, with excruciatingly beautiful skies, where farming fades to ranching. It is the home of native peoples, among them the ancestral Kansa, "the people of the South wind". Above all, life is celebrated and survived with great self-awareness, in wildly contrasting seasons. Vicious winters are survived to be momentarily forgotten in brutalizing hot summers marked often by decades of drought, punctuated of course by tornadoes and harvest. The achingly gorgeous autumns and springs remind you of the coming afterlife, and of the endless cycle of birth, death and re-birth. A big part of the seasons are the public schools, and the life they breathe out, and not much is more important than the music, the arts, and the sports of the schools. The incomparable will of Westerners to survive, and to reach for dreams as big as the sky, is bred by this endless cycle of seasons. And all the exuberance and color-filled romance of the fall was once again, on the fields of Marysville, being played out in one of the most serious rituals of life.

* * *

Concordia lined up in the new I-formation, two running backs behind each other, behind Quarterback Tom. The second quarter, and no score. The two teams snaked back and forth across the field. A Bulldog running back was down with an ankle sprain. A Concordia receiver, clotheslined pretty viciously, sat on the bench with an ice-pack on his neck, about twelve percent of the offense now sidelined. "Hut, Hut!" Tom called, stepped back, and rifled the ball toward Glen Owen, the surviving receiver. Tom was normally on the button with passes, but the inescapable eighth grade slight immaturity of muscle control put the ball a bit out in front of Glen, as he dove out from a slant-out pattern. Straining to catch the ball, it ricocheted off his fingertips, and spun erratically like a dazed buzzard, end-over-end. The Bulldog backfield defender plucked it out of the air, and forked down the field, ankle-tackled at the last second at the Concordia Junior High School eighteen yard line. Seventeen seconds later, the Bulldogs booted a field goal, which zagged its way looking for all the world like it would veer off west. But thanks to the ever-gusting south wind of the native Kansa , the ball lurched inch-by-inch back inside the goal posts just enough to bounce once off the west upright, and drop finally into scoring territory. The Concordia partisans bent over, clutching their stomachs, heaving out groans.

Coach MacDonald called his CJHS eighth grade squad together, saying, "Don't lose heart guys, we've still got the smartest and best offense in these parts. Mike, how's your neck?"

"Okay, coach," he moaned out with an obvious lie.

"Stay together out there. Clark, show 'em what you got," MacDonald cheered, with a raised fist.

Still, the two teams writhed against each other, shifting up and down the field, neither gaining clear advantage, as half-time neared. MacDonald sensed a need for "something different," a surprise quick-punt on third and long for Concordia which would drill the ball downfield fast. A quick-punt calls for the I-back to catch the hiked ball, as the quarterback lifts up his arms for the center to hike the ball backwards. Suddenly the I-back or fullback takes the hike, shifts to his right in a quarter turn, and kicks the ball with an end-over-end tilt. It sails downfield at a fairly sharp angle, not with the regular height of a punt, but with a low slanting zip, faster than a pass. This surprises defenders, they are not set up for anything like a punt. It can bewilder them into fumbling or chasing the ball, as it scoots down low and fast over the field. The hope is to gain field advantage, or perhaps, force a fumble.

The ball snapped, the I-back delivered the quick- punt from the thirty-seven yard line, and the ball zipped over the fifty yard line down field, slightly higher than expected, but heading out low and fast. As predicted by the laws of gravity, time and space, and of the lesser principles of trajectory and applied engineering, the ball arced out and flipped oddly down, down to the surprised face of a Bulldog defensive back. The ball perhaps took three seconds flight, as flat-punted footballs do. This gave the defensive back about one and a half seconds of recognition. Something called opportunity was coming his way, clumsily, and fast. Like most eighth graders, his vision was fixed on the in-coming ball. The lights of opportunity were flashing in his brain. For the world, things looked like the best laid plans of Coach MacDonald were about to find a different ending in a ball that was destined by physics to plop exactly into the hands of the unmoving Bulldog defender. He wouldn't have to even take a step. Just pick this soaring cherry out of the gorgeous sunset sky.

At that moment, a thing happened.
A timeless thing, beyond words.
It still gathers the mind,
*   and steals the breath, after all these years.*
It never happened before.
It was never even imagined.

In three seconds of flight, the low, zipping ball could be tracked with a sharp eye. From the hill on high in the Marysville stands, only the most astute observers noticed at first. "What in the name of God is that?"...a quavering, hoarse voice called out from near the top of the Marysville stands.

Many eyes turned out to the field. Hoarse shouts of *"Sweeeet Jeeeesus"* squeezed out of the crowd. A thick silence grew. On the sides of the field, and up in the stands, the breathing of all Coaches stopped. A slight, red and white streak was sizzling down the field like heat-lightning, down between figures who moved like they were mired in molasses. *The Streak was racing the ball.* For forty yards, *he was staying with the ball, moving at the same blinding speed,* as fast as a Greyhound loose after a rabbit on the plains. In the Great Upstairs, a lone figure named Mercury looked down nervously.

The unaware and hapless Bulldog defender, his vision riveted to the in-coming ball, waited with the confidence of a rattlesnake about to snatch a mouse...when the ball vanished from his eyes.

The Streak, in a blink of an eye, blazed out thirty more yards. Touchdown!

For several seconds, the crowd just sat. Or stood. Or tried to just draw breath, in *stunned silence.* Then all hell broke loose. The Streak was mobbed, by teammates, the coaches, both benches. Both stands emptied.

Pandemonium ruled the Kansas sod.

"Who in hell was that?" croaked out the main Bulldog coach, Mr. Blake.

"I don't know, but *that* was an eighth grade kid, for God's sake," yelled back his assistant coach. They were trying to elbow their way through a rising sea of bodies to the officials, who were standing mute, their arms down, struck dumb and still as fence posts.

"Is this legal? Who in hell has the rule book? How could he do this?" screeched Blake. Grabbing one official by the elbow, he shoved his chin two inches from the of-ficial-ear, to be heard. "Was he a legal receiver?"

"Good Lord, Blake, he *sure* as hell couldn't have been no fat-ass *lineman.* That fast, he had to be a back or receiver, so he *had* to be legal," shot back his own as-sistant coach.

By then, Concordia coach MacDonald had fought his way through to the officials.

"Nobody could possibly do this," Blake kept wailing.

"Guess what, Einstein. He just did," MacDonald shot back. "He's our wing-back."

The field was a boiling mass of humanity. *Mardi Gras had come to Kansas.*

The officials pawed each other, leaning and shouting into each others' ears, while the oldest one flipped frantically through the pages of a dog-eared rule-book. Mac-Donald spied his youth, off to the side being slid down from shoulders that had car-ried him around for minutes. Terry Householter.

Terry August Householter was born September 17, 1949. This slightly built youth, five feet and six inches and all of fourteen years, with a crop of red hair, an infec-tious laugh, and a love for friends, had a determination and a gift from the gods deep inside that burned like the very heart of the Sun. Coach MacDonald pushed through to him, not sure what to say.

"Terry, you okay?"

"Sure coach."

"You want to tell me what happened out there?"

"Coach, I just got tired of somebody not doing something. I saw the punt. I felt, just let me out there. I knew I could get to it. I only had to, uh, let it loose."

That day, in the fading gold and pink sunset, the Officials made a mistake. They tried to take the magic and slap a rule against it. They couldn't find anything in the book. It just didn't seem real to them, such a thing. So they made up a rule. With the touchdown over-ruled, Marysville got the ball back, twenty minutes after Terry had let it loose.

It never much mattered to us who won that day. At the time, I suppose we all first thought this was about Terry's incredible speed, and watching him go was better than any football game. But even then, we knew something bigger had come to us. With the kind of magic and heart that Terry showed us, nothing would ever be quite the same. And we would need what he would come to show us. *It was the '60s. We were at war, and at-war with ourselves.* As the years raced by, Terry was a regular guy and a good friend. In his senior year on the track, and in Vietnam, none of us would imagine, not even Terry, how his incomparable gift would light the deepest fires in his soul and the souls of everyone around him. He would help us find a common spirit, and a way through the bewildering times when hope is gone, and things before us seem lost.

And so comes this story of Kansas people, a town, a generation and a young man with a special gift, who helped us remember things which need to be remembered in the bright and the darkest hours.

Chapter 2
AGELESS, OUT HERE

The red-tail hawk perches high atop the elm just below the crest of the giant grasslands butte, the vast highland prairies home to a sixth as much life as the seas. The tree stands alone, bent to the north, gnarled and partly stripped by the ever living wind. Winds, and the terrible storms when they come, batter all that lives, or stands silent. Native Americans know the hawk as the sister who views things clearly in their finest realities from above and high in the crystalline skies. She is able to see the smallest from afar, is the fiercest defender of her young, and a messenger to humans from the spirit worlds. As the one who balances life on the Plains, the hawk is the ablest teacher of men.

It is early morning. The orange sun strains to burst into view. The breeze is a pale shadow of its rising power later in the day. Colors blend up through clouds on the far horizon, in a riot of senses for hawks and humans. Like a mirror lake at the foot of the Rockies, the spreading earth below, in its endless color rainbows of tall grasses and summer wild flowers, is a reflection of the sunrise sky. The grasses and wild flowers dance in undulating waves to the far rising sun. No camera, no poet will capture all the secrets of the northern Kansas Flint Hills.

Stoic and pure, the red-tail hawk spreads its wings to soar on the winds, and rise above the crest of the huge butte. Human hearts and eyes, peering through the eyes of sister hawk, would stop and falter at the scene when she crests the hill. The vision shifts from flowers near, to canyons far. The lessons of life, land, survival and beauty are spread out to view.

Far beneath, the hawk spies tiny mice, scattering away from humans. She lifts and folds her wings, and dives down ever-faster into the world of women and men.

Below, young men toil in the creeping heat. Rising early in the dew-less dawn, they are in the fields before sunrise. Sweating and hearts racing, they pace along quickly, tossing eighty and one hundred pound bales onto a flatbed, each arm carrying a bale. The gusting breeze helps swat back the flies, but that's what the jeans and long sleeve shirts are for, to keep scarring off the arms, and protect against flies. Knees help the arms lift the hay up four feet and more onto the flat bed. The rancher, holding forth on the trailer, arranges the bales in 3 x 2 opposing patterns, in layers. The layers build up high, but the crossing patterns grip the bales, holding them together.

The lads pace their heavy breathing to get oxygen and fatigue in balance some-how. Sometimes it's nearly impossible for them to keep up, to beat back the pain, and keep going. The thermometer rises above the high eighties even early, which is gloriously easy compared to the steel barn they will have to load these bales into, in the relentless, spiraling heat. It will soar above one hundred and twenty degrees inside the barn, later in the day. Unsweetened iced tea will arrive soon; the girls will bring it in. Fried chicken and all the trimmings will be there at the lunch hour. No one gets fed better than ranchhands throwing bales, who will work into the setting sun by six or seven p.m., when exhaustion will set deep into bones.

Each young man gets three cents a bale. At first, they return at night to nurse horrid blisters or wrenched ankles. Steadily, they learn how to hold off such terrors, and return to earn more with another job a few days later. So many things to think about. Twelve hours of this, three days a week, and four to five weeks over the summer, and the young men will grow in muscle strength and conditioning by a third. Other lessons come from the suffering, and the observing of each other each day.

The hawk, unknowingly, dives into this pain-filled, sweating world that mutually benefits her, and takes her prize of fleeing mice in the field nearby.

Jack Kasl, Steve Bauer, and I showed up at Hanson's farm at five a.m. this morning to throw bales, and joined Louis Hanson, our buddy, and his father, Mr. Hanson.

"Wow. Look. You see that?" Mr. Hanson points up. "Slow the tractor, Jack. Stop it, Stop it". Our eyes turned.

Our imaginations were captured by the diving hawk.

"Something, aren't they? We have to keep things like this well and pass them on to the next of us," Mr. Hanson mused. Our imaginations were tinged with awe.

"Wish I could fly like that."

"I've had dreams of flying like that all my life."

"Mine usually result in me crashing to the ground and I wake up."

"Well, mine let me go out over the hills. Sometimes it's so real, and I'm so sad when I wake up and see it isn't there."

"Any blisters yet?" I asked no one in particular.

"Yeah, starting one on my left hand," Steve said.

"Look, use this. I brought adhesive tape," I offered.

"What do you do?"

"Wrap it around the spot that's starting to hurt. Catch it now, it won't develop and burst."

Mr. Hanson interjected, "Jack, get it going again. We have some risk of thunderstorms this afternoon. That might put us back a few days. Let's get rolling."

Silent competition ensued, as the flatbed starting rolling again at a fair walking pace.

"You know what they said about Pinky," said Louis. Pinky was a giant, senior lineman from Concordia High School last year, State shot put and discus champion, currently a scholarship football player at KU. He could bench press four hundred pounds.

"He could throw bales eight and ten feet up."

"Lord," I marveled. "At least we can keep up here, huh?"

"If we do, we'll be better for football, but the real story this year will be track. You know about Terry Householter, right? And the other track seniors?" asked Steve.

"People say Terry's different than anyone. I can't wait for track. We got Diebel, he'll show 'em," I said.

"Did you hear about my cousin Craig? He dropped out of KU." It was Steve again.

"He did? What about the draft? It's coming, they say, and will affect all of us," asked Louis.

Steve said, "I don't know. It might happen to him."

"Is he ready for that? What's your dad say?" I threw out.

"Dad doesn't talk about it, which is kind of strange, him being in the army in World War II."

"Doesn't Craig say anything?" asked Louis.

"Not much to me," Steve replied. "I guess he thinks it's the right thing to do. One thing he says is that school's not for him. He's on a combine crew this summer, up in North Dakota."

"I don't know how you couldn't talk about it. You'd have to sort it out," I offered. He looked at me. It was getting obvious I had doubts about the war.

"Mom goes into panic attacks a lot about it," Steve said.

"I don't know about the storms. Louis, what do you think: *Is the Storm coming?*"

"Clouds are gathering all-right, but it's a little early to tell. See what it looks like later."

"I'm supposed to run the projector tonight at the Cloud Nine Drive-In, so it might mess with that too," I worried.

"By two o'clock, we'll at least have chicken, and a chance to look-over Louis's sisters," shot Steve.

The heat was picking up heavy now, but the breeze was not. The flies were back, too, biting through the shirts. No great wind to blow them away. A nasty choice... either ditch the heavy long sleeve shirt because of the heat, and face scarring on your arms. Or keep the long-sleeves and sweat it out in the terrible heat. In the end, you keep your shirt on.

At the edge of the far field, a truck was coming. It was the girls with iced tea.

"If the storm comes, we won't be dying in the barn at a hundred and twenty degrees, right?" Steve asked.

"Yeah," I grumbled, "but we won't be getting money either." Louis pointed to the heavens. "God, there is the hawk again, look there..."

There is a certain luck out here, besides the beauty. From this punishing but gorgeous land of the red-tail hawk, we get our chance to see and pick our way. Part of that better luck is that a few of us, in living and dying, learn from what's ageless out here, and teach the rest of us. We were lucky, in our town and troubled times, some of those few walked among us...

Chapter 3
AGAINST THE STORM

I wasn't too sure how good this would taste. Mulberry seemed rather offbeat, when Wendell proposed it a month ago. We had plucked the berries from his tree, just outside the north window of his house. He had pressed the stuff out with an old pillow case, into a funnel, into a cider bottle, and he hid it in his basement behind a burned out water softener. "According to the instructions in the Foxfire magazine articles, it only takes three weeks," Wendell said. Well, it wouldn't bother me, being a Catholic kid, we had relatives who brewed worse than this in basements. Besides, I grew up with asthma, and the Doc had prescribed Mogen David Wine. Mom always kept a small bottle for me in the refrigerator. I was familiar enough with wine. We Catholics had no strong objection to liquor in moderation, where I lived in northern Kansas. Not with French Catholics heading up the parade in our town, followed by German Catholics, and then the sprinkled Italians here and there. Even the Monsignor was seen to have tipped a few at church dinners. But Wendell was a Baptist. His dad was a deacon in the church and the town's outstanding banker. His mom was so straight-laced, my dad said, she wouldn't even go to a high school dance with him in the 1930s, much less drink. "God's Frozen people," my uncle Norm said. A joke spread among teens in Concordia about why Baptists, especially Swedish and Norwegian Baptists, wouldn't have sex standing up. "That might lead to dancing".

From what I could tell, all these wisdoms weren't far from the mark when it came to Wendell's mom. I figured we were safe enough as she had gone off to Salina for shopping, leaving me in Wendell's basement to help him check out "the product." First taste seemed a little yeasty, and over-sweet.

"Come on, let's drag some back to my room," he beckoned, turning left down the dark hall toward his basement bedroom, where scratchy sounds of *The Doors* wafted around us. Lots of exotic kids in this town, I thought, for what everybody on television thought was boring old Kansas. Being a new Catholic import kid to the public high school, I was learning a whole new world, now into the second week of ninth grade. Wendell, the mercurial cutting edge kid, part hard-rock demon, part Order of the Arrow Boy Scout, probably was the first teen in Kansas to memorize all the lyrics to the new Doors album. Wavy haired, rugged features, he looked a lot like an over-chiseled Michael Landon. He drew more girls from two hundred yards than a field of over-ripe alfalfa drew bees. Paradoxically religious to the third degree, he was my second Protestant best-friend. I was skirting the depths of hell, so the nuns said, by hanging around with these kind. So much for hell.

I was one of the faster kids in the Catholic school. But due to a few challenges down by the tennis courts, I learned that Wendell was more than fast, maybe fast enough to chase down rabbits. Other people of unusual traits lurked in this off-road, Western town, famous before 1967, only for having one of the first licensed pilots in America, a barn-storming rake and lady's favorite named Charlie Blosser. He periodically zoomed the town's church spires and businesses for a half-dozen decades after coming home in the '20s after the Great War.

Off I spurted, following this too-quick kid, to his room, a Kansas version of the Rock Music Hall of Fame. He had record albums splayed all over, half-stacked to the ceiling. He seemed determined to finish off a good bit of this yeasty-brewed wine.

"Have you heard the latest from the Doors?" he asked, while unleashing with one hand his new Doors album, and with his other hand he poured shots of Mulberry wine into Welch's grape jam glasses. Hand-washed by Mother Ganstrom, they were now being filled with a more heretical fruit juice. It seemed like Wendell was always doing at least three things at once.

"Yeah, you played that last night," I replied, hesitating (actually *four* times last night). "Can we try something else?" I hopefully asked. He stopped pouring so suddenly, some of it spilled onto his carpet. His intense eyes blazed deep into my skull. He was up to something. "How could I forget?" he blurted. "Sit here, don't move, I'll be right back." Once-again, the lazer-like enthusiasm of Wendell. He played Rock, quoted the Bible, and ran with all the same speed. He re-entered dragging two large suitcases.

"You said your dad was in the Navy?"

"Yup."

"Mine was in the Army, in Bavaria, and Austria. You remember the mountains in the Sound of Music?" We had talked about that last night. Julie Andrews, *The Sound of Music,* the story of the von Trapp Family Singers, and of course, *Those Mountains.*

Strangely enough, in Kansas, we *know* mountains. Not because we have them, but because almost every Kansan treks across the Plains of the western counties to vacation in the Rockies. If the prairies, the wind and sunsets are the Mother to your soul, your Father-spirit is found in the Rocky Mountains.

"Yeah. *Those Mountains,*" I said, my mind drifting to those craggy visions.

"Well, *Those Mountains* are actually home to what's in *here,*" he said, pointing down to the two large valises.

"Uh, Okay," I grunted, wondering what again, was coming.

Without a word, he went straight to work...popping open one case. He lifted out a dusty looking projector, scurried to plug it in, snapped open the second case, and gently lifted out small reels of film. He glanced over, raised his eyebrows and saying nothing, threaded the film, shifted the projector around onto some books, killed the lamp light and flicked on the projector. At first the images were a little out of focus, sliding around onto some kind of large back veranda of a house, with *Those Mountains* in the background. Then the film came into focus with a bunch of middle-aged men, in over-large military hats and uniforms, others wore suits.

"Take a guess who these folks are."

"Huh. Well, country-club Republicans?" Sure were lotsa them in town. Most were business-class Protestants, not working-stiffs like Big Al's father at the post office, or my dad at our small laundromat down next to the Brown Grand theatre. Wendell snorted good at the Republican comment, "No, not quite. These are home movies. *Deputy Fuhrer Hermann Goering's home movies.*"

I choked, unable to speak. Hermann Goering, the deputy Fuhrer of Nazi Germany, second only to Hitler, chief commander of the German air force, and top-Nazi authorizer of the Holocaust.

"Hey, don't knock over the mulberry jug, dipstick. I'll never get it out of the carpet. Mom will figure it out, and my ass will be grass," Wendell warned.

I stared intensely at the film. I *hated* the Nazis. My own Uncle Bill Green had been General Patton's jeep driver when they discovered the Nazi concentration camps in Germany. I knew about those bastards more than any kid in Concordia, maybe more than any in Kansas. A couple years before, I had *cheered* NBC-TV when David Brinkley had announced the capture of Adolf Eichmann, the monster- director of Auschwitz, nabbed by the Israeli secret intelligence services. I had screamed *"Mom"* so loud, and pounded the floor so hard in the TV room that she ran in from the kitchen white as a sheet, scared I had found my sister electrocuted or something. I was sure (I had rehearsed it in my imagination many times) that if I could board the H.G. Wells Time Machine, I could dial back to 1910 and go shoot Goering and Hitler myself. Could these monsters actually be on Wendell Ganstrom's wall, by some ridiculous twist of history, being spat forth from my own friend's home movie projector? Not just from mulberry wine, my mind was reeling.

"Dad's Army patrol was assigned to take Berchtesgaden, Hitler's mountain vacation retreat," Wendell was saying. "It is only a couple miles from where Julie Andrews was filmed spinning around, singing in *Those Mountains* near Salzburg, Austria. Goering was hiding out there, while Berlin burned and Hitler killed himself." He nonchalantly recited this like he was reading off a recipe from the Boy Scout Handbook.

I was speechless. The tin figures spun around each other, the camera jumping a bit from one to another. There was Eva Braun, here were Hitler's dogs, there was Hitler, here was a fat guy in a white military uniform, Air Marshall Goering himself, there was Hitler again. The crowd moved now to a dinner table, servants milled around, grey government types appeared and disappeared out of camera, an Italian-looking dude in a fancy suit...

"I can't believe this thing," I said.

"Not many people have seen it. As his patrol was taking control of Hitler's summer home, up there in the Austrian Alps, Goering fled from it. They weren't supposed to take anything, just protect it. But you know, souvenirs, man. You can't just sit there. So the films came to Concordia, via Pop."

"Shouldn't these things go to, I don't know, some big library or something?" I asked.

"Here, have some sunflower seeds." Wendell poked a bowl full at me across the coffee table. Always gobbling sunflower seeds. "Dad says film can last maybe forty or fifty years. I guess he's got time." I just kept saying "Jesus."

Wendell's dad was a tall guy with a grin as wide as a Kansas skyline, hair smoothed with a little too much Vitalis, and a waving-back-and forth kind of walk on legs that were seemingly too-long for his torso. Wendell inherited those legs, with a huge dose of quickness from some Swedish ancestral gene pool. Mr. George Ganstrom was a banker at one of three local banks downtown. It was strange that Wendell called him "George" rather than Dad. My dad didn't have much good to say about bankers, or some of the town's lawyers either, but a couple good guys like George and it might turn the whole picture of bankers around. He sure was darn cheerful for a Baptist. I had to admit being a tad bit shy of them, as the ones I knew would spend about ten minutes with you, sorta warming you up, before the Jesus questions started.

Not the Ganstroms. Mostly they offered you cheerful questions and an open refrigerator. Mrs. Ganstrom, a slightly frizzy blonde, with pop-bottle glasses, and a voice as soft and kind as the wind singing through the spring wheat, would speak out with "How's your mom these days? She's the sharpest thing since tacks." Or, "Have you heard from your brother Darryl since he's out to Wyoming, land surveying for the Forest Service, that-right?" Always something cheery, and a lemonade handed to you with no lead-up to the usual Jesus is your-personal-buddy stuff that leaked out of Baptists pretty quick. People here drew lines all-right, but not everybody walked inside them.

"Well, we better put this up. It's getting late," Wendell said, taking the film out and putting the machine on re-wind.

"More of that mulberry stuff?"

"Uh, later." Truthfully it was over-sweet anyway. We were both exhausted from double-football practices.

"We gotta get up for the wind-sprints and be out there by 6:30 in the morning you know," I said. It would be the second day of the dreaded windsprints. The famous Coach Betts was a believer in work, all-right. Football was the traditional king among sports at Concordia High School. Of course, the real challenger for king was track.

We sprinted up the basement stairs, taking them two and three at a time. He waived me off as I jumped on the two-speed, kick-back gear, purple Schwinn that I'd had since sixth grade. *Vindicator*, I named her. Out into the street the bike decided to veer north along Olive toward downtown Main Street. I loved the speed of the bike's second gear. I had great leg-strength, helpful for speeding around on bikes. I was a way-over-grown freshman, standing nearly five feet and ten inches and one hundred and seventy eight pounds. After two months of throwing hay bales, I had less fat on me than a desert coyote. I felt out of place in my class, too many hormones, too fast.

I belted past Washington Kindergarten, going up the elm-lined steep street, and topped out at the crest of the hill. My goal was to coast back down, going north, and then east past Gillan's bakery, to get a sniff of the sticky cinnamon flats they baked, then past the stoplight where the worlds' smallest Dairy Queen sat in a little hut no bigger than two phone booths, nestled up against the castle that the Episcopal Priest Father Hotaling lived in. Always a little scary, I couldn't stop the passing thought, as a Catholic kid, that the Episcopal Castle was the center of those Anglicans, Church of England, Henry the Eighth and his bloody search for a fertile wife.

As I swooped past the Castle, looking at the wonderfully cheery lights and gorgeous lace inside, I sternly shook my head, reminding myself how I couldn't stomach the spook-stories about Protestants anymore. I veered left at the Greek-pillared post office, remembering my dad saying that the church across the street was "packed with holy-rollers" on Sunday. "You could hear 'em whooping and hollering even at the high school up on the hill," he said. I wasn't too sure about dad's sarcasm on that, as I didn't know a group that didn't have "interesting" doctrines and rituals. Our town was sprinkled with every kind of Christian, non-believer, intellectual deviant, and nationality that God ever put on earth.

Vindicator veered down to the working class business section on Main Street. *This bike could coast forever*, I was thinking. I made all the lights somehow, and coasted down to what the richer folks in town called "across the tracks". The hot south wind, ever the breath of Kansas, pushed me down to Fifth Street where the bike veered right, going past the Baron's Hotel, home of the famous Oasis bar, a watering hole where jazz guys, black and white sometimes dropped in going from KC to Denver. The singing of the cicadas, long and slow, like a funeral dirge, rose and fell in my ears. I rolled past the lumber yard, under the WPA bridge, and hard-righted to go down the alley that led between Grama's house and the Catholic grade school. Mom and my aunt Mag had grown up in this house, literally in the shadow of the school and the Cathedral.

Grama often told my sister and me, "You young'uns today gotta learn some of your family traits to figure out some of what makes *you tick.*" The characters in our immediate gene pool were far from stodgy or boring. Mom was French, a dazzling black-haired beauty in her youth. And the French, I had learned by comparison to the Swedes, could *cook*. Dorothy Isabelle Francouer was her maiden name from Ed, my grandfather. You had to *be* French to even spell Francouer. Our family got started after 1917 when my grandmother Garnett Short, a flaming red-headed sixteen year-old, barreled down the sidewalk on her bike, and ran clean over my later-to-be Grandpa Ed as he stepped out of Nichols Pharmacy. Ed Francoeur was visiting fresh on leave from his second year novitiate in the Dominican Monks monastery in Atchison. After a few letters between them, Ed up and left the monastery and showed up at Garnett's front door, a sight to behold in monk's robes, asking "May I see your daughter, please?" Lord knows what went through great-grandma Belle Short's mind. Apparently Ed was a lot more impressed with this spirited red-head than the reflective life of the Dominicans, or none of us would be here. He survived the Dominicans, the Great Flu of World War I, and a stint in the Army Artillery, to come back home to the red-head.

Mom and aunt Mag were so French from Ed's influence, they spoke only French up through second grade at the school, where they were forced to learn English fast. Cooking was just one of her unusual talents. Mom often unnerved us, and bewildered her younger sister Maggie. Mom, by mysterious senses, could foresee future events, find lost-articles, track lost people, recite the Gettysburg Address by heart, and she knew all the names of the Presidents plus what they did since Washington. We were convinced she had a hidden third eye that could see where you had been that day. Lucky for us she had an amazing streak of humor. She could tell stories that would spellbind and still a crowd of drunken World War II uncles. As a child, I once or twice feared she was a wizard in disguise, but I learned she was more a spirited, mystical soul. She was decently principled, and Catholic to the bone. Above all, she was creatively *fearless.* On the night she graduated from high school in 1939 (where she typed ninety words a minute on a manual typewriter, and earned a 3.8 GPA), after receiving her diploma, she unceremoniously walked up to her great rival for my father, and decked the girl at her locker.

"I told you for years to leave Ryland alone," she warned coolly, and the girl fell pole-axed to the polished granite floor. The appalled Assistant Principal, not having many options, phoned my Grandfather Ed, the former Dominican Monk, and registered his complaint:

"Your daughter knocked out Geneva Martin after graduation." Ed, a gentle soul, replied, "Well, this is a serious matter. If Isabelle has decked someone, you can be sure they'd done wrong enough to deserve it once anyway," and hung up. Grama always said, "From the minute she looked at me, she was more than a hand full." Some of this from Mom rubbed off on us kids. Bigger parts than you know, from your parents, live on in you.

* * *

Near the school, all the houses like Grama's were two-story wood frames, packed with poor families, most of them Catholic, surrounding for blocks and blocks the giant golden-limestone Cathedral, Our Lady of Perpetual Help. If hard times came, you could hope maybe this Lady would step up. These houses lit up inside like pumpkins, with folks watching "The Dean Martin Show". Down the alley, a couple of kids played in the mud puddles of the alley, with little homemade boats made of shingles. One end was cut out at the back and a rubber band stretched across to windup a cutout rudder.

I stopped at the back of the school, looking right into Grama's backyard at the stump of the big elm that fell on Uncle Norm's new cherry red Mustang in the tornado of '66, crushing it like stepping on a June bug. Then I glanced to the left, across to the back of the two-story, red brick school, where the nuns would make you stand on your toes thirty minutes in the corner for talking in class, if you were a boy. There was a dark closet for you, if you were a girl.

And there was the bike rack where Sister Norma Euthanasia, or Sister Anesthesia, one of them anyway, found out my brother Roger's bike had a shifting picture of a naked lady inside the old Dodge wheel spinner attached to his bike. They used to have those down at dad's auto body-shop, before it became a laundromat. Lean to the left and the swim suit was there. Lean to the right, and it was one of the few places in town where you could see everything when the Lady Showed All. Rog had about a good four hours kneeling on hard tile for that one, at least until dad came down after Grama called home, demanding his driving wheel spinner back.

Concordia was a friendly town, but too often the lines dividing folks, spoken and unspoken, were clear. "Across the tracks" was one of the social lines, referring to the working poorer folks living on First to Fourth Streets, north of the rail lines, or around the Cathedral. I thought about how one such renegade hero, Mario Brichalli, had disappeared from Catholic school one day, booted out because he dropped a hand-made water balloon on Sister Euthanasia, from atop the third-story fire escape. Dead-eye Mario. Euthanasia was the School Principal. Mario was a long-gone hero to us school boys, for he had been exiled to "the public schools" where many thought of Catholics as "hard kids, some of them drinkers and smokers", or so the story went in "polite" circles. More lines, more rules, hemming people out from each other.

It was getting on about nine o'clock at night now, and I didn't really want to interrupt my tour of favorite areas of town. Looking over my shoulder, I could see distant flashes of lightning. "Count to eight," my Scoutmaster, Jim Snyder, had said some years back. "For every eight seconds between when you see the lightning flash, and when you hear the roll of thunder is one mile. Divide your total seconds by eight, and that's how many miles away the storm is." *Couldn't hear thunder now. Must be quite aways off,* I guessed. I spun the Schwinn around, and aimed out for Main Street. *Guess I'll buzz Main, and maybe spin up over the hill and down past the tennis courts in the park on the way back home. Head west, up on the hill above the football and track field, back to 1122 Willow.*

Hitting the lights right, I spun past Highway 81 and headed through town. I zipped past Everett's hardware, home of ten zillion antique parts, and Diebel's shoe store where Mr. Diebel kept a strange looking 300-watt X-Ray machine that surely was a reject from the movie "Forbidden Planet". It was out front in his store for little guys to see if their feet would fit into his cowboy boots. I then zoomed past Nichols pharmacy where its solid brass and gleaming pink, white and green polished granite Soda Bar marked the spot where my family got started by Grama's bicycle running clean over my later-to-be Grandpa Ed in 1917.

I sped past all that, including the palatial Brown Grand Theatre where I now ran the movie projectors. I took a U-turn back south a bit to head up the big hill, which topped out with Washington Grade School. I couldn't count clearly the seconds between the lightning and thunder now, but I was beginning to hear it slightly. A dark horizontal wall on the horizon was growing slowly, with an inside lit up like an electrical generator, and distant bolts of burnt red and white lightning buzzing around inside it. When you live out on the Great Plains, you get able to read weather like a nest of bees can read where clover is. *Something this way was coming.*

The Bullies and The Red Mops

I rolled down to the swimming pool, and thought about doing the night plunge, scaling the fence, and retrieving quarters and dimes which glistened a little on the robin's-egg blue bottom, but it was too dark, and the storm might be coming. That's when I heard some commotion and yelling over at the tennis courts. Little kids pestering each other, I figured. So, I tore out, going west on the sidewalk, and was burning a good twenty-something miles an hour when I saw a tall, lanky form skid backwards into the tennis courts fence. Startled, I just about veered off the sidewalk, and pulled over, braking sharply. Four or five dark figures were angling in the fading light toward a collapsed, skinny shadow which leaned up against the hail-fence.

"Kind of a nice package you got there, big boy," one of the voices sneered. I let the bike down and stepped closer to the fence to watch and listen.

From years of fierce self-defense in grade school, and braced by the spirits of Grandpa Ed and Mom, I was *not* inclined to put up with bullies. Fast, large, and stronger than my fifteen years, I had my imaginations bred early by Matt Dillon and Zorro, and by clashes with over-bearing Catholic grade-school bullies. These guys were older, and I wasn't sure what was up, but it didn't look good.

"Sure seems shiny enough to carve up for chrome pieces for my Chevy," a large brown-cast figure smirked. An even taller one in a red-and-white sweater kept flinging the skinny victim again and again into the fence. Three of the guys were pawing through a large case. The light was good enough from the swimming pool and street-light, to see it was a large silvered brass instrument, a baritone maybe.

"Leave her alone, you caveman bastard," a hoarse, shaky voice shouted out from the fence. The skinny victim was finding his vocal chords. Without counting now, I could see flash-echoes of the lightning, and hear waves of deep low rumbles off west, kind of a below-radar growl. I weighed my chances of swinging around the fence to go in the west entrance, some thirty yards away. I vacillated between waves of fear, there were *five* of them, and a growing certainty that I could do some damage to these sickos, long enough to attract the crowd exiting from a baseball game up the hill to the south. Not sure what to do, or what was coming, I walked around the fence toward the entrance. I was not drawing attention yet.

"You sure have a nasty mouth, for a *weakling fag*. Maybe you'd get your chrome thing back in one piece, if you hadn't opened your pie-hole," said the red-and-white sweater.

I knew the score now, it was getting worse.

There was a power switch to the tennis courts lights on the southwest corner. I could throw it, and take reasonable care of these creeps until somebody showed up from the ballpark. I was waging an internal war over how wise, and whether or not I had the guts to pull this off, when what looked like a '56 Chevy spun into the tennis court lot and circled slowly. I was scared and unsure, but I chose to "go for it", headed to the lights, and flipped the switch. The scuffling stalled out at the fence, when the tennis court lights blazed on. The Chevy veered toward the fence, and braked.

Two red mops popped out of the windows of the Chevy, surveying the scene. The one nearest, with the longest and curliest mop, shook his head and said, "Damn dipsticks, screwing around with some kid again..." Terry Householter, the slight but eerily confident red-mop, was stepping out of the front passenger seat of the car. I recently met this guy. He was hanging around sometimes with the older brother of my friend, Alan Luecke, when I visited Luecke's home. The other red-mop emerged from the drivers' seat. "Yeah, cripes," he grumbled. *John Luecke, Alan's brother.* These two started strolling toward the tennis courts, their hands in their blue jeans pockets. One of them was whistling a tune. Four sets of eyes turned from the victim, slowly out to the red-mops, and then back. And then four of the five hulks backed away muttering, and the tall one, in the red and white sweater, un-clutched the shirt of the victim. They ambled off the courts east, without much talk. Strangely, there was not one word, or look back. *Bullies in a pack don't back-off that quick,* I puzzled. I was glad I didn't have to keep up the courage to jump in there against these animals. I wasn't sure I could do it anyway. *What kind of luck, this guy Terry, and John just walk up there, and these creeps turn away from beating this skinny guy senseless.* It was an interesting mystery. But for now, I was just glad to breathe a little easier.

The victim limped to the big instrument case, and wiped what was inside with a towel from the case. He latched the case, and uneasily wandered in small circles, looking at the receding thugs until they were safely distant.

The red-mops popped back into the car. It rolled off west with a low growl, heading straight toward the growing, ominous turmoil on the horizon.

The chest-pushing vibrations of the thunder were too low to hear, and the weirdly snapping and buzzing back-and-forth of the lightning was all laid out in a horizontal black line, rising like a snake in pain, in the west. *Whatever that something was, it was getting closer.*

The Coming Storm

Time to kill the switch, and head up the hill to 1122 Willow, I decided. I snapped the switch down, plunging the whole scene into darkness. *The victim and I had skated out on this one,* I thought, as I buzzed around, grabbed the Schwinn, and pedaled madly up the long hill past the red-golden Madame of CHS on my right. I wheeled up between the two big blue spruces at the bottom of my driveway, and let *Vindicator* drop next to the wheezing air conditioner. I burned the corner in the breezeway, only glancing at the home-made track out back on the lot above. The coming Storm was still a bit distant from our town. The 1966 Panthers Football Schedule, in new stick-on plastic, adhered to a glass pane of our back door, greeted me, along with the whooping of Skipper, the Dalmatian wonder-dog who sported six toes on each foot. I rushed through the door into the golden-brick house on the hill, into the kitchen.

"Well, I wondered if you had sense enough to get out of the Storm..." Mom tossed out, not needing to finish the sentence. I was distracted by the TV showing black and white scenes of napalm roasting-out large stretches of Vietnam, and a panicked reporter giving frantic comments on the grisly scene. Sure was a lot more of this on TV this year. A black memory snaked back of a recent sobering visit to nearby Ft. Riley, "Home of the Big Red One", by our Explorer Post last June. We were made to visit a vicious mock-up of a "Cong village". It was a "training school" for GI Joes being readied for the tempest that was coming for them. That visit was a thunderbolt in our teenage heads: this wasn't TV anymore. We were shaking, green to our gills, after that little village tour. All of us were stabbed by unspeakable fears, night-or-day at the oddest moments, since the trip. In a split second, it could boil up the back of your neck and steam-away your mind and your eyes from your girl, or a sunset.

Mom's voice snapped me back. "The Ganstroms said you left forty-five minutes back. Out on a bicycle run again, huh?" She couldn't entirely suppress a grin.

"Heck of a Storm coming for us, Mom. It's all a-ways off, yet."

"It's coming, dear boy. Not sure I've seen worse. It's good you made it home." She paused, then said, "We've got chicken salad, and deviled eggs, and some broccoli and cheese, if you're hungry."

I rummaged through the refrigerator for Dorothy Isabelle's chicken salad, deviled eggs and such, and took a plate out to the large front window, which looked out across the football stadium, the track and the rest of the town.

I was the watcher, looking for what *the Storm* would bring.

A little while later, in a roar like a freight train gone mad, ninety-mile an hour straight-line winds with no conscience stripped the leaves from our stately elm out front, as the Storm slashed into the track and high school and city below. It lashed and lashed the track and town, like it was straining to tear us to pieces and sweep us all away. In terrible curtains of black slanted rain, the Storm tore away at the beautiful field and strangled the tall, silver flagpole, bending it over with a terrible strain, bending it permanently. The great and bright lights of CHS, high above the track and city, were twisted back. Our cedar shingles shook, as lightning every second stabbed and hammered the track field below.

"Look there, Chris, look." Mom pointed. We blinked, staring out. Strangely it seemed, there were shadows running, like undaunted track men, through the curtains of rain and terror.

Chapter 4
TERRY, DOG DAYS, AND A LITTLE REVOLUTION

Out from Third Street

Gusty twirls of cool wind spun outside the window. Terry Householter blinked himself awake, and feeling a slight puff of the cool blow through the window, he watched the lace curtain tremble a little in the air. Five in the morning, his grandparents, nearly eighty years old, were still asleep at 337 W. 3rd. He was due at work, at the motel Skyliner Restaurant out on the south edge of town in an hour. He had an early morning hour shift before school started three days a week. He was a bus-boy, clearing tables, bringing water, picking up tips. He rolled out of bed, tiptoed in to shower quietly and not wake his grandparents. It was a small house, with two small bedrooms, a living room, kitchen, front porch and detached garage. It had a long back yard, with a garden. In the north end of town it was "across the tracks", below and east a bit from the towering bridge over Highway 81. The wind blew a little harsher and colder here, coming down from the hills of the south and west end of town where the richer folk built themselves bigger houses after the War. His granddad Dolphas or "Bill" Strait was retired from the railroad, with a small pension. Grandma Jesse Strait was a high plains housewife, used to preparing game for meals on the white and blue trim ceramic gas stove. The handles were a beautiful mother-of-pearl set in chrome, the stove a thing of pride for her.

They sometimes went to the nearby Four Square church, or the Catholics' Our Lady of Perpetual Help cathedral. In all her glorious stained glass, the Cathedral spiked into the sky just three blocks east. She poured her heart out in the Angelus bells at noon, spreading a mystical tone-shadow and reminder of what's eternal, speaking out to the Protestants who were, in their churches, mostly without bells. From the north end of town across the secular business world of Main Street, and onto the south, her voice could be heard clear up past CHS, the track and football field, and even past the high hill of the country club.

Terry was respectful, but not religious. He was hoping to go hunting north of town with Ken Campbell on Sunday morning tomorrow, not breathing in the mystical incense of Sunday Mass. They would follow the deer trails out north and along the river, maybe scare up some pheasant for both of them.

Shivering in his cold room, he dressed in a white shirt, new Levis, and pulled on his tennis shoes. Grabbing his red and white wool and leather letter-jacket, he stealthily padded out the front door, leaving it unlatched, and tripped down the stairs. At a walk and run, Terry struck out over the two miles south to the restaurant. With no car, Terry walked or ran everywhere. More than half the time, he ran. As a kid, when his older brother Skip bussed down from Salina, they would run everywhere together... and that was "transportation". He ran out to the river fishing, to the park and swimming pool, downtown to Lester's sweetshop, and out to the bowling alley with the pool tables. It was still Terry's "transportation," unless buddies with cars were out cruising with him.

Soon he traipsed into the Skyliner backdoor, greeted his boss Mr. Shaffer, time-clocked in and headed into the food service area to bring in customers' water, and buss dishes from the tables to the dishwashers.

"Hey, Terry. How's life treating you? How's the team shaping up?" threw out Mr. Wilson. He ran a shoe store. He was sitting at a table of downtown business guys, with Mr. Tyler the managing editor of the newspaper. The clinking of spoons in coffee cups faded down a bit, as the larger crowd spread their ears to hear Terry's assessment.

"Hey, I'm peachy Mr. Wilson. We got a real-stud team this year. Maybe not like '65 'cause Pinky's not here. He's out mowing down Cornhuskers, I hear." Chuckles spread in the room, at that, except for Mr. Hepperly, whose face was the only one that shot beet-red at the table. The Hepperlys, the only Cornhusker graduates in town, always hung the Big Red University of Nebraska flag with the N on it, outside their house. Their daughter Melanie's boyfriend, Steve was the backup quarterback. He could rifle-shoot balls to the receivers on-target as well as senior Tom.

"We got receivers that haven't learned how to drop the ball yet," Terry winked, exaggerating, and scooping up dishes from one table. Mr. Diebel spoke out quietly to Terry in the hub-bub of chuckles, "Well if they do, you can snag up the ball and disappear before they can get sight of you..." Terry glanced sideways and smiled a little.

"So you think Betts has got 'em all cranked this year? Chapman looks mighty tough this year..." called out one voice across the room at the stool-bar.

"Green's an irritating color," Terry laughed, reaching to fill water glasses all around the table. "Causes rashes," he teased with a lilt in his voice and a wink, which sent more chuckles around. The boys from Chapman were *the Irish*. "But Betts, you know, is Betts."

"Does he run your asses off?" tossed out Mr. Swearingen. His store was electrical supplies and appliances, but his specialty was asking embarrassing questions in crowds.

"Not mine..." Terry teased, again. At this, the whole room burst into chuckles. Because everybody knew. As a lowly sixteen year-old junior last year, Terry took down the year reigning 220 yard champion at the State Meet in a revenge match on the anchor leg of the half mile relay leg at Manhattan. The earlier 220 dash itself had been controversial. A desperate-lunge finish had been called in favor of the older champion Senior from Haven. A snapshot later showed the young House, gaining spectacularly at the end, had caught him in a photo-finish. Photos don't lie. So later in the anchor leg of the relay, House caught him and smoked him and the Haven, and Wellington teams by five yards. Charlie Switzer's dad, a professional photographer, snapped the

photo: the ex-champ, his eyes-bulged out, was yards back. Stopwatches strained forward to catch House. Terry soared through the tape, serene as silk. Betts stood foremost among the watch-holders, his eyes fixed, and jaw open.

"Well, maybe I could borrow Betts for awhile," quipped Mr. Swearingen, "my ass could use a running down and shrinking..."

"You guys need more coffee? I'll be back..." Terry offered.

"Well. *Speed* it up," joked Swearingen, trying to stay in the limelight. Before long, Terry would have to hurry off to the high school for early morning football practice. It was the second week of school.

DogDays

Wwhaaaaanngg the alarm clock struck into my left ear. I whacked at it like I was trying to kill a mosquito. My left eye opened, and focused on the bad news: six a.m.. Early practice in an hour. The dreaded windsprints. I shook my head back and forth to unscramble my brain. The sinking feeling in my stomach spread like sour milk through my gut. Down at the foot of my green-iron bed in the upstairs breezeway room of 1122 Willow, the weak-yellow rising sun cast slanting beams on my shorts, shirt and steel-cleated football shoes. I had arranged them like the pictures I used to see of firemen sliding into their pants and boots as the alarm blew off.

I dragged out of bed, slapped on my black nylon sports glasses, skipped to the bathroom, and zipped back out to slide into the shorts, tee-shirt and tennis shoes. I grabbed the cleats and took the green steps down the stairwell two at a time, to the kitchen. Mom had laid out bananas, grape juice, and even coffee. I'd been drinking coffee to prop open my eyes and jump-start the blood stream since the four in the morning rise of the hay-bale throwing days last June.

One of two rituals were required of aspiring athletes for Coach Betts' league and state champion football and track teams: Throw bales in the summers for conditioning, often in one hundred-and-five-plus Kansas heat; and show-up ready to live or die by the windsprints of August early mornings. Those who had worked the summer with bales, ran miles for conditioning, and neither drank too much beer nor ate themselves soft, would survive the twice-a-day practices.

I gulped down the juice, poured coffee out of the green-steel Aladdin thermos, and patted Skipper the wonder-dog with one hand. After a couple of deep breaths, I finished tying the shoelaces, smooched Skipper on the nose, and I blazed out the backdoor, banana in hand. I headed across the backyard, jogging out and down toward Diebel's. I passed the oval track that Gary Diebel and I had built on the field just above, when we were six years old. We'd built it after sneaking under the fence in 1958 to watch track practices, and our CHS distance running high school wizard, the famous Bill Dotson, the first Kansan to break the four minute mile, national and world record holder, University of Kansas legend[1]. I never had beaten Gary around the oval. Nobody my age I knew could touch him, save for Ganstrom. I knocked on his back door. The red cedar siding on his house showed a certain glow in the sun. The door sprung open, and an amazingly muscled, swarthily tanned young man slid into view. He had curly dark hair and a pearly white six inch smile wandering across his face. "Yeah," he said, "come have some breakfast." He pointed to his mother's Greek pastries on the kitchen table.

Gary's mom was an exotic Greek gal from somewhere back East. I often thought Gary had poured into him the concentrated stream of all those Greek-athlete gods of olde that you study about in grade school history books. Thirty pounds less than me, he was still the only athlete, either upper or underclassmen, I had a hunch I might not out arm wrestle. He could pull a half dozen one-handed chin-ups in gym without breaking a sweat, and God knows how fast he would burn out the 100-yard dash this coming year in track.

We munched down one or two Greek pastries.

"You ready for the rack again?" Gary asked.

"Mmmf. Don't know. We'd better not eat much of this."

A red and white streak caught my eye. I glanced down, taking a glance at his red and white Pumas. These must have cost his dad, a shoe store owner, a pretty penny. Maybe one or two guys in three hundred miles had Pumas like that.

"Well," he grinned, "We will probably survive the stairs out there in the stands again."

"Some didn't yesterday. The McCoy brothers looked green."

"Yeah. Grant kept swooning over in Mikesell's math class."

"Well, we won't get cut, as long as we stay with the drills."

"And don't sprain an ankle. Let's go," Gary said. We ambled out his front door, across the lawn, and snuck under the stadium fence through that hole we had made years before to sneak into the field to get peeks of Dotson lapping people in the mile. On Fridays the secret hole was our way to sneak into football games. We ran down the west side stairs of the yellow-limestone stadium and out onto the field. Small groups of upper-classmen were gathering at the north side, and some of the underclassmen were hanging out under the goal posts.

The Tests were about to begin.

The 1957 Chevy rolled up and out strode Coach Betts and the entourage of assistant Coaches, wearing red and white nylon blazers, black dress pants and black sport shoes. Coach Betts was a legend across Kansas, with a dozen career championship football titles, an alphabetized list of football All-Americans going off to the Big 8 and NFL, and an unmatched track and field squad which had won nearly half of the last ten years' State track titles. Coaches of bigger schools in Wichita, and Kansas City secretly breathed easier knowing they didn't have to face Betts track teams; it might mean untimely unemployment.

Track in Kansas had become the sport of legends since the days of Glenn Cunningham, Archie San Romani Sr. and Wes Santee, the great early milers of the '30s and '50s. Kansas had plenty of open spaces to train great runners. Betts arrived, swept into town in 1957 from another coaching job, as if blown in by the western winds, out from Norton-way, near the Colorado border. In a year or so, his track teams were the elite of the state, led early-on by the legendary Dotson, the fastest kid-miler in America. Track was one way to condition football players. But year by year, football, the king of high school sports, soon had itself a restive rival for the throne in Concordia, in track and field.

Betts' drilling was legendary. Track, or football, he ran you nearly to death. You grew up with his voice in your brain, the echoes of his phrases following you the rest of your life. FDR said we had nothing to fear but fear itself, but for us, Betts *was* fear itself. Normal mortals could call him Coach. If you were in his better graces, you could say Coach Betts. Truth was, whether any of us really understood what he was teaching us about sports or life was doubtful.

Coach was trucking himself toward the goal posts.

"Okay, men and girls, your time has come. Line up."

Gary and I looked at each other. "Let's stick together," Gary whispered.

"Don't stretch us out too far, Gary."

Clumps of some of the other underclassmen gathered with us. They knew Diebel could lead them at a fast enough pace to keep within sight of the upper-classmen, enough that Betts wouldn't order-up a tongue-lashing and extra work for laggards, but not stretch guys out into a pace that risked collapse or worse. Anyway, Coach always eyed the upper classmen a bit more than sophomores and freshmen.

The Drill. You worried about it in June. You got queasy in July. You ran miles in fear, to get ready for it, in August. You hoped you could survive it, to continue in school through the day, and come out the other side for after-school practice. The start was the goal line.

"You know what to do. Whistles up," Betts called out. The whistles blew at five, then ten yard intervals, blowing out the mark of the leaders, letting you know where you stood. In between, you hoped your name didn't get called out ("We're seeing ya, McCoy") because that marked you out for extra laps around the track.

The Whistle. Out five yards, back five yards, out ten and back, out to the fifteen yard line and back, as fast as legs could move. As fast as the emerging sprint leaders would lead the group, themselves grimacing in agonies. Out to the fifty yard line, and then back down in five yard reductions. 1966 was not a year of luck for *The Drill.* Upper-classmen had the likes of Steve Collins, our premier halfback, Price Pickard our agile, powerful fullback, and Householter. Underclassmen had to follow or keep up with Diebel, Foster, and Ganstrom. Not good for those who lived off beer a bit too much in the summers. The one minute rest after the first cycle was always an interesting moment. Groans, labored and frantic breathing, and those poor devils throwing up. Then the thirty and ten second countdowns. And then Diebel, Foster, and Ganstrom were up again, trying not to vie with each other, the rest of us trying not to die. Three more rounds of this, and those who swooned (fakers or not) were off to the side, for a "rest" and special treatment coming. The survivors were led over to the Stands. The Stairs loomed. The west side could hold nearly fifteen hundred people, and had eight aisles. You trudged up thirty flights of stairs, and down, with the best of the best leading. Snake up and down from north to south, and then snake back, and then repeat, ending back on the north side and out to the track. A two-minute break, more groans, more up-chucking. Then repeat the whole cycle of torture.

By the finish, those-who-swooned were shucked again off to the side, nervously awaiting their fate. The survivors were given a cheery pep talk, revisions of the play-book, an invitation to the Fellowship of Christian Athletes meeting that night, and a summary of what would be concentrated on at afternoon practice, for linemen, back-field and receivers. Drills would all be the same for everybody, but the freshmen team would eventually be separated into their own defensive and offensive drills. Those who swooned now got a tongue lashing from Betts.

"Too many twinkies last summer, huh?" Then the inquisitions. You knew you'd better tell the truth, as the whole town had eyes, and many of them reported back to Coach. Betts stalked the suspected slackers like a Louisiana big-house executioner.

"So, you didn't start hay-bales until July, Schmidt, that's right?"

"Yes, Coach."

"When you gonna start next summer?"

"First of June, Coach."

"Too much beer-hall work on those combine crews up in North Dakota, right Bruce?"

"Yessir."

"Think you want that again next summer? "

"No, sir."

"Well, you girls have six timed laps around the track to do here, and you'd bet-ter keep the pace up. Coach Forbach will have the watch on you. Finish that, and you can come to practice this afternoon. Now, get it over with. School starts up in forty minutes."

The torture was impeccably well-timed.

We survivors loped off to the showers. No room, no energy for bullying from up-per-class thugs out here in morning practice; the prima donnas suffered as much as the benchwarmers and underclassmen. Sparks flew under our cleats as we trekked across the cement sidewalks, across the asphalt, and up into the shop and into the showers. A few renegades had slid sideways over to the corner grocery store, to grab cokes or candy bars or sunflower seeds to replenish themselves.

Conversations broke out around the lockers, underclassmen in the smaller central lockers, and the A-team juniors and seniors in the larger caged lockers a little east, all of us dressing quickly after showers.

The shower and locker room walls were festooned by Coach with a few pictures and long-posted and yellowing mottos, and phrases that we ill-understood, such as:

"When the going gets tough, the tough get going."

A signed picture of Gayle Sayers: "CHS, Live your dreams."

"If not now, when?"

"Character is the only thing."

"It's up to you to pass it on."

"Champions are made, not born."

You could imagine an invisible Watchman or guardian angel standing in hopeful silence at the waves of young men of class-after-class, year-after-year, as they squinted at the signs, trying to suck meaning through hormone-fogged brains.

Brett Swaggart moved through the crowd, naked, brandishing a wet towel, followed by several of his goons. Unusually good-looking, crew-cut, red-headed Brett was one of the heirs to the throne among upperclassmen, a star split end receiver, arrogant to the bone. He snapped the towel in a vicious whip, right on the butt of one of the skinniest freshmen receivers. The lad lurched in searing pain, a purplish red welt instantly spreading. No time now for more serious bullying and chest-thumping, just a warning shot for what awaited future victims. Eyes of underclassmen shifted sideways as he passed to the showers, snorting something about new boys from across the tracks. Several of us, among them Diebel, Foster and I, glanced at each other, coolly-eyeing the goons as they passed, oozing their snears and chuckles. My ears started to ring all by themselves. Something terribly cold and steely rose up the back of my neck like a ghost, and I felt it taking note of Swaggart's viciousness all by itself.

"Let's scoot," said Gary. "Almost time for the assembly."

A Little Revolution

This morning Evelyn Freeburne was heading into CHS in the pickup driven by her mom. This was only her second week at CHS. Like some, she had come in from the one-room country schoolhouses which were about to die off. Our families were long-time friends, and our dads were in the class of '39. Her two year old picture showed forth her character, a girl in a plaid dress with intense brown eyes, and short dark brown hair. Her face seemed to radiate an inner happiness and penetrating spirit that said, "I know the world. I'm getting used to it. It better get used to me." In the picture she sits with her hands folded, next to her piano. This was the first photo of her past her infant year. She began playing the piano at age twenty-three months. She never stopped. Her parents were Welsh-French immigrants, her uncle a very big player in Kansas politics in the legislature. They were understood as reasonable and reasoning Republicans, a breed that would dwindle perilously a few decades hence, grain farmers on the plains who had their daughters reading poetry, taking piano lessons, and reading encyclopedias at young ages. Such were some of the "farm girls" in Concordia.

The pickup hopped around, dodging potholes in the white-crushed limestone road coming from the low hills east of town, eventually becoming Eleventh Street, winding in from the prairie. The rusted 1954 Ford pickup passed the Rocks, a strange formation of thrust-up boulders, piled upon each other in jumbled nuggets, some stacked like poker chips, as they flowed up a hill. The Rocks were many things to many people, and one use was as a famous "watering hole" for youth seeking beer, or other forbidden pastimes. More than one unexpected pregnancy had its beginnings in the romantic pathways between the Rocks. There were no sure theories of how the Rocks were formed, in an otherwise endless vista of rolling plains punctuated by trees along riverbeds. Some said Indian spirits had re-arranged them, maybe in anger after the days of the dying of the buffalo. No white men were ever known to move them around, as they stood six to fifteen feet tall each, when not piled on top of each other. The winds could whistle through the Rocks with strange low and high overtones, when they sped up to their almost-daily and steady forty miles per hour. Spirit voices were heard among the winds.

"How do you feel about CHS?" asked Evelyn's mom.

"I dunno. Some of them are friendly. I like the survey of physical sciences. I like Mr. Miller's music theory, and choir," Evelyn said. In reality, she was still gathering impressions. She wasn't telling that the home-stitched school dresses she had weren't getting the eye of some of the richer girls out from near the country-club. Buying the booster-club uniform of trim red sweaters, pleated red skirts, and white and brown leather shoes was something beyond the finances of her farm family.

"I hope I can fit in." She didn't want to push her mother on buying the uniform.

"I'm sure you will, dear. You are so bright, people will come to know you."

Evelyn wasn't sure about the "fitting in" thing. She loved her music, science, and art classes. The foreign languages classes were something she wanted to try next spring, the smarter and kinder kids with a sort of curiosity about the outer world seemed to take those classes. Mostly she was happy with the Baldwin Grand, available on the stage. CHS had choirs, an orchestra, plays, and music performances on that grand stage, the master and commander of which was the Baldwin Grand piano. The '54 swerved hard to the right. Her mom jerked the wheel, avoiding a sizeable jack-rabbit nearly as big as a medium-sized border collie. The Ford chugged its way up and down the hills east of the town, and down across US Highway 81, called the "ribbon of light" or the "great white ribbon". It was the south-to-north artery that ran from the Gulf coast of Texas, up to the land of a thousand lakes up north. Looming off to the left was the truly gargantuan, eight story Convent and communal grounds and farmlands of the national headquarters of the Catholic Sisters of St. Joseph. The Catholics were a full forty percent of Concordia, making it a truly off-kilter township and county. Most of Kansas was a polyglot nation of European Protestants, punctuated with strong islands of Mennonites. Evelyn hadn't got to know Catholics yet. Her soul belonged to the Baldwin Grand, in the near-palatial stage and theatre of CHS. She stayed after school to practice, hour after hour, on the Baldwin. The school plays hadn't started up yet.

The '54 chugged a bit as if it was half-missing on the fifth cylinder. "Your dad's going to have to do something about this engine. He's just no mechanic," Mrs. Freeburne said. The pickup wheezed past the WPA–built, limestone swimming pool, tennis courts, and brown-brick bungalows. It crept up the hill going north to the water tower, which splayed out northeast of the high school front entrance. "I'll drop you off here," she said.

Evelyn grabbed her books, and strolled west toward the front entrance, where an unusually large crowd had gathered.

* * *

Inside, Gary and I swarmed up the football locker stairs, and headed out toward the main marble lined hall, where the stage and auditorium opened out. The intoxicating smells of eggs and cinnamon rolls drifted up from the cafeteria, to blend with the odor of freshly waxed floors. Dark walnut doors, marble tiled floors, and gothic-looking chandeliers held bright forty watt multitudinous bulbs, evoking the idea that maybe hundreds of candles would have cast light in an earlier age. The crowd milled around in the hall, separating into informal groups by class. Whiffs of perfumes floated past, producing strong, unrevealed hormonal reactions in scores of young lads. Kids broke off into subgroups, music kids, science geeks, sports jocks, school paper gurus, arts or theatre. Lizbeth Ellison, daughter of a local surgeon, surged past. She whirled around and grabbed my arm and breathed hurriedly, "It's really horrid, what they're doing to us girls out there." Her breath was like wine. Her gorgeous robins-egg blue eyes blazed into mine, her blond short hair whisping around us. Lizbeth was an outstandingly bright student, a wonderful flute player in the band. Her face was bright red in patches of anger. Small she was, but powerful, and her red fingernails dug deep into my tanned arm. Nobody but nobody messed with Lizbeth when she was cranked.

"It's crap. And nobody can do anything about it," she said. She stomped on the marbled floors so hard it slightly vibrated, and stormed off.

"What's that about?" Wendell sidled up to me.

"No clue, Stud-ly" I replied. I strolled to the left a bit to get out of the stream of traffic. Suddenly, a foot stuck out in front of my ankles, and I managed to barely step over it so as not to fall on my face. Conditioning from Catholic School. Always watch out for pranksters, keep your balance up and your feet light, watch with your eyes around corners. It was Wild Man Jack Kasl, teasing us. Not a threat, just a prankster. "Keeping you trained and on your toes," was his motto. Jack had a smile happier than sunrise.

"Jack. What's the story with the crowd over there?" I asked. He was always in the know. Bright as a comet, sort of a radar for human psychology, Jack knew about everybody in the school.

"Well, it's all about Kramer. The Assistant Principal." He leaned forward. "He did too many pushups in the Air Force Academy, I think. He's out for revenge".

We asked several girl friends. The answer was strangely uniform: "You don't want to know."

I spotted my younger sister, Sue. We had been watching each others' backs since grade school. Only ten months separated us in age. I slid past a couple of her friends and tapped her on the wrist.

"What's up, Sis?" Her coal-black long hair snapped around like a whip.

"He's an ass," she snapped. My sister was no doubt a little too hard-bitten and plain spoken, but she had been raised wrestling with three older brothers, and surviving the thugs of Catholic school playgrounds.

"Who do you mean?"

"Dick Kramer, the new Assistant Principal, and his back-up boys up there. They're measuring girls' skirts. Some are being sent home for having skirts too short. I barely passed by hiking mine down aways. Older girls say Principal Overbrook isn't interfering on this. Monica got sent home because her sister's skirt from last year was too short, but her sister's was five inches shorter. If I got sent home, Mom would kick my butt and then come down here and kick his butt."

Fifteen minutes to go, to the assembly at 8:30.

Out front, the crowd around Evelyn was backlogged. Almost all girls, very few guys. The Assistant Principal, Dick Kramer, and two assistant Assistant Principals, were brandishing measuring tapes. Evelyn had merged slowly to the front, oblivious at first to what the crowd was going through. She was immersed in reading an epic poem assigned by Miss Fletcher, the legendary, unmarried masters degree English literature instructor who had taught at CHS since 1934. Not until Evelyn was two feet from the front step, did she shut the book, and look up. She was staring directly into the eyes of Dick Kramer, school Assistant Principal. He smelled slightly of English Leather cologne, cigar smoke, a sour shirt, and bad breath.

"Okay, honey," he said to her, "kneel down."

The words struck Evelyn as hard as any words could. Her father was a reasonable man and would never say something like this. Kramer might as well have asked her to chop the head off a kitten.

"What?" she burst out. "You want *what*?" Her voice rang out across the steps, and out across the grass, and disturbed the flagpole some, and drifted out into history. The second *what* carried a force akin to one of those Navy foghorns used in World War II on destroyers and battleships. Astonished, and appalled to the bone, Evelyn stood her ground, and looked into the eyes of her adversary.

"What's your name, honey?" She paused again for several seconds, not believing this effrontery. *What kind of thing could call itself a man, and ask for this?*

At age seven years, Evelyn had packed her bags, and announced with some sadness that she had to leave the farm and Concordia, because it wasn't quite the right place for her. Her parents couldn't quite catch on at first to what she was saying. She loved them dearly. They didn't fight much. But somewhere inside, Evelyn knew she wasn't fitting in. None of the schools had given her classes with enough of the sciences and the music she was interested in, and none of the piano teachers could do her any good anymore. She thought she had to go out to bigger places, where she could take in more of what she wanted to know. She had an Aunt in Chicago. She was going to go live in Chicago.

So, she packed her bags, and disappeared in the purple sage, walking down the road toward the Greyhound bus stop on the country road south of her farm. An hour or so later, her parents pieced together what had happened, and what she had said. They took off in the '54 looking for her. They didn't have to go too far. She had made it only about three miles. They snatched her up and tried to talk to her about what she wanted, and where she thought she was heading. She said

Chicago. They had museums and things like that in Chicago. That's where she belonged.

This was the personality this gung-ho U.S. Air Force officer-turned-Assistant Principal was now trying to stare down. He had encountered no such female force of nature before in his world.

Kramer repeated himself a third time, out-loud, to the attentive Ocean of Silence that now reigned to the north of the CHS entrance.

"What's your name, honey?"

"You don't call me honey again. My name is Freeburne. You should know better."

Kramer was struck dumb. "Freeburne?" he asked. In the reptilian insides of his brain, the name was being sorted through the local establishment that he recollected. Suddenly he remembered the connection to the Kansas senator. And that other school board member with the same name.

"Uh…" he stammered. "Well, your skirt looks okay."

"Stop *looking* at my skirt. Maybe somebody should call your wife. Excuse me, I have books to put away and I need to study."

Evelyn walked past him, and the tape measures, and the assistant Assistant Principals, and right on down to her locker, unmolested.

Suddenly, the announcement came over the intercom, "We've got to start the Assembly now. We will continue this tomorrow. Be certain that your skirts fall below your kneecaps. Enforcement of this will be complete."

Several in the crowd figured out this was a skirmish in a war that wasn't quite going as planned.

* * *

Managing to evade a revolution at the front doors, the Administrative "skirt enforcers" hurried themselves into the building, urging students to file into the vast auditorium, "time for the assembly." Assemblies were motley collections of announcements, and student groups. Students did not gather together by class, but instead broke into groups…band or choir students in one place off to one side aisle, jocks filing in up front and center. Renegade personalities and the farm and vo-tech kids held out in the back, being the least interested in the cheer-leading endeavors of the Administration.

The fact that temperatures were already soaring toward ninety degrees didn't help the air, or the restlessness of the student audience. Glad to be out of class for the moment, but increasingly feeling the rising humidity and heat, the students wouldn't last long in the place. The noise of the big fans on the stage fought a little against the sound system. Assistant Principal Kramer strolled to the podium, tightly poured into his black pants, with shiny wing-tip shoes, white short-sleeve shirt, and black, Mormon-narrow tie, his shirt pocket festooned with a penholder that had a gilded brass United States Marines emblem. Quickly, with military precision, he rattled off the announcement topics:

"Good morning CHS students. We are having a great beginning to a great new year. Our school has some of the greatest teachers, students and activities anywhere, and I'm sure many records and memories will be made this year. Before new teacher introductions, we have a few important announcements. First, window fans are an option in this difficult heat. We recommend that you eat your lunches at school because the cafeteria downstairs is below ground and it will be cooler; our lunches will no tbe cooked, but will be "cold cut" meals, so you can get a little break from the heat by way of the cool lunch room downstairs. This year, we are proud to say we have new buses and vans available for road trips this year, for the sports teams, and band and choir groups, and science classes. Also, you seniors should know that Recruitment day for universities will be one month earlier in November this year. Now, without delay so that we can get on to our classes, we will introduce our new faculty."

The new faculty were paraded on-stage. Some were displaying mildly defiant paisley ties; those were the younger men, new from that infamous home of all things radical, the University of Kansas. The new women teachers were in compliantly longer skirts and high heels. Each stepped forward and smiled around into the auditorium as they were introduced. Slight squirming noises were breaking out in the back of the auditorium, among the more restive rebels. In truth, Kramer was sweating it out, and stalling for time. His experiment in "compliance" on the front steps with the women had frazzled his image badly, and he sensed it. His voice raised in pitch a little, as he tackled the ever-creeping Beast head-on:

"As you know, CHS stands for excellence, and the best of opportunities for all students. We have some of the most talented students anywhere in Kansas in academics, sports, band, music, theatre, agriculture, shop, and the arts. We have wonderful teachers, and dedicated coaches. But as you surely know, there are some elements in America today who want to bring down our young people, from living up to excellence. They question the American life of pride of country, and proper morals, and excellence. Some even question our President. They want a kind of wild life. You can see it in the music, and dress, and rebellious and disrespectful attitudes that they carry to each other, and to their parents. These kinds of corrosive attitudes, the kind that tear people down, will not be a part of our school. As you know, we will not allow such things as smoking on our premises, nor bad language, or rebellious haircuts among the boys, or dress that is disrespectful of yourselves or others…"

Guarded whispers broke out in one of the back rows.

"What about your dad's garage at his store? Can you get into it at night?"

"Yep. Told him I was fixin' to work on my bike gears. He's at VFW meetings Wednesday and Thursday nights. We're clear."

"Brady and I will bring supplies. Dad's got spray paint cans that I can get."

"We can cruise after."

Up in the front row, Brett Swaggart muscled a shrug sideways and broke a Cheshire-cat smile in the face of the coal-black haired, chunky-muscled buddy who sat next to him. "Kramer, what he says. We can use this." The chunk of dark muscle smiled back. Off in a side row, Pete Foster and the red-mops exchanged questioning looks and quickly-raised eyebrows with each other. The intrepid cousins Lizbeth and Evelyn's lips pulled into narrow, tense lines. Their breath grew shallow in their noses, and tiny interior flames lept up in their hearts, as hot as sparklers on the night before the fourth of July. Kramer droned on...

> "...some of these things will be monitored this year a bit more closely, haircuts among boys, and dress-lengths among girls, especially. You can expect the best this year, for your-selves, and from CHS teachers and administrators. You are now dismissed to your classes."

So once again in the heat of August, another gauntlet had been thrown to start yet another Great War. But this wasn't 1914, and this trench warfare wasn't in Europe. This time, the trenches were dug in over the dignity and rights of "just girls", on the un-noticed vast plains, where pioneer grand-daughters were the frontline warriors.

Chapter 5
SEARCHERS, REBELS, AND
NIGHT SKIES

Searching for Something

The day raced on. Kasl, Bryant, Evelyn and some of the rest of us trickled into the Survey of Physical Sciences class. It proved promising, partly because of the blend of wacky-mad student scientists in the room, one of whom kept dropping a rubber brick weight out the window tied to a ticker-tape that measured acceleration, as the teacher droned on about a feather dropping in a vacuum bottle. After several launches, the renegade rubber brick managed to brush off the ball cap of Ol' Jake Brakewell, one of the assistant janitors two floors below. It just missed braining him senseless, as a small group of janitors strode out into the parking lot below. Both Jake and the launcher of the rubber brick were lucky, as it merely bounced around on the ground near Jake's cap. The rubber brick was quickly sucked back up the wall and disappeared into the launcher's skinny white groping hand. The launcher was lucky in another way: Ol' Jake Brakewell had a bad stutter. Jake was trying to catch the attention of Mr. Collins the chief janitor, who had strolled on ahead of Jake into a pickup truck. But the class bell rang before Jake could calm himself down enough to get the story out to Mr. Collins and have him send somebody up to the class room to catch the guilty one. Students swarmed again into the halls, and the launcher got off "scot-free".

Next came choir practice in the bright, shiny tiled Choral room. Holding court was Mr. Everett Miller. Miller held a masters degree in music history, and choral direction. Miller was wildly popular. He earned a spirited loyalty college coaches yearn for. He greeted people daily by name, with a sharp and teasing glint in his eye. A paradoxical soul, his fun-loving side blended well with witty sarcasm, and people skills. He knew his rough choral talents, musical prodigies and sports-jocks alike, as a well-trained Kentucky horse breeder knows each horse. Standing just at five feet and eight inches, his coal-black eyes and Italian silk tie dazzled the students, who were filing into the choral room.

"Stand taller, Bryant," he said as Greg shuffled past, "You can't expect the women to flock after you, unless you exhibit better posture. Besides, it improves your tenor range." Bryant was a bit taken aback...but sure enough, his posture improved, along with his high notes.

"You know your dad sings darn good in the Methodist choir, Swaggart," said Miller, with a wink and a smile, just loud enough for Swaggart's buddies to hear. He had all their psychological and motivating push-buttons down cold, even for the bad-ass jocks who, strangely enough, also flocked to his choir practices. The Man was a wizard. He could play the room of personalities like an Ozark Mountain Fiddler, salting choir practice with charming bits of music history. He set up the sections against each other in sportsmanlike competitions. More than in church, or on any ball field, the annual-motley crew of social antagonists were unified by his mastery. Harmonics and overtones, the young charges discovered, could produce a soul-stirring high equal to any blend of tobacco, beer and furtive sex that a Saturday night party could give out. Miller was on a mission, his goal to challenge the motley crew this year, shaping them into a school choir like no one could ever imagine.

Students filed in, took seats, jostling each other with gossip, giving occasional stares at a movie projector that was wedged into the tenor section. Miller was decked out in a white silk shirt, his brilliant yellow Italian silk tie, and sporty red burgundy tassled alligator loafers. He strolled patiently, looking at them eye to eye, shaking his head a little, and pausing for silence. Then he started in on them.

"I have a little film for you today. Hamilton, you're the projectionist and popcorn man at the theatre. You can run the machine, can't you?"

"Yeah," I blurted, and popped up to fiddle with the machine, and Miller hit the lights.

After a few minutes of sound and fury on the screen, he said, "Some of you surely recognize this...it is the bombing of London in the late Fall of 1940."

Grim aerial battles high in the sky were lit up in flashes of explosions; bombs rained down and bloomed in terrifying flashes that obliterated government and civilian buildings. Even small parts of the great Westminster Cathedral were damaged. Stricken white as sheets, terrified mothers and government workers scurried underground to subways and basements. Miller allowed the catastrophe, the burning buildings, and the sobbing civilian women to go on display for awhile in antiseptic black and white. With the flip of a hand, he had me cut off the machine. The lights came on.

"How many of you had fathers overseas in the war?"

Most hands went up.

"Kasl. Your dad was in Austria?"

A grim-lipped "Yup" floated out.

"Any, shall we say, effects?"

"Huh?"

"Does he show any troubled reactions?"

A long pause, "Yeah. He wakes up at night, screaming. It takes Mom awhile to calm him, bring him around. It's usually a loud noise that triggers him. He gets scared, sees things that, you know, aren't there..."By now, the gossiping had dropped off. Miller had their attention, at least.

"I have a recording for you, by a little known group, called the Whitehall Choir. It was formed during those very dark days of London, around Christmas time, 1940. These were just ordinary people, government workers, secretaries." He sat down at the piano and played a few bars.

"Anybody recognize this?"

"Greensleeves," a voice called out.

"Yes, but it is also 'What Child is This', the Christmas song. It was part of their program. How 'bout this?" He struck a few more bars.

"Good King Wenceslaus."

"Correct. That was also on the program, but it wasn't all of it." He strolled to the turntable and spun the old '78. Hymns soared out of the past, dimmed by scratchy-white sounds. After the hymns, he flipped the recording over.

"Remember, this was recorded near Christmas, during a break in the Nazi bombing of London by the Nazis. It was part of a lunch-time event at the War Planning Board, some of the near-by buildings were in rubble. These voices are the government and military people of the London War government. Amateurs. Just people trying to survive the terror of the war, both physical and psychological. But this next piece from their program is, well, special." He handed out brief notes to the class. The bristling new Fischer speakers were flipped on and the old '78 record spun again. Out-sang voices whose timbre showed no fear, in tones and rhythms that stirred the deepest subterranean parts of their souls. Any closer to the cemetery, and maybe the music could have roused the dead.

> O Fortuna velut luna statu variabilis, semper crescis, aut decrescis; vita detestabilis nunc obdurat et tunc curat ludo mentis aciem, egestatem, potestatem dissolvit ut glaciem.

> (Fortune, like the moon you are changeable, ever waxing and waning; Hateful life, first oppresses and then soothes, as fancy takes it; Poverty, and power...it melts them like ice.)

At the stunning conclusion, Miller lifted the needle. Silence filled the room like a November fog.

"You're wondering what this is. It is *Carmina Burana*, the great work of Carl Orf. These people were trying to survive by drawing on the spirit of some of our greatest music. They were surviving Christmas, between bombs, tears, and joy."

He leaned over an eighteen-year-old young woman who aspired to be the senior class valedictorian. His tie swung back and forth, as if it were ticking off years. Ignoring her White Shoulders perfume, and crystalline blue eyes, he asked, "What, with this concert, do you suppose they were trying to express?"

A very long minute ticked by with no answer.

"Courage," offered Jack Kasl from the back.

"Well, well..." Miller replied thoughtfully. "Maybe. Maybe it runs deeper."

He stepped to the tenor section. The jocks, of course, had defensively armed themselves by sitting in the back-bench rows. The political activists and energetic minded types filled in to the front.

"Okay. Your chance, men, since one of you spoke up first."

Once more a long, stale minute passed.

"Well then, try this." He stared into the eyes of the second sopranos, then he moved slowly back to the tenors.

He stabbed a finger at one of the second sopranos, and then at one of the tenors and said, *"A time will come when you will question your sanity, your self-direction, and what's important. What did these people turn to when they were frozen in fear?"*

More silence.

Miller's voice rang like a prophet. *"Come on. You people are Kansans.* You are grandsons and granddaughters of pioneers and abolitionists, and progressive Methodists, and fearless Catholics, and Congregationalists. Some of this ought to be in your bones, if it hasn't been too washed out by your daddy's MasterCard. What source did these people turn to? "

"Weren't they praying to Jesus?" a young lady's voice called out.

Miller paused long at this one.

"Perhaps. Some of them. But this is London, the center of a world empire. Some people likely were Jews or Buddhists, don't you think?" Slowly, that sunk in.

Miller spoke in low tones, "Look for it in the music. Courage you say. Interesting, Mr. Kasl..." as he pointed at Jack. "Well, as we do the music this year, you all just keep thinking about it: What you will need when your time comes? I'm afraid you *will* need this music, people. What is deeper than courage? Is it hope? What else is there, between a people, that counts? What can bail out your sanity?"

Miller paused, then continued, "This year, we will take on the full, double Grand Piano version of this musical mountain. Good money is that you are the first Kansas high schoolers to ever try the great *Carmina*. We will have twenty minute extra sectional rehearsals after lunch. Sopranos and tenors on Tuesdays, basses, baritones and altos on Thursdays. We might even slip into your churches for a rehearsal on weekends, sometimes, to give you more reasons to feel your way into this." He passed out copies of the musical scores, as the dazed students filed from the room. "Don't lose the copies or I'll roast your butts."

He then spoke the golden words: "We will have try-outs for the double grand pianos, starting next week. So, potential pianists, please step forth to get piano scores."

Evelyn Freeburne was the first to seize a copy from the piano even before he completed the sentence. She held the piano score close to her heart, like it was her newborn baby. With the soul of a pioneer woman, she strode down that narrow and dark tunnel and out into the sunlight.

A Little More Revolution

At 3:15 p.m., the final bell rang. Students dispersed like birds fleeing from a lightning strike. They rushed out the brass and wood doors, into myriad sub-worlds. Some scurried to farm homes to help work the fields or the livestock. Others went off to work in cafes, or car shops. Some went home to hobbies. Some broke out the cigarettes, and cruised the side roads and streets, killing time, wondering how to pilfer beer from downtown bars. A clandestine gang of whisperers scurried off to find supplies, to build their renegade instrument of rebellion in Tim Brady's dad's garage, out back of their family-run liquor store.

Evelyn Freeburne sat the grand piano on the CHS stage, breathing life and marrying her soul into the leaping harmonies of *Carmina Burana.* Her hands pounded out the complex chords for hours, until the pink clouds and turquoise sky put the sun to rest.

* * *

After the bell, I struggled with taping the ends of my toes against blisters. The worst threat of football practice, in the annual new football cleats, is the horror of blisters. If you are not careful, new shoes not broken in can make you bleed through the leather by the end of your second practice, and your chances dim of making placement on the team. We were now into the second week. The shoes were a little better broken in. In the musky, dank dressing room, I hurried with the tape, and then pulled on thin wool socks (wool avoids blisters). I pulled on the tight trunk pads, strapped on the hard nylon-shell rib pads (keeps your ribs from being crushed by helmets), then shoulder pads. That years shoulder pads were the new wide, hard-nylon "killers". Have to get help pulling on the tight outer jersey, and tug-on the super-tight spandex pants so the thigh and knee pads fit well. Then slap on the helmet, insert a dentist-fitted mouthpiece (teeth are nice to keep), a drink, and I was running out the door, across the asphalt street and out one and a half miles to the far west practice field. I was running the distance over steaming asphalt that every now-and-then sent up head-spinning fumes. Up the hills, past Diebel's, past Dr. Owensby's gorgeous tudor house which held his brilliant brunette daughters. *Keep moving, it raises your heart rate.* A painful process, but you can feel yourself take in oxygen better and the pain dims out. I needed the faster heart rate and oxygen balance by the time I made the practice field. I had to get there before Coach Betts's van did, or it'd be extra laps for being "slow". A gusty south wind broke the ninety degree heat. The westering horizon showed glorious cumulus clouds towering-up to sixty thousand feet, stabbed-through by slanting rays of gold sunlight. Hawks were tracing circles in the magenta sky. This hypnotic canvas distracted any of us from the pain of short breath. Beauty with pain is very Kansas.

"Hey, Grant, you hanging okay?" I asked, catching up to Grant McCoy. Grant was a bit chunky, but brave.

"Hey, I'm better than the cattle my dad's chasing now," he tried to joke. Grant was already breathing heavy with pain, sweating a river, but still cheerful. He had a crew cut, and a dazzling smile with teeth so bright and uneven it could back up fierce yard-dogs a bit. I learned to look past Grant's teeth because he had such a wonderful laugh and wit, and man could he pull pranks. Took me three days to figure it was Grant shooting spit wads at me in the cafeteria. Every day, in Mikesell's math class, "cross-hair Grant" shot a few more spit wads onto the picture of President Johnson, building up a pile on LBJs face.

"We got the downhill now Grant. Let's speed it up..." I said, not wanting either of us to be late.

We ran onto the practice field, but had to dodge left as a growling engine raced next to us. Pulling in was a metal-flake cherry-red with chrome trim 1966 Dodge Charger, gorgeous enough to get your oxygen back in one big gasp. Out pranced Stuart Whiteside, one of the wealthier boys in the senior class. His daddy was a high-ranking executive in an auto parts store chain. Grant and I exchanged stares. It registered on us that with being a senior, privileges must come. We *ran* to practice, but he *drove* his daddy-bought new Charger.

A whirlwind of dirt spun down the road, and skidded into the field, wheels braking. The coaches had arrived. Betts huddled the coaches together, giving instructions, then the assistant coaches zipped out like a swarm of hornets toward us. Out came the call from Betts, using a bullhorn to boost his voice, "Linemen on the south and west stretch, backs and receivers in the center field, punters and kickers in the east end with a couple freshmen ball retrievers. Move it! Time for drills."

Forty minutes passed in a blink of an eye. Linemen, freshmen to seniors, were run ragged through tires, side-sprint drills, and shoulder-blocking sleds, in a continuous circle. Quarterbacks, running backs and receivers split into A, B and freshmen squads, continuously doing run, and pass plays. All were getting shouts of encouragement, explanations, quick demos, and an occasional helmet-thumping and lecture. At the end of running three circles of these drills, the gasping and groaning groups, sweating like moose on the run, were allowed to drop to one knee and take two-second squirts of water from brass squirt-pumps. Punters and kickers were happy to not suffer this, but they were getting weeded out by observation of who could really kick. Everybody knew that even worse pain would come at the middle of practice in the tackling, blocking, and circle-hit drills, and at the end in the sprints and the long-drag back to the school for showers. Every half hour, we got only the two second spray of water, but no real drinks. No pain, no gain.

Over it all, Coach Betts observed this spectacle with binoculars from a platform fifteen feet in the air, carrying on occasional conversations with assistant coaches. Once in awhile he descended to stride to one of the drills and watch individuals up close. He spoke directly only occasionally, throwing out humor, or constructive observations. He only tongue-lashed laziness, or bone-headed stupidity.

"Rodney Hess, can you read?"

"Yessir."

"You got the playbook?"

"Sure."

"Study it at night do you?"

"Yes."

"Well, not enough. On the A-47, you cut left and out sharply after five yards down, but you don't wander off going left like a cow in the field."

He grabbed Hess by a shoulder pad. "See that thing out there? What is it?"

"A cow."

"Good. You see it wandering?"

"Yes."

With a smile and a wink, he said, "Well buddy, that's what you *do not* do. You sprint down, fake it to the right, and cut-left as fast as your ass can move. Hess, demonstrate this two times, for our freshmen here, so they don't wander like cows. Tom, make sure you pin-point the pass where Hess is *supposed* to be."

Sure enough, the demonstration made the point. A-47 was not-forgotten.

After these drills, we were suddenly shunted into half a dozen groups, and led off into the tackling, block, and circle-hit drills. The smaller freshmen were separated and went off east. But the likes of Diebel, Grant and I, and the bigger freshmen were mixed-in with the sophomores and upper-classmen into the blocking drills. Even the first string running backs had to practice blocking. Two equal lines of guys faced off against each other, one behind another, one line trickling back east, one back west. The Coaches picked Byron Beauchere, a junior split-end receiver, as line-boss in charge, and left the scene for the first couple rounds. The battles began.

"You ready, Gary?" I asked, he being nearer the front.

"Yeah, no sweat." We all counted heads in the opposite line, to see who we would be "lucky" enough to be lined up against. Eight yards apart, each combatant crouched down in the lineman three point stance, getting ready to sprint forward and hit the opponent with the strongest block you could throw in a four yard headlong sprint. As a contest of collisions, it is a sort of madness, a test of courage, and brute strength...a real King Kong battle.

In its intended form, the blocking drill was supposed to teach you how to be the "great defender" of those weaker than the tacklers, such as the quarterback. It is your responsibility to block powerful onrushers such as linebackers or defensive ends who were mindlessly bent on flattening hapless quarterbacks, backs or receivers. The senior line boss kept mental notes of "winners and losers." Some of the battles sent shots of frozen fear into anybody's veins, regardless of how strong they might be.

Clumped together like younger fish, we worked our way to the front, Gary ahead of me, Grant in back. Diebel's turn came.

"Show 'em Diebel!" Grant and I called out. He was lining up across a junior safety, probably ten pounds his superior.

At the call "Hut!" Gary was out three yards, accelerating and kicking dirt back like a western road-runner before the other guy even took his first step. I knew it was gonna come out this way, a bottle rocket might just have kept up with him. "Sheeeez," Grant whispered. Diebel met his opponent head on, somewhere around twenty five miles an hour, even before the guy was on his fourth step. Mass times great speed sure is something. The starting safety flew up several feet in the air, back two feet, and landed flat on his back. He wheezed like an arthritic bloodhound for a good two minutes, trying to get air back regular into his lungs. He got hauled off to the side.

Gary shook some dirt off his sleeves and walked around to the back of the line, grinning like a calico cat.

I was next. I wanted to continue the show, but not all-out. I looked out, and there was the black-haired buddy of Swaggart. A tough guard, one-hundred and seventy five pounds, two years my senior, two or three pounds less than me. *Was he one of the goons who were out on the tennis court beating that skinny guy senseless last week?*

I was not as fast as Gary, but I could toss an eighty pound hay bale five feet up with one arm. With thirty one inch thighs, I got a notion one day that I could lay flat on the cement floor of the CHS shop and leg-lift both of the regular John Deere tractor's rear wheels off the ground as a test of strength, and for exercise. I tested it out a couple times anyway, until somebody noticed.

I was still pondering the black-haired guy when the line boss called, "Ready. Hut!"

I clicked down, sprinted out, and met the maybe-goon a little past the gentleman's half way point. A seasoned guy, he was low and tough but not fast. I ripened my guess that this guy *was* one of the tennis-court goons from a few days ago, so in the last two strides I put some extra grit into it and brought my forearm up from below and whacked the guy into the chest at about eighty percent power maybe. He flew straight up and smacked straight down flat on his chest. He scrambled up quickly and whacked at me with forearm thrusts. I backed up a little and belted him up in the air again, and he flew not as far as the first time, and landed flat on his back. "Next!" cried out the line-boss. I wheeled around to go to the back of the line. The black-haired guy scrambled up, coughed some and loped off, glancing back at me.

The corner of my eye caught Grant, getting down into a kind of over-spread spidery stance. I looked across to see who he was to face, and sure-to-God, there was number 22 crackling his knuckles, and grinning out from his tall menacing frame, Brett Swaggart. For size, he was one of the biggest receivers, among the more ominous juniors and seniors. I stopped cold at the edge of the circle, not moving to the back anymore.

"Ready. Hut!" came the call.

Grant ambled forward, trying to pick up steam. Swaggart came out of his stance like a bull gone berzerk...one hundred and eighty five pounds, six foot and moving like a freight train. Grant was caught head-on at the chest, with Brett's forearm under his chin strap. Grant flew back like a rag doll, his helmet wrenched a bit clockwise around his head, covering one eye. Swaggart then actually ran over him, cleats and all. He wheeled around, and screamed, "Get up, you pussie! Stand up for yourself." Disoriented, Grant erected himself, and gamely half-flung himself, staggering, at Swaggart, who freight-trained Grant again, bringing a round-house forearm up from below and from the back like a discus thrower. He seemed intent on taking Grant's head off. On impact, Grant's helmet went flying. He bit into his lower lip, because he'd lost his mouthpiece in the first collision. He just lay on the ground, not moving, bleeding.

A tall, powerful streak flashed into the face of the line-boss.

"You idiot! You shoulda stopped this at the second hit!" Pete Foster screamed, ripping his helmet off. Spitting sparks and red-faced, he confronted the senior line-boss, who was a back-up first team tackle.

"What the hell's wrong with your brain? Do you even have one?" Foster fumed at him. "Somebody call in the trainer!" Half the crowd was mesmerized by Foster's totally fearless confronting of the "authority," while the other half of the crowd still watched Swaggart and Grant. Just when it seemed Foster and the line-boss were coming to blows and the crowd gravitated to them, Swaggart walked up to Grant splayed out on the ground, and bent down and hissed out *"Pussy!"* With considerable strength he swift-kicked Grant in the butt, for more humiliation. Grant couldn't breathe, the wind was knocked clean out of him. I wanted to lunge at Swaggart, but was diverted with a crowd to go get Grant up and over to the sideline. He was trying to breathe, slowly shaking his head trying to see, a bloody drool spinning out of the side of his mouth. Gary had run off in a blaze to find the trainer, who ran back with towels, his first aid box, and a squirt pump.

Hartshorn, a line coach, had converged on the scene, directed more trainers over and, at some personal risk separated Foster from the year-older tackle, which was probably a healthy idea for the line-boss. We were ushered back into the blocking line for more drills, the coach trying to bring order back to the scene.

My ears were ringing again, head buzzing. The cold icy ghost rose up the back of my spine again. I was being taken over by the hot-headed stranger within. Gary was back saying, "Good Lord, did ya see that..." several times. Noticing my strangeness, he kind of shook me, saying "Are you here?" I kept saying "Gary...Gary..." I heard myself talk, like I was somebody else. We were back in line. I was staring at the grass, breathing shallow and fast, trying to find clear thoughts. Blood pounded so hard in my ears, I had trouble hearing Gary. Finally, he plunged full into my face.

"What's with you?" I looked at him straight on, and replied, *"This* is gonna stop."

"Okay..."

I pulled him to the side, and counted down the opposite line. I got to the sixth guy, and found number 22. I turned to Diebel, tugged his jersey, said, "Come on." I counted out six places from the front of our line, and squeezed up and whispered, "Excuse me. Gary and I are stepping in here to give you a couple minutes rest. Be thankful."

At the word "rest" I forced into the line and made a space for Gary, waving him in behind me. The line inched forward, and when two guys were left ahead of us, Diebel poked me in the ribs. I turned around. "Just watch my back," I said.

At the front, I looked out at Swaggart. He smiled too much. I dropped into a stance and took a bead on him. The cold ghost was in full power now. My vision narrowed.

I let an awful lot of it go at "Hut". The collision was a thunderous whack. We were both thrown upright. I was a little faster and caught him on the uptake with a right forearm and shoulder to the rib cage. He staggered to the side, but we were at it again. We whacked each other savagely up, down and sideways. His forearm shots rattled my helmet and vision. I stalked him, with vicious upward and leg lift-powered shots. I forced him into a backwards circling retreat. The battle escalated for almost a minute, the crowd watched, stunned into silence. Battles were not supposed to go on this long. After the second circling, I backed up and raised my attack level a real notch. *No more playing around with this creep,* my cold ghost told me. I blasted my helmet and right shoulder pads into his ribs, enough to launch him up in the air and back two feet. He scrambled back a bit to regain balance, wincing. The ghost whispered again, *"Very Nice. Not too much. Let him think there's still a maybe. Next time, finish him off."*

I pulled my mouthpiece out and just smiled. By then the line-boss steamed into the center screaming, "Enough!" Swaggart side-stepped him, and leaned over to snear, "You're new around here, aren't you?"

"Maybe to you...pleased to meet you..." I spat out. I shoved the line-boss off me and strode around to the back of the line, the steam and the cold still curdling off my back.

A piercing air-horn blew, and a bullhorn announced, "Freshmen and sophomores to the sidelines! Full speed defense and offense A teams report to centerfield for scrimmage. We will run a few plays."

The side-show was over.

We underlings rambled off to the sidelines. The bull-horn Authority had spoken. Foster and I looked each other over on the sidelines, former Catholic-school survivors. Pete walked in circles, flamed out in frustration, shaking his head. His dad was a doctor, so he was appalled at how the coaches had missed how Grant get mauled. I walked in circles too, in a separate struggle, breathing out my ghost.

"Having fun out there?" Gary half-nervously joked with me.

"Yeah. Fun," I replied with deep breaths, "It was probably good for me to stop. How's Grant?"

"He's sitting on the sideline, chewing on ice, over there," Gary pointed.

I looked over. He didn't seem completely back in the saddle, but he was crunching ice from a cup, and carrying on a conversation with our classmate Mac Campbell.

"Things could be worse," I told Gary.

The House makes his Move

Attentions diverted to the field. The A team offense had to be one of the better fielded in the State. The Offense had big, dual effective receivers at tight end. It was to run the new I-back formation; the backfield featured a mobile, intelligent, accurate quarterback, and a stable of fast and powerful backs. A few sophomores were nabbed to join the quickly assembled team defense. It wasn't as strong because some of the A team defense members played both ways and were on offense at the moment. From the sidelines, we underclassmen gulped in water and air. We watched the speed and the power of the running backs, led by a line averaging at two hundred pounds, as they plowed away in several draw plays, gaining seven and eight yards each try. From the center of the field, on the next play, quarterback Tom drew back quickly and tossed a pitchout lateral to the big junior half-back Steve Collins, who ran to the opposite hashmark away from the benches, and suddenly handed off the ball to a slight wingback running in from the far opposite side...a reverse!

At the moment of the hand-off, reality shifted on the field, as Terry Householter, the senior wingback, took the ball and down-shifted. The helmets of helpless defenders rotated left rapidly, and eyes followed where legs could not. *The House was on the move.*

He ripped around the side of the crowd in a sharp arc, accelerating like a scalded cheetah. The House soared past human pursuers, losing them in gaps that increased by three and then four yards each second. Whistles dropped from the mouths of coaches. Betts stood high in the platform, his arm outstretched, pointing West like an Old Testament Prophet, silent as a limestone post as the winds swept the field. The two best defensive safety backs, Ganstrom and Foster, hand-picked for speed and agility, tried to pull an angle on Terry coming across the field. As they got within a couple arms lengths, he shot them a smile, and kicked into overdrive like he was a motorcycle, accelerating on each stride. He floated into the end zone, some fifty yards away from the handoff.

The crowd was silent. Foster and Ganstrom, the safeties, trailed out behind him, decelerating, hands drooping, staring at Terry in the fading sunset. Diebel, next to me stared down the field as if a UFO had just landed in his front yard.

"Jesus...H...Christ" floated out from the platform above, and over the silent crimson helmets.

Terry loped back, flipping the ball up and down, smiling three miles a minute. He hadn't even broken a sweat. His red-mop of slightly curly hair spilled out as he took off his helmet; elbowing and grinning at Foster as he trotted past. Betts descended quickly down the ladder and motioned for Terry, the offense, and coaches to meet him in a mid-field huddle. Betts strode fast to the group. Small clouds of dust breezed away behind him in the wind. Many of us underlings streamed in from the sidelines. He strode right up next to quarterback Tom, smiling at him. Betts glanced over the crowd, and looked at Terry for a second that stretched into the next couple centuries. The song of the cicadas spiked up out of the trees, as he spoke into the ever-living Kansas wind.

"Boys...we can do something with this..."

Terry smiled out at everybody, and everybody smiled back.

Now, we were all on the same page.

This Friday night was not a game night. The first game was one week away. For the time being, we were no longer a bunch of tribes in a civil war. Terry's display of brotherly cheer and magic had washed out all the memory of bullying and battles, as we showered and sped off to the weekend, all of us splintering off to follow dozens of different fantasies. The A & W would see its share of hot cars. The River Road out by the Railroad bridge east of town would welcome its batch of seniors & juniors who scammed beer from Brady's liquor store, the farm kids likely turning in earlier for chores that were certainly expected of them the next morning. The Cloud Drive-In north of town featured "The Good, the Bad and the Ugly" with Clint Eastwood. It would grind on deep into the night. On Saturday night, *The Fabulous Flippers* were supposed to help "burn down" the National Guard Armory with another blow-out stage show.

The Cloud Nine Drive-In would not have me at the projectionist box, un-air conditioned, with yellow outside bulbs still drawing June bugs and moths. After supper of mom's rich tamale pie, I packed up and headed off to Hanson's sand pit out west. My '49 Plymouth just about knew the way all by itself, as it wheezed around deadman's curve on Highway 28 west of the old skating rink and grain silos on the edge of town. I was out to mess around at the lake and camp with Wendell and the boys.

We would speak of secret heart-throbs like Lizbeth and that new dark eyed AFS girl from India, the usual conversation for guys our age. We would also speak about something different in the winds: What was Everett Miller up to with us? What was this with Terry? We would hold watch on the scintillating stars and wispy streams of the Milky Way deep into the breezy night. We knew it would help us with all this somehow. The night sky comes to live and speak steadying things in all of us out here, in the good and the troubled hours.

Chapter 6
IRON MEN, THE FABULOUS FLIPPERS, AND AUTUMN SATURDAY NIGHTS

The Iron Men

The screen door banged behind him, as Jerry Jones headed out across the front porch. He tripped down the creaky steps and sped out on foot, following the ruts that the pickups had cut through the front lawn. The south wind rustled the leaves in the elms above, which lined the quarter-mile dirt drive out to the limestone road. No humidity in the drylands today. It was five a.m. and getting colder outside, mid-thirties. Only the rooster cleared his throat to greet him half-way down the road. Even the dogs still slept. Mercury and Venus loomed as bright distant spotlights just above the eastern rainbow horizon. The sun was struggling to be born, shoving streaks of orange-pink up through the resisting blues. Meadowlarks scattered from the trees as Jerry's steady pace beat out a tempo in passing the elms. As he jogged south into the gusty light wind, crickets sang cheery and slow in the passing ditches. The white seagulls, always a mystery to folks from the coasts, circled lazily in the sky. In a mile and a quarter, he was to meet up with a year-younger runner and neighbor kid from Jamestown, both of them out for cross-country.

Cross-country at CHS. Even the words speak fear-of-pain to normal folks. The Iron Men. The ones who show, but speak little of pain. Every day they pound their legs, ankles and feet literally into the ground. Miles upon miles, three miles and more for each training session, sometimes twice a day. Cross-country in the fall, and distance track in the spring, these were the Siamese twins of sacrifice. The courage to endure this is the kind of desperate power of the heart that is called forth only by climbing the Himalayas, or surviving battlefields, or giving birth. Shin-splints, broken blisters, terrifying cramps, wrenched ankles, twists in the knees, burning lungs, and searing leg muscles for hours and days...no one knows these better as dear-companions than the lonely iron-men of cross-country. And Jerry Jones was its most devoted and disciplined Disciple.

To the Men of Iron, Jerry was a man of steel. Five foot seven inches, sandy red hair, and freckles, Jerry had a quiet smile, a gentle humor, and a warm handshake for any and all. Only a few in the long history of CHS runners trained for it with more love, and only a few ever trained with the same steely will. He was heading gingerly toward the distant mailbox, topped with a turkey buzzard that stared at him from afar. This was the crossing point to pick up his buddy in the six mile training run this morning.

47

Soon the young iron men met up at the mail box, the turkey buzzard never-blinked, and flapped off only in the last second.

"Hey, Jake."

Thumbs up.

They strike out south.

Distance-men don't talk much as they pound it out. Two quarter sections of fields equals one mile south, plus one quarter section west, two back north and one east will together line out six miles. Nobody gets lost much out on the plains, because every kid learns that roads and directions are predictable in waffle-grids, north, south, east and west, and that people still stop to help travelers broken down on the road. All natives live with a compass in their head, and hope for help in their heart. Even in a fierce blizzard, runners can run roads blinded by the snow, and if they know their pacing, can end up back home and open their eyes within sight of their own mailbox. Out here, feeling lost is a bit less common.

Switching side-glances, Jerry and Jake stride out and enter a state of what Californians call Zen, where pain and the world are seen from inside, as well as from a transcendent eye. Halfway through the six miles, at the same moment Jerry watches jack-rabbits peel off into fields and sea-gulls soar through the wild blue, his internal pain fades and he feels the rush of the second wind. He pushes his strides out, and Jake fades slowly in small puffs of white dust. As they round the last section quarter, Jake pushes to maintain lost distance and maybe hold steady the gap to Jerry. On to the mailbox. Jake pulled in about a minute later, and fell in next to Jerry. They leaned on the mailbox, gasping to catch their breath, coming out of their transcendent mind/pain world.

"How's it going at CHS?" Jake asked.

"They're all-right with me running it out here. I had to talk pretty hard to Coach Smith, though. The city-boys can make those country club training runs on Saturdays. But, you know, Dad wants me out here for chores."

"Are they okay guys?"

"Some. It's hard sometimes. There are quite a few country-clubbers. And they know who's who from way back, as kids in schools. You know. They don't always talk straight to you."

"The girls?"

Jerry let out a long sigh and shook his head. "Yeah. Sure are lots of perfumes."

"So, are they flocking at ya yet?"

"Come on."

"Did you know about the Flippers tonight?"

"Yeah, the flyers are all over."

"So? You got the Big Beast, don't you?" The Big Beast was the '52 Chevy pickup Jerry's dad had as backup.

"Yeah, but our dads will want us doing chores Sunday morning, even before church," Jerry replied.

"So scratch out the Flippers, huh?" Jake grinned.

"I don't know. Maybe if we work through the afternoon, we could talk them outta tomorrow morning's chores."

"It's worth a shot."

"I'll call for you after supper and I'll see if I can wangle Dad for the Big Beast." Jerry sounded hopeful.

"Well, at least with that we'd have options in town. We can always say we're hitting the Dairy Queen or the Cloud Nine Drive-In. You want to see what the crowd's like at the Armory, don't you?"

"I guess so," Jerry reluctantly replied. "Honestly, I've never been to one of those dances. I hear they can get kinda wild." Jerry stalled, worrying about getting spotted with guys with beer. *I'm staying a million miles from that. No problems with Coach Smith hearing rumors.*

They stood up straight from leaning on the mailbox; they had finally caught their breath. The breeze picked up a little, but something had just changed in the winds. Long gone were the smells of summer...sweet clovers, freshly mowed hay, and corn to pull from the stalk to chew a few sweet bites. A distant field of stubble burned and the wind filled with the smells of harvest-time: ripened summer hay, a trace of smoke, black walnuts crushed near the sides of the road, yellowing pumpkins, and fallen leaves.

This change of spirit arrived with the cold on this morning, draping itself over the two young men. The wind carried the change, and an unmistakable rush entered their souls: *Now it is autumn, with football, harvest, and cross-country.* The spirit and scents of autumn on the plains come alive in a subtle, profound awakening which calls people to reflect. Braced by the whisperings of fall, the young men's passion *to run* quietly deepened, and thrummed to the bottom of their souls.

"How's your chances, on the team?" asked Jake.

"Well, I plan on working at it."

"They have a lot of runners, don't they? They always do."

"Yeah, ever since Dotson ran in the late '50s. Ten minutes flat in a two mile, up and over hills like we have? That's hard to beat. Some of them have a lot of guts, that's one thing. There's one guy, Lyle, you can tell he loves it, and he runs like a deer. The younger guys are hungry to run. It'll be interesting. Then we have track, next spring. It'll be sorted out by then who the leaders are."

"So we'll be up and running tomorrow again?" Jake cautiously asked.

"Yeah. I guess so. As long as I get the chores done. I just tell him, I gotta run, Dad. You know farmers. All they think of is something else to fix, some other critter to take care of. It's endless." Jerry sighed deeply.

"I think the sun chases my dad instead of the other way around," Jake observed. "He won't even go to church, unless Mom gives him the look."

Jerry backed away from the mailbox and turning to jog, he called back, "I'll phone ya around suppertime, okay? I'd better get back. Dad'll be up."

Searchers

I crawled out of the sleeping bag at dawn. Jack Kasl's snoring had joined the chorus of crickets, boosting me up from sleep. The limestone fire-ring at the edge of Hanson's sandpit lake wasn't dead of fire yet. Blowing the coals to life, I stoked up a fire, warmed the bottom of my boots, and rummaged through the backpack to bring out instant coffee, bacon, and a glass jar with eggs. I was always the cook, a legacy of my French-cooking mom, plus years of Boy Scout camping. Bacon and coffee smells drifted over Kasl and stopped his snoring.

"Mercyyy... the Trail Cook's at it again," he crowed, whacking Hanson on the butt. Louis had slept next to him.

"I thought you farm boys rose and chased down roosters for breakfast," Jack teased.

Hanson moaned weakly, without replying.

"Well, I'm not the cook your mom is, with her Czech bieroks and zelnikis," I said to Jack. They were my favorite foods. "So, have you dried off from your lake plunges last night?"

"Wish I could do it again. It's a little nippy now." Jack pulled on his boots.

Last night, Jack had spotted a long rope swing on the far, twenty-five foot high bank, which swung out from a pin oak branch that stretched out over the sandpit lake. He had us scramble over there, and we built a bonfire on that side. Jack spent much of the evening whooping and singing various verses from Italian operas and from Gilbert & Sullivan musicals, as he swept out on the rope and launched himself, like Tarzan, flying out into the water. There was no stopping him. He soared out, then back to the bank. Then another Gilbert & Sullivan verse, and he was flying out again into the starlight night. Most of us followed his lead for half an hour. Jack kept it up for almost two hours. It was a last fling back at a fading summer.

A quarter moon rose as the fire died down, and we eventually swam back to the other side and dried off. We re-stoked the bonfire on the camping side, where our sleeping bags were.

Under the stars, the silver sound of wind through the cottonwoods, like waves on the shore, whispered the special deep whisper of an old friend. Through the deep fall night, when an Alberta clipper from Canada was dropping the temperature forty degrees, the fire steadfastly burned. Our conversations drifted, and the crickets sang us to sleep, one by one.

* * *

As the bacon fried up, pretty quick we began moving in around the breakfast fire, seeking heat. Wendell had brought in more wood, and the flames blazed higher, teaming up with the rising sun. Greg Bryant took to running chords on his guitar, spinning through folk music history. Hanson was stoking up his Danish meerschaum pipe and smoking another round of the legendary, deep-black raspberry flavored Flying

Dutchman. He was Danish Lutheran, a sectarian breed, for sure. In his family, he was the most out going, philosophical and accepting of others beliefs. He too was an Iron Man, a half-miler in track seasons. Last night's discussions, after the Tarzan-phase, had turned to soulful topics, such as differences in our religions, Everett Miller's *Carmina*, the bullies of the locker rooms, rock music, Mr. Kramer's odd-ball tilt toward Ghengis Khan, and the deep temptations and feelings toward the wondrous girls such as Lizbeth, Audrey Jean Zimmerman, Lizbeth's older sister Mary, and the AFS gal from India.

The bacon and eggs were downed with a good jolt of A-1 sauce, and the coffee swilled some practical sense of the day ahead, back into us.

"We'd best get back into town," Wendell said finally.

"Mom wants me back to mow the lawn," I confessed.

"Farm chores are waiting. I don't want Dad driving out here for me," Hanson sighed.

We scurried to clean up. I drove Greg back with me. We reviewed our musical plans for next week, with *Carmina* and folk trio rehearsals.

"You still want to visit our youth Wednesday Baptist Bible study group to describe Catholics and the Vatican Council's stuff?" Greg asked.

"You bet. I'm there." I was hoping for, but not betting on, open hearts and minds. We were living in a strange time, with deep and cold conflicts and fears.

I ended up back home mowing the lawn for Mom, and helping with laundry and trash-burning. After lunch, I called Alan Luecke.

"Hey, big guy. Are you up for music this afternoon?" "Up for music" meant that we would spend a couple hours listening and discussing mostly jazz and blues history.

"Yeah. Come on over," Al said.

Alan Luecke was a best friend since eighth grade. I was indebted to Al for coaching me in the more nonchalant ways to put your arm around girls at the movies and maneuver in for closer operations. We were conspirators in jazz history, what with my dad's and Al's combined two hundred album collections. I spent as much time burning through his refrigerator and album collection as any place in town. A tall, lanky guy with coal-black hair and flashing blue-green eyes, he often broke a mile-wide grin that he borrowed from his mother, with whom he shared a heart of gold and courage. He was Big Al to me. In eighth grade track Big Al and his unending legs had burnt out a new half mile record better by three seconds of any previous middle school mark. He was the kind that was quiet about his talents. He could recite the history of virtually any rock or jazz band, group, or star in his numerous albums.

I hopped on Vindicator, and buzzed over to his place, north of CHS. I knocked, then breezing in through the front door, Alan led me through the kitchen. There sat Terry, off work from the Skyliner, and his best friend and Alan's older brother, John. They were eating Wonder Bread and bologna sandwiches, and downing chips.

"Hey, you guys," Terry called out, "what are you dudes gonna be doing?"

I didn't talk too much with seniors, but some of these guys were A-Okay.

"Listening to records," I answered.

"No kidding. What?"

"Oh, various old jazz and blues."

"Yeah? How about the Beatles?"

"Well, yeah."

"We're gonna *do* some music, later," John said. "Heard of the Flippers?"

"Yeah, sure."

"Well, you guys may be too young," Terry said. "Maybe we'll squeeze you in one of the Armory's windows or something." He winked big at us.

"I gotta run the Cloud Nine Drive-In movie projectors tonight," I replied, disappointed. "Maybe Al and you guys can sneak out there, huh?"

"You run the movies? Cool. Maybe we'll come out and harrass ya!" Terry joked.

"I could let you in after ten p.m. when Mr. Roney goes home," I said. "Call the number, you'll get my sister at the concession stand. She'll let me know and we'll get you in." I winked back at him.

"We don't know yet," John said. "There might be lots going on."

Alan and I nodded. We weren't really sure what that meant, so we drifted off to the stereo room.

High Plains Minutemen

Across town, the secretly hidden instrument of rebellion was under-construction.

"I'll spray paint the back of the shirt. Gimme that can," called out the skinny one with the wry smile.

The bigger guy flipped him a spray can, an old one from the auto body repair shop his dad used to own.

"Let's stash it in the trunk of my '57 Chevy. I'll be sure to get it where it needs to go real early next week," the bigger guy said.

A third shorter guy was standing watch outside the back of the *Highway 81 Mixer Shop*, which was an extension store selling soft drinks and snacks, connected to Brady's liquor store across from the Skyliner Restaurant and Motel. The rear-side of it had a small storage area and garage, where this spraying and construction was underway. The '57 was parked out back of the store in the gravel. It sported several long whip-like antennae. One of them was a CB radio.

In the little garage, the construction crew labored to finish. The bigger guy was a real wit. He was humming a song as he helped patch and tie the pieces of the instrument of rebellion together. It was made up of stuffed paper, a carefully drawn charcoal sketch of a face, a white shirt and bow tie, blue jeans, a Roi Tan cigar, a Pabst Blue Ribbon tall can, and a Jack Daniels bottle. After the third Pall Mall cigarette, the watchman tapped on the glass pane of the back window.

"You dudes about done?"

"Come around back," called out the skinny guy.

The back door opened, the instrument was hustled into the trunk, and the big V-8 roared to life. The wheels spun gravel as the '57 drove away, aiming for downtown pool halls, its secret weapon safely stashed away until its deployment.

The Doors to Ray's Mystical Chicken

Peanuts.

Sometime during the War, the rumors said, Ray had visited "down south." One theory among town folk was maybe he drifted out to the countryside on weekends, to try out southern cooking by dropping in on Mom-and-Pop cafes and road side stands, which are spread about every two hundred yards on all roads throughout the South. Ray LaBarge, a boy from out West, comparing Western cooking to that of the South. Ray would have caught on that usually the best recipes were from the small black family establishments. Maybe at one of those roadside stands, he learned one of his hidden secrets of his fried chicken: peanut oil. The other theory was, Ray was French. Nobody knew which theory of how Ray learned his culinary sorcery was correct. It's what the Catholics call "a mystery".

Ray's mystical chicken for twelve years now had Concordia folks, plus some of northeast Kansas and southern Nebraska, flocking to his café at noon. Ray's Café was a block east from Longton's Bakery and two doors west of City Hall, on the north side of Main. Mom, whose French bones knew more than most folks brains about cooking, said Ray's was the best fried chicken in a thousand miles. The recipe had more than just one ingredient, though. For years folks had prodded and bribed Ray for his secrets. You could patch some clues together, if you hung around a lot and listened to patrons. Usually he joked and dodged any questions about his recipe. Some said he once mentioned white flour with fresh sage. A nun from the Sisters of St. Joseph Convent told Dad and others she heard Ray once say corn flakes. Others said cracked black pepper. My big clue came when I saw a red-headed waitress wink once, lean over and breathe out to a table of local bankers the words "peanut oil."

Ray's Café offered varied, home-made dishes. Each daily lunch plate special was a buck: Roast beef & gravy, salisbury steak, meat loaf, chicken and noodles. All of them were tasty. But the queen of them all was the fried chicken. I had begged Dad since I was six years old to drop in every week or two and buy me the two-piece chicken plate. It was a tradition, for Dad and me, and I was pretty successful at keeping it up. I had close on to eight years of Ray's mystical chicken by the time I was fourteen, which no doubt came close to three hundred pieces of chicken, speaking conservatively. Eight years allowed me to eavesdrop on uncounted conversations, in my search for *Ray's recipe*. I was out to be the detective who would finally unearth Ray's culinary secret. When I was eight, Dad stepped out to the car, and I scurried behind the counter. Ray and the waitresses were serving customers, so I whipped back into the kitchen to see what I could spy. On the floor were large bottles of a thick-looking oil, labeled *"Lou Ana "* from Opelousas, Louisiana. They were stacked next to butter-flavored Crisco boxes. *Bingo.* I had cracked the greatest secret since the Manhattan Project. With

Ray's chicken, there was a powerful crunch involved, and a buttery-garlic-sage flavor that could not be found anywhere else. I thought I had the secret down cold, and told Mom. In the end, even Mom couldn't duplicate the flavor by using my discovered "two-oils". Apparently there was more in the secret than just two oils. Ray's chicken remained the great unsolved riddle in northern Kansas.

All manner of things blew in through the doors of Ray's Café, with its wide, south-facing screen, and its glass doors. In came the wise women, and town philosophers, the Doctors from the hospital, and even the Bishop from Salina. The best deep-dish pies in the west were arranged in crystal cases on the wall or in the round tower glass cases on the green marble bar. When Ray rang up bills at the register, if your receipt came up with a star on it, you got a free meal.

In the winter, frozen west-by-northwest blasts funneled in. In the spring it was the cooling south wind. In the fall, colorful leaves. Always something or somebody important blew in through that door. On this particular Saturday, as in every Saturday lunch and Wednesday supper, Coach Betts strode through the door, on the hunt for Ray's mystical chicken.

Betts grabbed a center table, and ordered up the two-piece special. In a few moments, George Ganstrom swept in and sat at the table with Coach.

"Well, George, how did harvest look this year?" Bankers knew how harvests went.

"Decent enough, with wheat. The thirteen-year cicadas were not much of a problem, and rains were enough. So Coach, how's the new generation of athletes? Football look good? Track?"

"Football's looking good." Betts eyes narrowed. "Track, I tell you George, 1967 will go down as *the* year of track in Kansas history, that's my guess. There are so many miracle kids out there in the Kansas high schools, and we got a half dozen of them, sprinters this year, each one of them a state record breaker. Your boy is among them, not to mention Householter." Betts crunched a big bite of Ray's chicken. The silence grew while he chewed slowly. He wasn't thinking chicken.

"I've seen eighteen years of track talent around this state," Betts spoke up. "Some of them have been the greatest talents in the nation. Kids like Jim Ryun, and Bill Dotson, and Duane McIntire, and Charlie Tidwell in the '50s, and the miracle black hurdler, Bill Kimble, last year." He dropped his fork, leaned low across the table, and whispered, "I don't know whether I should say this to people. It's really hard to say this. But I've never seen a miracle kid like Terry. We'll see. I just hope we can keep his head on straight. The other kids too. These days, the kids seem different."

"So, what's your best guess. What's different?" George poked around in his coleslaw, with his eyes wide open.

"Ten years ago it was more about cars, TV, and rock. Now it's hard to put my finger on it. They're harder to motivate sometimes, more independent. Seems like more temptations are out there. And some are scared, with the war heating up and talk of a draft on the minds of the seniors."

"I know..." George whispered, sinking into dark memories of seeing all this before in World War Two.

One of the young waitresses, looking like Emma Peel in *The Avengers*, breezed past in a hot mini-skirt, giving the men a dose of just what was on the minds of the new generation. Finally George, with half-mixed feelings, found breath enough to wheeze out an appropriate question.

"So, do we need to crack down more, guard against some of this looseness?"

"Whatever's going on, I think they need to know self-discipline, what it means to work for what you want," Betts replied softly.

"Our ministers say it's all about moral corruption. Satan is loose out there," said George, playing that one out, stirring his coffee, and buying time to think. Finally it came to him. "Hmm. Playing blame games doesn't change anybody's mind. I guess if they are occupied and really challenged in groups, then that's a start. Kids aren't dumb. They learn what's good and balanced, if given a chance. And if they survive their first car-driving years."

Betts nodded to that. "Preachers don't know all, do they. Religion doesn't hit everybody. I'm sorry, George, I know you're a religious man. And I've agreed to promote the Fellowship of Christian Athletes. But I think getting them to strive for excellence, and to endure, like the farm families that stuck together through the dustbowl, is a key. It carries over to help families and neighbors. It keeps them focused and not drifting, and away from beer, marijuana. When that burning inside hits 'em, to go for their best, that's the turning point for them. I told the track team in the spring of '59, the year after I came, that one of their classes could be State Track Champs. I told 'em it was simply their choice. 'Which class will choose to do it?' I asked them. And you know, that freshmen class that year, the class of '62, was the first to do it."

George wondered if Betts saw himself as a high-plains philosopher. George joked instead, "Well, if the fumes hit 'em first, and that's what starts burning, then you are preaching to the lost."

"Fumes?"

"Car fumes and perfumes."

They mused further, as the coconut pies showed up. "Still..." George muttered, more to himself, "somehow, things are complicated today."

Adventure

"We got this 'bootleg' copy of the new one you just heard from an unknown garage band. Will they make it big some day? You call and tell us at..." The radio in the '57 Chevy blared out the song "Born to Be Wild" by Steppenwolf, from the legendary "Giant 50,000 watt KOMA, 1520 on your radio dial, America's station, from *Oklahoma Citaay*..."

The Chevy spit gravel as it left Brady's garage, and cruised north on US 81, heading into town, with its hidden instrument of rebellion in the trunk. The Chevy had the egg-shell cobalt blue base color, with chrome trim on the sides, and the hardshell white-cream top, and wide white sidewall Goodrich tires. It was decked out inside with several wireless radios and gizmos attached to the front dashboard, including a CB radio for long-distance communication, a police monitor, and an adapted Chrysler under-the-dash air conditioner (pirated from dad's old auto shop). It also had a set of double-dice hung from the rear view mirror, a side door spotlight which could swing out from inside the car. And last but not least, it had a pirated naked lady wheel spinner attached to the steering wheel, the one that got Roger in much trouble with Sister Euthanasia in grade school. They were cruising north on Highway 81 for Cooley's pool hall downtown when suddenly, Tim Brady grabbed the fake alligator skin covered steering wheel, and tugged it to the right. The Chevy spun into the gravel lot of Charlie Blosser's Army-Navy-Rangers supply store, and skidded to the front door as Roger slammed on the brakes.

"Hey dung-head. You should give me notice, not just grab the wheel," Roger snapped.

"There's stuff I gotta get in here, for tonight at the Flippers deal. Besides you're an ace at braking, so cut the whining." Tim grinned. He whipped out the door and hustled inside the low, white cinderblock building, with Roger trailing and still bitching about just missing a fire hydrant.

Inside, the front glass cases of Charlie's held a wilderness of exotic outdoor items. The intoxicating smells of leather, moldy-waxed canvas, cigar smoke and spilled coca-cola mixed lightly in the shop air. The glass cases out front held bayonets, Bowie knives, World War II sidebelts and canteens, odds and ends of uniforms, pocket knives with spoons and forks, ivory handled Roy Rogers sideguns, long-knives with Roy's face etched in black on ivory handles, and boxes of Black Jack Licorice and Juicy Fruit chewing gums.

Along the top and sides were hung parachutes, and racks of flight jackets, including a rack of World War II leather flying ace jackets, and another rack of the spiffy "Eisenhower jackets" of Army Officer wool. His store packed a trillion pieces of trivia from Boy Scouts, both world wars, and the arts of mountain men, all gathered into large boot cardboard boxes and displayed on tables. Back on the walls were hardier pieces of equipment, such as military issue small tents, fire-axes, cots, and boxes of K-rations. Arrayed on one wall were art renderings of fighter planes of both world wars, and the USS Missouri with her big guns blazing at beaches in the South Pacific. Charlie's prize possessions were hung above the cash register. One was a photo of the infamous First War's bloody Red Baron Manfred von Richthofen, the killer German ace. Next to it was a signed photo of the Baron's killer, the hero Captain Arthur R. Brown of the courageous Canadian Air Force.

Tim stepped closer to read the words written on the photo again, probably for the forty-ninth time: "Charlie, you were right, Irish ale leaves you with bigger headaches and bustier ladies. Yours, Art."

Roger wasn't much into war stuff, but he ambled forward to stare at this photo, his mouth open. Charlie stepped out of the shadows, chomping on the stump of an unlit Dutch Boy cigar. His sure movements and quick direct stares revealed the reflexes of a First War fighter pilot.

"What ya need this time, kid?"

Tim drummed his fingers on the glass top case for a couple seconds and wheezed out, "Uh, you got anything we can use for night excitement?"

"Depends, kid. You gonna be outta town, in the country?"

"Sure."

"Don't lie to me, kid. I got too many years of crap-detecting skills up here." He tapped his noggin. "If I sell you stuff, you'd better not mention me. Dog houses and cars can have accidents, you know." He winked.

"Don't worry. We'll definitely be outta town," Tim replied.

"Follow me back. Knock anything over and you buy it." Charlie waved them into the store. They trekked back through the rows of stacked boxes on tables. Back behind an old player-piano was a glass case with a tarp over it.

"Okay. Name it, kid."

"Well, we want some M-80s, and maybe something with a little more punch," said Tim. Charlie's long, strongly-cabled arm snaked under the dusty tarp, and extracted a small box of M-80s.

"That'll be three bucks."

"Oookaay.,." Tim said. "Ya got anything else?"

"Yeah. For ten bucks," Charlie replied, smiling.

Roger and Tim swooned a little over the price.

"I'll spot ya some. But you're gonna have to get it back to me in a week," Roger said.

"Okay, Charlie," said Tim. "What's possibly worth the ten dollars?"

"Step over here, young men, see the options." His long arm whipped out again, and laid two strange looking devices on the tarp. The first had a long cylinder shape.

"They got commercial uses. Farmers used to use 'em to scare off crows," Charlie droned-on, like an old-time snake oil salesman. "I'll sell you one of each of these, but only once. This one's called a Cricket Ball," he laid out the second one, "and this is a really rare one, called the Smooth Mills. You'll be just fine with these as long as you don't use them with anybody nearby and you go behind a tree to launch them. I ain't selling you the more dangerous ones," said Charlie.

"What *are* these?" Roger asked.

"Oh, they're rare enough nowadays. Made by the Brits. The bastards can't make a car that starts, but they sure did these right. They're early First World War grenades."

"*Holy crap...*" Roger gasped.

Tim leaned back on the case, staring at Roger. "Sure we oughta do this?"

"Look boys, a sledge hammer couldn't set 'em off. You gotta pull the pin out. Even then, you got eight full seconds. These very early ones had less shrapnel, so they were as much thunder as threat. Now do exactly what I say: throw it down over a hill, then hit the dirt or get behind a tree and you're safer than a baby in a mother's arms. It'll scare the feathers clean off a buzzard at a quarter mile."

The ten dollars changed hands, and they were out the door.

Cooley's Pool Hall

"Come on, I'll whup ya at pool," Roger called out, as the '57 spun down the hill, and into town.

"Ah, bullshit," Tim replied. "Which place?"

"Cooley's. We can try the ice trick, see if it works there." Rog winked

"Yeah, that'd pan out good for the Armory later." Tim was referring to the coming big blowout at the National Guard Armory featuring *The Fabulous Flippers*, the greatest show band of the midwest. They were coming in that night for their third stand at the Armory on the south edge of town, just beyond the bowling alley and the Skyliner, out at the city lake and airport. The Chevy turned left before the big bridge at City Hall, and buzzed west three blocks, turned right heading toward the tracks, and pulled into Cooley's on the southeast corner of Fifth and Olive. The rippling Pabst Blue Ribbon display and the Hamm's Beer, *Land of Sky-Blue Waters* display, with its bubbling waters, tall pines and roaming bears, called out to them through the glass windows.

They opened the grid-screen door, and strolled into the darkened bar, where green-mat pool tables spread out under see-through colored Bud and Schlitz lampshades above. On the ceiling, low-powered, whirling broad-blade fans spun slowly above in the summer months. They lay in silent hibernation for the Fall. The bar had quaint snacks for sale: pickled eggs, beef jerky, smoked oysters, as well as cigars and chewing tobacco. Thick blue cigar smoke hung in the air and drifted in clumps near the patterned steel ceilings. The smoke was sucked erratically by a reluctantly spinning exhaust fan in the back of the store.

A couple of older guys sat on the bar stools. Two younger guys in red and white wool and leather sports jackets hung out in at a pool table, shooting balls. Tim strode up to the bar, carrying a slightly rusted green and white Coleman cooler, trying to catch the eye of Ike, the owner and bartender.

"Hey, Ike. Dad wants some ice in the cooler, Colorado ice," Tim called out.

"He hasn't got any, huh, so he sent you?"

"He's trying to get mom's car started. The Colorado ice truck didn't stop at his shop this week. Just a little personal amount will do fine." A "cooler of ice" was slang around Concordia booze dealers, especially on Sundays, for a request to fill the bottom of a cooler with beer or other known favorite beverages, and cover the top with less-criminal ice. Cooley's was one of the few places that had regular deliveries of Coors, a fairly hard to get brew out of Colorado. The Coors truck driver was a third cousin of the owner, who often left other liquor stores, pool halls or dance halls short on the product, but he never left Cooley's short.

"You sure this is for your *Dad?*" Ike asked.

"Well, you can mark it on his tab here, although I'll pay for it. That should clear up who it's for..." Tim and his dad had an "understanding" to split the beer.

"Okay, sure." Ike grabbed the cooler and headed to the ice machine.

Roger and Tim ambled around the pool hall, observing pool games. Roger looked over the nickel bowling machine, and fed it a couple nickels. He loved to bowl with the little balls and pins.

Ike strolled back after several minutes. "I left your ice cooler out near the back door. You can pick it up there. His out-stretched hand took the five dollars that Tim waved in the air. Roger finished his game, and the two teens ambled toward the back of the store.

"Up for a game of billiards, Tim?" Terry Householter called out, as they ambled past the backroom table.

"I took your money last time, didn't I, kid?" Tim joked.

"That's not how I remember it, exactly," John Luecke smiled out. "Seems like you got cooked by the House here."

Terry and Tim were ace players, who took stabs at each other occasionally in pool games at Cooley's and out at the Bowling Alley. Nickels were often bet. The best offer was Indian-head nickels. Roger always had an eye out for Indian-heads, when he and the rest of our family sat down before church on Sundays and counted out the coins taken in from dad's self-serve washers and dryers at the laundromat. Rog slipped Tim a couple Indian-heads, which he carried around in an old coin purse. When they were laid on the banks of the billiard table, smiles broke out, and the game began.

"I'll load up and come back for you. Don't lose the Indian-heads again, Lone Ranger," Roger coughed out this sarcasm to Tim who had taken on the "Lone Ranger" nick- name as a pool shark. A few minutes later, Roger closed the trunk on the '57 and started to head toward the back door. Tim burst through the door, his hands in his pockets.

"Ah, so, me Tonto sees..." Roger drew-out the sarcasm, "that Keemosabi has lost Tonto's Indian-heads, *again*. You owe Tonto big money."

"I almost never can take that kid," Tim grumbled. "He learned from his brother. He sank seven in a row in about forty seconds, before I had a shot."

"I guess he's fast at more than one thing." Roger smiled wryly. "You still owe me."

"Well, if there's any beer left over, you can have it."

"That might work. Let's go cruise. We can pick up some burgers at A & W and head out to the Rocks to kill time before taking to the Armory later to catch *The Fabulous Flippers.*"

"Sounds decent," Tim said, and the '57 growled down the alley, heading east.

The Fabulous Flippers

Eight-thirty p.m. Up at the big National Guard Armory, on the east side hill above the airport park lake just south of town, cars were everywhere. They parked in the grass, on the roads leading up from Highway 81, and along the fence south near the airport runway. They crammed in around the tanks and Army water trucks near the building itself, and even out on the Highway north and south for a quarter mile. Outside the building, teens and early twenty-somethings gathered in clumps, eyeball-ing each other and the cars. The cars were a wonderland of Detroit jewels. Terry and John had squeezed John's '56 Chevy into the crowded Armory parking lot by going down the drainage bank on the bottom of the drainage culvert, and angling up across the open field to the black-top lot. They got out, and strolled through the lot. They nodded at Jerry and Jake, as their rusty pickup passed, seeking a spot to park.

"Jesus," breathed John, half-way through the lot. "Did you see that metal-flake gold '65 Barracuda? It had a custom-air scoop, and tags from Oklahoma."

"I like the '66 and '65 Mustangs. The red-cherry one has South Dakota tags. Lord, people drive here from all over," Terry replied. Whistling loud, they eyeballed and passed a long, purple-hood '65 Bonneville, but suddenly they were stopped dead by a crowd surrounding a smaller vehicle. They pushed through the groups, and caught a glimpse of the jewel of the night. It attracted jocks, gals, and musicians alike. It was a jacked up 1960 Plymouth Valiant, in powder-flake turquoise, with red-and-yellow glitter-flames on the doors, Tiger Paw tires, and a cut-out hood with a chromed engine sticking up through the hole.

"Whew," whistled John. "You see that? Never imagined such a thing. That's a Chrysler 426 hemi engine drop-in, with a super-charger. *The Monster*, forced into an en-gine-well designed only for a six-banger!" The big Chrysler hemi engines could crank out well above six hundred horsepower, the most powerful engines Detroit ever built.

"Sure beats the slant-six, huh?" Terry replied, referring to the Valiant's legendary gas-miserly standard six-cylinder engine.

As the drivers revved the super-charged, alcohol-and-gas fired engine, it belted out mostly dust and air. The power-mad engine actually twisted the car's frame into the front torsion bar suspension. It heaved out deafening roars like a Tyrannosaurus Rex, and scattered teenagers back onto the grass. People fifty feet away had to cover their ears. The driver and his buddies show-cased the crown jewel of the night by inching down the blacktop in front of the Armory entrance door. Even the ticket tak-ers and bouncers swarmed out to snatch a look as it inched past. Like Moses parting the sea, the Valiant parted the crowd, its flashing red, blue, and white small bulbs encircled an Iowa plate on the back. It growled south, periodically scaring the natives, as it prowled and roared to the night.

Terry and John were pushing slowly through the crowd to the ticket booth. The entrance was gilded with rotating, flashing colored lights, which surrounded the door frame. A neon sign above blinked out "The Fabulous Flippers".

"Hi, Terry." Sky-blue eyes, and the gorgeous shy smile and purring voice of Lizbeth Ellison called out to him.

Terry and John glanced at her. A nest of younger friends that included Liz, her sultry sister Mary, Alan, and the Foster brothers were perched to the side of the entrance. Mary elbowed Terry and smiled.

60

"Hey, guys," Terry called out. "I'll bet you want in, huh?"

"You guessed it, sharpie," Mary said.

Lizbeth blinked her fairy-eyes up at Terry and smiled. Not able to pass by her exquisite perfume and dazzling eyes, Terry grabbed his sidekick John by the collar, and leaned in to whisper to the crowd.

"We'll see what we can do. Go around south to the kitchen windows and wait about fifteen minutes. If something can happen, it will. We'll give it a shot." Terry flashed his famous smile, and smiles shone back, all around. Then he winked. "See ya, I'll bet." Jerking his head toward the entrance, he signaled John to follow him in. They showed their driver's licenses and paid for their tickets, pushing past the bouncers who checked identification. They slipped through the narrow passage way into the huge, steel and concrete Armory.

"What are you up to, wise guy?" John asked.

Terry reached into his back pocket and pulled out a five-inch square of thin plastic.

"I cut it from one of the new plastic orange juice jugs at the Skyliner. Figured we'd run into your brother, or some of his crowd. You know the bouncers won't let 'em in without drivers licenses, and most of 'em don't have one yet." Terry smiled craftily. "Follow me to the kitchen door." They ambled over, weaving through the crowds. "Now stand in front of me, and flex that big chest of yours. I don't want anybody catching me. You should watch more *007* movies, to pick up cool ideas like this."

John complied, adopting a wide-straddle. He crossed his arms on his chest. Eyeing the crowd carefully, and seeing it was clear of anybody older than twenty-five, Terry slid behind John, and slipped the thin plastic into the crack of the kitchen door, then slid it down past the lock tumblers of the door. He made a couple of tugs downward. The plastic forced the tumblers back from the frame. He popped open the door slightly, then looking back for cover, he whispered, "I'll be back in two shakes. Just stand here. I'll knock three times. Open the door when you're sure it's clear." Terry slipped inside.

He skipped over to the kitchen windows that faced south, spun the handle, slid the window open, and stuck his head out. "It's Santa. Are you elves ready?"

Lizbeth planted a cool smack on his cheek, and some of the little crowd scrambled together, to boost each other through the windows. They scampered to the door. Terry knocked, and in three seconds the crowd slipped inside, popped out beside John, and formed a line that hid the next ones sneaking in. Thanks and winks were exchanged all around.

"Don't go out unless you're leaving. You don't have hand stamps to get back in," John cautioned the group. Mary replied, "We owe you," and the crowd scattered out.

On the far side, big side tables were laid out with cokes and small paper bowls of potato chips and french onion dip for sale, a nickel each. The band was approaching start-up time, milling around on-stage.

"Let's head up closer!" Terry called out.

Alan had sprung himself in somehow and now hung-out with them. They all nodded, and moved closer to the stage.

"These guys are *out-there*," Alan tried hard to explain. "The horn section is so good that people scream, and the singers are amazing, Danny Hein hung with Leon Russell in Tulsa, and Denny Loewen, they've got the greatest voices. The drummer, Jerry Tammen, will tear your *shirts off.* It's all R & B. Best stuff going."

Terry and John nodded.

"You're the man, dude. You spend enough hours scouring blues records," John admitted.

"These guys tear up the entire middle of the country from Texas to Canada, and Wyoming to Kentucky," Alan continued. "They draw crowds as big as the Stones. The entire rock music world copies them and, believe it or not, they're from Lawrence, Kansas. It's all about the music and the stage show. Hold on to your shorts."

The legendary eight-piece band was spectacularly arrayed in shiny boots, blue velvet suits, their cream color silk shirts had ruffles with different color edging under the neck. Under bright spotlights, their gleaming silver or gold horns, and sparkling chrome and candy-apple sheen drums dazzled the crowd. They milled around, taking positions on stage, settling in with final tune-ups. The mike was grabbed, and Loewen barked, "We're *The Fabulous Flippers* here for ya tonight, in scenic Con-cordia Kansas!"

The crowd went ape.

"We got *The Harlem Shuffle* coming for ya, *but*...to start off, we got a very special opener for ya tonight, first time anywhere in mid-America, by special permission of good buddies of ours. We're pushin' this for 'em. It's coming out this next month. It's an amazing kicker, and you'll have to bribe us to tell you who's bringing it out on the airwaves, and who wrote it. But here it is, for the first time on our tour, all for the greatest of the greats, and you'll be buying it for the next fifty Christmases..."

Alan's eyes bulged as if he was about to lose heavy steam. Terry and John raised their eyebrows. Suddenly, the drums split the night, the guitars soared, and colored lights and players danced in mesmerizing patterns on stage. The vocalists belted out lines and traded leads, and the fantastic horn players rotated from horn-to-horn, flipping their horns in the air, screaming out perfect harmonies. Amped up enough to threaten the fuses and seriously dim the front office lights, the band tore holes in the roof. The building, and even the hill, shook with riffs, lyrics and cheering that would be repeated for generations...

I'm a soul man, I'm a soul man...**Isaac Hayes, Sam & Dave**

The crowd was hoarse in seven minutes. The band roared on into the night.

Chapter 7
NIGHT MOVES, LIBERATION, AND MYSTERIES

And the Good Times Rolled

At the ten o'clock evening break, the *Fabulous Flippers* crowd spilled out of the Armory into the night. Most of the clumps of fans hung around buying records, drinking clandestine beer in the cars, ogling the cars, or each other, or heading out to the nearby park for some nocturnal activities. Most, not all, would prefer to return to the band, this night. A few small groups headed down to the lake, one hundred yards below.

Roger and Tim, who had come in a little late from the Rocks, headed out to the lot with a few gleams in their eyes. As the beer was sucked down, small groups got a little rowdier. One group started a small fire on a lid snatched from an Armory trash can, and were roasting hot dogs. The *Valiant* was revving its engine again, and conducting a self-guided tour of the roads in the park, with "little honeys" who would crowd into the car as it circled back to the front entrance from time to time. Another crowd was trying out KOMA Radio 1520 on a custom-installed radio and speaker combination, and swilling a few beers. Tim and Roger drifted from one group to another, dragging along a brown paper bag with some of the still-fairly uncommon Coors in it, for sheer interest and conversations.

"You still got the other sack in the trunk?" Roger asked.

"Sure do," Tim answered. "When's a good time to get into that?"

"Maybe just as the crowd thins, going back in."

"We do want to watch out for Krasny and Co." Bill Krasny was the Chief of Police. His deputies themselves were a rowdy crowd.

"They'll be going in the building, or following what looks like too-drunk drivers going out on the road, which is starting about now. They won't be hanging around the lot," Roger predicted.

"Man, let's go up and see that crazy Valiant," Roger said. "Dad used to sell those in the Dodge dealership, before he switched the business to the laundromat. We had the first Valiant station wagon in 1960 sold west of the Mississippi. Dad and I took a bus up to Omaha to get the car off the train from Detroit, supposedly for the dealership, but he drove it home, allegedly 'for Mom'. Mom pitched a fit. Said she "didn't need no new expensive car." But Dad wouldn't take it back. She got so mad she flung his bowl of spaghetti, meatballs and all, at him across the table. He ducked that one.

It was the French in her, Grama said. She apologized, we all laughed, and we got the new car!"

"Sheesh, that's excitement all-right, my mom never flings anything. Yeah, let's go see this thing," Tim said. As they strolled up to the north side entrance, the Valiant was coming around the curve. The screams of the engine were deafening, as the car unloaded, and loaded up again for a new cruise. Roger ogled the Chrysler drop-in huge alcohol-boosted V-8 engine that stuck up through a cut-out in the hood of the Valiant. Tim eyeballed something else, off north a bit in the field. A bunch of younger guys had started up the Armory's huge double-sided lawnmower, and were driving it around in the field north of the Armory. They had idled-down the machine, and were running in to see the Valiant.

"Hey, Rog. Get your eyeballs off the Valiant there. Come on, I've got an idea..." Tim said, tugging on Roger's sleeve.

"Whassup, Lone Ranger?" Roger asked. Tim just pointed north, to the idling huge mower.

"Aha, *Silver*," Roger said slyly. "We got ourselves *Silver*, Lone Ranger." Silver, of course, was the Lone Ranger's horse. They split north to the field.

Hopping on the mower's driver-seat, Roger fiddled with the gears, revved the engine and cried, "Climb on back, Lone Ranger." Tim shook his head, hopped aboard, and hung on as Roger spouted the famous "Hi Ho, Silver, and away..." and popped the clutch. The mower growled off at top speed, mowing across the field like a demon in the night, straight toward the Armory.

"We'll give those bastards in the Valiant something else to remember!" Roger called out, and he spun the wheel and headed onto the entrance road, and drove the mower through the big crowd near the front doors of the Armory. Blinking his lights, and revving his engine erratically, and cutting off the power to the mower blades, Roger warned the crowd he was coming through.

"Yee-ha!" he called out, with a fist raised in the air. "On to the Valiant!" The startled crowd spread out making way, and raising toasts of beer. A few managed to jump on-board. Like a crazed bumper-car race, the mower plowed on into the dark, with a couple extra stragglers hanging on for good, guzzling beers. Roger weaved it around on the snaking roads of the park, and closed the gap on the Valiant.

"Agh. Side-trip!" Roger yelled, as he suddenly branched left, driving the mower up a bank of grass.

"What the hell you doing now?" Tim yelled.

"Radar shed. Radar shed." Roger shouted cryptically, pointing. The airport had a radar installation for weather forecasting, part of the National Weather radar system. It was a pork-barrel gift to the town in the late 1940s, partly because ancient-pilot Charlie Blosser wanted it for "his" airport, and partly because a certain United States Senator resided in Concordia, Kansas.

"We're gonna buzz the radar lady. She can't come out, because she can't abandon the radar readings. A little excitement, she needs it," Roger insisted, with his head and a smile cocked to one side. Tim shook his head again.

They buzzed up past the radar shed, but had to whizz out on the tarmac, and around the fence to get to it. Roger tied a red neckerchief from his back pocket around his face, and grinned. Approaching the building, he buzzed the shed at high speed, and then buzzed again, slowing a little. The radar lady stared out of the window, wondering what in blazes was going on. As he drifted past, Roger shot her the two-fingered V for victory sign. She scurried backward from the window, reaching for a phone.

Spinning around, he called out to the dazed and motley beer-guzzling crew still riding the mower, "We'd better put the pedal to the metal if we're to catch the Valiant!" as he blazed down the hill. Roger cut across roads, trying to catch the Valiant at a winding lower road the car was traversing, and then cut back through the park into the adjoining Armory parking lot. The mower hit the rise of a former tree stump, and went airborne for a second and splat back down on the grass with a terrible crunch. It lurched around doing wheelies until Roger regained control.

"Can't take *tooo* many of those..." he cried out, grinning from ear to ear. *When will the cops show up?* Tim worried. *Maybe Roger guessed right, maybe they're distracted by trolling for drunk drivers leaving the Armory just now.*

Roger bent himself to his task. He angled down-hill, gaining ground on the Valiant. He pulled up next to it on the shoulder of the road, and engaged the giant mower blades. He buzzed in close to the Valiant, kicking grass clippings into the car through its open windows. The passengers inside were startled to the bone, some shouting and laughing, others trying to brush grass out of their hair or cleavages. Rog gave the driver a thumbs-up sign, kicked off the mower blades, and spun a U-turn to climb up the grassy hill toward the open Armory parking lot above. He left the Valiant weaving and stranded on the asphalt, the driver reluctant to follow him up the slightly spongy ground.

"We'll drop off, and split for the crowd," Roger yelled to the whooping and still beer-gripping passengers who clung to the mower. "Never fear. They'll never figure out who we are." He pulled the mower up to the west side of the Armory parking lot, and killed the engine. They leaped from the machine and vanished like ghosts into the boiling crowd near the Armory, their joy and laughter sprinkling across the sparkling night air.

Lakeside Sentinels

Down at the lake waters, things were somewhat different.

Off to the north side of the lake, hidden behind some bushes, was a parked, tax-payer supported official car. In it were two officers of the law. This was one of three city police patrol cars assigned to the rock concert, which remained in the park. Two other patrol cars were off trolling for drunks on the road. The parked police vehicle was supposed to be doing the same. Instead, inside were two officers of the law of the opposite sex who were starting up something rather un-authorized. This was the police car *not* responding to calls from the central dispatcher, which had been relayed from the airport radar lady.

On the north-east side of the lake, a gathering of high school athletes had formed, mostly juniors and seniors, about two dozen guys. A small fire warmed the chill out of them. Only a few were from Swaggart's circle. The others in the crowd like Big Mick, Byron Beauchere, and Rodney Hess were down to earth, regular guys who had a more individual and independent mind. They sat around the fire, drinking the beer they carried down from their cars after leaving the dance at the break.

Stoking the fire up a little more, Brett Swaggart looked up.

"Hey, Stevens, break out the Bud from your cooler. No cops in sight for twenty minutes."

"Sure," Stevens agreed, and stepped over to grab the cooler from behind a bush.

"It's nice to get a break," said Big Mick. "Man, I'll tell you, from work and workouts, I'm beat. The band is a fantastic outfit. Nobody in the bars, or in Salina or Junction City around here sounds anything like these dudes. The horn guys, and the drummer, Holy Mother..." Mick passed around some Budweiser bottles.

"Yeah, and we don't have to be out suffering the sprints tomorrow, on Sunday morning, that's the best part," offered Brett. Groans and nods of sincere agreement spread around. "I'm breaking out the hotdogs over here, you guys can run your own sticks. Ketchup and stuff is on the picnic table."

"What are we doing down here?" asked Stevens. "Some of those Nebraska and Iowa honeys up there are what we oughta be nosing into."

"No kidding, Sherlock." replied Hess. "Hey, Mick, you wanna help me go scout some *poontang*. Some of them maybe ought to like beer."

"Yeah. We'll be back, with improvements," said Mick. They loped off up the hill to the Armory.

Stumbling down the hill that moment, and passing a stand of trees on the opposite side of Mick and Hess who were going up the hill, was a lone, slightly younger and paunchier figure. Grant liked to fish and spend time out on his dad's farm ponds. So he was heading down to the Airport Park lake, to skip rocks, and break away from the social scene of the older kids at the lots above. Tunes from the Flippers rummaged through his head, so he was oblivious to the crowd he was skirting around which had the built the fire nearby.

Momentarily, the entire lakeside crowd's attention was caught by three blazing Sentinels in the sky. The first two were pure white, and as bright as the burst of an electric arc welding torch. The streaks quickly cut across the sky from northeast to southwest. The third streak that followed in their wake was amazingly different: a spiraling, yellowish ball that fizzled—out fantastic yellow and red sparks. A sound like a sheet tearing next to your ear split the night, as the brilliantly-spurting third traveler etched the clear, black and starlit sky, unfolding like a sparkling inter-planetary whip.

"Lord Almighty, Roger, look over *there*!" Tim cried out, and pounded him on the back at the sight of the first two meteors. Roger was bent over, pulling out a second sack from the trunk of his '57.

"Ouch!" he cried, and spun quickly, to swear and swat at Tim in retaliation. But then Roger's eyes caught the glittering white tails of the fading first two celestial sentinels. Then he stood stunned by the passage of the dazzling yellow and red traveler.

"Whooaa," both guys moaned and stared at the fading sparkles. Rog whispered, "Mother Nature. Hell of a sight."

"No joke. It looked like it broke up over Jamestown, out west."

"Well, it was more like *over Denver.* It's hard to tell how far away, and big these fast-movers are."

"The fast-movers don't live long, do they?" observed Tim.

"No. But I'm standing here with this stuff stuck in my head. Probably until I die." Roger turned to Tim. "Makes you wonder how big it really is out there, huh?" He slammed the trunk shut. "The crowd is moving back into the Armory. The cops are nowhere. *Time to try out these puppies...*" Roger thumbed for Tim to head down to the lake with him. They traipsed off down the hill, headed just north and west of the barely visible fire of Swaggart's crowd.

Peach Brandy

Inside the police car, forty yards west of Swaggart's fire, and behind a clump of bushes, things were warming up. Police officer Dave Swazey, age thirty-six and married, had dialed in KOMA, and pulled a bottle of peach brandy out from underneath the driver's seat. He was proceeding to ply third year officer Jean Somerset, a single female. Officer Somerset pondered how game she was and entertained somewhat better feelings for the brandy than for the assignations of officer Swazey. Slowly, the eternal dance of the sexes was playing out.

As officer Swazey was pouring shots of brandy into two crystal shot glasses with the gold-lettering *"The Long Branch Saloon"* emblazoned on one side, Grant was ambling toward the lake edge, skirting only twenty feet distant from Swaggart's fire. He was hunting for stones to skip on the lake.

Lakeside Fires

Swaggart and his black-haired football buddy slurped down another long draft of five percent alcohol Budweiser, and milled around with the group close to the fire. Most of the guys were still roasting up hotdogs, and wondering if Mick and Hess were having any luck attracting out-of-town honeys down to the lake.

"Didja see that kid pass by us?" the muscled black-haired one asked.

"Nah." Swaggart replied.

"I think it's that pussy-kid, on the football team."

"Which one? There's so many."

"You know, the one you kicked the shit out of."

"Which one? There's so many..."

"The fat one, the pussy you went after on the first day, the youngest one of the McCoy brothers."

"Yeah," Swaggart smiled. "Let's drag him up here." They gathered a couple other willing goons, hoofed it down to the edge of the lake, split up, and encircled Grant from two sides, closing in quietly.

"You know, you do have some guts coming out here, kid, where the big boys are..." Swaggart commented to Grant from behind. Startled, Grant whipped around. He stared through the darkness, and matched up the half-light figures with terrified memories from football practice. His heart skipped two beats. The crickets sang cheerfully against the oddly terrifying moment.

"You want some beer, kid?" Brett spoke in low tones, and then broke a smile. "Come on up. Yup, you got guts." Brett and his muscle-buddies wrapped strongly gripping arms around Grant's shoulder. They pulled him insistently up the hill toward the fire.

"We ought to offer a little hospitality to a young guy with guts, don't you think, Axel?" Brett asked of his black-haired sidekick.

"Yeah. Sure. Hospitality."

"So, didja bring some pussy out with ya, Grant?" Brett asked. The goons chuckled.

"Uh, no." Grant's knees were turning to jelly. His mind raced between Brett's phrases. At one second Brett sounded like he was offering some big-brotherly adventure, but the next second Grant could read the double-meanings behind each comment. *What's really going on here?* he worried. As he was tugged toward the crowd, he scanned hopefully for familiar faces, perhaps a friend of his brother. His divided and racing mind searched back and forth between hints of safety, some route of escape from the crowd, the terrifying words, and the iron grips around his shoulders. His heart pounded on. Brett's grip pulled him to the fire's edge.

"Hang here, I'll get you a beer."

In two seconds, Grant glanced around, with the hope of running. But Brett was glancing back at him, the goons were nearby, and Axel muscled in next to him and bumped him in the shoulder. *This guy is a weirdo, he just stares straight ahead. He's not even looking at me.* Grant was getting dizzy with fear.

Brett was back in Grant's face. It was like Brett had instantly beamed over from the picnic table, fifteen feet away.

"Here, kid. It'll put hair on your chest!" Brett coldly joked, handing him a bottle of five percent beer.

"He needs more than another beer, for that to happen." Axel sneered, still staring straight-ahead like a robot.

"You're man enough for a couple, aren't you kid? You didn't come out here for nothing, did ya?" Brett bantered. "Too bad we don't have any pussy to offer you, yet. But that might be coming. Hey, this could be a big night for ya, huh kid?" Brett slapped him on the back hard. "Don't run off now. I'll get ya another tall one."

Brett disappeared a little too quickly in the dark again. Amidst the cheerful crickets, Axel spat on the ground next to the fire and stared stiffly into the night.

Two minutes passed in soundless agony. *Even Brett jabbering at me is better than this weird robot-man just standing here,* Grant thought. Occasionally, another couple guys came back to the fire. Two of them stayed now to roast up more hot dogs.

"Hey, Grant," one of them called up. Grant nodded at the friendly voice, and thought of sliding over to them for a possible safe escape. *This is a little better.* Suddenly, Brett was back in a flash again, straight out from the dark.

Law and Order

Police Chief Krasny headed south of the Skyliner on Highway 81 leading back to the Armory. He'd just shelled out four tickets for violations, one of them for driving under the influence. Three tickets were for out-of-staters, whom he had followed, or stalked, as they came out from the concert at the break.

The fourth ticket went to a local gal, daughter of a big-dog grocery man. He let her go with only a warning. *What perfume. What a smile, red lips, white teeth,* he fantasized, dreaming that he could cash-in with her for giving her only a warning. *Maybe next time I'll get lucky when I pull over her custom Mercury Cougar.* He shook his head to dispel the fairy-tale. He was hunting more teenage game, as he drove past the first north entrance and cruised south. He scanned the park for suspicious vehicles. He passed some shadows of vehicles and a small fire down by the lake. *Bet your ass there's shenanigans there, teenagers with beer, humping each other in the shadows. Better whiz around, come back.* He drove to the south entrance, shut off the lights, and spun the squad car around, pointing it back north. He planned his strategy. *Sneak up. Cut through where the drainage ditch levels out and meets the bank of the dam at the road. Crawl past the bushes on the lake edge. Check the fire. Spotlight anybody getting illegal booze or pussy...*

Grant

"Here's another tall one, kid. Better down it. It's not polite to waste money." Brett spoke close into Grant's ear, "You gotta learn polite. Right guys? Right Axel?" The goons cackled again.

"Damn skippy, bet your ass," Axel replied.

"See Grant? Axel learned polite years ago. He doesn't say much. Just does what needs to be done, and is very polite about it. As you get older, you'll like polite, and you'll want no smart-ass from the younger crowd. Right, Grant?"

"Uh, yeah."

"That's how things stay under control. There's all kind of crazy shitheads that want to break things up, get things outta control these days. Smart-ass niggers, protesters, hippies, the worst of them are the fairies." Brett paused.

"You're not a fairy, are you Grant?" Brett sneered.

"No. Course not."

"Axel. You think he's a fairy?"

Axel's robot head rotated around, his eyes motionless until they locked on Grant.

"I don't know. He's suspicious. He whimpers. Fairies whimper."

"Well, if you think he's a fairy, shouldn't we run the fairy-test?" Brett asked.

Only a minute ago, the other guys with hot-dogs had drifted away from the fire, when Brett had gone off on this "crazy shitheads" and "outta control" speech. The question hung in the air. Grant's heartbeat pounded in his ears. Bitter fear rushed back into his soul. His vision narrowed into a sort of tunnel, and the blood drained from his face.

"The fairy-test." Axel droned. "Yeah, this kid needs the fairy-test."

"I ain't no fairy. I've got a girlfriend! You can ask my brothers," Grant defended himself.

"They're not here, so we can't ask them, right Axel?" Brett blurted.

"I don't see them." Axel's robot neck rotated again, looking around. "I don't see nobody, except us men here." The goons cackled again.

"You don't have to be scared, kid. The test is easy." Brett said.

"Yeah, easy." Axel growled. Grant could see Axel's hands flexing and unflexing in the firelight. His heart raced frantically. He started to feel sick and real weak at the knees.

"All you have to do is be polite. Once the test is over, you don't have to worry about proving you're not a fairy again. Proof positive. Everybody's happy," Brett sneered.

"Let's get it over with..." Axel and the goons grunted. They wrapped their arms around Grant's shoulders from both sides, and started to pull Grant down to the lakeside, and west away from the fire. Toward those bushes on the north edge of the lake.

On the Hill

"Hey, Rog, look down there..." Tim called out. "You see something moving down by the lake edge?" They were skipping down the hill, past the parking lot, down toward the north side of the lake, carrying the second sack from the trunk. Roger paused to scan.

"Nah. You're seeing things. Your eyes are wandering from all those beers you downed at the Rocks," Roger sarcastically shot back. "Pick your feet up so you don't fall and break a tooth or something. Take some deep breaths, get the oxygen cooking in your brain. It'll be fun to get into this. Hand me a beer from the sack, not the other stuff yet."

They crept down to the lake side, and up behind some bushes.

"If we see any cops, we'll just leave all of it, beer and all, behind this tree, and walk coolly back to the car and come back later," Roger explained.

"Damn good plan. The other is just a bit higher octane than the beer. It'd be more trouble than getting caught with beer, for sure. The tree's the answer. Nobody can see the sack so low, behind the tree."

"We got about twenty feet downhill to the lake, too, over these bushes. Surely nobody can spot us from the lake. We're safe. Let's sit here."

Roger and Tim spread the goods out and sipped the beer. Nearly thirty feet below, and down below the bushes, Chief Krasny, with his car lights off, was creeping around a bend of bushes with the engine quietly on idle. He reached for the heavy spotlight, shifted the focus to distance, and was getting ready to aim it at the fire when he pulled up to it. Suddenly he spotted a few shadowy forms ahead, making jerky movements down by the lake edge. He pulled the cruiser ahead slowly...

Night Moves

They forced Grant down by the lake edge, near the bushes. "Listen kid, keep your mouth shut, be polite, and you won't get hurt," Brett threatened. He ominously repeated it.

"The test is," Axel grunted out, "You lose your pants and shorts, and if you don't show a stiffer, you'll get your shorts back. Fairies can't help showing a stiffer to guys, just like real guys can't keep it down when a girl's checking him out. That's proof positive. If you pass, then you and your shorts can walk somewhere. Everybody will hear you're not a fairy. Things will settle out. If you don't pass, we'll help straighten you out quick. *And* if you tell on us, well, we'd just have to tell the whole school that you *showed* us your stiffer, out in the open. Then you can deal with that," Axel snarled, the goons chuckling.

Grant was sweating it out, getting dizzier. Axel and the boys loomed over him, flexing their hands.

"Dudes, let's give him a choice. I been thinking..." Brett said.

"Thinking? What's there to think about? What choice?" Axel replied, getting itchy for the test.

"He kicked up a fuss coming down. And he drank down two beers, right off. True?"

"Yeah." Axel grunted.

"Fairies don't kick up a fuss, do they? They *want* it. Right-o?"

"Well, you got that right."

"And, fairies don't stick around drinking beers with tough guys. They get sick easy, and run for it, especially when real guys figure them out and start to deal with 'em. Correct?"

"Damn right!" the goons echoed like barking dogs.

"Well, studly Grant here, he kicked up a fuss. And he drank like a man. And he didn't upchuck and run for it. But, he also didn't fight, either..." Brett was working out his thinking.

"So...and this is *logic*, Axel, guys, pay attention. I think Grant's maybe not a fairy. A fairy wouldn't act this way. And, Grant's brothers would've pounded him into turds by now. And he wouldn't be out for football either, if he was a fairy. I think we ought to give him a choice."

"Aw, hell, Brett. If he ain't a fairy, he's probably thought about it," snarled one of the other goons."

"Yeah. He needs some straightening, anyways," growled Axel. "What choice you talking about?"

"Well, I say he can choose between getting the fairy test, and the pussy test," Brett announced.

"Yeah, I see...the pussy test is tough..."

Grant swallowed hard, the terror of this un-ending torture was killing him. He spoke out through his fear, controlling the waiver and pitch of his voice. "You guys talk too much. Come on, what's the deal?"

"Here's the deal." Brett spat out, "The pussy test is, *you fight. Prove* you're a man. Who knows, you might kick our ass a little. If you win the fight, you get to keep your blue jeans on, and we get to bleed some. Lose, and we'll let you keep just your underwear on. Then you can find your way back to wherever. But win or lose, folks will hear from us that you're not a fairy or a pussy. We'll tell everybody you're a man, and that you could fight and take it. On the other hand, you could choose the fairy test, instead. That way, you don't have to fight. Just take your medicine. But remember: if you choose the fairy test, *you damn* well better pass it, with no stiffer in sight..." Brett threatened.

"*Yeah,*" Axel growled, the goons grunted and flexed their hands again. "What's it gonna be?"

Shaking, humiliated, dizzy from fear, and angry, Grant took long breaths. For a few seconds, Grant calmed himself by listening once more to the cheerful song of the crickets. For a moment he dreamed of the beauty of the fabulous meteors in the infinite Kansas sky, a half-hour before. These helped him face the awful choice.

Then Grant took a breath, and spat on the ground between Axel's feet.

Squad Cars in the Night

In those fleeting seconds, Chief Bill Krasny was pulling his squad car ahead slowly to the strangely jerking shadows at the edge of the lake beyond the bushes ahead. Then he noticed the dark shadow of a vehicle appearing in the starlight on his left. The size of the vehicle startled him, and he swung the spotlight around, and fingered the switch to flash it on.

Inside Officer Swazey's squad car, sufficient peach brandy, music and nature had evolved things to what the Catholic kids call "rounding third base" and "heading for home plate." Officer Dave's shorts with Colt 45s on them were hung on the external spotlight, and Officer Jean's panties with pink hearts had just headed significantly south.

"Did you just hear those splashes, and crunching noises?" Officer Jean wheezed out, between slightly broken breaths.

"Fish are jumpin', babe...and so's my heart..." Dave whispered back, tugging the pink hearts a little lower.

Thirty feet up the hill, Roger set his beer down. "That's a good one. And so are these. Here's yours," he whispered, tossing one to Tim from the beer sack. "And this one's mine. Let's just 'twist the caps' off these together, and go for it."

A big catfish splashed near the north edge of the lake. Two seconds later, two heavier splashes hit the water about fifteen feet apart, and began to sink like rocks to the bottom. Just as they sank, the night was torn from private and tantalizing darkness into blinding sunlight that arced across the inside of Officer Dave's car. From beyond, Chief Krasny had clicked on his spotlights from both open car windows.

The Chief's eyes bulged, as his two blazing 500,000 candle-power spotlights illuminated a naked lady's foot and ankle poking up inside, and a pair of boxer shorts hanging outside of what surely had to be another police patrol car.

Frantic whoops soared out of that car. The whole car rocked a little as a red, and then a slightly balding head bobbed up and down into the light. Intermittent blasts of the car's horn blared out into the night.

Suddenly screams for help ripped the night, from the other side of Chief Krasny's car, screams so desperate that it caused Krasny's heart to leap into his throat. The Chief tore his disbelieving eyes away from the rocking police car. He frantically thrust around the spotlight, and re-focused it from small beam to broad beam, and zoned it down the edge of the lake straight ahead into the screams.

In the mud, Grant had taken several terrible punches to his head. The half-bright bully pushed his face down close to Grant and shouted more than once, "You like them apples, pussy?" But Grant whipped his fore-head at Axel's nose with all his strength. With a tremendous crack on the nose, Grant shut Axel up.

The goons closed in, and Grant's pants were disappearing down his legs, as Brett and another goon on the other end, were tugging. Grant's left ear hurt terribly from a punch, and he was sure a tooth was loose. He was mortified that Axel was going to near-kill him now if Axel quit coughing and gasping from the nose shot. Grant hoped he had cracked Axel's nose enough that maybe only Brett and another goon were left to fight. In a second, Grant found himself staring at Axel's blood-gushing nose in a blaze of light so brilliant that Grant could count the bends in single strands of Axel's hair. Stunned, Grant glanced left, and his heart soared with hope. Such an awesome, brilliant light could only mean *help had finally come.*

I'm losing my mind, Chief Krasny told himself. *These are lunatics,* he kept saying to himself, as he spun the spotlight back and forth between the bizarrely rocking police car, and the screaming youths fifteen feet straight ahead. He rubbed his eyes in disbelief. *The poor bastard on the ground, he's getting dragged along by some bizarre creep pulling his pants down to his ankles.* Krasny fumbled for his bull-horn microphone and hit the clicker and screamed, *"All you crazy bastards are under arrest. The whole boat-load of you.*

Drop to your knees on the ground. Anybody moves, and your ass gets filled with buckshot. You shitheads in the car, crawl out now and..."

At that second, up the hill, and ten feet from the '57 Chevy, Roger and Tim spun around. In real shock, they saw floodlights panning back and forth below. They heard the crazed and shaking voice of Chief Krasny on the bull-horn spewing out *...crazy bastards...drop to your knees...ass gets filled with buckshot...* Roger stared. Tim kept saying "Jeeezus." Suddenly, they grabbed each other, shouting *"Jeeeezus."* Like mad-men, they lunged for the Chevy.

Liberation

At the bottom of the lake, the old British-engineered World War I fuses on the big grenades, after waiting patiently for five decades, fizzled, and choked for eight seconds...and exploded with a bone-rattling *KA-WHAWM.* The explosion rocked both police cars, deafening them all. After the double *KA-WHAWM*, all were in shock for a second. The dazed Chief spun his spotlights around, searching. Everyone on the beach looked up to see something really crazy: a ten foot tall, well-lighted wall of water and mud was cascading down from above.

Now this *is not my average Saturday night's patrol in north central Kansas*, Officer Jean wistfully thought to herself.

Mud and water filled the cars. Catfish flopped on Chief Krasny's dashboard and the seats of his cruiser. Catfish flopped on the roof of the other police car. Three little ones flopped around inside the car next to half-naked Jean. Even Officer Dave was greeting a few floppers, in front of his eyes, as he dropped to his knees on Krasny's orders, on the slithering mud.

For Grant, this was National Liberation and the Second Coming all wrapped into one. All the goons but Axel and Brett fled up the hill like spooked coyotes. Axel was still coughing and gagging from his near-broken nose, and breathing muddy water.

"Hoooray, God Loves Me! Jesus really Saves!" Grant whooped a couple times. Brett was flat on his back, covered in mud, trying to pull himself out, and scrape off enough to breathe. Grant had held onto the last leg of his blue jeans at the explosion, only to lose the jeans as Brett flopped backwards. Grant pawed around to retrieve his pants, but gave up as he saw Brett groping himself up out of the mud. Grant took off like a scalded rabbit, under cover of the bushes. He sprinted up and along the dam and down to the highway. He was heading somewhere, thankful for his shorts, and his Liberation. Forty seconds later, Brett finally extricated himself from the mud, and looked up the hill toward some noise.

Up at the Armory, the flashing lights, the screams and then the huge double explosion had people jumping up and down, screaming like lunatics, and dragging more of the crowd back outside. Some were pointing down at the bizarre scene below. To his horror, Brett saw streams of people flowing down the hill. Brett scrambled, grabbed and dragged Axel up the grass slope, and threw him in the back seat of his car. He fumbled for his car keys in the ashtray. The crowd was less than a hundred feet away, and coming fast. Brett started his engine, frantically backed up, and tore out to the south exit, putting acreage between themselves and Concordia.

Grant got his. And the cops are getting theirs right now, Brett assured himself. Rolling down the road, Brett dialed-in KOMA on the car radio as it blared out another big hit, "Don't Let Me Be Misunderstood", by The Animals.

Back up on the hill, Roger and Tim idled the Chevy, and watched the events like it was the UFO landing in Washington D.C. in the old movie "The Day the Earth Stood Still".

"Well, hell. Those puppies worked, just like Charlie Blosser said!" Tim cheerfully crowed.

Krasny's light faded slowly, down at the edge of the lake, just as the crowd started arriving.

"Whaddya say, Lone Ranger? On to Cooley's?" Roger chimed out. He gunned his Chevy's engine, and spurted down to the highway leading into town. Tim glanced back. The "Fabulous Flippers" neon sign still split the night. The band was starting to roar again.

Mysteries

We were closing up the outdoor Cloud Nine Drive-In movie theatre.

"Here's the keys, Jack, just go around locking the doors. I've got to rewind this last reel, and shut down the projectors. I'll meet you at the '49 Plymouth."

"Let's split. We can pick up some malts at the A & W before it closes, and buzz back to my house. Mom's got some zelnikis in the 'fridge we can warm up," Jack offered. I grinned big for that and we were off.

After slapping out the coins for the malts at the A&W, I started up the '49.

"Hey, Jack, got something to show you, before we go to your place. I, uh....had this experience last week. And it's a bit unnerving. I drove Helen Foster to see it after our Catholic CCD classes last Wednesday night. We saw it with our own eyes. She was pretty freaked. I want to see what you think."

"Fascinating," Jack replied with a wink. It was his word of the year.

Three blocks west on Sixteenth Street, and we were there.

I pulled up at the intersection on Sixteenth Street, at the furthest south east corner of the Protestant cemetery. Off to our left and south was a steeply rising hill, one of the last of the Flints. The word was the hill was soon to be decorated with a new junior college. Down behind us was the little dammed-up lake behind the Shady Court Inn motel. It had a small collection of tiny bungalows for rent, a little south of the blinking lights of the Hillcrest Bowling Alley. We slid out of the car. I jumped and sat on the hood. Jack strolled over, and I pointed up the hill into the cemetery.

"Look right through there, just to the right of the first tree." I spoke quietly. "Tell me what you see. You might have to look for a couple minutes, but just keep looking." Jack squinted, saying nothing for about a minute and a half.

"I don't get it."

"Well, keep looking. Be patient."

A few seconds later, Jack jumped off the hood.

"Well, holy Christ...you see that?!" Jack whispered loudly. He was jumping around nervously, which wasn't like him. Then I saw it, and jumped off the hood to join up with him. We edged nervously up to the fence. The slight gusting south wind was alive, even at night. It rustled the elm's leaves just ahead. I noticed this carefully, as the rustling of leaves was my reality-check.

"Okay, Jack." I whispered. "What's going on with the tree up there?"

"What do you mean?"

"I'm checking reality here. What's happening to the tree?"

"Okay, the winds in the leaves, they're rustling..." Jack spurted out the phrases nervously.

"Uh-huh. Now, tell me what you see to the right."

"It's glowing. It's flat-out glowing," Jack mumbled.

"Uh-huh. What else?"

"It almost fades. Then it comes back really strong. Then...in no pattern it fades again after awhile."

"All-right." I pressed on. "What color? And what is it?"

"Well..."

Even "Cool-Hand" Jack, the psychology genius of the school, the sharpest knife in the drawer, had to swallow a couple times before whispering out his answer.

"Well, I'd say it is a deep dusty red," he paused, "with a little motley brown in it. It's not an even color. But mostly dusty-red. And..." Jack swallowed again, "it is a small, leaning-over tombstone."

"Yeah. You got it. Same as last Wednesday night with Helen. I'm telling you, Jack, I came by with my sister Sue the next night, last Thursday night, and she laughed me out of the car and all the way back home. *Because it wasn't there.*"

"You're kidding."

"Well, it was *there*. But it was not glowing. It was glowing Wednesday night, but not glowing on Thursday night." I explained. "I've been too shook to go back until tonight, when I had you along. Ol' level-headed you. And now you see it too."

"This is, un-natural," Jack whispered carefully.

"How 'bout *we don't stay here?*" I pleaded, and no sooner than the words were out, Jack grabbed my arm. He slowly pointed up the hill.

"Look there, to the right, up past the glowing stone. Past that tall statue. I saw something moving." We stared. Nothing. Suddenly we heard a hissing sound, and a dark form, tall, and mottled white and black, took off running.

"What'd you see?" Jack breathed.

"Uh, I think it's a guy, but his bottom half looked weird. Like he was maybe half black, and white, or mixed up, and his top half-seemed to..."

"Disappear..." Jack finished. "It's time to leave, I think." The wind had picked up, rustling the leaves a bit more.

"I believe you're right..." I said slowly, turning to the car. We fired up the engine, backed out, and were gone down Sixteenth Street, heading east to some comforting streetlights.

* * *

Two blocks north, and heading west at the same time were Terry and John, with Wendell and Red in the back of John's '56 Chevy. Red was a prankster everybody loved, from Wendell's class. The '56 buzzed along the north edge of the cemetery.

"So, boys. Whadya say about dark beer and chili dogs?" Terry sang out.

"Mmff." Wendell replied, smiling happily, shaking his head from side to side.

"Wonder what the hell the ruckus was down by the lake?" Terry asked. "Anybody hear?"

"Some smart-asses set off some explosions, way bigger than M-80s, folks were saying," John replied. "Cop cars were down there. Guess it was pretty cool."

"Yeah, well, so were the Iowa ladies you loped off with there, *Big John...*" Terry stretched out the words.

"Holy shit!" Red muffed out, barely able to talk past a mouthful of chili dog.

"Behind us, behind us..." he waived and pointed with his hotdog. John slammed the brakes, screeched the tires and the car skidded to a halt. Terry looked out the back window. Wendell, Red and Johns' heads popped up and looked out too.

"Hold still, I'll get there," Terry said, as he was half-way out the door. He zipped like lightning over to the strange-looking figure that was bent over in the road. John and Wendell followed out. Red stayed in the car working on the chili dogs.

Terry reached the strange apparition, as it was bending up from picking up a shoe.

"Good God, boy. What in blazes happened to you?"

It was Grant.

"Aw shit. *Damn.*" Grant was spurting out the words. He didn't want to be spotted.

"Come on, guy. We got a ride for ya here." Terry offered a hand. They climbed in the car.

"Jayzus..." Red muffled out, still downing a chili dog.

"You were on the losing end of a mud-wrestling match, or what?" Terry asked.

"Not exactly."

"Well, what the hell happened? You don't get stranded in your shorts, with mud all over by accident, even in a month of Sundays. Something happened to you." Terry tried gently to pull the story out of him.

"Some guys."

"Some guys, huh." Terry turned to John. "I'll bet some guys. I'll bet *which* guys."

Terry turned back to Grant, saying, "They got no class, Grant. *No class.* You don't have to worry about this getting out. Somebody's gonna settle their hash..."

"Yeah, 'you're in good hands with All-State' here. Nobody will know," John cheerfully said over the seat to the mud-drenched youth. "Where can we take you?"

In twenty minutes, they dropped Grant at his farmhouse mailbox.

* * *

Somebody told somebody. Rumors spread like wildfire about what happened to Grant, among us younger guys. We felt sickened, scared stiff, and bewildered. Among a few isolated friends, we could talk about this. We thought Swaggart, his boys, and other wackos were out there in just enough numbers to be dangerous, and they were getting more perverse by the week. Humiliation like this psycho-war and getting beat up was hard to talk about to girlfriends, sisters, or parents. In fact the girls, and the parents, never knew. They were as clueless as Bambi, because we didn't tell 'em. If you got the courage to squeal, the fear was, you would be the next instant victim.

That kind of fear shut a lot of mouths. Most of us were frozen in silence. Personal bravery and uncanny strength might work, and enough of it might back this off for some of us, I was thinking.

"Give them their own medicine, kick their ass into next week. More of that has to work," I told Gary.

"But what about our friends who can't protect themselves?" Gary would sagely ask. He had a point. Grant was lucky to escape. This guy Terry, he and one or two others would step in on the side of decency, once in awhile. A lot of us noticed that. "The vast portion of the older ones are not like these few goons. Most are decent dudes, some great guys, Lyle, Terry," Gary said. "It's the few creeps getting away with it, under the coaches noses, they'll hurt somebody bad."

I had to agree on all this. Still, it was getting worse. Would Terry or somebody do more? And what difference could one or two guys make when the coaches themselves and the school administration were either not noticing, or were tolerant of it by silence. *Which way would this sadistic little uncivil war turn?*

Jack's house that night was a little oasis, free of worry and fear. Zelnikis were warming in the toaster oven. Root beer was out of the fridge, and I was pouring it over ice in two glasses. I headed out Jack's back door, and slid up the ladder to his flat roof above his garage. We had spread out sleeping bags up there, to watch for satellites, scan the Milky Way, and catch the occasional falling star. Jack was up the ladder in a jiffy with a large plate of zelnikis.

"Well, that was bizarre, that glowing thing," Jack commented. We were still uneasy and disoriented about the weird stone and the weirder figure running between the gravestones.

"I don't know what to do with all that, exactly."

"We've got a lot of strange deals going on, unusual stuff. That's the thing," Jack sagely observed.

"Yeah. Not anything *ordinary*, like tornadoes. And hundred mile-an-hour down-drafts."

"Ball lightning."

"Blizzards that cover barns."

"Guys that out-run jack rabbits, and genius girl pianists."

"Yeah. And zelnikis..." I bowed to Jack's mom.

We munched on into the night, observing the great mysteries displayed in the black velvet, diamond-sprinkled vaults above.

Chapter 8
A SHIFT IN THE WINDS

"It doesn't take a Weatherman to know which way the Wind blows." **Bob Dylan**

Evelyn's Sunrise

The pickup door wheezed like a rusty iron lung. Evelyn winced as she stepped into the truck from the clover, her brown scuffed shoes moist from her trek across the lawn in pre-dawn light. She turned the key, and on the third grind, the engine coughed into life. She tried to jam the column stick-shift gear into reverse without grinding and whining while backing up. She spun the wheel, using the gold metal flake American Eagle wheel-spinner encased in honey-colored Lucite. The gold flake caught a flash of the arcing light of the rising sun, dazzling her eyes for a second. Other greetings of the high plains autumn morning spun her senses, as she clutched the pickup, and sped down the road. *Sometimes it's so lonely out here, and other times I swear I could never live without this land and the sky.* The crunch of crystal white quartz gravel, the warbling and effervescent tones of the meadowlarks, the sweet smell of clover and alfalfa hay bales, and the diamond-bright morning star ruling over the magenta and turquoise sunrise called to her. They lured her away from the task she had risen so early for. It was time for practice.

Through the nights, so that she wouldn't drive her parents crazy, she lay in bed practicing again and again in her mind, the almost frightening, deeply sweet but aching, discordant chords of *Carmina Burana*. Evelyn was gifted with perfect pitch, and almost-perfect first time recall. She could hear, and her fingers could feel every frantic chord progression through that vast, dark work that dredges the depths of the soul. The piano didn't have to be with her. In her mind, in her room touched lightly by the night song of crickets outside her window, she worked on the nuances, expressing power and passion into the wee hours of the night. *I'll try it this way, in the morning,* she assured herself, as she finally drifted off to sleep.

The bumpy ride next morning, over the potholes in the limestone road of Eleventh Street going west into town distracted her, as she tried to turn her attentions from the beauties of the dawn, to the fiery, technical demands of the great *Carmina*. Circling the huge, shouldering mass of Concordia High School, she turned the corner going east, on the north side on Fifth Street, and braked the pickup to a stop into a parking stall. Six AM. *God bless Mr. Miller, no doubt he's not got permission to give out keys to students to enter the building, for something like practice.*

She trekked up to the front glass door, and twisted the brass key to the left, shaking the door a little, until the bars that have stuck for generations retreated and the door opened. She shut the door, checked the bar, and strode slowly through the atrium double door frame. She turned right in the dark, and groped her way down the hall, past the Assistant Principal's office. She felt with her left hand along the lockers until they gave way to the back entrance door to the central auditorium stage. She opened the door, and slowly felt her way through the dark to the light switch up high on the left inner wall, and flipped it on. There, on the north side of the stage sat the huge Baldwin Grand. She sat, and laid the *Carmina's* score on the grand piano's bench next to her, not opening it. In a few seconds, from the soul of a pioneer's grand-daughter and the fifteen year-old hands of an unassuming genius, the vast empty Victorian auditorium, as grand as any in Chicago, rang deep to its moorings with the blood-stirring passages of the towering *Carmina*.

In the Trunk

On the high hills west of town on Eleventh Street, two miles out, the steel grid screen door of Radio KNCK slammed shut. Built with steel-reinforced concrete, and faced on the exterior with the yellow-cream colored brick from the Concordia brick factory, the small building thrust a rugged shoulder up from the grassy sod. It was designed to withstand high winds, and the possibility of a passing tornado. Kansas gets an average of ninety three tornadoes in June alone. "Tornado alley" stretches down through Oklahoma. This double-stretch of states is visited by more tornadoes per hundred square miles in the summer months than any real-estate on earth.

Damn, that screen door spring is too strong, thought Roger, as he loped out to the '57 Chevy. He'd just finished the floor cleanup, and had spun a few records "on the air" before Mr. Wendell Wilson showed up for the six-fifteen a.m. weather forecast, crop report, and local sports report. He sniffed at the gusting south wind as he sat down into the driver's seat of his '57 Chevy, and became distracted by the mixed scents of the car's leather and rich, ripening clover and alfalfa hay blown in through the car window. A few lusty crickets still sang in the early morning breeze. Just before slipping into the driver's side, Roger shook his head a little, to gather back a thought. He slid back to the trunk, and popped it open. *Just to check it again… Yup, she's going up, tonight, it's about time for their come-uppance. Better head off to school.*

* * *

The day spun past like a top. We were rooted in Mr. Everett Miller's choir rehearsal, with ten minutes to go.

"Okay, my maladjusted lyrical penguins. That closes down 'Frostiana' based on Robert Frost's poetry. The soprano and alto sections will practice the first section of the *Carmina* tonight at Our Lady of Perpetual Help Cathedral. We need to start practicing where decent acoustics can rattle you a bit with the giant harmonic ghosts of the *Carmina*. Those Catholic bishops know how to erect buildings with acoustics. So let's be nice, and thank the fine and astutely learned Father Long tonight, ladies, as he opens the Cathedral. Seven p.m. Don't be late. Oh, and yes, tomorrow Master Fischer here, and Madam Freeburne will display something you won't forget, correct?" He glanced and winked at both parties. They nodded back in unison. "You'll hear the opening and closing bars of the piano shoot-out of the *Carmina*. We'll play the old recording of the Whitehall symphony's piano duel first, and then let our able prodigies see if they can show them up." He waived his chorus wand, dismissing them with, "You're free now a little early, before lunch, so head-out. Go mix perfumes, do some arm-wrestling, whatever you-all do. But stay in the multi-purpose room and just be dang quiet for five minutes. You don't want Messrs. Betts and 'The Sarge' to get on to you, so you never get to slide out early again." The Sarge was Miller's sarcastic name for the Assistant Principal Kramer.

We all filed out and down the hall to the multi-purpose room, and gathered in groups in chairs around the round tables. Tall and purposeful, with a laser-like stare, and closing in like a cheetah on the hunt, Wendell strode to my table and pulled up a chair.

A Fellowship of Strangers

"Hey hambutt, got something for you. I went to this Fellowship of Christian Athletes thing last night."

"Yeah? What was it like?" Being Catholic, what the Protestants did together in their semi-exclusive groups was still mildly exotic and intriguing to me.

"Well, I've been to lots of church-goings. But this wasn't exactly about Jesus," Wendell remarked. He always had a stem-winding way of telling a serious story. The more stem-winding it was, you learned after awhile, the more deadly serious was the issue, the confrontation, or the disaster. Wendell seemed to be in grade seven stem-winding mode on this one. He hadn't been at that level for awhile. I was a little worried.

"All-right. Go on." I was bracing a little. Wendell went on.

"Several of the coaches were there. Forbach too. Not Betts. He was off somewhere. Swaggart seemed to run the meeting with the coaches. We talked awhile about, you know, 'staying a certain distance' from girls, the problems of smoking and beer. We talked over whether Jesus was a guide in our lives. And then Forbach talked about how God's guidance was needed for our country, especially with the overseas communist threat. How his parents had to flee Russia, back in the '30s. How the same thing might come down on South Vietnam, and spread over here. That we had to pray about that. And be ready to support God's work and our country's resistance to atheistic communism."

My head flashed fast through several reactions in about three seconds. *He's talking to me about this stuff because I'm one of the guys worrying big time, trying to study up on this. He thinks I've got some conclusions, but hell if I do. Still, maybe we can think this out some, together.*

More and more of our conversations among friends were about trying to fish the right thing out about this communist threat thing. Father Long was going to be holding a series of youth workshops on this stuff. I hoped that would help us think. Father Long had rattled the town the past week, by inviting the participation of different youth groups from various churches, and a few other pastors. One of them was a Mennonite. We didn't know jack about them. Suddenly my thoughts were jerked back by Wendell's obvious stress about something unusual last night.

"It turned weird with Forbach making this speech," Wendell continued. "So I asked him, 'Well, I don't know all about this war, but didn't Jesus heal the ear of the Roman soldier enemy that St. Peter had chopped off, when they came to crucify Him? He didn't ask us to draw the sword even to our attackers. He pushed St. Peter's sword down to the ground. And then He healed the ear of the enemy. What does that say about going somewhere overseas to get involved in a war when we haven't been attacked?"

"You said *that*?" I asked in amazement. "What'd he say to that?" I had to admit, this rock-star and chick-magnet knew his Jesus.

"He grabbed me by the shirt, and dragged me off to the side." "You're kidding." I felt an electric jolt just hearing this.

"Forbach literally hissed and screamed in my ear. He said, 'You *do* know about the kid from Belleville who died in Vietnam last month, don't you? Do you have any idea how a parent would feel about this who has a son serving overseas? Do you have any clue how using Jesus like this can divide families? And how a divided family can feel? It's smart-ass stuff like you're saying that's tearing families apart in this country, and giving the communists strength.' "

I shook my head in silent disbelief.

"I wasn't really sure what to say, or do," Wendell whispered. "All the room was looking at us. He was spitting in my face, and grabbing my shirt. A few months back, I came across a rabid possum in the alley back of my house, with its eyes all bulged out. He looked just like that possum. I really wanted to punt him good in the balls. I can punt a football seventy yards, you know. But I remembered the Roman soldier and Jesus, and that calmed me. I told him, 'You. Take your hands off me.' Forbach just shrugged, and did so. Then I said louder, for the room to hear: 'Well, Mr. Coach-Christian. I don't hear you quoting Jesus on these ideas of yours, just yet. Maybe I'll be a bit more convinced when I hear you do that.' I just went back to my group and sat down. He said 'shit' and went outside for awhile. Then Swaggart started mumbling about staying away from cigarettes again, bad for the team performance, and all that. It all kinda went downhill from there."

"Uh-huh. I'll bet," I replied. "I'm floored by this. What the hell is with these people?"

Wendell shrugged and shook his head.

I was stopped cold. I heard my own voice as a strange, distant echo, "Yeah. What the hell is this?"

High Noon at the Grocery Store

The lunch bell rang.

"We'll talk about this craziness some more, Wendell," I said. "I'm heading home for lunch today. Dad's gonna be there." Wendell nodded, still thinking the whole thing over. As we drifted with the crowd down the hall to the lunchroom, I split to the left down the main hall, and wove my way through secondary halls, and out a side door. I crossed the street south, and turned right, heading up west past the football field. I was looking forward to lunch. Mom had made some killer ham salad with her meat grinder, for sandwiches. Tons better than the floating meat loaf today, at the cafeteria.

Halfway up the Eleventh Street hill, I was passing the "mom and pop" grocery store, when the screen door sprung open with a whoosh. Out trotted Axel. He was dressed in blue jeans, white tennis shoes, and his leather red and white letter jacket. He had sunglasses on, and was moving at me with a scowl on his face.

"Hey, you," he said, sidling up to me and pointing his thumb back over his shoulder, "Somebody wants to see you in the store. One of the varsity team members."

"Uh-huh," I mumbled, pausing to look him up and down. *Great, more craziness.* This was suspicious. The cold ghost was awakening a little. It whispered, *Well, this could be interesting, but we'll have to keep our wits up.* I looked Axel up and down a little more, letting him know I was thinking. "We'll see. Lead the way, senior," I teased in Spanish, bowing a little and raising my arm to the side with a little mock graciousness.

"Agh. Let's go," Axel coughed back with a sideways jerk of his head. I strolled into the store, a couple paces behind, watching carefully.

We went to the back of the store where the popsicle and ice cream bar freezer was, and slouching next to the freezer was P.J. O'Rourke, a junior lineman. He took his sunglasses off, which he didn't need inside the store, and glanced at me.

"Oh. The new kid on the block."

"Uh-huh, that's me."

He ignored that and started in on his speech.

"Coaches don't want you underclassmen messing with girls a couple days before game days."

"Yeah. That rule is for all of us, right?" He ignored that.

"Just want to make sure you remember the rules. It's possible, you might be called in on the defense. Defensive end. Not likely. But who can predict an injury? And you gotta be ready to go, and not pussy-whipped."

"Not to worry," I replied cheerfully.

"You know some of the cute Baptist and church-girls, right? You tail around after them, don't you?"

"*Tail* after Baptists? Hmm…Look. They're just friends. I'm a Catholic. Like the Fosters. So…I get basic approval, only as a friend. If you know what I mean."

"Yeah, well. They're off limits. The coaches want discipline."

"Yeah, that's probably good for us all to remember," I suggested with a wry smile. "Look, I'm outta here. I gotta go for lunch. See you boys." I walked back out of the store, tired of this little charade. Strangely, Axel followed me out three seconds later. He trotted up the sidewalk to catch up with me.

"You're kind of a smart guy, aren't ya?"

"You want to talk? Walk." I replied, and kept on up the hill. He followed.

"Look, Axel," I said, "You're a junior, I respect that. You can think for yourself. If O'Rourke wants something outta me, how come he's not out here dealing with me? Huh? How come he sends you? He's man enough to come see me on his own, isn't he? " I kept walking.

"Uhg." Axel grunted. "Coaches say we need discipline."

"Okay," I said.

"We don't need smart mouths."

"I said okay. Now if you want something more outta me," I said, and stopped, and turned and smiled at him, "look me up on the practice field. I just love fun and games. But make sure it's for your own reasons. See you around."

I loped on up the hill, and into the golden brick house. Ol' Skipper greeted me with a thousand licks. I couldn't remember how many encounters with bullies I had in Catholic school. I had gotten so used to them, it was like automatically swatting flies. Mom had taught me immense kind-heartedness. But maybe it was Uncle Bill Green's horrifying stories of the Nazi camps which had helped grow the really dangerous, avenging cold ghost in my soul. I worried some about this thing, how it could viciously arise, and reach out to take me over. It was weird, and hard to control.

Pop came in the back kitchen door, it was almost never locked, and we never even thought about it. He hung his grey zippered jacket on the back hanger board on the wall. "The Hamiltons" were spelled out with a white vinyl laundry line cord that was stapled to the black hanger board. Older brother Darryl had made this in eighth grade shop in '55.

"Hey, Dad."

"Hi, Crisco."

I was reluctant to go too much into it, but I did bring up the grocery store encounter. All Dad said was, "Well, there's always troublemakers." Dad was a practical guy, not a psychologist like Jack Kasl.

"Let's get out the ham-salad. You're Mom's a winner on that," Dad said cheerfully. I couldn't agree more.

The Magic blew in

It was Tuesday, so the varsity game with Salina Sacred Heart was a long ways off on Friday. Practice that afternoon was glorious. An early Alberta clipper blew in during the afternoon, one of those which brought in high clouds and some kind of northern magic. It switched the in-coming wind from the southwest to the northwest. Usually, the hard and punishing drills and conditioning sprints would drive us to exhaustion in the suffering heat. But our conditioning was improving. More than this, we all realized something about the day was special. It brought us an experience of the power of life we might never feel again. No matter hard the drill, or direct the calls of the coaches, all of us, even the coaches would catch ourselves raising our eyes to the heavens, just pausing to take in the magic infused into the air and sky by the north winds. Even Swaggart and his band of goons seemed mellowed by what blew in.

Like a sip of cold wine, the cool, bracing northwest gusts cut into our breath. So many fantastic sensations pummeled us: a neon turquoise sky, all striped with yellow, white and pink streaks of clouds. The clouds were pulled and stretched-out into parallel wispy spider webs. They ran in streams like a horizontal rainbow. They tumbled into brighter colors as they neared the orange setting sun. Against the startling turquoise heavens, the gathering and vivid color contrasts in the clouds stole our attentions.

This was another world, blown in from above, from the far and pure Canadian wilderness. From below, the mixed, intoxicating smells of hay, autumn leaves, fallow, plowed earth, and a distant fire blew across our feet and swirled up into our helmets. Even the dirt felt cool and friendly today.

It was more than a distraction. Each of us was more alive than ever before, in the thrill of our efforts, the love of the game, and in the unfolding mysteries of the great Western land and skies.

One Clear Night

Diebel and I found ourselves trekking home together, after practice.

"Our freshmen team's shaping up, don't you think?" Gary asked. Generally, we had a separate set of game drills on the practice field, in preparation for our own games parallel with the older B and A Varsity teams. Once in a rare while, a freshman might be called into suit up for B or even A team substitutions, eg, "sit on the bench" until more senior players got hurt.

"Yeah. We'll take Salina Sacred Heart, with you running wingback. You'll run circles around them, just like House will," I said.

"Yeah, well, I'm not House," Gary replied. "But I plan to take a crack at his freshmen 100 record (9.9) come track season".

"Well, speed ball, if anybody can, maybe you can."

"The juniors and seniors were different today, don't you think?" Gary asked.

"Yeah, and the coaches. Now this is camping weather for sure, isn't it?" I had suggested the answer in the weather. But also, Gary and I had been in his Methodist Scout Troop 31 for several years. It was a real shift for me, being Catholic. But I was accepted in, fast. Gary had gone on less campouts lately.

"We neared the corner of Eleventh and Willow. Rumor had it that Eleventh Street was the 38th parallel, which on the other side of the world, was the border where the last great war had ground to a halt between the North Korean Communists, and South Korea in 1953. Gary's house, strangely, sat on that border.

"Hey, you wanna come in for spaghetti? Mom's fixing it tonight..." Gary asked as we rounded the corner on Willow.

"I'll have to check with Mom, I'll phone you," I replied, and we parted with a thumbs up. I dragged myself up the hill, cutting across Tyler's lawn for the millionth time, jumped up the wall and skirted under the giant elm and past the blue spruce that Mom planted when she heard Sister Sue was "on her way" merely a month after I was born. I scooted in the back door.

"Yup. I haven't started the goulash yet. Ryland's still not home. Who knows where your sister is, probably riding around on that damn motorcycle with that degenerate Spacek kid." Mom was a bit judgmental about Sue's boyfriends and activities, compared to us boys. This was an on-going issue I was bound to avoid right now.

"Don't worry, Mom. She's got a cool head." Mom shook her head, and drew in that left side of her lips into a tight, un-approving thin line.

"So, is it to Diebel's for supper for me?" I asked, partly to disconnect her from her obsession about Sue, and figure out what was coming.

"Sure. Just be back before ten tonight," Mom said. I phoned Gary.

"Can I bring some ice cream?"

"Sure."

"And hey, ask your Mom if you can come up here later. Since it is a cool night, maybe we could spread out the cots in our breezeway, and break out the telescope."

"Great idea."

We had been "camping out" in our screened in breezeway since we were little guys, it kept the bugs off us. But it allowed us to be outside, see night skies, meteors, run around the neighborhood in the dark, etc. We were getting older. But the old great habits wouldn't die easily.

After Gary's mom's terrifically spiced spaghetti, and after politely refusing Gary's dad's usual teasing offer for a few beers (he was German), we dragged Gary's camping stuff up to our breezeway. I dug my sleeping bag, and both cots out of the basement. We headed out on our bikes, and toured up and down the hills in the area, spun past White's house down on the creek, out two miles to the "five corners" intersection where a pony express mail route heading into town had cut diagonally through the typical north-south and east-west dirt farm crossroads. We were back by dark, as a few lingering fireflies floated close to the ground in people's front yards. We set up shop in the breezeway, with my Gilbert astronomical telescope which my folks had bought for sixteen dollars in 1960, out front on the driveway. We pulled a couple folding chairs out next to it. We were ready for Moon rise, or Saturn, or whatever. We set up cots, lit a couple candles, and broke out the crunchy Jif peanut butter and jam for sandwiches.

"So what do you think? Will practices, and these weirdos get better?" Gary asked.

"Hell if I know."

"Well, the Swaggart boys, and the rest of the varsity seem more focused on the upcoming game. Salina Sacred Heart is a bigger town, a bit bigger school. Newspapers have them rated third in class A."

"It'd be good if we can run over their freshmen team on Thursday," I said, "to make their varsity wonder what's coming." On defense, I was better, mainly because I could fling people out of the way while zeroing in on quarterbacks. But Gary, at wing-back on offense, was a real star. He could run circles around opponents, and as strong as he was, he could break through most tackles. He'd caught the eye of Coach Betts, more as future varsity than as potential backup in case of severe losses.

"So what'd you think about Ganstrom's confrontation with Coach at the FCA meeting over Vietnam?" Gary asked, with a chuckle, as he sprang for the peanut butter. "You know him pretty good don't you?"

"Yeah, well. You don't push him on religious principles. He's against killing, for religious reasons. Also, his dad, you know, had rough experiences in World War II. So Wendell is touchy about war."

"So, what do you think about the war? You read a lot of this political stuff," Gary asked.

"I'm still thinking about it. Father Long is against it as immoral, because we weren't attacked really. He's been holding these open discussions. Next week, we're going to see some documentaries about it, and other youth groups are invited. But the Baptists have banned their kids from that. He likes to have us read, talk, think about it. Communism is atheistic, and pretty deadly. I'm not really sure, to tell you the truth. Mom says "that son of a bitch Lyndon Johnson" a lot, because she lived in Texas in World War II for awhile. She learned to not trust Johnson as a politician, and she thinks he has manipulated this war. She says I should go to Canada, if the draft starts and gets me or Roger in it. How about that?"

"But. If you go to college, aren't they talking about not drafting college guys?"

"Yeah. I guess. I hope so."

"We'll probably whip them in a couple years. How can a jungle country, with people in huts hold up to us? We got Green Berets, Marines, and now Army and Air Force. And the B-52 Bombers, you remember them from Omaha?" Gary was referring to our Explorer Post trip up to Strategic Air Command base in Omaha last winter, before the summer trip to Ft. Riley where we were given our terrifying tour of the "Cong Village".

"Well, I'm more scared about the nuclear arms race." I was a fanatic on this. We all had been frightened out of our minds in the Cuban Missile Crisis. Late at night, Dad had frantically built the nuclear bomb shelter in the basement, which we used for tornadoes now. He had stocked water down there since then, in emptied-out Clorox bottles from the laundromat. I never saw anyone so scared as Dad was when he was building that atomic bomb shelter. I had read all manner of stuff about nuclear missiles, proposed anti-ballistic missiles, etc. I was kind of a walking encyclopedia on it. I was sure Gary was tired of hearing me out about it.

"Let's go check out Saturn. It's dark enough now, and it's above the horizon. We can probably see the rings," I offered as a change of subject.

We scurried out to the chairs and telescope. After awhile, I was able to focus in on the rings of Saturn. My old reflecting telescope was pretty good. We sat around for an hour, honing in on different star systems. We could even see the Andromeda galaxy with the naked eye. Eventually, we just sat there, looking up, hoping to see meteors. About one a.m. we were tired.

"Man, look," Gary grabbed my arm, and pointed, "Above the tree..."

There in the north was a gold-sizzler.

"It cut across half the sky. It was putting out gold and silver sparks..." Gary said in real excitement. "I don't think I've seen one bigger."

"It's just so *clear* tonight, maybe it's this northern front that has come through. I wish it was always like this..."

Rebellion Aloft

In those moments, Tim and Roger had wobbled a little on the extension ladder they had unreeled and leaned against a light pole.

"Jay-zus..." Tim cried out. "Did you see that fireball up there...?"

"Hell, yes," Roger replied. "But hold the damn ladder steady, will ya?"

"Damn betcha, chief."

"For the third time, Geronimo..." Roger chimed out, as he swung the rope with a rock attached. This time it arced well up and over the streetlight. The rock quickly spun the long rope to the ground.

In less than a minute, the sarcastic facsimile of Assistant Principle Dick Kramer was twisting in the wind, holding a Jim Beam bottle in one of his hands, as he was hoisted up the street light that stood squarely in front of the hallowed front door entrance to Concordia High School. The instrument of rebellion was aloft.

Chapter 9
THE WHEEL SPINS

For the times they are a-changing...   **Bob Dylan**

The locker room windows, at the lower entrance between the band room in the junior high building and the high school building were unlocked. They have always been for decades. It makes for easy entrance for runners, and weight-men seeking to practice on their own time. The secret honor code, iron-clad and subject to un-named and innumerable punishments, is that you keep your butt out of the rest of the building. The honor code always holds. Lyle Pounds, Rivers, Hondo, and a batch of underclassmen including Alan and Louis arrived in sweats or shorts and t-shirts about six a.m. They congregated around the windows; a couple of them slipped in to grab better running shoes, or "moleskin" to ward off blisters. Ribbons of the smell of breakfast rolls baking wafted into the cool, black-dirt scented autumn air.

"Mrs. Letourneau is baking again," Lyle said quietly to the group, sniffing in the air. Word-less grunts and head-shakes were the replies. A distant steel door slammed. Jerry came skipping up the steep walk and drive, around the corner of the shop.

"All-right, let's get it on," Louis called out. One group split to run south on the "cemetery road". Another took off to the southwest, snaking around the football field and out over the golf course, threading themselves out to Five Corners and back. Forty five minutes later, the cemetery group was angling back toward the shop, while the Five Corners group led by Jones and Pounds spun an extra lap just for extra sweat, around the north side of CHS. Half-way down the north-side sidewalk, something caught Lyle's eye. "What the devil is that?" Lyle called out, slowing down and pointing up. The group slowed, and gaped skyward. A slow twenty seconds passed.

"Sheesh. That's a puppet, or something."

"It's a drunk one. Check out the Jim Beam bottle."

"Uh, boys. Somebody's ass is gonna be grass on this one. That's the image of Dick Kramer, 'Mad Dog', the Assistant Principal," Lyle offered. Snickers and snorts spread around. "Uhhh...I think maybe we oughtta just head around the building..." Lyle suggested. Within twenty minutes, most of them were showered. Several of them ran back around to the front entrance. They joined up with a slowly growing crowd that stared up at the sarcastic emblem of rebellion, and milled around, speculating about what was coming next.

* * *

For most of the morning, there was nothing but silence from the high school front office. Nobody had spotted Betts, or Kramer, or the school counselors doing their usual prowling of the halls, and nabbing miscreants who lacked hall passes. Teachers whispered. Students passed notes and whispered even more carefully. Rebels snickered, and some made deviant hand-gestures in small groups. At ten-forty five AM, the American Government class students in the second floor of the northwest corner classroom spotted a big truck pull by. An extension ladder came out. The back row students craned their necks out the windows to watch one of the janitors spring up the ladder, cut down the offending instrument of rebellion, and toss it in the back of the truck. The truck rumbled off east.

Six minutes later, the intercom speakers in each classroom clicked on.

Coach Betts's voice rang out, "Attention, students and staff. An all-school assembly will gather in the main auditorium in five minutes. Classes are cut short before lunch. Teachers, guide your classes quietly to the auditorium over the next five minutes. Thanks for your cooperation."

Tensions, snickering, whispers and curiosity were running fairly high that day, as students filed into the auditorium. A quieter than usual hush spread over the crowd as Assistant Principal Dick Kramer, wearing his Mormon-thin black tie and white shirt, strode quickly up to the podium. His black, wing-tip ornate shoes glinted in the lights, and his hard-steel heel caps nailed into his shoes' heels clicked more ominously than usual on the hard-wood stage. He snapped on the podium microphone, and a wail of feedback screeched out over the crowd, spoiling his well-orchestrated Executive entrance. Grim-lipped, he stared out at the assemblage without expression. His eyes narrowed into slits like a bobcat about to spring on hapless squirrels, as the crowd endured the fluctuating wail of the feedback. A sweating and black-spectacled Mr. Robbins, the anti-war forensics and debate coach, gyrated around in the sound booth, twisting knobs. He was trying to isolate and down-play the squawking microphone. The beast was finally tamed.

Kramer tapped on the microphone, spouted "test" a couple times, and dove right into his speech. The Government class had just finished a section on pre-civil war conflicts. I guessed that more than one student had passing thoughts similar to mine, *Kramer's eyes are bugging out...he looks like John Brown, the crazed Kansas Abolitionist...*

"Concordia High School will not tolerate acts of hooliganism, and disrespect of authorities." Kramer paused long, for effect.

"This infection of rebellion is spreading among misguided young people in some parts of our great land. It will not come here. This is not San Francisco." At least three fourths of the students were scratching their heads, or staring blankly at their neighbor, trying to figure out this one. Kramer cleared his throat.

"If any of you have any information on who is responsible for this provocation, it is your responsibility to come forward. We guarantee all information is strictly confidential. The hooligans will be identified, and corrected. Things have returned to normal. You may now break for your lunch period."

Lunch was a macaroni, cheese and hamburger combo, with green beans, salad, strawberry jello, half bananas, iced tea, chocolate milk, strawberry milk, dinner rolls, and peanut-butter cookies.

This time, the jocks and the artistic-music people were more sprinkled in among each other than usual around the lunch tables, trying to figure out the passing events.

"This Kramer guy takes himself real seriously, doesn't he..." mused Pete Foster.

"I thought the thing was just funny," said Hondo Johnson. Hondo was a middle distance running machine in track, just behind Jones, Pounds and Rivers. He was your basic cowboy to the bone. He was too good at football as a guard, to be allowed to run cross-country.

"What do you suppose they'll do to the guys who did it?" asked Diebel to the guys at our table.

"They'll never find out. Nobody will rat on them!" offered House, who had overheard the question, while passing by with a tray. Terry bent down and smiled this out to everybody. He winked and skipped on.

Wendell, Greg and Louis had been carrying on a separate conversation about this, at our table.

"Some of these school board parents will back up Kramer, you can bet your toosh on that," observed Wendell. His dad was on the school board. Greg chimed in with a different view. "These kind of guys don't like to be opposed, for sure. But some of the School Board are parents of girls, like Dad. There's anger from them about how the daughters are treated these days." His dad had been a CHS government teacher, and was now the President of the under-construction community college, which temporarily was holding a few night classes in the CHS building.

"There's never a dull moment around here, is there?" I said. It was my catch-all phrase when I didn't know what to say for situations which looked impossibly sticky and tangled.

Later that afternoon, before we were finished suiting up for football practice, Coach Betts, who was also one of the Assistant Principals, strode through the locker room. He announced, "Assistant Principal Kramer has asked me to ask you, if any of you boys hear any rumors as to who these guys were that strung up the mockup of the Assistant Principal, to please let me know. We need to let malcontents know that defiant and disrespectful pranks like this don't get off scot-free. I'm sure you boys understand this. Nothing good comes without discipline."

All of us really were clueless. Obviously, this had been kept under-hat.

Pete leaned across into the back row of small lockers. He smiled and raised his eyebrows up and down like Groucho Marx, and whispered, "This whole deal's getting worse. You guys got wind that the fire department was called in to hose-out a fire in the back seat of somebody's car out south in the parking zones. The Fire Chief told my dad at lunch that apparently some high school kid had been smoking, and probably left a cigarette dangling in the back seat ashtray. Wonder who that genius was..."

"This will only tick off Kramer and Betts even more. They're sticklers against smoking," Wendell cautioned. No doubt, I thought. Anybody caught smoking in the building is expelled for a few days. Anybody on sports teams caught smoking is also at risk for at least temporary suspension from a team for more days.

We were hitting the asphalt for the two mile run out to the west practice field in five minutes.

Losers Only Now

Coach Betts was highly agitated. Smokers, the fire department embarrassment, and the hooligans taunting Kramer, all stuck it to the Administration in the same day. At lunch, Betts got vague reports from somebody who hinted that underclassmen were widely flaunting the rules about dating girls in mid-week. *I've seen enough of rebellion. Don't want this spreading through the teams*, Betts thought. He had mulled over his plan to nip all this in the bud with help from some upperclassmen and his assistant coaches. Now at football practice, he was launching the plan.

He blew his whistle, calling all groups together on the practice field.

"Boys, we got a little skill building and character exercise here. We gotta sort out who has fast reactions, and who can take it when the going gets tough. Coaches, break 'em down into three Circles. We're doing the Circle Drill. Coach Forbach you come with me. We'll select the first group. You other coaches split up the rest of the crowd when we're done."

Betts and Forbach stood aside, and herded about half of the Varsity with him into his Circle. Betts himself then hand-pointed certain sophomores and freshmen into this group. Foster, Diebel, Ganstrom and Liedtke and myself were picked. Ambling around, we sort of gathered in a group. Liedtke was an Eagle Scout, and dated one of the Hanson twins. He was fast like the other three guys, certainly more than me. We wondered about our selections. The remaining crowd was led off by the other coaches.

"Line up, ladies, in a big friendly circle..." Betts called out. "Rodney Hess, you take the middle first. Show these younger ladies what the Circle Drill does for you. Coach Forbach, you run this group. I'll watch a bit, and float between the groups." Hess was a varsity defensive end. He was tall, rangy, strong, shrewd but decent-hearted. He hopped into the middle.

Suddenly, Coach Forbach shouted out a number, and then a second number, and then a third, and a fourth. Each number was a jersey number. And calling the jersey number, each man took off and flew full tilt at Hess in the middle. The upshot was that Hess couldn't know who was coming, nor from where he was being attacked. Hess in the middle of the circle had to look around quickly, and adjust to four speedy, and sequentially incoming attackers, each of whom was hell-bent to flatten the man with a full strength body block. Hess took the hits as well as he could, being able to anticipate and locate the first three. But he couldn't recover in time for the fourth hit.

At the fourth, he was flattened pretty good, but he got up gamely, looking around for anymore incoming assaults. There were none.

"Great reactions there, Hess. You'll be good for the punt return team with those quick recovery abilities," Betts commented. "Now ladies, you see how it works. Let's see what you're made of..." Betts grinned directly at our group of underclassmen, strung together on one side of the Circle. Forbach then called out first Diebel, then Wendell. Forbach then called out and matched the assaulters to have approximately similar body sizes to Gary and Wendell. Both guys with their fantastic reaction times, and toughness were able to hold their feet through the fourth assault, though they were pretty wobbly by the fourth hit. Coach Forbach paused, and then called out Liedtke.

At first, I noticed that he called out some of the biggest varsity guys to hit Liedtke, and that he was calling them too fast. Don was down slightly by the second hit. At the third hit, he was coming up into balance, and looking around when he was flattened. Then Forbach called a fourth hit. Don never saw him coming. He was launched forward a couple feet and immediately flattened. He staggered up, and was pretty dazed. His chin strap was loose, but he wasn't limping.

"Some of you guys need to learn to follow the team rules during the week." Betts called out the admonition in vague but threatening terms. Don shook his head, and stalked off from the center, picking up his mouthpiece from the ground..

Betts drifted off to the other two groups. Coach Forbach then called out my number. I strode to the center. *This is weird. The coaches don't get it. It's a setup. The goons have pulled something,* my cold ghost inside hissed. All fear fled me, replaced by a strange, heightened vigilance, and a rising burning storm inside me. *Okay. Time for fun and games...* whispered my inner ghost.

Forbach repeated for me the deal he arranged for Don. I had my new sports glasses. At least I could see. The first guy I decked like a rag doll. The second was not as easy, but I deflected him sideways. The third guy was Big Mick. At six foot and four inches, and a rangy two hundred and five pounds, he was by reputation the toughest bar-fighter in a hundred miles. A solid, decent guy, he was the first string end, and the younger brother of an All American running back now at Nebraska. I spotted him motoring in from my left back side. I adjusted in the nick of time and met him with what I could. It was an interesting side-swiping collision. We both were staggered sideways, but were still standing. After the whack, I vaguely heard Forbach call out the fourth guy's number.

It was Swaggart. He was coming from somewhere. I couldn't spot him, but I could hear him hissing like a freight train. My senses weirdly shifted. I could monitor myself in the next seconds, almost like I was outside my body as somebody else watching. The cold ghost whispered again, *Some unknown scum, maybe this guy, has manipulated all this. It's all to torture younger guys, or push us away from younger girls they want. And who knows what they want with younger girls? Is this crap ever gonna stop?"*

In a quick scan I couldn't see him. He had to be behind me. I flipped around frantically to land in a forward leaning crouch. In a split second, he steamrollered in, but I wacked him with all the up-thrust I could muster. The cold ghost was in full-rage. I caught Swaggart in the ribs so hard it sounded like a sledgehammer on a car hood. In the same instant he clobbered my helmet like a falling Sequoia. He flew three feet to one side, and I swooned over. We were both down. I crawled up, head ringing, and tried to focus. I spotted him, spat on the ground and moved toward him. He was coughing, on the ground, trying to stand and breathe. "Ready for more?" I hissed coldly at him. Swaggart looked up at me dazed, in a fog, and clutching his ribs. "*Lord Almighty...*" Diebel wheezed out low in the silence that blanketed the crowd.

"Next!" shouted a nervous Forbach, short-circuiting anything further. He called Foster's number. Pete was steaming like an Alaskan coal-fired power plant in mid-winter. He hopped to the center, and took down four in a row, just chopped 'em down like cornstalks. Hardly breathing, he took his mouthpiece out and spat on the ground after the fourth.

"You guys probably don't need any more injuries," he joked, and walked off on his own.

"Character building, huh, boys," Forbach cheerily called out, looking us younger guys over. "And now you know how you have to react quickly out there, on special teams." Several of us grunted. Liedtke still seemed a bit stunned. I said nothing. I found it hard to believe the coaches didn't know how they had been manipulated into this charade. Betts loped back, and blew his whistle. The crowds gathered in.

"Coaches, split the groups back into the three offensive/defensive units, and take up spread out points in the field and work on offensive patterns. Hop to it."

"There'll be more time for him," said Slim Gerhardt, nodding toward Swaggart, and grinning at me as he sidled past. A tough and decent guy, Slim was a year older, a lineman like me. I nodded back. I was still looking to get a grip on myself.

* * *

Diebel and I walked it home again, after practice, pretty much in exhausted silence.

"Well, this probably burns it out with those creeps," Gary said.

"You really think so?"

"Yeah. Probably. What more can they do? They know who they can't push around much, by now at least..." He winked. I was surprised at his insight. Maybe he was right. What else could they do, except victimize weaker guys? Only time would tell.

"What are you doing tonight? Want to go on a hay rack ride?" I asked Gary. I'd been invited to go with the Methodists on a hayride, through the Snyders, our old Scoutmasters.

"Nah. I got a geometry test tomorrow. Gotta crank on that."

"All-right, speed-ball. See ya around."

I scooted up through Tyler's back yard, glancing out where we had built our old running track in Wentz's yard to the west. You could still see the trace of the angled worn track in their grass-covered yard.

Keep Your Eyes Wide Open

After supper, I buzzed down to Wendell's to escape all the craziness in my head. Wendell's was always the great escape. He would talk religion, ethics, nature, environment, camping, girls, strange European race cars, rock music, track...and girls again. I could escape my strange ghost inside by keeping to our larger world of wondering about the fate of the humans. And, there was always a fire to build, and a sky to look into for answers. Tonight was the Methodist hayride.

We hopped into his Carmen Ghia, which Wendell and George had somehow recovered from a wrecked condition in a Topeka salvage yard. It was black, with black leather seats. Being British, it didn't run all that well, or start that easy. But it was the perfect visual symbol of Wendell's sprinter prowess.

We motored into the hills north of Concordia, to a farm, following the handwritten notes of instructions which I got from the Methodist newsletter after our Scout troop meeting. The sky was deep-ocean blue above, and fading into lighter shades of blue and orange-pink on the western horizon as the sun slid down the sky. Venus and the moon stood out low, but were dropping in the sky to the west. A wide swath of Canadian geese flew high in a long V overhead, heading south. A sign of an early winter to come. We pulled into the farmhouse entrance road, and bumped our way up to the barn, where a small blazing fire cheered the on-coming sunset. Kids surrounded the fire with marshmallows and hotdogs on sticks. The barn's perimeter was sprinkled with carved out and lit up pumpkins on the ground.

Wendell was greeted by Dorothy Nelson, his girl. I tagged along.

"Here's some sticks guys, go for the marshmallows or dogs," Dorothy sang out. She handed me a stick, and collared Wendell, dragging him off for a little private conversation on the other side of the fire.

I stirred the fire with my stick. *Seems like more of the people here are from a class or two older than me. I don't know all the faces and names yet.* After a bit, I roamed over into the barn, to look over how they stacked their hay in the upper lofts. After a couple minutes, I heard announcements about starting up the hayride, so I strolled back outside. Wendell and Dorothy waived me over to the hay rack. I rounded the back corner of the flatbed, as people were assisting each other up.

"Hey, Chris," Dorothy said, "You know Audrey, don't you?" I turned.

"Hi," a soft, melodious voice spoke. She stood behind me in Mr. Miller's choir. She was a year older.

Audrey Zimmerman had limpid-pool green eyes, and red short cut hair which had shining, slight tones of gold in the direct sun. I had heard she was a whiz in science and math classes. She stood behind me in choir. She had a terrific sense of tone and expression in her singing voice, and an unnerving way of smiling and looking out at me from the side, and from upward glances. I also knew she had been dating somebody. So I felt off-limits.

Even so, we sat that night, next to Wendell and Dorothy, and carried on chatter like meadowlarks, nestled into the hay, watching stars come out.

"That's Pleiades, the seven sisters." I pointed to the north-east. "The star at the bend in the handle of the Big Dipper is actually a double-star." I droned on with astronomical trivia, pointing out stars and night sky features. I had been into astronomy since I was little. I had to be boring with all this, but Audrey listened avidly. She really liked to nestle up close. We talked over the fears of the war, and Wendell's debate about it with Coach Forbach. We talked over music, and the amazing Miss Gwendolyn Fletcher, who held a Masters degree in literature and had taught now three generations of CHS students. In two solid years of courses, she had all her students read dozens of classic English novels, American novels, plays by Shakespeare, epic poems in Old English, and such. We learned to write essays like college students.

But these topics faded, as the gathering mysteries of the prairie night stole our souls. The blanket of stars winked into life in the purpling velvet heavens. The hypnotic song of crickets, and the mystical calls of Owls reached out of the vast land to mystify and silence us. The wind whooshed down the dark, great hills, and across the valley, and spilled into the cottonwoods, carrying to us the soft rustling of their leaves, and the deep scent of clover. The hay rack bumped and ground into the darkening night, as distant farm lights blended with stars into a seamless, deepening sky.

"If you try, you can imagine these stars and lights as being all around us, and we're just a hay rack drifting in space," Audrey whispered. I glanced out and around with her, and her vision was just so. *A girl with the soul of a poet,* I told myself.

On the way home that night, the Carmen Ghia growled its way down the dark gravel roads, spitting back dust as Wendell shifted and gunned the engine through its gears. We watched the canopy of the moonless and infinite stars, as we passed insignificantly beneath.

* * *

Wednesday zipped by, with no rumors that any accused or suspected perpetrators of the "dirty deed" against "Mad Dog" Kramer had been smoked out. There was a scribbled message, in purple lipstick on the mirror in the *boys* north bathroom, that said "It was Robbins", the discreetly anti-war forensics coach. Everybody knew he was a graduate of that infamous breeding ground of communists, socialists, basketball kings, intellectuals, homos and hippies, the University of Kansas. Some even said he was a founding father of the left-wing and war-protesting SDS when he was there. Other names popped up on blackboards, and notes taped to walls. Rumors abounded, but the day ground on, the mystery was unsolved, and the silence grew loud from the Administration.

Practice that day was rained out. The rain came down so hard at two-thirty p.m., a child's tricycle had been seen from classroom windows tumbling downhill on Eleventh Street, awash in the down-flow emanating from the football field and hill streets above. The rain increased so much, you lost sight of the doors of cars as the flood rose up as high as the floorboards.

"Rains like a cow pissing on a flat rock," blurted Hondo Johnson, in Miss Fletcher's American lit class, when the trike floated by. Half the class split their sides in silent laughter, and some of them went into cramps. Miss Fletcher, ever-the embodiment of decorum and steel-bottomed feminist wisdom, broke out in a rash over several silent seconds. She finally replied, "Creative use of a metaphor, Mr. Johnson." The class dissolved again into painful, cramping laughter.

At ten minutes to the final bell, Betts' voice called out over the intercom, "The football squads will report to the gym today, to run patterns, and stairs." Twenty minutes later, we were all following Householter again, who led the entire team running up and down the aisles of stairs in the large basketball gymnasium for forty-five straight minutes. Terry and Hondo Johnson didn't break a sweat through the whole drill, but a lot of us swooned over, succumbing to lactic acid pain and immobilization. Betts and the coaches hardly noticed, as they mulled over which short pass patterns could be run indoors, and which lineman training drills could be shunted over to the old gym. After forty five minutes of patterns and drills in both gyms, followed by twenty more agonizing minutes of fruitlessly following the grinning Householter on stair drills again, we all wheezed and staggered our way to the showers.

Diebel and I slowly walked back home, enjoying the startling thirty degree drop in temperature, and the chilling northwest wind. Wordlessly, we patted each other on the back, and headed into our homes. Mom had whomped up her famous home-made egg noodles and turkey that night, graced by cornbread. We ate on TV trays, painted with black matte background and yellow and red roses, and watched Chet Huntley and David Brinkley on NBC nightly news.

"Troops in Vietnam are up to 164,000 and climbing," Brinkley sang out in his famous sing-song baritone. "The government has plans to be calling up over 40,000 men per month in the new Selective Service draft, by December, according to Pentagon officials..."

"That *son-of-a-bitch* Lyndon Johnson!" Mom spurt out. "He's sending boys to fight a war that he lied about starting. Congress never declared this. We got no business going over there, and dropping bombs and napalm on women and children who live in huts. Good God, this will be a disaster for us all. If I had a gun, I'd shoot him myself," she declared.

"Mom," I tried to distract her, "you're noodles are great."

"He's an arrogant, self-blinded son-of-a-bitch," she repeated. Mom was deeply Catholic. She rarely used that particular phrase on somebody, unless she was supremely appalled. Like the time she saw Lee Harvey Oswald when he was arraigned for killing a policeman and JFK in Dallas, or the time that she walked past on Main Street one of the town's unscrupulous lawyers that she got into a tiff with over dad's inheritance when grandpa died back in the 1950s. She then modified her colorful assessment of the President, "Well, he has done the black folks some good, when Truman couldn't get the job done. I'll give him that." Dad just ate his noodles in silence.

NBC's David Brinkley continued, "Vietnam war protests, large ones at that, have broken out in many cities around the country in the last several days. These are mostly led by organizers of the SDS, on various college campuses, such as the University of California-Berkeley. They claim they will organize up to one hundred such protests within a month on college campuses. Our correspondent Sander Vanocur has a special onsite report at the Berkeley campus..."

"Let's switch channels. I don't want to see Johnson's face on the tube anymore..." said Mom. Dad stepped up to the TV to run the remote electric rotor that spun the antenna on top of the house, so that it could pick up the Lincoln, Nebraska station instead of Topeka.

The Spinning Wheel

The next day at school, just before lunch, the Intercom broke an announcement to all classes. It was "Mad Dog" Kramer.

"Attention, attention. The hooligans have been apprehended, and summarily dealt with. There will be no public announcement as to their identity. However, they have been suspended from school for the remainder of the week, and handed over to the authorities. Justice is served. Order is restored."

For the whole day, Roger hid out from Mom. At school time, he parked his '57 over by the school, but then took a bike downtown. Nobody was the wiser, until that night. Late in the afternoon, Dad strode into the West Side Inn, a small greasy spoon that had legendary hamburgers and homemade pies one half block east of the laundromat. One-eyed Curley was the owner and cook. He was always springing pranks on customers, and vice versa.

"Hey, Ryland. You heard about the ruckus up at the high school?"

"Oh, yeah. They'll probably smoke 'em out. Betts has his ways," Dad replied.

"Anybody in here, hear any rumors as to who they suspended? They actually suspended a couple of them." Curley was a one man headline news service.

"Nope," the crowd echoed itself.

"Well, I don't know either. But Ryland, I did see your boy whip down the alley this morning on his bike, about forty minutes after eight o'clock. Where do you suppose he was heading during school hours?" Curley winked to the crowd.

"Well, hell if I know. He's supposed to be in school. He left for school this morning." Dad mulled this over. After a couple of winks, and a few "Uh-huhs" in the room, dad slowly drained his coffee, and headed out the door. In a couple minutes, he was cruising the alleyways, looking for where a youth might play pinball, and hide out his bike. After the third bar establishment, he spotted Roger's bike, nestled in between a few trash cans on the east side of the Oasis bar in the Baron's Hotel on Fifth Street.[2] At five-thirty that night, the dinner table conversation was pretty cryptic, as Sue and I learned Roger wouldn't be playing his trombone in the marching band on Friday night at the football game.

"He was one of the guys that put up the sarcastic figure of Mr. Kramer," Mom explained, stirring gravy for the chipped-beef and gravy over biscuits for supper that night.

"Reaallly?" Sue said, clearly impressed.

"I'll be darn," I replied diplomatically. I had wondered if he had something to do with this.

"Well, he got his medicine dished out. He won't be doing such things again," Mom said. Sue smiled at me.

"He's still in the band?" I asked. "And still in school?"

"Yeah. He'll be back in the band after tomorrow night's game is all. He'll be back in school on Monday. I guess the Assistant Principal could have done more to him. But there are a lot of pressures coming to bear, over there. Anyway, that's the story."

"I wonder who else was in on it?" Sue asked me after supper.

"Someday we'll know, maybe," I guessed.

Change in the Winds

At five-forty p.m. in the CHS Assistant Principal's office, Dick Kramer knifed open a special delivery letter the high school secretary had just received and put in his mailbox, a few minutes before. Kramer pulled out the letter. It was written on the letterhead of the Concordia School Board. It read, "We have received several complaints from parents of girls at the Concordia High School, regarding your policies with respect to the enforcement of dress codes and other treatments as relates to the high school girls. Some concern exists among Board members regarding the propriety..." Kramer dropped the letter. The first hearing would be in three weeks.

Bonfires, within

Thursday afternoon our freshmen team edged out Salina Sacred Heart High School at their home field. Diebel caught a down and out pass in mid field, and sprinted his way past a half dozen defenders to the six yard line with seventeen seconds to go. He was ankle tackled at the last second. Dead-eye Mario Brichalli booted a field goal, and we were headed home, having staked a fair warning for ourselves and for the Varsity game coming to CHS on Friday.

Our bus pulled into our home stadium, just as the all-school bon-fire was about to start at seven p.m., up on the northeast practice field above the stadium, exactly in front of Gary's house. We spilled off the bus, and ran up to the field area to catch the goings-on. The pep band, decked out in white sweaters and red ties, was playing some Tijuana Brass numbers, and popcorn and hot dogs were out on tables. The Fire Department pump truck was nearby on Willow Street in front of Gary's place, with some pretty sleepy looking firemen leaning up against the truck. Liedtke, Diebel and I had grabbed some popcorn, and hustled over to the log pile, as Forbach was sprinkling some kerosene on the stack. In less than thirty seconds, the pile of sticks, logs, and old school chairs was pumping sparks and yellow-red flames twenty feet skyward and rising. Bone tired, and nursing bruises and blisters, we just stared at the crackling flames, not listening to muffled conversations or the occasional bursting laughter of a crowd of girls.

Coach Betts strode out from a parked Bonneville station wagon, and positioned himself well in front of the fire, and began his speech through a megaphone.

"We just got word from Coach Frohardt that our freshmen football team took down Sacred Heart's freshmen in the last seconds with a blazing run by Gary Diebel to the six yard line, and then they buried those Knights with a field goal!" The crowd erupted into cheers and roars.

"Tomorrow night, it won't be like that for our Varsity, I have to admit reluctantly..." Betts was winding them up. "You can ignore the city papers. Because we're gonna kick their butts." The crowd roared approval. A newspaper, a used popcorn bag, and a half eaten hotdog flew into the fire. A few seconds later, a bigger deluge followed. One of the popcorn bags bounced off Betts' red & white CHS baseball cap, and the crowd just laughed with him. At that moment, a couple of the senior linemen unrolled a banner and held it aloft. One of the linemen lit up the banner with one of those eight battery steel police flashlights that could cast a beam a half-mile. It read,

"Better Bet on Betts' Butt-Kickers"

Betts and all the crowd broke into chuckles and applause.

Betts took up the megaphone again. He looked down, around, and down again. Some long seconds passed. You could tell he was thinking something over.

"You all know that I can't give speeches like Robert Kennedy. I'm just a farm boy from Norcatur, out west. You ought to know why you are fortunate. You are grandsons and granddaughters of immigrant pioneers who fled to this country to escape something pretty bad. They wanted a chance to find and pass on great possibilities to you, to us, their children. We're all different, different religions, nationalities, rich, poor, abilities and talents. But you all come from people who had unusual courage, to move from comfortable places to out here on the vast rugged plains. Out here, we all learn to pull together. Maybe you don't know it yet, but these things are born and bred into you. That's our secret. The big city papers say we aren't much. I say, tomorrow we will show them who we are."

Don, Gary and I exchanged silent glances, and gazed around the crowd. There were some cheers, and some fist-punching in the air, and several bouncing cheerleaders. But mostly, these young people were just looking at each other, and shaking hands.

Game Time

One of the great pleasures Mom had in the golden house on the Willow Street hill were the many years of listening to the high school marching band practice in the ripening and gorgeous fall mornings. The practices were in the stadium, literally out our front yard, down the long hill.

Come game time, the great bright lights, which had been bent slightly to the east by the great storm, blazed out. You could read the fine print of the newspaper stock reports from the lights coming through our front living room window. The roars of the crowds smothered any conversations or television program. Some game nights are shining gems, talked about for generations.

* * *

The crowd filtered in around six p.m., dragging blankets, baby things, portable seats, and Coke coolers (with an occasional beer buried deep under ice). The drifting gusts of a bracingly cool north wind blew the streaming scents of chili, baked potatoes, corn and hot dogs, and cotton-candy around for blocks. Growling engines of Mustangs, Barracudas, and an occasional motorcycle grunted and popped in the fall night air, as vehicles squeezed into every available square inch of parking on the upper practice fields, streets, curbs and private yards. Grizzled, pipe-smoking grandpas or smiling church-lady volunteers in red bibs manned the white and red small ticket booths at unlocked gate entrances around the high, hurricane-wire fenced stadium and fields.

Diebel and I met up with Alan, Louis, and Don Liedtke at our pre-arranged time of six-thirty p.m. at the northeast front gate. We entered without paying, just saying "freshmen team." We wore our stiffly new cardinal red wool, and white-leather arm CHS sports lettermen jackets. Liedtke had the most powerful calf muscles of anyone in five hundred miles, as he deliberately walked everywhere on his toes. It was his strategy for constant leg strength training. Don was but a tenth of a second slower than Gary in sprints. Alan and Louis were fresh off a cross-country meet, where yet again the crop of Iron Men had wiped out virtually all teams except a large Kansas City school, at a meet in Chapman. Alan grinned his way past a half dozen girls, setting off eyebrow-raised glances amongst the rest of us, as we loped around the north track. Gary pursed his lips into a spreading smile, and shook his head in slight amazement, at the obliviousness of Alan to the swath of girls glancing back over their shoulders at him.

We leaped up the stairs up the middle of the west and home side of the stadium, three and four steps at a time. We settled in near the top. I whipped out the pair of dad's Navy World War II binoculars from under my jacket, and passed them around. The Sacred Heart Knights were doing drills at the south end of the football field. The CHS Panther varsity had not yet entered the field at the north. Luecke was eye-balling the Sacred Heart team with the field glasses. Sacred Heart was in Salina, a much larger town, and was a somewhat larger school.

"They got some 220 pound linemen down there," Alan wheezed out.

"Come on. Let me see that," I asked for the glasses.

"Check Number 82. Been a lot of corn dogs going into *that* boy," Louis quipped.

I scanned for number 82. Several other large dudes came into focus as well. I studied them.

"Well, some of those boys got tummies, too many Little Debbies..." I offered.

"Think you could take him, huh?" Gary ribbed me with an elbow.

"He doesn't look fast. I don't know, Don. What do you think?" I passed him the glasses.

"Yup. Too much gravy and corn dogs," Don smiled out.

"Uh-huh..." Alan skeptically replied. "If 82 fell on you, you'd be wheezing for awhile."

"If he ran three blocks with you and Louis, he'd be wheezing inside of twenty seconds, I'd say," I joked.

"Aha....he's a defensive end," Alan smiled, rifling through the program. "We'll see how he does against Rodney Hess."

The Varsity squad was funneling in the north gate. The pep band, positioned near the gate, struck up the CHS fight song. The cheerleader squad gushed, and sprang into frenzied cheers, pumping up the all-girl cheering section decked out in their lustrous red sweaters and skirts. After twenty minutes of preliminaries, the game was on. The CHS Panther captains won the toss, and chose to receive at the north end, a slight wind to their backs.

The game went well that night. Quarterback Tom rifled a pass to Big Mick on the third play of the game, and Mick literally trampled two hapless safeties into ground chuck, as he motored for an early touchdown strike. That held the lead until late in the second quarter, when a Sacred Heart interception brought them down to the Concordia 30 yard line, and they ground out a touchdown. The hitting on both lines was brutal. On one catch, Mick busted one of the star-crossed safeties so bad the victim's helmet flew ten feet and rolled toward the Sacred Heart bench. A little CPR, and he was stretchered off to St. Joseph's Hospital out west, still breathing, his tongue lolling out the side of his mouth. Just under the two minute mark to the half time break, and with the game still tied, Coach Betts called a time out. He spoke to the assembled team, huddled on the sidelines, "Boys, we've got perfect field position on the far hash mark. Their defense is wheezing worse than an old mule. We're better conditioned. They're thinking of getting that cold Coke at the half. It's time to launch the play. Tom and Steve Collins, just get it to Terry, just like you practiced it two hundred times."

The "Porsche manuever" is what Gary called it. It was the double reverse, designed to confuse a defense as to where the ball is. As we saw in practice, Quarterback Tom was to run to the deep, open field side and hand-off to Collins going opposite, and then Collins gives the ball to Householter going back opposite again. Terry then breaks out into the large open area.

The open area where no man alive, then or now, could hope to catch him after House kicked on his after-burners.

We saw it coming again from high in the stands. Diebel leaped into the air, and shouted to the silenced home crowd *"Watch This!"* His shout had barely spread to the cheerleaders, when House took the ball. He shifted the ball to his right arm, and *exploded* toward the home-side open field like human lightning. He sizzled around defenders like a Nike missile. He passed clusters of two, and then three defenders who took a stride or two after him and they dropped to a dead stop, to just stare.

We stopped breathing. Terry took the turn a good ten yards from the sideline, with forty yards to the end zone. He had already passed two-thirds of the two teams in less than three seconds. Their safeties down field were desperately sprinting at 90 degrees to head him off across the much narrower width of the field. At the turn, the House shifted into high warp drive, seared over the field and passed the safeties like a scorched greyhound, *accelerating with every stride, as smooth and untouchable as the Queen's silk. Forty yards, three seconds.*

The crowd was silent as Dodge City Tombstones, until House almost hit the goal line, stepping out of bounds at the three. Dispelling disbelief, the masses erupted in a frenzy. Ten seconds later, we were in the end-zone with a steam-roller, go-ahead touchdown by Collins.

Those in the crowd who'd seen this from Terry four years ago when he was just a skinny eighth grade kid, felt a tremendous confirming relief: they had not been stone-cold delusional back then after all. But for those who'd never seen this grown-up Terry blaze out at full-hearted power, it was just plain hard to fathom.

Terry and the rest of the offense zipped back to the bench. His helmet was off, curly hair flopping in the wind, grinning his way with the other varsity running backs into popping flashbulbs and a tumultuous crowd.

There's something about this guy, and it is more than ungodly speed and an easy dazzling smile. I can't quite get it down, I kept thinking. In this sizzling moment, the four of us stared at each other, eyes wide, no words. It was a prophecy of things to come. That night mighty Sacred Heart lost.

Chapter 10
COLD WINDS RISING

There was a considerable amount of reveling that night. For starters, Mr. Culbertson paid to fill the huge Jacuzzi tub in the locker room with iced-down Cokes for the whole team, freshmen and all. Gary, Alan and I drifted into the locker room following the Varsity and band after they flooded over to the high school following the post-game celebration. The police had allowed a spontaneous circling of the field by a batch of ecstatic fans, driving hot cars. The brand new demonstration Camaro from the Babe Houser dealership, various Mustangs, Tom Hutchison's '65 Plymouth Barracuda, Jake Bray and his Triumph motorcycle, and a police squad car all circled the field for fifteen minutes, blaring horns.

Several out-of-town newspaper reporters surrounded Coach Betts in the locker room, taking notes, asking questions.

"Would you say your defense, and surprise plays made the difference, coach?" a Topeka Daily Capitol sports reporter asked.

"How 'bout you ask them?" Betts replied, waving over the team.

"Defense, defense, defense..." was the echoing reply.

"What about the trick plays? What do you have to say about Householter?" another reporter shouted out. The room grew silent.

"He made a difference. He had a good night. What do *you* have to say about Householter?" was Betts crafty reply.

"Well, how about... *'a new Clark Kent appears in Concordia, faster than a speeding bullet'* ...how's that, coach?" joked a Topeka reporter. Betts smiled, replying "Yeah. Maybe that's a bit much..." He shook his head back and forth, as chuckles ripped through the room. House just coughed, threaded through the crowd, and headed for the showers in a towel.

Betts radiated, as he leaned over to the reporters. He paused for a long second, and said something in a quiet voice below the general hub-bub. Long slow nods, and eyes wide-as-moons were the replies from the reporters.

We grabbed some Cokes, and headed up to the old gym above, for the dance.

The famous Red Dogs were playing that night, for the after-game dance. Cars cruised around the high school, and down on Main Street, engines snarling at each other like rabid wolves. Luecke and I split for my house after awhile, and we snuck downstairs and quietly played dad's old swing era '78s on his turntable in the bomb shelter. After an hour, we slipped upstairs to the upper north room that had a window that looked out and down over the town. For quite awhile, we mulled over music, girls, and the war. The clock spun. We mumbled our way toward sleep on sleeping bags spread before the window. Alan said he'd be up for cross-country runs by six-thirty in the morning. At five a.m., Jerry would be out to run, before his farm chores. Terry would be up and running his two miles out to help open the Skyliner Café. Over on Jail House hill, high above Highway 81, somebody was launching fireworks.

Stone Hearts under Siege

In the morning, I had to mow again. But not before I buzzed out on Vindicator, to the top of the hill just south at the Country club. I was out to watch the sunrise. Alan had took off to go run with the cross-country crew. I watched them thread past the golf greens, trekking out on cemetery road, glad I could watch the mystical rising colors in the east, and glad I was not an Iron Man suffering miles on the Kansas hills.

After mowing the lawn all morning, and scarfing mom's tuna salad for lunch, I reported to the Cathedral for *Carmina Burana* tenor and soprano section rehearsals. Mr. Miller was a stickler for holding extra rehearsals, sometimes on weekends. He was grinning a mile wide, wearing brown and white loafers, white pants, and sporting a Hawaiian shirt at the top of the Cathedral limestone steps at one p.m.. Soon Father Melvin Long arrived, carrying a large brass ring of keys. A young man, with curly brown hair, Father Long had come to Kansas by a mysterious and winding road. A Jesuit trained priest, he had a certificate in Christian history studies from the Sorbonne University in Paris. As much theologian as priest, he was a man of peace. He cut a swath through the crowd, smiling and greeting kids on all sides. The doors of the Cathedral creaked open. He flipped the back lights on, and pointed the crowd up the spiraling stairs to the choir loft. The slanting rose-colored light shone through the Rosetta stained glass window above the choir loft, melding with the scent of myhr from decades of incense. The scents, light and shadow were familiar and soul-settling to me. The Protestant kids seemed semi-stunned into reverent silence by these sensual traces of Christian centuries unknown to them, brought alive by the Cathedral. Few of them had ever been near, much less inside a Catholic Cathedral.

A breath blew against my hair from behind, as I threaded up the stair case. I glanced back. An impish smile and a wink greeted me. It was Audrey Zimmerman.

"I think you've been here before, no?" she asked, teasing.

"A few times."

Audrey was Episcopalian. According to Father Long, they were "Catholic-light" believers, who had been re-habed into legitimacy by the teachings of the Second Vatican Council of 1963. According to the old catechism and church histories, they had been dangerous heretics, following a blood-thirsty line of Anglican Kings. To me, Audrey was less a dangerous vixen heretic, and more a friend and tantalizing girl with a fabulous brain.

"Some are missing today," Audrey whispered.

"Well, it does seem thinned-out." I looked around at the choir pews being filled in.

"What do you think is up?" I asked.

"I think some of us are scared of you," she replied. "But not me..." she breathed at me with wine-like breath.

"Scared?"

"Oh, come on, think." Audrey pursed her lips and raised an eyebrow.

"It's the Cathedral," I offered.

"Well, partly. The Cathedral is beautiful. It's that some minds and hearts out there are not. There still is a lot of fear, Catholics vs Protestants, instilled into us as kids. We had it. You had it. Others had a lot more of it. It's these crackpot preachers to blame, really. You know, 'Jesus is all about love your neighbor, except for those devil-people we fear or hate'. Crackpots in shepherds' clothing is all those preachers are." She leaned in close to my ear, and breathed sweetly, "And I must say, your Church's teaching that all children in a marriage must be raised Catholic is no help, it sets up fears and lines between us all." I couldn't do anything but nod.

"Someday, some-bodies will bring all these walls to an end," she said sharply, her gold-flecked green eyes glistening.

In our day? I wondered.

Evelyn was warming up the huge Italian organ. With a gleam in her eye, she cranked up the volume, and blazed out a dazzling sequence of the *Carmina*'s soul-rattling chord progressions. The angels in the Cathedral looked to the heavens, and the very air shimmered around us.

Skirt-Gestapo Blues

The brilliant autumn days in Kansas were skittering by like fallen burnt-orange and red maple leaves in the undying winds, like the days in our lives.

The next morning passed before Sunday Mass, with sister Sue and I perched at the dining room table, counting dimes, nickels and quarters. That's how Dad made deposits to the bank, from the laudromat's weekly take, with Sue and I counting up the coins. We learned to do math in our heads lightning fast. We were able to count proper change in our heads at the grocery store as fast as the clerks could figure it with adding machines.

This morning Sue was decked out in a new Scottish plaid dress with white collar, a new creation of mom's Singer sewing machine, from which she sewed about a fourth of sis's clothes. We gathered in the coins from dad's bags, like squirrels snatching acorns.

"You're running movies tonight, at the Brown Grand, aren't you?" Sue asked. "I've got another night tonight doing concessions there." The Brown Grand is the four story maid of honor among Kansas theatres. Built in 1909, constructed by mom's great uncle, it is the most ornate, elaborate theatre between St. Louis and Denver, surpassing any in Kansas City or Omaha. It sports a silk, hand-drawn thirty foot tall painting, behind the red velvet curtains, of Napoleon at Waterloo, which draws to the ceiling. The proud lady, like so many lesser sisters, had been reduced to hosting movies by the late 1920s, as the traveling theatre productions had long-since gone-under.

"Yup. For sure, I'm there. Gotta splice some reels before the seven p.m. showing," I replied, piling up quarters, and sliding them into paper tubes. "I like the Scot plaid dress mom made ya, nice greens and blues."

"I don't know if it'll pass muster, or not," Sue replied. "Kramer's gone rabid again, sending girls home for short skirts. I'd like to kick him where the sun don't shine, but that wouldn't do what with Roger laying low from the Jim Beam/Scarecrow-in-the-sky stunt he pulled two weeks ago, and me being his sister."

"Uh, yeah. No doubt. Kramer's really worse, huh?" I asked, sheepishly, having to admit that I hadn't been watching this scene for awhile, and was out of touch.

"If girls are breaking down, and not coming back for a few days tells you any-thing, yeah, right. How'd you like to kneel in front of that son of a bitch? There's a drawing in red fingernail polish of him getting stabbed, that won't come off the walls of the girl's bathroom, that the janitors are going ape to scrub off somehow, but it's not coming off. Something's gonna give, sometime. Somebody's gonna freak on him."

* * *

Monday morning, the civil war on slow burn between the young women of CHS and Kramer heated up. Kramer and his boys were facing down fuming girls at the front steps again, forcing them to kneel to have their skirts measured. It was obvious that vengeance was in the air, as three janitors were the targets of sizzling side-glances, as they sweated to clean off with razors, a hardened slash of Xs and Zs painted on Kramer's exterior window in red nail polish. The "evil protest" was probably foist-ed sometime over the weekend. Unnoticed by the skirt-gestapos, an ever-increasing stream of young ladies were sidling in through one of the southwest glass doors which had become mysteriously unlocked, and held open by a piece of cardboard placed so the door wouldn't shut. It had a sign taped to the inside of the glass. It read, *"Zorro opens doors for women! Reprobates measure skirts! Know who your friends are!"* It was signed with a slashing Z, in cherry-red nail polish.

For two solid days, Kramer and the skirt gestapos were so dense they couldn't figure out why the stream of women entering through the front door had slightly dwindled each day. Rumor mills were clamped tight. Nobody talked to anyone over eighteen years of age. One rumor spread that Zorro was an un-named brother, who used the forever secret entrance of the guys' locker room window to sneak in and strike a blow for freedom for his increasingly enraged sister. Another rumor was that Zorro was Kramer's own freshman daughter who some thought couldn't stomach the humiliation of her CHS Panther Sisters any longer. She was rumored to wink and say, "I know nothing, I say nothing," when asked.

That morning, seven-thirty a.m. Tuesday, was day two of the simmering civil war. Roger pulled up the '57 Chevy into a parking slot south of the door. He was hoping to get in through the band door entrance, by knocking on the window for

Mr. Ensign who was always early, to let him in. He hoped to skate past Kramer at the front entrance for a couple more weeks anyway. As the Prime Miscreant, Roger desired anonymity, for awhile.

As he opened the car door, he spotted something. *What the blazing devil is that behind the bushes?* Roger stopped cold, squinting. He crept up to the bushes slowly. Dimly coming into his focus was a pair of plaid pants, and a pair of binoculars poking through the bushy leaves.

"You can't get a good fix into the girl's bathroom from *that* angle, you have to go to the *west* side windows!" Roger sarcastically sang out.

The bush shook, the plaid pants rose, and the binoculars fell tumbling from nervous fingers, into the bushes. It was a sheepish-looking Coach Forbach. Roger loped off, chuckling to himself, angling fast for the band room doors. As the rumors spread of Coach Forbach in the bushes, most of us came to figure that an apoplectic Kramer had shanghaied a couple hapless teachers and coaches to take up spotting positions at six in the morning, across the street with binoculars, in a plot to nab Zorro. But Zorro apparently knew how to read tea-leaves, for on Tuesday morn, he or she was a no-show. No slashing red Zs that day. Over the remaining fall months, Zorro would reappear randomly, leaving doors open with slashing red Zs, and stranding a few humiliated teachers or coaches, embarrassed in the bushes.

* * *

That day we had a crushing football practice that ended with a full twenty minutes of merciless sprint drills. After practice, Gary and I straggled out of the shop exit from the football lockers, and walked slowly up the west hill of Eleventh Street, nursing blisters. The two blocks seemed to deliberately lengthen out before us.

"Do you mind if I come up to your place, and we can check out Roger's short wave receiver?" Gary asked. I had been telling him that among the electronic gizmos that Roger spread out in boxes in the upstairs rooms was a short wave radio he picked up at the auction house out west on Eleventh Street, at the bottom of the hill before the climb to the radio KNCK station. At nights, especially on Christmas Eve, when Mom and Dad always took off down to the Elks club to take in their once a year spiked eggnog and several other annual hard drinks, we dialed in Radio Havana Cuba for their Christmas Eve broadcast. It was exotic, tuning in the semi-forbidden communist radio propaganda, and hearing strange Christmas doings in a country that supposedly was deeply atheistic. It felt as chillingly weird as a broadcast from the other side of the galaxy.

"Yup. We can give her a whirl. But we'll have to wait until after sundown, when the short wave reception clears up," I replied.

"You think we can pull in Cuba?" Gary asked with trepidation and curiosity.

"Maybe. I haven't tried since last about last Easter to get them. Last week I pulled in some really strange sounding belly dancing music, maybe from outta Egypt or somewhere," I replied.

Our spirits pepped up a little, and we took the climb a bit faster. "I'll check in with Mom, and be up as soon as I can," Gary said, as he angled off at the corner to head into his house. I angled with him, and took the backyard route around Tyler's house, skipped past the cherry trees and into the back door.

"Hey, Mom." I cried. "What's cooking?"

"Grandma Francoeur's goulash," she called back. "How was football?"

"Ughhh...I'm beat. Grrreat on the goulash." I responded. Images flooded my head, of trekking with sister Sue through thirty mile per hour winds, snow crystals stinging, across the schoolyard in a winter blizzard, to Grandma's house across the alley. We would stamp our boots free of snow inside her porch cover, hang our frozen mittens over her hot-as-fire gas floor heater, and watch her take out her goulash and Jiffy cornbread from her porcelain white gas stove with blue trim.

A knock was at the back door, and Gary let himself in. He radiated politeness. Mom grinned like sunshine as she tousled his black-as-coal hair.

"You guys watch TV for half an hour, supper'll be ready by then. Scoot," Mom said as she pointed us out of the kitchen.

We spun the roof top TV antennae motor. The Lincoln Nebraska NBC station signal etched into view like a snow-storm fading out, with faces and voices coming clear through the snow. It was news time, and the sales-pitch chanted,

"NBC TV evening news with Chet Huntley and David Brinkley, from our Washington studios..." Gary and I sank into the green couch. Gruesome scenes of napalm exploding in oily-looking streams of fireballs, and soaring over treetops popped into view, as the correspondent ground on...

"Here in the central highlands, US B-52s unleashed hell's greatest fury on what American officials say are concentrating forces of the North Vietnamese Army, and Viet Cong in this region. The Air Force here says that air power can root out the majority of hidden enemy forces with napalm's infernos, leaving smaller mopping up operations to US Army forces. Marines will later penetrate any areas that suspected hold-out Viet Cong forces might escape from, and root them out easily... Back to Washington, and to you, Chet..."

Gary and I looked sideways at each other, wordlessly.

"Here at home," Chet continued, "the radical student nationwide organization, the SDS or Students for a Democratic Society, have claimed credit today in announcements by spokeswoman Bernadine Dohrn, for numerous spreading large protests on university campuses. There are four of them just this week, a dozen of them total this month, on campuses spread from New York to Ohio, Michigan, Indiana, Kansas, California and elsewhere, as the lottery draft is due to accelerate in December. Here's Miss Dorne, at her news conference..."

Gary and I sat breathlessly as the attractive, well-spoken Bernadine Dohrn measured her words of fire in eerie, moderate tones: "...hell-fire fell from the sky burning women, and children in their villages...corporate-sponsored death by flames... capitalist pig profits fattened by war...Our white fascist government 'Christian leaders' wreak their genocide on yellow Asian brothers and sisters, using our black brothers as cannon-fodder…"

With our mouths open and eyes wide, in shallow breaths we suffered, taking in the sulfuric images of Hell and revolution, as they stormed into the room. Unnamed fears and revulsions slid mercilessly into our heads like spears of dry ice. I felt beautiful dreams fade in my heart, and slip away for Gary and the rest of us.

Mom's voice, carrying the warm promise of home, cut through this evil black tempest like an undaunted New England lighthouse…*"Supper's ready."*

October's Shift in the Winds

The pace of living in Kansas, the autumn traditions, the usual scenes of our lives in and out of school seemed to unfold in expected patterns that week. The glories of the landscape and season seemed to harmonize into what a sensitive soul would call "normalcy". Yet, events in our lives carried the resonance of vaster, titanic forces. The visionary souls among us were carrying forward the great, unstoppable tides of change. This new dance of life ran quickly.

* * *

Evelyn's genius displayed itself in the early morning hours in practice on the grand piano on the CHS stage. The early janitor, Mr. Collins, who opened the doors early, and went about morning bathroom cleaning chores, knew she was there. *Every day she's here, I should turn her in. I could get in trouble if Mr. Betts ever shows early, and finds that I don't turn her in, but this music, it's so… something. And to think she's just fifteen…* He swept the hall near the stage door, again, for the fifth time, to listen.

Jerry rose early that week, for his almost-daily cross-country morning runs before chores, his rising earlier than the week before. He pounded out more miles each week, like a machine.

Diebel and I started our campaign to rise early and sneak over into the school through the locker room windows, and lift weights three mornings a week for an hour, to build our strength. Monday had been the first day, a successful one. Nobody was around save the discrete Iron Men who came in through the same window for showers, after their early runs. Tim and Roger had laid low for weeks, trying to stay off the radar of anybody resembling an authority.

The tempo of normalcy beat on. The Hanson twin sisters, so Louis had informed us in the lunchroom on Tuesday, were rising early to study their Bibles in the hopes of "saving souls" by getting them to accept Jesus, as their personal Savior. The lost souls of their designs were either "sinners", or members of a "suspect" Church, including myself, Luecke, Mac Campbell, Terry himself, all the Fosters, and among others to my surprise, Swaggart.

"You wonder why they wear that White Shoulders perfume to Bible studies when friends from other churches visit," observed Wendell, "and now we know. They aspire to get your attention…"

"Such clever women," Jack interjected with a sly grin, "and is this tactic scriptural? Ah yes, I remember now, it's in Devious chapter 2 verse 10…" Even Louis had to chuckle at that.

I ran the movies in the Brown Grand on Monday to Wednesday, and some Friday nights. Kasl showed up at the projector booth Wednesday night, in a surprise raid.

"Wuh-hah, ha!" he shouted, thrusting open the iron door, and jumping into the projection booth. "Startled ya, huh?" he teased. I shrugged my shoulders, shaking my head quickly. In fact, he succeeded.

"I know you too well, studly." He smirked. It was eerie how much he looked like me. We often masqueraded as fraternal twins, as a joke.

"You're *never* going to get over that scene from the movie *The Blob*, are ya, despite all your muscles…when the Blob seeps into the projectionist booth, through the vent behind the projectionist in the movie theatre, and swallows him up… maybe you'll get over it, but…" He leaped at me, making slurping noises. *What a wild man*, I thought. Jack knew this creepy scene from the famous Steve McQueen movie haunted me, especially when I was trapped up in the heights of the projection booth, three stories up. The movie scene had a theatre that was a dead ringer copy of the Brown Grand. I never could shake the unrealistic fears.

* * *

Our freshmen team skunked Belleville 16 to 7 on Thursday. In the last quarter, it began to rain. We managed to slog down the field in mud in the fourth quarter, the score tied, when Mike Hepperly drilled a pass to Bruce Johnston, who skipped nimbly past three tacklers and slid into the end-zone. Three plays later, Liedtke recovered a Belleville fumble, and Mario Brichalli booted a field goal an astounding forty-seven yards, in spite of mud, and a bad wind. We couldn't help leaving a thin pool of mud oozing outside their locker room after the game.

Most of us didn't go to the Belleville Varsity game, an away-game, that Friday. I ran the tiring, three and one half hour long early evening screening of "Romeo and Juliet" that night, at the Brown Grand. It was director Franco Zeffireli's drippy, too-sweet silver screen version of the classic play we were to study in Miss Fletcher's class next year. I was exhausted, after seeing and running the darn thing four times, in the last two weeks.

Wendell, Louis and Jack tooled up to the projectionist booth in the last five minutes of the showing Friday, about nine-fifty p.m.

"Hey, Hambutt. You surviving this Hollywood schlock?" Wendell asked, breezing through the iron door. Making quick movements like a cat, he had on a new pair of Pumas, something like Diebel's pair. Jack ambled in behind Wendell.

"Shut the door, boys...there are three minutes of this thing left to run, nice timing," I said.

"We got the Carmen Ghia. Want to hit the A & W?" Wendell asked.

"Sure," I replied, taking some reels off the re-winder and loading them in their metal cases.

"Hey, is this stuff hard to work with?" Louis asked, peering through the safety glass into the carbon-arc light.

"Uh...it's a little tricky. Took me six months. You got the complicated machines, you got reels to splice, and you don't want to damage film. You do not want the film to jump off the cogs and scrunch up in the machine. The 32 and 64 millimeter films are worth a thousand dollars a foot in some cases. "

"Jesus-Mary-Josephine," Jack cried, his eyes widening.

"It's insured, Jackson. Not to worry. But you betcha, I'm careful. I love this place. I don't want to lose this job."

I packed up the last reel, and dialed down the voltage on the carbon-arc lights. We thundered down the red-flower carpeted four flights of stairs. "See ya later, Sis," I called out to Sue. She was still tallying receipts, and would lock up. She gave us the eyebrows, smiled, and kept counting.

A few minutes later, we pulled into the gravel lot of the A & W, next to Christenson Oil, out on south Highway 81. We ordered root beer double floats, onion rings, and hamburgers. Jack whipped out a paper sack, "Extra!" he cried, waving the bag in front of me. "Zelnikis."

Wendell and Louis groaned. Jack and I beamed. A biting cold wind blew hard through the window, as we called in the order. We were halfway through the zelnikis, burgers, and root beer, when a car wheeled in next to us, spitting gravel.

A tall, rangy and athletic figure sprang out from the car, and sprinted over. It was Pete. He leaned through the window, looked us over with wide eyes, took a deep breath, and said, "Guys..." he swallowed hard, pausing, not able to say something.

"What's up, Pete?" Wendell asked nervously. In all the years I knew Pete in Catholic school, I never saw him ashen-gray, or afraid. Pete took another deep breath. The cold wind whipped harshly through Pete's hair, whistling in through the car window.

"It's Terry. Betts threw him off the team."

Chapter 11
PER ASPERA

Valleys of Shadows

There was nothing but silence from us all. The icy wind whistled erratically through the window, and sang a high lonely whine in the power line above the Christensen Tire lot. A flat metal trim piece on the side of the A & W roof banged, seeking revenge. Pete hung his head down in the window, shaking it slowly back and forth. A stinging acid crept up my throat, and my ears rang. Wendell looked straight ahead, through the glass, unblinking.

"Come on inside, Pete. Don't just hang out there, it's getting cold." Wendell said. Pete called back to the car he arrived in, "I'll catch a ride with these guys." He then walked quickly around to the other side of Wendell's car, and we squeezed him into the back seat, next to Jack.

"This is not possible," I croaked out from the passenger front seat.

"All-right, what's the story?" Wendell called out. Jack looked intently from one to the other of us. Pete sighed, and said,

"The word from my brother Charlie is that guys were joking around in the back of the bus after the game on the way home tonight. The bus had just arrived home, pulling into the school, and one of the coaches heard something like 'you've got cigs?' and reported it to Betts, who came back to investigate. House stood right up and said they were his. Betts said something, Terry said something back which Betts didn't like, and Betts came back with, 'For this, you're off the team. We can't have these kinds of examples, and lack of commitment.' Terry had a tiff with Betts a few weeks back before the Superior, Nebraska game. This time Terry really stomped off, saying football wasn't his main thing anyway. Charlie said some of them are worried this means Betts won't let him back on any team, maybe not even the track team, unless Terry...backs down on this," Pete whispered.

"That's all the time you have left, my pretty..." Jack said. Pete stared at him, puzzled.

"He's quoting the Wicked Witch of the West," Louis explained, "Jack does that. Quotes famous movie lines a lot. It gets the point across. Jack's a philosopher."

Pete said low, and sadly, "I get it. We're all in dire straits. Damn." Pete looked despondent.

Silence reigned for half a minute. Pete continued, "Time will tell. Terry loves track more than breathing, I think. So maybe he'll change." Pete was trying to reason through his panic. "But he also doesn't like people slamming down on others, he will not go for that. Not even from Betts. He'll put Betts on the line."

"You know him better than the rest of us," I said.

"Yeah. Probably. I have trouble guessing how this will go down, though," said Pete quietly.

Wendell gripped the wheel of the car, still staring straight ahead, with a grim seriousness, like he was scanning for a dangerous predator.

"I believe it's out of our hands, gents," Wendell said, slowly. "This clash between Terry and Betts is serious. I can't think clearly now, thanks to stupid movie quotes rattling around in my head..." Wendell whipped around, and raised his eyebrows accusingly at Jack, "...and *you're* to blame, infecting my brain with movie junk, boy."

"Infest. I infest you. Not infect." Jack smirked.

Pete sighed again. "This all is not very funny."

Jack nodded, and with a long, quiet breath, said "Yeah. You're right. We'll know more next week," said Wendell. "Let's drive north to my little cabin, we can build a fire against the cold." We all agreed on that.

* * *

October blew past us like a scared rabbit. The fabulous kaleidoscope sunsets sang their chorus only briefly that fall with the brilliantly lit, neon-yellow and wine-red maples. Early snows set in by November first. Events that normally would cheer the souls, like Sadie Hawkins Day, when the young ladies of CHS sponsor a carnival, ask their favorite guys along, or "plant one" on the guys cheek and lead him off for a long-desired secret but permissible conversation, came and went with a bit less shine and cheer to them. With Terry thrown off the squad, the football team slowly spiraled down-ward. They won only half their games. Terry had mysteriously vanished from the halls of CHS, with rumors abounding as to his fate.

Well into the month, on a bone-chilling and grey Saturday morning, after finishing up sweeping, and burning the trash out back for Mom, I was heading into the house, with Skipper on my heels. The phone rang. It was Kasl.

"How about we crank up Wendell, and see if we can get the crew together again for a night at his cabin?" I agreed. It was time again for a therapeutic pow-wow. By seven that night, we found ourselves out on the plains, in the big hills northeast of town, at the little cabin. The cabin had been Wendell's older sister's Swiss outdoor playhouse, now made larger by a front porch. It had ornate Swiss carvings, and the steep "mountain roof" characteristic of Swiss high-altitude homes. The paint had faded over the years. Wendell had moved it out on a flatbed, at the edge of the woods, in the hills, on some family-friends' land. He and I were setting up dutch ovens, for a "Canadian" style mixed-meat stew, and for peach-blackberry cobbler. These were "bragging-rights" recipes left over from our Scout days. Louis chopped wood, started the fire, and threw on charcoal. Wild Man Charlie Dixon was back from gathering black walnuts, and was stripping their dried dark hides, and trying to crack them with a vice-grip into a bowl. Louis's black-berry flavored "Flying Dutchman" pipe tobacco laced through the chill autumn air, adding a delicious scent to the smells of fallen leaves, fallow rich dirt fields, and black walnut shells' smoke from the fire. The stars were popping out like diamonds, in rank-order of their brightness, against a bluish-darkening sky, graced by the bright queen Venus.

"I gotta show you guys something," I said, pulling out a folded piece of paper. "Bryant, you remember the come-to-Jesus-or-you'll-burn talk, by the youth minister at your church, that I got trapped into last week, after the Brotherhood trio practice?"

"Yeah. That was embarrassing. You were my guest. I was hoping our songs could be inserted into the youth choir Sing Out he planned. At least that's what I thought was going on, when he agreed to let us practice there, and hear some of our songs."

'Well, that was one thing," I said. "I have to confess to another. While I was waiting outside his office, after practice, I figured he just wanted to talk with us for a few minutes about which songs might be included, and you went off downstairs. And well, I roamed around a little in the store-room there, and noticed a shelf of pamphlets. Here's one of them..." I tossed it over to Greg.

He read it silently for a few seconds, and turned as pale as a shaved cat. He passed it around. It went silently by Louis for a read, who spat into the fire, and then Wild Man Dixon, a progressive Methodist, and Wendell both scanned it. Together they groaned "Ah...Cripes," and then Kasl snatched the thing. Jack's jaw grimly shifted back and forth, and as he flipped through it, he muttered, "Well, well..." and handed it back to Wendell, who threw it in the fire.

Some years back, Wendell had hand-painted a white cross on a green background, in oil paint. He named it "the Order of St. Patrick" in honor of the Irish Saint. But it really was a symbol nailed above the cabin door, of our mutual pact to understand and accept whatever differences existed among us, and to appreciate what the other persons most personal beliefs were.

Wendell walked over to me, put his hand on my shoulder and said, "That stinks."

"Yeah, no kidding," was the general echo.

"It explains a lot of stuff we run into," I said quietly. "Especially in the stand-off-ishness of girls. It comes out sometimes in other ways, like the little 'warm salvation message' that I got from the youth minister, or the stuff they dish-out when they pressure you to attend Fellowship of Christian Athletes."

The pamphlet showed a young married couple at a Catholic altar, with the title "Beware the Whore of Babylon." Inside was a dialogue-narrative between a mother and a daughter about a "true Christian daughter" who had sadly fallen in love with a Catholic boy. It was laced with phrases explaining how the Church was "a tool of the devil", that children of a mixed marriage of a "true Christian" and a Catholic would be doomed to hell because the children would have to be raised in "apostasy". It advised young people to "simply avoid friendships and assignations" with Catholic boys and girls, no matter how pleasant they were as people. Such connections would lead the daughter or the son into drinking, or dancing, or other certain hell-fire behaviors, and into false doctrines, with all their off-spring flung into the eternal torture with them. Inside, I was uncomfortable that it was only a few years ago that the Catholic Vatican Council had disavowed exactly the same kind of Catholic brutal fear-mongering against Protestants. But there was no such reciprocal acceptance in this vicious screed.

Louis walked over, and handed me his carved meerschaum pipe, and his black-berry Dutchman tobacco.

"Here, boy. This was my grandfather's best pipe, from Denmark. Give it a try. And don't listen to creeps. *Don't even hear them.*" Louis radiated kindness. A little voice in me, maybe from my Granddad Ed, spoke a quiet cheer about this. I long reflected on what Louis said. There were so many great-hearted people in town, the Snyders, Charlie Everett and his infinite hardware store, the Whites, Mr. Switzer the photographer. The real souls of Kansas.

The fire crackled for a great while. Charlie cracked the black walnuts and tossed shells on the fire, and the stars winked into life in the silky vaults above.

"What has anybody heard about Terry?" Wendell called out the question.

"Headed out to his brother Skip's place, in Junction City, I heard," Charlie Dixon said. "His cousin Hess told me, in shop class. Guess he'll team up with those pretty fast black brothers over there, and make them invincible at the State track meet," Charlie guessed. Bewilderment, a sense of alienation and loss had settled into most corners of CHS after Terry's story had made the rounds.

"Some folks just miss his sunny disposition," I said. "The Lueckes are hard-pressed. He practically lives over there. From what I hear, the family wanted Skip to take Terry in, and help him ease into the Junction City scene. Maybe deal with some of his habits."

"The distance guys are even down," Louis reported. "Some feel that discipline is important, even for super-stars. Others feel the 'hammer' was whacked down too hard on him, too quick, you know, that it was more about personality conflicts. A lot of that seems to be going on these days."

"Look," Wendell paused, anguished and searching for words. "We have such a chance at taking State, in track. It's scary without him. Maybe we get our one chance, against these bigger schools and all their attention. For some of us, our running talent is our only chance at a college scholarship. But without the fame of a championship team, without Terry, the big university scouts will keep their noses poking around in the likes of Wichita, home of Jim Ryun, to give out track scholarships. Not in back-woods Concordia. Our dreams can die on the vine. They all think we're nobodies, out here."

"Some mutter around like they're glad 'he got his'," Jack reluctantly reported.

"Let me guess." Wild Man Dixon started in. "Some of the country-club set. The ones who have more money. From the right side of town. The better churches. The people who claim to not drink, but carry on pretty good 'at the river'. The ones who arrange for their girls to 'go away' if they 'come into a family-way'. The people who don't like that Terry isn't a big back-biter, and is cheerfully quiet about peoples 'questionable behaviors'. Maybe he stands against their ways..." Charlie now drew long glances from us. He was the perspicacious son of a U.S. Army Colonel. Charlie had traveled the world, and ate dinner with His Highness Haile Selassie the Grand Emperor of Ethiopia. Charlie knew something about 'social circles'.

"Things sometimes aren't what they seem," Jack whispered.

"Didja hear about Betts, and phys ed class?" Charlie asked all-around, seemingly changing the subject.

"Uh...no..." I answered for the rest of the now-silent group.

"Didn't hear about the pool?"

"The pool?"

"The swimming pool. Betts had a little accidental encounter. He took a dunk," Charlie smiled.

"Huh?" we all burst out.

"Yeah. Maybe it hasn't gotten around yet. You hear things where I work, that you won't otherwise hear," said Charlie. He busted tires at Christensen oil, his first job. Good money. And, the rumor mill spread pretty fast from the 'town leaders' taking coffee at the Skyliner Café, over to near-by Christensen's Oil.

"The way I heard it, this guy Tim Brady was kidding around with *somebody's brother*, near the pool in phys ed class, and one of them slipped and stumbled and fell on his elbow, and the other guy trying to help, accidently bumped and plunged Betts into the pool, fancy suit and all. It was all judged an 'accident' because of the elbow..." Charlie raised his eyebrows.

"Some-body's bro-ther..." Dixon crooned again, as he leaned over, and stared smilingly at me.

"Aw crap," I groaned. "Not again...I haven't heard *a thing* about this." I was never going to be shed of Roger's antics. I even wondered if he had some connection with the mysterious Zorro. *But Roger never talks. So who would ever really know?*

"Like I said, sometimes things aren't what they seem..." Jack smiled.

"Oh, *quit...*" complained Greg. Even so, I felt Jack had put his finger on something.

"Well, maybe this helps with the 'rebellion', I guess, such that it is," Jack continued.

"It's all a mess. Maybe the dunking says something, to all of us," Louis observed.

That night, over two of Ray's Café four-piece, ultimate-golden fried chicken dinners, these were the very same words offered to George Ganstrom, by Coach Betts.

The Fire Within

West of Salina, that same night, Terry was playing catch football with his younger half sister Sharon at his grandparent's farm. Supper time was approaching.

"Enough of this," Terry called out. "Where's your fishing pole?"

"Over in the barn."

"Let's grab that, dig up some worms. We can catch supper, I'll bet."

"Yipeee..." Sharon cried out. "I'll be right back with 'em." And she sprinted off to the barn. Memories of Terry danced in her head, of him riding around with her on bicycles, showing her off in Concordia to his friends. *I'm lucky. He's the most fun brother anywhere.* For years, Terry had been separated from his sister, by circumstances of his mother re-marrying and having many younger kids to tend. *I'll bet she'll grow up to be a heart-breaker.* He watched her skip off. *She's such a great sis. I wish we had more chances to see each other, the family's been split so long.* In the silent moments before her return, he turned to reflections. He partly regretted the beer-drinking binge in Salina with friends, the night Betts threw him off the football team. It wasn't exactly fair that the county judge had later confiscated the six-packs for himself, the ones he and John had launched into the stream, as the sheriff pulled them over on Highway 81 and wrote them up, spying the beer, and seizing the evidence. *Even the sheriff got left out! Gonna have to get past stuff like this, I imagine. Funny, but not so funny.*

He waited serenely for his sister, cardinals singing, winds whispering. His heart was flooded with the deep ache of missing friends, back in Concordia. He swallowed hard, tears misting his eyes. *I guess I gotta try to fit in, in Junction City. Skip's great too. I probably ticked off Betts so much, I can never go back. Drives me nuts with all of his rules, and hard-ass slamming on people, how could I stand it? But man, all the guys, I can't just bail on them. I can taste it. We could set things down in track in Concordia that won't be touched in a hundred years, if we could just get back together, and get along.*

He looked down at his red and white letter jacket lying on the ground where he and Sharon had sat, as they looked out over the mysterious, rolling Smoky Hills west of Salina. Last year's gold medals from the State championship relays, and his silver from the 220 glinted up at him.

Terry closed his eyes, as his dream came over him again. That mysterious part of his spirit which bore the speed of a Greek god, which cried out to be "let loose"...

"Wake up, wake up!" Sharon was tickling and poking him. "Here's the poles and stuff..." she said, her eyes glistening with hope and a little adoration.

He blinked, and came back into more of the regular world. "All-right, sis, let's get to it." He grabbed the coffee can, and they skipped down to the shore of the pond, to dig around for worms.

* * *

The last days of October brought us a blizzard. Seven inches of snow, blown in by icy northeast winds. "Alberta clippers", the old ones say. The winds blew so hard, the glass panes rattled, and the snow filled into the window-sills. Dad's Valiant 1960 station wagon, the one that caused Mom to clobber Dad with a flying bowl of spaghetti when she found out he'd bought it in Omaha, stood out in the driveway like a frozen jackrabbit. The snow had sifted in through its windows from the pressure of the winds, filling it one-fourth with snow. I had to scoop it out with a tupper-ware pitcher, its ice crystals almost like talcum powder. At sundown, when I stepped out on the front porch to scan the heavens, the late autumn skies had clumped-grey clouds, and eerie whistling winds sang through the naked branches of the maples and elms. They held semi-invisible dark spirits who whispered of unmentionable fates creeping down from above.

Mom beat back the whispering ghosts of fate with her late October traditions of cheer. With the house decorated by colorful leaves and pumpkins, the night of Halloween was filled with her bright red candy apples, and caramel-pecan apples, sacks of home-made cheese and caramel popcorn, hand-made pecan and coconut dark chocolate turtles from her oven, and pumpkin pies tickling your nose with special tangs of nutmeg-pumpkin-and-cloves. Skipper was decked out in an *Underdog* costume, to greet the little door-bell ringers in their angel and devil costumes, trudging through the snows, on All-Hallow's eve.

Armed with these cheery sights and smells, sister Sue and I plunged through the deepening glooms of that November, the creeping war, and the unsettled rebellion against viciousness, which had settled down on us. The gloomiest apparition was the sinking spirit from the loss of Terry in those of us who lived our years dreaming to run for the stars on the track, as a family of brothers.

Mid-November came and went with all its bluster. Even Swaggart's little band of minions seemed to lose their taste for torturing younger victims. The choir practices formed up the massive harmonies of the towering *Carmina*, as the pianists pounded their dual parts into shape. By mid-November, Mr. Miller allowed the two pianists, Evelyn and Phil Huscher to take their "challenge run" against the backdrop of the London Whitehall Choir *Carmina* recording. Sweating like tortured souls climbing through Purgatory, the pianists dueled the war-time recording of the orchestra and choir. Evelyn drilled the chords with a clarity, speed and accuracy so startling, that half the choir sprung up from their seats in spontaneous applause at the climax. She beamed like a mother who had birthed triplets.

In the same days, the snows blew back, and the Iron Men were out again, pounding south and west in the early morning hours, coming into classes red-faced and fresh from showers, but still sweating. Dauntless, they carried our hope on their backs, spreading its seeds to the rest of us in the face of that bitter November.

Things felt out of normal as Thanksgiving approached. All the rumors of the war and the draft, odd events, and unusual glooms created an unsettled spirit behind our whispered conversations between classes, and in the school lunch room the week before Thanksgiving.

"What are you guys doing for Thanksgiving?" I asked Wendell and Pete, at the lunch table.

"Not much. My sister's coming in." Wendell replied.

"Mom's bought *two* turkeys, and several bushels of fixings, so we're required around the house," Pete said.

"I'm thinking of camping one of the nights, maybe hunting pheasant," I said. "Maybe we can steal out to Hanson's sandpit."

"Of course, all-right by me," Wendell replied. "Maybe we can spring you lose from some chores, one night?" Wendell asked Pete.

"We'll have to see what we can pull off..." Pete winked back, and asked, "Betts is talking about starting up informal running of stairs in the gym, for sprinters, have you heard?"

"Yeah, he talked to me in gym class," Wendell replied, in a non-committal tone.

"Some of us are weightlifting, trying to get past bench-pressing 200 or 250 pounds, in the shop. Heck, I've been throwing discus, once the snows blew back a bit," I said.

"You're a fanatic," Pete observed. I grinned back at him.

"I guess I could do running, too..." I offered. "Diebel's gonna want me, and the other freshmen sprinters to take a shot at getting in condition for the relays, since freshmen teams count for points in most meets. But Betts hadn't said anything to me. I'll check with Gary."

"It's hard to get up and get committed, like the distance guys, when you know Terry's not...." Wendell said slowly, the corners of his mouth crinkling.

"Hell, you can do anything, Pete...you're not just a jumper." I scurried to change the subject, and relieve our tensions about Terry being gone. I turned to Wendell, pointed back at Pete, and continued, "This bruiser came up and threw shot put once with me, and I'll be hanged if he didn't toss it three inches short of my best throw that day. Or maybe you should try out for sprints, Pete. Your brother was pretty studly last year as a relay guy, with Terry, and Ken Campbell sometimes. It's in your genes, I'll bet." Pete was just unusual.

"Uh. Maybe," Pete said, distractedly.

"Well, Betts said he'd put the lights on at the gym, if anybody comes out. By State track association rules, he himself can't organize anything. I'll try to get up for it. Maybe I'll see you guys out there today," Wendell said, grabbed up his tray, and headed out of the cafeteria.

I drifted off to talk to Gary, to see if his dad could order me some Converse gym shoes at his store.

"Yeah. I think so. He sure got me the Pumas."

We were joking around with one of the class officers, Terry White about the prospect of persuading the school administration to let in a vending machine, with the new Gatorade, and maybe Cokes, for students.

"I think we can squeeze this out of them," White said.

"Well, I've heard they are distracted pretty strongly by pressures from different mothers around town." I said. "The scuttlebutt from my Mom is they don't want their daughters being harassed by school officials. There's a battle of Waterloo coming over this, so they say."

"So what's that got to do with a vending machine?" Terry asked.

"Well, maybe they'll be so distracted, they won't put up yet another fight over vending, especially if we pitch it as Gatorade for athletes, after practices," Gary said.

"See? Gary's a politician, phrases things better than most," I said.

We were discussing the ins and outs of this, when a commotion tumbled down the stairs, created by non-other than Wendell. He sped over to us, with that laser-look on his face.

"Boys. Moses just parted the Sea again, upstairs..." Wendell said, enigmatically.

"Huh?"

"Walking through the front door, smiling like a Cheshire cat..." We stood in silence, not sure what was up.

"Come on up to the front office..." He waived for us to trot up the stairwell.

We took off like rabbits, and spun around the corner, practically splaying several girls out on the tile, earning grimaces from them. We sidled up to the main office door, and crowded in to peek through the window to the side, toward Betts office. Wendell pointed at a figure who was cutting through the doorway, into Betts' side office.

Gary glanced back at me, eyes wide.

"In a suit, no less. Terry's back."

* * *

Coach Betts was finishing a phone call. From his open window gushed in small puffs of the chill November air. Laced with a trace of ozone from a brief chill rain, the air held that intoxicating, strangely bracing tang that picks up the energy in your blood. He had his back to the doorway.

Terry timed his entrance when he heard the "click" of the telephone handset being placed on its base. In black-polished shoes and a starch-white button down collar shirt he had on loan from his brother Skip, Terry strode swiftly through the doorway, and up to Betts's desk.

Betts heard "Hi, Coach!" in voice tones that ran an electric jolt down through his midsection, all the way to his toes. Betts whipped around, and his heart skipped a beat. He had to blink his eyes several times. *He's decked out like a banker*, thought Betts, the unspoken words stuck in his throat. Terry's instant sunshine smile, the shock of curly red-and-light brown hair dangling to the left, the black nylon glasses, his chiseled features which bore a certain resemblance to the famous Buddy Holly, and that infectious cheer and confidence that radiated like sunrise breaking through clouds, all made Betts' heart skip several more beats as they shook hands. Betts sat down. He was wordless for two seconds, and his knees were a little weak.

"Terry....glad to see you. What brings you back here? You're supposed to be..." Betts looked at his watch, "...at Junction City High School right now."

"Skip and I have talked a lot about all of it, Coach. I'm here. I'm serious," said Terry, his eyes flashing up at Betts.

"Go on," Betts said low, lacing his fingers together in front of his nose.

"I have to be here, Coach. I can't be there."

"I'm not sure what I can do for you. Besides, you know the rules here. You know what it takes," Betts replied.

"It's not just about me. It's about us. We'll take State, Coach. I can help. What-ever it takes, Coach. Whatever you want. I'm here to do it. I can't run with the Junction City guys. They are not us. I'm not them."

Silently, Betts looked out over his laced fingers at Terry.

"Tell me what you'll do. Tell me what your goals are. Then we'll see if I can be of any help, or not."

"I'll follow your rules. The team will, too. And we'll take State by storm," Terry said.

"No smoking. No drinking. Follow my advice, all the way through, starts, relays, everything?"

"Deal."

"Not yet," Betts replied, reaching for a sheet of paper. "Tell me what *your* goals are. Tell me what you can do, what times do you want to set?"

"I want to break whatever's all-time best," Terry said.

"Write down the 100. Then the 220, then the 880 and mile relays. Throw in the long jump, and listen up." Betts zeroed in.

"The 100 is 9.6 seconds. That's the all-time, cinder track State record. You re-member the fabulous hurdler Bill Kimble, the black kid, 1966 senior from Hoising-ton?"

"Yup." Terry replied.

"He tied it, at the State Meet. National best is 9.4, still tied by Jesse Owens back in 1934."

"I'll beat the 9.6 one day. I'll try for the national," Terry replied casually.

Betts blinked at him. *You're it kid...* he thought silently.

"What about the 220?" Betts then asked. "The Kansas all-time best is either 20.9 (20.7 200m) by Bob Hansen in 1962 or Kimble in 1965 but reports say they were wind-aided. Probably it really is the 21.1 by Roger Timken last year and Henry Weibe in '55."

"Well, I'll do better than 21.1 for sure (20.9m)."

"By the way, if you do, it could be the national record," Betts said, breathlessly.

Terry just smiled.

Betts' heart literally raced inside. *They don't come like this but one in a billion.*

"We'll have to see, Terry. You'll have to give it all you got. We have the 'horses' here to go with you in Collins, Ganstrom and others. Maybe the best ever," Betts said.

Terry pursed his lips, and nodded ever so slightly.

"How bad do you want it?" Betts asked.

Terry leaned forward, raised his eyebrows, and said, "Just let me out there..."

Betts twitched his lips, and looked at Terry straight on.

Terry's cheer, slight smile and fearless soul radiated back like a thousand-year solar flare.

Betts nearly jumped on his desk. He grabbed the calendar, and started counting. He was sweating a little around his neck collar, as he tallied up the days. He counted them again.

Terry was starting to look puzzled.

Betts tapped his pencil on the desk, and said, "We got six weeks and five work days exactly...until the State Indoor, Terry," Betts intoned. "If I write a letter today, requesting that you transfer back to Concordia High School, and then IF the State high school activities association receives the letter inside of five days, and IF they approve the request within these days, then we will meet the six week transfer request deadline. We got a fighting chance, kid. I've saved a few butts over there a time or two, at meets. I'll call and tell them to look for our letter dated today. That's all I can do. Then it's up to Uncle Sam, and to them. But we've got five days play on our side. It's a decent chance." He then leaned forward, and pointed straight at Terry...

"I believe you, Terry. *Don't forget.*"

"That's not ever gonna happen," Terry replied quietly. Terry rose, shook hands with Coach, spun on his heels and headed out. He stopped at the door, and looked back at Betts, out from that deep-buried spirit in him that burned from far-away, lighting up his eyes.

Betts saw that look in Terry's eyes, and found his words, "I understand, Terry. It's great you came today. Some of the guys will be running in the gym on their own about 3:15 after school..."

"Yeah..." Terry smiled, and strolled down the hall toward the waiting noses pressed into the glass panes of the front office door. Eight seconds later, the phone rang at the state high school activities association headquarters, in Topeka.

Chapter 12
THE SIFTER OF SOULS

The All-Connecting Tunnel

Gary, Wendell, Luecke, Louis and I sprang up the basement stairs, past the track record board, from the damp and cramped boys athletic locker room, where we'd stashed our running shoes and such in the early morning. This day was the start of *Track, the great venture.*

Wendell strode in front, radiating his unstoppable purpose.

"Ready?" Louis elbowed me, raising his yellow eyebrows, lengthening his already long strides.

"...the times that try mens' souls..." Alan replied for me, with his flashing grin and glint. I grunted agreement.

"Diebel's got the shoes, all-right..." Louis continued, as Gary's flashing pearly whites, and luminescent Pumas shone in response.

"Yeah. He'll be out in front, and hard to miss," I muttered.

Our banter helped us glide through "the walk", the glass-covered skywalk that connects the old part of CHS to the new. The walk itself is a symbol that links every CHS current generation to past and future generations, and for none is it more important than the undying line of track men and women. At the end of the glass tunnel, we'd spring through the doors into the vast new gym, and skip down to start the running of the stairs, the first heartbeat of Track season.

Surreal discoveries zipped through our young heads like ghosts. We bore a special, grim anxiety and nausea in the pit of our stomachs, which waged mortal combat with our hopes and dreams. Every early December, in the walk through the great glass tunnel, the semi-sweet emotions swept you up like a tornado, into the high drama ahead. It was a vague and wordless feeling: *This walk will echo in us for many years.*

Above the glass, the gray, lumpy skies echoed with fading, muffled thunder. A cold rain, near freezing, extended us a chilly greeting to deepen the bittersweet dramas ahead.

Track is like mountain climbing: an unyielding marriage of suffering, heartbreak, and sky-scraping joy, which is beaten out on a forge of pain and sacrifice. *Track is the sifter of souls.*

This year, the State outdoor Championship loomed ahead like the heights of Mt. Everest. Our hearts pounded as we strolled through that great, all-connecting glass tunnel. The weight was great on our hearts. This year we would hear a quiet voice calling, and we had to be equal to the call.

The Gathering of the Clan

By three-twenty p.m., the track clan was gathering below on the gym floor, clumped somewhat into classes from freshmen to seniors. Pretty soon the class gatherings broke apart to re-gather more into groups of talents: hurdlers with hurdlers, sprinters, etc. We had to do these training runs on an informal, voluntary basis, because state rules would not allow coach-led organized trainings this early. Betts and the other coaches were nowhere to be seen for weeks. It was a crappy rainy day, with early morning freezing, although the clouds were starting to break up, and the rain dropping to mist. For the start of things, all parties would run on the gym stairs, for conditioning. The field men of discus, shot put and spear-chucking would do the least running, they would split soon for weight lifting, down in the shop area. Sprinters and the distance men started with stretching. The field event guys took off for a few laps of loping up and down the stairs. After a few laps, they slowed down, their faces taking on mottled white and red patches, as they sweated and gasped profusely.

This was a unique year. Rumors were that the Catholic high school was going to shut down, due to financial shortages. This year, a slew of new Catholic kids had floated up to the public Concordia High School, joining a few others of us who had trailed in a few years before.

As Gary, Wendell and the rest of us sprinters did hurdlers stretches on the gym floor, the talk and rumors spun through the air like the wispy seeds of cottonwoods.

"I know these guys," I offered to Gary and Wendell, and nearby Charlie Switzer, referring to the new influx of Catholic talent. Not that we didn't already have talent. Wiry, tall, dark-eyed Charlie was a self-effacing, multi-talented senior runner, who, shy though he was, could blast most anybody off the track. Charlie's grandfather was a collegiate two-mile champion at Kansas State University in 1909. Charlie had the gene-pool greatness buried in him. He was second at the State Meet half-mile last year. He was taking a run at the sub-two minute half mile record of Bill Dotson's 1:58 on dirt, back in 1957, which stood then as a Kansas high school record. Strangely, Dotson, who after high school was the first Kansan to break the four minute mile, had been entered to run the half mile *only one time* in his high school career, with this mark. (Runners had to choose between a half mile, or mile race in one day). Who knows what his 1:58 high school half-mile a half-century ago would have zipped down to, if incomparable Bill had been been given a chance to run it more than just once? Charlie aimed to crack it. And he also was a threat to most anybody in the state in the shorter sprints.

"You got the Fosters, Charles and Pete, they can run like antelopes," I informed this unknowing crowd of Protestant kids, about the newly arrived Catholic talent. "If only we could get Johnny Schmidt over here from Notre Dame High," I pointed out. Johnny had placed in sprints and hurdles in last years' State Meet for double B smaller schools.

"Yeah. We'll see," cheeky Wendell said. "Let's get this show on the road," he said to Gary. They jumped up, and with Chuck Switzer, took off for the stairs, waving all the distance men and sprinters together to join in.

The gym offered eighty single steps to the "nose-bleed" sections at the top. They were arranged in eight aisles. The leaders were followed by the crowd of sprinters and Iron Men, with the jumpers, vaulters and weight-men bringing up the rear. The leaders tore up the stairs with a loose and very fast footwork, zipping up and easing down the stairs in snakelike endless fashion. Running "the stairs" in track was even more painful than in football season. In track, the "real men" would grimly sort themselves from "the boys." A dire contest set in: sprinters showed off their fast footwork by accelerating to the top, to break away from the rest of the struggling crowd. As time and legs wore on, the Iron Men gained ground on the sprint leaders, Ganstrom and Diebel, who took turns outracing each other across the gym floor to the other side to begin the scaling. The Iron Mens' superior conditioning kicked in, so their endurance and considerable speed eventually closed the gap. The Iron Men mixed in with top sprinters, and a small group of stable "leaders" emerged. They began expanding the distance between themselves and the lesser or younger talents. It was a public confession of your lesser manhood if you allowed yourself to straggle back too far.

"All-right you speed-ball studs, why don't you follow us in a new twist?" Lyle Pounds challenged, and he waived the lead group out the top double doors, into the school halls. Now the trial truly bore down. The long, winding school halls and stairs in both complexes of buildings ranged up and down three stories. They became a battlefield, *the sifter of souls*. The lengthy halls set the terms of battle in favor of the Iron Men, who were used to pouring it on over long distances, rather than burning out their energy in high speed bursts up stairwells where the sprinters dominated. Now, the sprinters struggled through the halls to even keep the Iron Men in sight, gaining a little on the stairs against the distance men, but losing real ground in the stretches.

The protracted war spread out through many halls, trekked back across the glass tunnel skywalk into the Junior High buildings, and down into the basketball gym again. In the suffering, the numbers of leaders had narrowed to several Iron Men with speed, and a couple sprinters with endurance.

So it was Doug Rivers, Ganstrom, Diebel, Pounds, Jones, Charlie Switzer and Pete Foster who scrambled into the gym, as the true leaders of a long wake of valiant sufferers. At the top of the west side of the gym, the group saw something, and slowed as they tumbled down the southwest staircase. Across the dim, unlighted gym, in the northeast corner, a slight figure in cranberry red silk track shorts, and red and white Converse flats, soared like a Chinese bottle rocket up the far staircase. They watched this scarlet wraith flash across the top, and down the far stair case. The crowd met up with the lone runner on the center gym floor. A minute or so of whooping and hollering, backslapping and poking ensued. You'd have thought it was a re-union of giddy Alaskan sled-dogs who had lost partners overnight in a blizzard, but found themselves in the light of day.

"You happy to be back?"

"Bet your tushies, dudes," Terry saltily replied.

Comments rained down like a pent-up western hailstorm:

"Thought you were a goner."

"Thought Betts had it in for you."

"Was it the suit that got you back in?"

"Bet the black *and* white girls over there in Junction City had the hots for you..."

"I couldn't take it in Junction City. It's just not you guys," Terry replied softly.

"Why did Betts let ya back in?" Steve Collins let out the naked question. It stilled the crowd. Steve, a junior, was by reputation the second fastest sprinter in the talented CHS line up, and was among the fastest sprinters in the state. Six foot, crew-cut, blonde and muscular like a Norse god, Steve was the lead rusher on the football team, and a mild-mannered steam roller.

"Maybe he just likes my smiling face..." Terry quipped.

Laughter spread like bees over alfalfa fields. The rest of us runners straggled in late from the stairs, and catching the last of this conversation, we broke into chuckles between wheezing gasps for air. We were thankful for the moment's reprieve.

All were in awe of the resurrection of Terry onto the CHS gym floor.

"Naw, seriously guys. I'm back in. I might even be able to run the Indoor. Betts wrote a letter to the big gurus in Topeka, for me," Terry explained.

"Then we have a serious chance to win both the indoor and outdoor State Championships this year," intoned Ron Green, the lanky, dark, deadly-intense student and hurdle master.

"Yeah. I'm here for the same reasons you are..." Terry spoke simply and quietly into the silenced crowd. Several long seconds passed.

"So...why are we holding off from all the fun?" Terry joked. *"Let's roll..."* He whipped around, and zipped up the stairs. The crowd trailed after him. Without breaking a sweat, and beaming like sunrise, he swept up and down the stairs like a March wind for twenty minutes, as the crowd struggled to keep pace. Even Wendell was wheezing. Joy rayed out from Terry like a solar flare, one in a billion, born to run.

At the top of the stairs on one of the laps, Jerry broke forth with "The sun's out! Rain's outta here. So am I..." As the other Pied Piper in our big tribe, Jerry diverted the Iron Men out the door under the now-sparkling blue skies, for long runs. Secretly, more than one of them were giddy to get relief from Terry's cheerful, blazing runs.

The long, stupendous climb had begun.

* * *

Day after day, the training runs and the weight-lifting spun on and on. Even the trainers would show up, down in the dank locker room. Led by cheerful and shrewd Steve Thompson, the wily Rick Radcliffe and Logan brothers, and steel-willed and jocular Ted Easter, you knew you would get better "re-hab" with them if you were injured, than if you shipped out to the doctors at the clinic near St. Joseph's hospital. The trainers could bandage a sprained ankle perfectly inside of fifty seconds. They could banish the gruesome stabbing pains called "shin splints" which plagued the legs of the Iron Men as they pounded on hard pavements. Trainers would run the deep-power portable jacuzzi, which was no beauty instrument to ease the twinges of housewives complaining about lawn struggles with weeds. This jacuzzi was a high horsepower industrial pump that plunged deep into the horse trough that served as the treatment pool. Ol' grinning Steve would dial the water temperature up past 140 degrees, and aim the stream power of the jacuzzi, which rivaled a small Mercury outboard engine, at whatever you had that was bruised or torn. In you'd go, limping, hardly able to walk. In fifteen minutes of suffering the pounding heat, out you'd come with your particular damaged limb now turned beet-red from increased circulation. Usually you'd be out on the road again, hopping around like a spring rabbit.

The aesthetic purity and sheer-discipline of the self training, which ran through the late months of November, all through December, and into January, could have rivaled anything thrown at recruits in the Marines. The ethos, held by most of us, was the regimen was a matter of pride, and our secret weapon. We were to *be there*, honed in body, and steeled in soul, when the shackles came off for the official start and coaching of our skills and events in late January. The ethos also meant no beer, liquor, smoking, and no excessive "messing" with the ladies. Pity whatever rival school thought they could be our "competition" at the official start of track season. We would bury them by our advantage from months of Spartan self-training. Most of us aimed to faithfully survive this land of grim discipline.

December's Secrets

I drowsily watched and listened to ice-crystal snowflakes sizzle against my bedroom window and pile up on the glass on the second Saturday of December, when Mom knocked on the door.

"Hey, sleeping beauty. The phone's for you. It's Gary. And *you* need to get up and shovel the driveway at least, and vacuum the floors. I'll get you a waffle going, you hop out and answer Gary." I fumbled my way down the hall, to our only phone, a black-dial desk model outside the kitchen.

"So. You up yet, lifting weights, or playing your clarinet or sax?" Gary chimed. I worked a weight set every day in the basement, since fifth grade when my brother Darryl gave me "barbells" at Christmas which he made from cement and heavy old bolts poured into giant bean cans connected with bamboo poles as the bars.

"Uh. Not yet," I mumbled. I was never a morning guy. "What's up?"

"My Dad has a new camper in the back yard. It's wired with electricity. I'm holding a 'campout' sleep-over in the camper tonight, with playing cards, radios, chips and stuff. I'm inviting you, Ted Easter and Luecke. What do you think, can you make it?"

"Uh, yeah. I'll ask Mom. Probably okay. I'm not much for cards though, you know."

"That's all-right. Just sneak in Roger's shortwave, and we can try that on them. I can bring the RISK game too, you know, conquer Asia again."

"Sounds pretty good."

"I'm going downtown around noon. There's the Christmas parade, and Santa's supposed to arrive for little kids near the First National Bank, like he always does. You wanna do that?" Gary asked.

"Who's Santa this year?"

"I dunno, let's go guess."

Mom interrupted us, overhearing about Santa. "Yes, I'm making the Christmas parade. Got shopping to do. You guys surely are welcome to ride down with me, or Gary's mom."

"I'll ring ya back after breakfast on all this, Gary. Okay?"

"Sure."

I pretty-quick showered up in the cold basement shower, and wolfed-down the cream-and-pecan waffles that Mom had whipped up. I decked myself out in my winter camping blue nylon shell Alaskan long- hood parka, jeans and boots, and zipped out to shovel the ice-crystals off the sixty foot steep driveway. This took forty minutes. I fell several times dealing with the icy, steep driveway which angled down between two large blue spruces. After the third fall, I traded my boots in for my high ankle football shoes with cleats, for better traction on the icy slope, and went back to shoveling.

After clearing the driveway, and warming up with mom's spiced hot cider, I called Gary. With Mom driving, we slid down the driveway in the '49 Plymouth (the one with the naked-lady wheel spinner on the steering wheel), and picked up Gary to go downtown for the Christmas parade.

The Christmas parade was the official excuse for the opening of the holiday shopping season, sponsored by the downtown merchants. The Junior High Band marched in their old red and silver uniforms, playing "White Christmas" and "Rudolph the Red-Nosed Reindeer". Everybody politely listened to their slightly off-key, off-rhythm renditions. Then "Santa" pulled up in a horse-drawn wagon decked out like a "sleigh", and slid himself into a white throne setup on a little stage outside the First National Bank southeast corner at Sixth Street. The stage had fake snow, and a couple grade school girls dressed up as bogus elves in red and white suits. Mothers with babies and children lined up for "time with Santa", while Mr. Switzer popped pictures for those willing to order. George Ganstrom, vice-president of the Bank, and the main payer of the "expenses", stepped out and beamed heartily about Santa. Most of the little guys and gals lined up to see Santa were dressed in absolutely adorable elf, or snowflake costumes, with some boys in Davey Crocket garb and coon-skin hats. A few little babies were nervous about Santa, and crying for momma.

The city streets had absolutely mesmerizing, home-made light decorations, translucent stars with multi-colored flashing lights inside, which were paid for and hand-made by the intrepid Great War veteran, Charlie Blosser. The stars were strung on wires decorated as pine boughs, and hung between city light poles, and criss-crossed Main Street. At night the city street radiantly beamed flashing multiple colors back to the twinkling partner-stars in the Milky Way above. Charlie's lights mystically lit the Christmases in the city for decades.

Gary and I trailed past Santa, in our annual quest to sniff out who he was this year.

"Dr. Foster, don't you think?" Gary guessed.

"I do think. But he's a little paunchy, for the doc maybe," I wondered aloud. The Fosters blanched and spun out denials whenever you asked them if Dr. Foster was Santa that Christmas.

That December night, Gary's back yard camper fairly gyrated with rock music from radio KMOA, as our crowd played Black Jack, and RISK into the wee hours. For that night, at least, anxieties about the war, the bullying, and the revolution seemed far away.

Chapter 13
A THOUSAND YEARS DEEP

New Year's 1967

Bacon and scrambled eggs. How can the smell of scrambled eggs and bacon get up here above the houses where I'm flying? I wondered. I sniffed carefully. *Sure enough, that's bacon,* I smiled, and soared nimbly over the high maple trees south of the swimming pool, and curved left to fly northeast to the far, silvery tower of Our Lady of Perpetual Help Cathedral. *This is right?* I puzzled. A sudden sinking feeling flooded my innards. I took a slow breath, squinted and forced my right bleary eye open. The scent of bacon stole my nose, as the back of a well-cut head of black hair swam into view. *Yeah. Gary Diebel's place. No Cathedral.*

I looked down from the cot I'd slept on. *Potato chips, empty bowl of French onion dip.* I looked up. *TV set, sports broadcasters jabbering...* "...the marvelous 1966 Kansas City Chiefs, last night buried the Buffalo Bills 31 to 7 for the AFL Championship on the first night of this new year..."

Damn right, they did. Darn if Diebel's color Sylvania television isn't fabulous, with that startling crimson of the Chiefs uniforms. I sucked in some more smell of bacon, and dredged up a bit more clarity of brain. *Sure love those dreams about flying.*

I poked Gary. He rolled over, and popped open an eye.

"Hey, speedball. The Chiefs kicked butt."

"Yeah," Gary grinned out over those startling pearly whites.

We had holed up in the rec room just off their kitchen last night, and held forth a watch party for a few more guys, to see the Chiefs take down the Bills in the 1966 AFL season championship game, which we all knew would lead to the first Superbowl, and the collision with the legendary Green Bay Packers of the rival NFL. We were excited "just a bit".

"I think your mom's got some bacon going."

"Uh-huh."

"You know what we got today?"

"Uh...uh-huh."

It was an *official extra* New Year's Day that year, Monday January 2, 1967. It was the official opening day of legitimate coaching of the Track season. Even though school was off, Betts would be unleashing on us his vast arsenal of coaching weapons and strategies.

"We'll practice starts in the gym. Get the big lecture, and demonstrations," I observed.

"Yeah, and he'll run our buns off," Gary answered.

The day before, on the regular New Year's day, we were hanging out and looking over *Sports Illustrated* articles about the Chiefs at Gary's house, when the phone rang. It was Wendell and Louis. They invited us out to ice skate, and practice hockey on the frozen Airport Park Lake. By one p.m., at five degrees above zero Fahrenheit, the air at the lake was a bracing chilled champaign. The large crystal snowflakes piled thick puffs on the limbs of trees and sparkled out mini-rainbows of light as we skated past. Gary and I formed one team, and Wendell sided up with the indefatigable Iron Man Louis. Thus the two speedballs were balanced, one on each team. At least, I was quick off the start. After three hours of frantic ice hockey, Louis' endurance prevailed over my quickness, while Gary and Wendell cancelled out each others' blazing speed. In the end, Gary and I lost by a single point. The marks of the skates on the ice left a great, silvery spider's web, as we headed back in the purpling and scarlet sunset that evening to "the game".

Today, however, play times were over. What lie ahead for us, we only knew from rumors. Betts was surely the most astutely learned high school sprints coach in a thousand mile radius. We would soon be apprentices of the vast encyclopedia of "Sprint Magic" that was buried in Betts brain from decades of detailed study. A thousand times and more, we'd experience the detailed demos, and eye-ball-to-eye-ball corrections of the minutest aspects of "The Start" and "The Baton Pass". In our dreams at night we would re-live the techniques of starting blocks placement, hand placement, angles of the body tilt, how to dig out in the first steps, the uppercut of the lead arm, how to listen for the gun, how to run swift and efficiently, how to speed up. As crafty as any Olympic or University coach, Betts would steep us in dozens of these fine-tuned secrets. We would see films of our own starts, and baton-passes, and repeatedly compare them against the films of the techniques of the great Olympic and University champions. Where Betts got the budget for all these films, and technical books, no one knew. We'd be drilled, again and again, in myriad techniques, lashed on by his catchy phrases. This Merlin of Sprints would bellow *"Loose! Loose!"* from the stadium in the midst of races, giving us another secret edge of speed, and echoing in our heads to our graves. We were to learn, and to be *invincible.*

A Kansas Merlin

After bacon and eggs at Gary's, I sped home, and Mom assigned me to shovel snow off the front walk again, out past the great blue spruce. By one o'clock, Gary and I were crunching our way over the half-plowed snow to CHS two blocks away. We were to report to the new, great CHS basketball gym, dressed out in light track gear, where Merlin, eg, Coach Betts prowled.

We trekked our way through the shop, and the cold grey corridor to the dressing room, and whipped on assigned grey shorts and T-shirts with the CHS Track and winged running shoe red emblem. We scooted across the all-connecting glass tunnel to the gym, feeling that special weight of tradition and queasiness again, and tripped down the stairs to the gym floor. Betts had already been directing the distance Iron

Men to the opposite end of the gym to meet with Coach Smith, and the field events guys back to the shop for weightlifting. We sprinters, relay guys, and hurdlers milled around under the south basket rim, or did stretches. Betts' whistle, and gravelly voice rang out, "Start 'em up, Coach Smith." He turned slowly around to us, in a silky red nylon windbreaker, a red and white Panther ball cap, bearing a sly smile. His bulldog-block chin thrust out from a blue-steel close shave, and his shifting glances bore into our eyes. A great, pregnant silence loomed.

"We're here again, guys," Betts intoned. A silvery mix of confidence, dread of pain, and adrenalin shot warmth down our throats and limbs, like hot coffee swallowed on a dark blizzard night.

"House, Switzer, take these guys around to the north wall there, and then through the multi-purpose room photo wall, and then over to the old gym. *Don't let 'em say nuthin'.* Any man talks, you name him, and we'll see how he likes the stairs with me, after practice." He let that sink in for awhile, and then went on.

"What you're doing, gentlemen, for the next twenty minutes, is looking. Just look at the track championship banners on the wall here. Then go look at the photos, and the state champions. Then go to the old gym, and look at the record board on the wall. Notice the 1921 long jump record there. Maybe Terry will surpass it this year, maybe." Electric side-glances were swapped between Terry and Betts. Coach continued, "That's forty-five years of a long-jump record, and it's still just shy of the all-time Class A school best. Then, Terry, Charlie, you run them *slowly* past the class record board, freshmen, sophomores, etc, just above the dressing room."

Long moments sizzled on, and Betts walked up and down in front of us, looking at us one by one, smiling here, nodding there, or raising an eyebrow. The only thing he said in four minutes was, "Nice shoes, Diebel. You'll need them to chase down some guys 'round here..." Snorts and chuckles broke out, as well as the light from Gary's high-lumen pearly whites.

"Merlin" strode back to the free throw line.

"Here is what you are doing. Two things. *Number 1:* you are learning that the CHS track men are the New York Yankees, the Green Bay Packers of track and field in this state. If you're here claiming you can wear the silky reds, you've got people that you *owe* things to. Charlie, when you get them up there, show 'em Bill Dotson, the first sub-four minute miler in this State and in the Big Eight when he was at KU, national record holder, and before that, the fastest high school miler in Kansas and the nation in 1958. *And he was from here where you stand.* There are some shoes to fill around here."

Betts paused for a breath, then continued, "*Number 2:* you'll be asking yourself, 'Where am I going to stand on these records'? You ask yourself: What time do *you* want to run? What distance are *you* going to throw? And when you feel you are done with them, Charlie, Terry, bring the men back in here." Betts turned around, and walked the floor alone.

After twenty silent minutes, we were led back into the big gym, sober as St. Joseph on the night of the news from Mary.

Betts strode out from the long basketball corridor with Coach Smith, and they parted ways at mid-court. Betts walked back and forth slowly on the free throw line in front of us. He then spun around and waived out to Coach Smith, "Bring those long and lean ones over here too, Bill. So I won't have to shout to reach them." The Iron Men loped over, smiling cocky, mingling in. Betts looked us all over a couple more seconds.

He then kicked in, "If you're lucky, you love to run, or throw. That's good, to love it. But there's more to this than loving it. You have to *want* what you've seen on the boards. For yourself, for your friends here. For the great ones before you, who loved it, and sweat blood for it. You have to want it. Maybe for what you can be, for those coming after you, tomorrow, and beyond. It will come, if you want it, and if you pay the price for it. But right now, it's just one thing. It's your choice."

He looked down, and sighed. A mist came over his eyes, and his steel-grey jaw relaxed. He seemed sunk in something deep, and far away, not sorrow, exactly. The janitor flipped a bank of new lights on just then. That's probably why it looked like a sudden light had brightened his eyes.

"Each of you will meet with me this next week, and I will hear what you have for goals. I think I kind of know what Jerry wants, already," he joked, and whipped his arm around to point to Jerry's T-shirt: *10:05* it sang out in black. "My question Jerry, about your two-mile dream is…" and he strode up to Jerry to put his arm around him, "How often do you wash that thing?"

For the next hour, we sprinters and hurdlers were drilled by Betts and House-holter in the secrets of setting your starting block spaces right, the proper lean, muscle tone, quick reaction to hearing the gun, and the first three strides out. We were amazed, at all the little things. More than an hour later, coach blew the whistle and called us together.

"Good start today, guys. We will be doing drills on these skills, just about every day. I'm determining here in the next two weeks which of you will be going to the State Indoor. This is not a competition for the freshmen, but you could go observe this great event with us. Next, I think we can take a page from the distance men, and send you guys outside to run, as the sky has cleared some. Go pick up your sweats in the dressing room, and seniors, I want two groups. One of you lead a group west out past KNCK radio station to Five Corners and back. Another of you lead out south to the cemetery, spin around it three times and head back. You all should be done in an hour, or less. No stragglers, and I'd better see some sweat. Get hustling."

At the dressing room we grabbed our sweat pants and hooded pull-overs.

"We'll meet up in the shop, and divide into the two groups," Charlie Switzer said in his soft way, with a glinting smile. "I'm lucky today, I get to run with you guys, not Jones, Rivers and those boys."

The crowd milled around in the shop, a few of them trying out the weights with the weight-men.

"Drop the acetylene torch, boys," Collins growled to a couple sheepish miscreants. "We don't want any explosions…" The group hopped around like a litter of giddy puppies.

"So, who's going where?" Collins asked.

"I'm going south," Charlie laid claim. "Whoever wants can follow."

"I'm gonna sweat out the younger guys," Terry announced, drawing surprised glances. "Ganstrom, Diebel, you freshmen, sophomores, head out with me." Terry grinned, and strode out the steel door. Most of us followed, a few splitting-off to go with the Switzer group out to the cemetery.

We were taken back. Terry could have had a stronger run with the upperclassmen. We figured we would be split up between the two groups, to be the "stragglers" trying to keep up. We sure didn't anticipate Terry would choose us lowly underclassmen to run with. Upperclassmen, especially the "big stars" never did this kind of thing. I couldn't guess why. Trying to keep up with him would be impossible, if he chose to push us. So we'd just end up with more stairs at the end, compliments of Betts, if we straggled back too far. It looked like a trainload of suffering was barreling toward us.

"Come on, dudes," Terry called, as he jogged loosely down the steep shop driveway, "We're heading west, pals." It was a good half-dozen of some of us freshmen and sophomores, with Gary, me, Don Liedtke, plus Wendell, Ron Green, red-headed Charlie Foster, and Terry. We buzzed west on Eleventh Street at an easy-lope, not saying much, as we passed the small grocery store on the north side.

"Gotta grab some sunflower seeds, boys, on the way back," Terry announced

"Sounds right to me," Wendell cheerily called back.

"And pick up a little ice cream, Coke, some Zagnuts and Cherry Mashes…" smirked Charlie, a guy who always went his own way.

We spun past Gary's house at the corner.

"Check out those Christmas lights," I said. The Diebels always lined out their bushes and trim around their house with alternating red, green and blue lights, the slightly bigger, flame-shaped ones. It was edging toward dark. In the high plains west out here, nightfall in this season was by four p.m. or earlier. Diebels' lights shone early after Thanksgiving, and all the way to Valentine's Day, as the first and last bright sentinels of cheer in the darkening, frozen nights. In this much-troubled winter, they shined all the brighter.

We crunched our way over the sidewalk snows, journeying west, wordless in the moments. The sky shaded into sapphire blues, the north winds carried a deepening chill. A waning moon, and the daring Saturn and Mars fought bravely to display their diamond-bright courage, above the cranberry and gold sunset.

"Let's step it up a little," Terry said back to us. We traced past the hospital and set out on the road that passed now north of the football practice field. I glanced at Gary, and Wendell, and we inched up more to the front of the pack. We picked up the pace, and with it, the special moments of life out here came calling.

The asphalt, blown-dry by the bold north winds, slid by under us. Our paces, bodies and minds eased into the hypnotic song of "second wind". Our view of all things shifted. Now we ran in the shadow of the young god Mercury, as the snow turned to diamonds, and the air to wine. Our souls spread to join the land that breathed in and out with our own silvery breaths.

We glided up the base of the hill, over a stream and up toward Radio KNCK, a high sentinel that overlooked the town.

Terry glanced back at us, a wry smile breaking out.

"Okay, Diebel, Ganstrom…all you guys…let's see what you got!" he challenged. He paused for a second, and chimed out *"Let's go…"* Terry paused for a split second for us to kick in.

Wendell and Gary took out like avenging angels. With Terry, the three of them lit up the hill, kicking bits of asphalt back at the rest of us as we faded in yards by the seconds. After half a dozen accelerating digs, Terry smiled out to his right to the younger blazing duo, and then he burnt up the hill in a silky blast of speed, opening a lead like an SR-71 Blackbird. Halfway up the long hill, Gary and Wendell neck and neck, led the rest of us by fifteen yards, and Terry led them by nearly as much.

At the crest of the hill, Terry spun down and turned around to watch the dynamic duo behind him shoot up the hill in a flat dead heat, still accelerating, still kicking back bits of asphalt.

"Jeezus!" Terry yelled out, his fist pumping the air as the two speed demons tore up the hill, unrelenting in their quest. They shrank into the distant crimson horizon. In several long seconds, the rest of us caught up with the stolid Terry, who stood with fists on his hips. We joined him to stare into the distance at the eerily vanishing, un-wavering twin speedsters.

"Wow. Those coyotes think there ain't no quit, huh?" Terry chuckled. "Didn't know I was igniting that kind of deal. Wonder how fast those two will be in a couple years…"

The rest of us were doubled-up in gasps-and-bends, so we couldn't say much.

"Let's take five, at least. You boys been workin' way too hard," Terry sang out.

"Okay…" we replied in shaky voices.

We sat on our butts on the asphalt, sucking oxygen, as we watched distant twin dots bounce closer on the road. In a couple minutes, they were loping side by side, an occasional arm around each other.

"Bet you studs are glad you got that outta your system, huh…" Terry joked, as they skipped past us, side by side, grinning like Cheshire cats.

Redemption

After practice, Brett milled around in his front yard, wondering how to *not* go back in the house. *The bike!* he thought, with a rising cheer in his chest. *It's been awhile,* he mused, as he veered around to the back yard, and pulled his bike out from behind the woodpile. He hopped on, and coasted down the long, high hills just southeast of Jailhouse Hill, to Main Street down town. *On the bike I feel free. Like a bird, no guilt, no devouring angers. Just free. Man, I just had to get away from the house. Mom carping on me, how my grades aren't up to my older sisters and brothers. Damn. Always me compared to the six of them. That's all she does.*

"You'll never be as bright as Sara, if you don't buck up and study. You'll never be a great athlete like Richard, if you keep eating like that," Brett whined in mocking, high nasal tones. *God, will this shit never quit. I just wanna bust something.*

He stilled this agonized voice, and felt the sweet wind in his hair, as he coasted down the long stretch of streets, to the downtown. He cranked his bike left, crossed the highway and pedaled down the alleys going west between sixth and seventh streets. He was heading toward the Baptist church, for a little variety. *Let's see what downtown alleys have to show that's different than storefronts.* Halfway down the last downtown alley, just back of the Hamilton laundromat and Brown Grand theatre, he glimpsed a grey lump in the brick alley road. He almost ran over it, thinking at first it was some rags. An alarm went off in his head at the last second. Brett lurched the bike to the left, and plowed into a wire fence, spilling forward and cutting his forearm on the fence.

Crap. He dabbed at the blood with a handkerchief. *Musta been a big, frickin' squirrel, or...* he stepped closer *...Holy Moses...it's a cat.*

One of Brett's great loves was his faithful cat, Mortimer. Mortimer had arthritis now, but he still slept at the foot of his bed. *"Looks like Mort,"* Brett groaned, and he bent down with his non-bleeding hand, petted the cat, and looked it over. *Maybe a girl kitty.* "Lord..." he croaked, noticing blood trickling out from the cat's head. He bent closer. "Oh no, her eye is hanging out!" Brett lurched over and wretched several times in the alley. He returned to the cat. *This little kitty has been chopped-up somehow, maybe by a fan, or a machine belt, and ...some bastard tossed her out into the alley for dead.*

"You're still breathing, sweetie...man, what are we gonna do?" In a total panic, Brett fished around in the alley for anything that might help the kitty. He rummaged through the big dumpster behind the Theatre: nothing. Then he spied a trash can, across the fence. He hopped the fence, plunged through the can, and came up with a Captain Morgan Rum box. *Sheez. Somebody's been having a good time...* he guessed, and stumbled back over the fence line. Slowly he scooted the barely breathing cat sideways into the box. *She can't last very long.* A deep desperation spread over him. Brett's heart was pounding fast. He stared into the box.

A stunning thought shivered through him with that strange, static-electricity that takes your breath and dims your eyes in swirls. *That Bible verse one of the guys read out at the FCA meeting the night before...Matthew 25-something, I think...*

"I was a stranger, and sick, and you did not look after me...
I tell you the truth, whatever you did not do for one of the
least of these, you did not do for me. And such as these will
go away to eternal punishment, and the right-doing to eternal life."
(Matthew 25 v. 43-6).

Brett swooned at this revelation as if he was felled by a brick. *The least of these. Good grief...* He snatched the box in one arm, leapt on the bike, and pedaled like a madman. He headed north past Sixth Street, and veered west on Highway 9. Sweating like a race-horse, and dodging potholes, he sprinted on the bike three miles west to the nearest veterinarian.

He sped like a robot until he hit the vet's office door. For the next three days Brett stopped by the vet's office, checking on the cat. On the third day it happened. For Brett it was a miracle. Brett was sitting alone, near the window of the doctor's office after football practice, staring at the weeping-gray sky, and waiting for the kitty to show some sign of life. Then it happened in seconds.

Like a miracle of Moses, the sky above cleared, the winds blew from the North-west, and a gorgeous sunset shone through the doctor's window. At that second, the vet's nurse ran out singing "Hey! Your cat. She's sitting up! " Dumbfounded, Brett stared at the sky out the window, stared back at the nurse, and ran into the backroom. Spread out on the table, she blinked sweetly at him with one eye doing all the blink-ing, and meowed.

That night, Brett introduced Mortimer to his new, somewhat chopped up looking little sister. "Hey, Mort. This is Scooter!" They contentedly slurped up the Half and Half that Brett had swiped from his mother's fridge. *This is something,* Brett marveled, as he watched two of his best friends in the world, slurping away. *"The least of these..."*

Looking Somewhere Deep

Terry was at it again that night, bussing trays and filling in as a waiter at the "Skyliner" restaurant. On a borrowed bicycle, Terry was able to spin out fast to get to work.

"You mind if I have some of the ham and beans and cornbread, after the rush, Mr. Shaffer?" Terry asked. Charlie Blosser owned the place, but Mr. Shaffer was the night manager.

"Don't have lunch money today?" Mr. Shaffer inquired. Terry shrugged his re-ply. He'd spent his lunch money on his favorite sunflower seeds, and to slip Gary and Liedtke some dimes for Welch's grape popsicles, when he paused the worn-out sprinter's group at the little grocery north of the track, on the way back into the show-ers from the practice run out west.

Mr. Shaffer looked him up and down. *Not a lot of kids work their ass off like this kid, no parents, and his grandparents not well-heeled.*

"Sure kid. Eat some green beans and strawberry shortcake too, if you want. We got a lot, and it's way-better that you take it than the trash man. Terry, take some home for your grandfolks, too." *It's not long enough, for Christmas around here,* Mr. Shaffer reflected, turning back to his order sheets.

"Thanks. Thanks!" Terry replied, beaming. He snatched a piece of cornbread, to replenish a little energy, as he zipped out to the customers. Tips had improved over the Christmas break. He'd stuffed some of the money in a jar under his bed. He was saving up for the best pair of running shoes he could afford, for later in the spring.

Even during the work, and the jokes with customers, Terry's day-dreams broke into his routines. *It's sweet to run, don't have to grind it out. Just let it loose, all by itself, and takes me with it. Everything zips past. Open it up once in awhile, and watch the fireworks.*

"So the track squad looks good this year?" a customer shouted out. *How many times do I get this one? But he's a nice guy.*

"Yeah. I'm pretty sure you can bet on the guys this year," Terry replied softly. *Pedal to the metal for me. Will I get enough training for the State Indoor? Damn, if we don't get the yes letter soon. This year, what will happen when I push the whole thing wide-open, and just let her fly? Well, surprise, surprise...* Terry snapped back to the present. A freckled, smiling face shone out from under a Russian fur-hat, on a lithe figure who blew in through the front door, and shook off some outside snow. A wink. Sure enough. John Luecke.

John strode up to the counter bar stools, waving his auburn hair in a "come over" motion to Terry. Both of them grinned out with hundred-watt smiles.

"Working hard, or hardly working?" John teased, as Terry slid over.

"Hey. I do both, you know. Want some grub?"

"Yeah. Ham salad sandwich, and some fries." Terry scribbled the note, and stuck it on the round-wheel, and spun it to the cooks across the counter in the kitchen.

"So, uh...interested in some decent, uh, grain-based refreshment, tonight?" John asked.

"Uh, yeah..." Terry replied. *Yeah, I know. Ya shouldn't do this to yourself, sport.*

"It's no Moose-piss this time..."

Terry stalled, leaning on the counter, making like he was scribbling another order. Stalling more, he tossed back, "Uh-huh. Not if it's Schlitz, PBR, or worse. I got my standards, dude. I can't do much anyway. I'm out to..."

"....I know," John cut in. "You'll do it too, jet-fueled or not."

Okay. I should put the skids on this right now. Where do I want to take this...? I can't blow it. Terry shifted his weight around on the balls of his feet, not saying anything, thinking.

"It's that new stuff...Michelob Dark. You know, as the ad says, 'Don't be afraid of the dark...' " John joked, knowing that exotic beers were Terry's soft spot. "It's from Brady's, you know. Always some interesting stuff in the back of their liquor store."

The sandwich and fries slid out on the counter, buying a few more seconds of time. Terry stepped and reached over slowly.

"I got something I really should do, after work. I'll take care of it first, and if it doesn't take too long, I'll drop by your house, and we'll...give her a shot," Terry offered.

"Okay... I'll be there, chief, if you can. You got the bike, right?"

"Yup." Terry raised his eyebrows up and down, Groucho Marx-like, smiling slightly. "Gotta split. Catch up with customers, make some green..." A finger in the crowd pointed up for attention, "Hey, Terry. Any decent coffee?"

"Uh...well, it's black. It's hot. TV's Juan Valdez brought it in here, after he jumped off the burro... Be right there." he joked. He shook his head so-slightly, as he strode back to the big Cain's Coffee and Hills Brothers coffee urns on the counter.

Just after the nine o'clock closing, Terry grabbed a sack, which carried the ham and beans and cornbread for his grandparents, and took out on his bike. He crossed Highway 81, and wove through the streets near the cemetery. He pedaled slowly and a little nervously past the grounds of the imposing eight story behemoth Nazareth Convent, the continental headquarters of the Sisters of St. Joseph. The towering building is the largest Convent property of a Catholic order of nuns between Chicago and San Francisco. It is surrounded by a hundred acre stand of orchards, gardens and livestock buildings. This brown-brick and limestone giant, called the "nun-factory" by local miscreant Catholics, casts a mysterious spirit across the breadth of the town, and into the souls of the citizens, Protestant and Catholic alike. The main services of the many Sisters were the generous operation of the St. Joseph Hospital and clinic on the west end of town, and teaching in the Catholic grade school.

Terry drove the bike through the sparkling snow, up past the golden madame of CHS, and straight on to the cheery Christmas lights of the Diebels' home. Up the front walk, he parked the bike, and rang the doorbell.

"Why, Terry!" Mrs. Diebel sang out, upon fixing her dark-brown eyes on him through the opened door. "Come on in, we'll get you some hot chocolate and brownies. Just took 'em out of the oven."

"Oh. Wow, thanks Mrs. Diebel. Do you mind if I set this sack here? It's for my grandparents."

"Sure. I'll get Gary. He's in the basement, running his electric trains. Hey, maybe you'd like to see them? Have you ever seen them? He's been building the set since he was five years old," Mrs. Diebel chimed, as she led Terry through the kitchen.

"You bet," Terry said, intrigued.

"He's down there. Watch your step. Gary, Terry Householter's here. I'll bring you down some snacks in a jiffy," she called out, pointing Terry down the stairwell.

"Man, how are you? Glad you dropped by," Gary beamed out. He crawled out from behind his acreage of meticulously landscaped HO Gauge trains.

"Cripes. This is amazing. I thought maybe you had a couple feet of these things," Terry wondered aloud.

"I've been going at it for a long time. Let me show you some of it," Gary replied. A good twenty minutes passed, as the two drifted into the tiny, wondrous world of trains and villages. The brownies and hot chocolate disappeared without a whole lot of attention.

"This last one is a replica of a steam train, which ran in the 1940s to speeds over one hundred and thirty miles an hour. Sure wish it was still around today, as there's nothing like it now..." Gary explained.

"Well, you know, this is kinda why I wanted to drop by for a bit. Something I wanted to tell you," Terry spoke out slowly, in soft broken phrases. Gary blinked back at him.

"Wendell's a sophomore, and you're a freshman."

"Yeaaahh. But you know, we're only a couple days apart, on our birthdays."

"No kidding?" Terry replied, a bit mystified. "Huh. Well..." he continued, "I really think the two of you have the abilities in you, to break my class records. If you put yourselves to it. And really, if you're a class year younger, that just gives you more time, and uh...growth."

"You're serious?"

"Yeah. You've got the look in your eyes. Certainly, you got speed. Both of you, really. You see, I know what it's like. To have this, inside you. Nobody else really does, believe me." Terry paused. The silence sang in both of them.

"Let me try again," Terry turned full-face toward him, his mind and heart churning for the words. "Uh....I've seen them all, out there. There's a few fast guys. You know, regular speed balls in the normal sense. I'm talking about *something completely different*." He paused again, struggling to find words.

"I don't just run to win. Don't get me wrong. Unless I'm disqualified in a race, or am sick or something...uh....*I will win*," Terry said with an easy smile and a look in his eyes that reached a thousand years deep. "I run because *it* inside me is completely different, and it makes me feel alive."

"It is a gift from God," Gary whispered.

"I'm not strong on knowing about that. But I can tell you about it, anyway, because I think you have the same thing. It's *beyond*. And I see the *beyond* in you. So basically, kiddo. I think you can pull it off." Terry's eyes shone brightly again for a second. And then he grinned out like a sunrise, "If you really want it..." Gary breathed deeply, searching.

"I gotta split, man. It's snowing!" Terry said. "You got a cool setup here. Thank your mom for the good stuff, if I don't see her upstairs."

"Yeah. Glad you like it. Thanks. I'll head up with you."

The snow was coming down in huge flakes, the size of a nickel or more, as Terry dropped the bike down near Luecke's front porch. He headed to the door with his food sack in hand, and rang the doorbell. *Just for awhile. One or two. The kid up there on the hill, he's got the stuff.* The door popped open, and John grinned out through the snowflakes.

With a pretty clear head, and the sack with food still warm, Terry made it home before the midnight bells of Our Lady's cathedral rang clear through the heavy snow that night. When Gary told me about this visit by Terry, we puzzled about why Terry would take time to run with us during practices, and why Terry would come by to see Gary this way. We weren't "the big boys". It came to us that Terry worked a different way than most guys. Terry had a steel hand in a velvet glove that reached out in a quiet way. He didn't make a big deal of it. It just happened, and maybe you didn't see it right off.

Gary woke several times that night, searching deeply. Every time, he was pretty sure he found the same *something completely different* in himself, which shone out from Terry a thousand years deep.

Chapter 14
LONG AND WINDING ROADS

Clandestine Deliveries

A week later, classes were underway. A chaotic world bore down on us from above that strange January, and a swirl of local rumors bubbled up from below. At Christmas, Mom had bought me a subscription to *Time*. Wendell had managed to parlay some of his Christmas money from his Baptist parents to subscribe to the brand new, left-wing renegade *Rolling Stone* magazine.

"How are you getting *this thing* delivered to your house, without your folks going ape?" I pointedly asked.

"Hey. Not to worry. Our Order of the Arrow chapter, right?"

"Yeah..." He was throwing me off again.

"Well, you're Secretary, true?"

"Yeah...and..?"

He rolled his eyes a bit. "You're not catching my drift, boy. We got a Post Office Box. *And you got the key.*"

"Oh, man..." I bent over, groaning. The Order of the Arrow is the honorary secret and service society of the Boy Scouts, and we were two of the local head honchos.

"No use my folks, or yours, having to see this," was all Wendell would unrepentantly say about this clandestine delivery. I caved. He had a point. We needed information, from different sources.

That winter we devoured both magazines, scouring them for their stunningly different answers about how we were at war, and at-war with ourselves. Devastating political winds were blowing in America. Two vast forces vied for the command of our attentions: the grand enterprise of track, and the maelstroms of our wars, internal and beyond.

In the days, we sacrificed ourselves to the grueling endeavors of track. In the nights, we and our friends agonized in our talks about the demonic winds pouring down from above. We did most of our "agonizing" in Wendell's basement, usually to the sounds of Steppenwolf, or The Doors.

Thanks to our *Time,* and *Rolling Stone* magazines, we were developing a clearer focus on the bigger world and its chaos. Race conflicts, and civil rights in the nation were a weird, puzzling fog to us. We had only one black family in town, and that was ten years ago. Dad had hired the guy into his auto paint shop job, before the car business switched to a laundromat.

"Yeah, that nigger could drink, but boy could he spray paint," was about all my Dad ever said. Such was my initiation to our older generation's race attitudes in our family.

In the magazines, new revelations came to us weekly. We stood aghast as we learned how our big coastal cities burned in race riots last summer. We were stunned to read that the murdered Malcolm X (who simply enraged most of our white fathers, who said he was nothing but a black devil in robes), had inspired a legion of young blacks to turn away from hate, to brotherly love in true religion. Last November, Muhammad Ali had returned from his overseas vanquishing of European and British opponents. We were mesmerized by him. But the more we read, the more we became unsettled by his siding up with the weird race and anti-semitic bigotry of the Nation of Islam. Big nightmares haunted us more and more, due to the current vast increase of troops to 500,000 in Vietnam, and to last months' "Christmas present" from Lyndon Johnson, of the universal draft. Worst of all, we feared the rumors that the dreaded doomsday weapons, the apocalyptic Minuteman II missiles, guided by smart computers, were creeping their way into silos sprinkled around Concordia. A good part of our hearts and souls were sucked toward despair by these dark and dire horrors.

Still, the greater half of us held on to recent glimmers of hope. We marveled that America was landing lunar orbiters on the moon about every month, though we fell broken-hearted when the three Apollo 1 astronauts burned alive in their capsule on the launch-pad that January. In shining hope, the human possibilities were reborn in us by the new visions of *Star Trek*. Along with the whole world, we awaited the Beatles who were now in hiding, recording a great magic. "The Beatles are my religion," Terry told Wendell in practice. We too were entranced by their greatest musical revolution since Beethoven, and by their pushing higher the giant wave for peace and love which was finally pouring out from the great religions, and from music. Undimmed, these lights were rising to battle the deepening shadows.

* * *

Rumors in school carried whiffs of the greater chaos.

Tuesday lunch in the school cafeteria offered us goulash and cornbread. I sat alone for awhile sipping iced tea. In a second, I caught a whiff of White Shoulders perfume as a lunch tray slid down beside me. It was Audrey Jean Zimmerman.

"So. You have a good Christmas?"

"Decent enough. Had to run movies a lot, though. And you?"

"Too many cookies. Interesting things, though, were the *Carmina* practices, and a lot of luxurious time to read. What are you thinking about these days?"

Definitely a shrewd leading question. Wonder if I should really tell her. I've been thinking of her since the Methodist hayride.

"Hmmm," she hummed in sugary tones, "must be something in your head. You're still quiet..."

*Heck yeah. Last time in choir, on the stands at the stage, you pressed up behind me. Whad-
dya say to that? These older genius-girl vixens get the ol' heart racing fast.*

"Well, well. The Panther cat's got your tongue. I'll just be patient," she replied,
forking a maraschino cherry into her mouth, and melting me with her deep-pool
green eyes and light auburn-red eyebrows.

"Uh, Audrey, would you like to go bowling?" *Not the best idea, but it's all I can choke
out at the moment.*

"Bowling?" she asked, melodiously. "Well, you'll have to coach me. I'm maybe
not the whippiest at that."

"How about Saturday? I can pick you up at six-thirty."

"You're on," she smiled.

*Good. Maybe we can talk out a few of the rules, here. Man, my breathing's not steady. Miss
Zimmerman, you're still the alleged-girl of a senior.*

"You know," she said, "I'm in the school play *Our Town,* this year, a small part.
But it's pretty profound, really. Our practices seem to run a little later than your track
work. Maybe you could stop by to watch a little...after your practice is over?" Her
smile was inscrutable, and the tone of her voice hinted of things rich and deep.

"Sure."

"Okay..."

Then her eyebrows knitted together, and a serious shadow cast across her face.
"The rumor Dad hears at the cafes, is that certain women-folk are in the hunt for
Kramer's scalp. Ol' Mad Dog has sure been quiet ever since before Christmas, don't
you think?"

"Well, now that you mention it, we got no weird speeches out of him at the start
of school a couple days back."

"Here's another deal going down. You should know that your Father Long's invitation to our Episcopal and other youth groups in town, to join up with the Catholics
and watch the movie *The Graduate* and discuss it after, is causing quite a stir. Some of
the other church leaders are pretty appalled."

"What?"

"Hmm. Maybe Father Long didn't let on much about this to you or your youth
group, but we got a letter from him. His idea is to have preachers and priests face the
issues of the movie straight out, in conversations with youth. You know, dear, issues
like sex, adultery, capitalism, the church, the hippie life. 'Better to air the issues, and
take them on than let the controversies spread, un-discussed', I think his letter said."
Audrey continued, "And our priest read the letter to the whole Anglican congregation
from the pulpit on Sunday, and cheered him on! That's next Wednesday actually, at
our church hall, after the first evening showing of *The Graduate* at the Brown Grand
theatre. And by the way, Mr. Chris, won't *you* be the one to run the movie at the
theatre?"

I gulped. Things were starting to sink in.

"You gotta be right...I hadn't...really...known much about this," I wheezed out.

"Well, the talk in the shops downtown among the ladies, Mom says, is that the Baptists, the Lutherans, and the Seventh Days are appalled and up in arms. They demand their churches ban their youth from seeing this movie, or attending this ecumenical dialogue among youth groups. In this town, your Father Long is either the biggest Kansas hero since John Brown, or a back-door agent of perdition, in the lights of some of the church ladies and youth ministers. I say, let's have more of Father Long!" Audrey Jean's eyes sparkled.

"I haven't seen anything like this since our nuns went ape over the movie *Cleopatra*, four or five years ago," I replied. "Just before school was out that summer, the nuns all pounded us about how we would roast in hell if we looked through the Sears catalogue with lust in our hearts at ladies modeling bras and underwear, or if the girls wore the new bikinis that summer. If that wasn't enough fear of hell to cover the summer, they spit fire over how the American Catholic bishops had ruled that if we went to see Liz Taylor starring in *Cleopatra*, it would be a mortal sin of near-occasion."

"A what?"

"Near-occasion. The idea is, if you put yourself into temptation, like staring at certain interesting parts of Liz Taylor, that also is a sin...not just the real doing of a sin."

"Oh, brother. I bet more Catholic boys went to see Liz Taylor in record numbers just because of this. And no wonder all the Catholic girls I know act like they *want certain things, but say they don't*. This censorship is ridiculous, and I think it works opposite to make us teenagers want more of stuff like this." Audrey paused for a couple seconds to let this sink into my head.

"I've read reviews about this movie *The Graduate*. So, my question to you, dear, is: Suppose you go to this movie, and you see Dustin Hoffman get seduced by the older, married Anne Bancroft. Watching the movie will be a mortal sin to throw you in hell, even if you don't run right out and bed down with the nearest gorgeous neighborhood wife? Correct?"

"Well, no. They haven't said that this time. That was about *Cleopatra*."

"Oh, I get it. Anne Bancroft doesn't have eyes purple enough to tempt you into mortal sin, but Liz Taylor does."

"Well, I don't know what to say. I just run the movies," I weakly replied.

"Well, because of the movie and Father Long, I'll bet you there have not been so many phone calls between Protestant ministers, church deacons, and Catholic priests in this town since Ma Bell strung the first phone lines to customers here."

The lunch bell rang, putting an end to Audrey's review of turmoil in the town.

Audrey rose with her tray, but leaned down to whisper low and warm in my ear, "So you'll drop by to the stage after your practice? And come down to the church after you run the movie next Wednesday, to see your Father Long in action?"

"Yes, and yes," I replied, a little breathless.

The Brotherhood of the Baton

It was simple, but a little mind-boggling. Coach Betts had the opportunity of a life time before him on a silver platter. Like a genius rock hunter who toils for half a century, Betts had unearthed the track equivalent of the South African 7,000 carat diamond in Terry Householter, plus a diamond vein of other lesser gems. Without voicing it, Betts was out to train us at the same skill levels of the NCAA and Olympic contenders.

After a week and a half of indoor practices forced by arctic conditions, a rare sixty degrees Fahrenheit was the top-out temperature on Thursday January 19. As fast as spring rabbits, we took to the newly-paved asphalt track. Yesterday and the day before the town was blasted by a forty mile an hour blizzard, two feet of snow, with drifts over cars and a temperature plunging below zero. Nothing like an overnight seventy degree swing from arctic subzero conditions to gulf coast balminess, to boost your attention span. The greenhorns and immigrants from the coasts who visit out here come unglued by these extremes. The old ones just say it breeds character.

This morning, due to the ingenious anglings of the implacable Coach Betts, a track alumni had snow-plowed off the east and west straightaways of the new asphalt track at six AM. We gathered there now, gaping at the stupefying contrasts between the warm air, the mostly dry track, and the melting snow-drifts plowed back onto the fields and parking lot.

"We got a chance for something important today, boys. Mother nature is being nice to us. So let's dig in and get into it. Can't start too early on this," said Betts. "Now gather up, and listen."

Coach circled us into a group around the west-side 100 yard dash starting line.

"We are fortunate this year, we got the makings of great relay teams for the half-mile, mile, and maybe the two-mile and medley relays. You're gonna learn the near-scientific art of great baton-passing. This is one key to how teams become champions. *Listen carefully.* Before I start, let me tell you why this method is our greatest secret weapon. There are three tremendous advantages..." intoned Betts, with the reverence of a priest doing a baptism.

"One, you will practice this method, until no mistakes happen. *This means in a real race, mistakes don't happen to you, they happen to those other guys!*" We all chuckled at this.

"Two, when you get the method down, *you are not forced to slow down to complete a pass, like all the other teams.* Only this method lets you complete a pass at the highest speed between the two sprinters. With this method, you will gain one to two yards against any opposing team, *in every baton pass, every time. This means we gain four to eight yards against every team, in every race.*

"And three, this means you will win *every* race!"

We glanced at each other; we were getting it.

"Terry, you line up here on the track to receive the baton pass. Wendell, you're passing it." He led Wendell about eight yards back of Terry. "Let's do this in slow motion." Betts started up his explanation.

"Gentlemen, this is an all-important eight yard mark behind Terry." Betts used red chalk to make a mark on the cement edge of the asphalt track. "This is the 'go-mark' for Terry to start running. It will be a little further back or closer, between any two different runners. When the approaching runner, Wendell, hits the go-mark, Terry the receiver blasts out at top acceleration. The goal is that Terry matches Wendell's top speed in six to eight yards, exactly at the moment that Wendell catches up to Terry. *That magic moment is the fastest baton pass. How to pull this off is what you must learn.* Finding the exact best-distance to place the 'go mark' is the critical factor to have a perfect and fast baton pass. The point is, in practices, Terry...*or any receiver...* must eventually work out in practice and in his head just how far back to place his go-mark."

Betts paused before this all-important demonstration. He walked to each of us, staring in our eyes, saying quietly, *"Now listen. And watch."* He marched back to Wendell, and led him forward near to Terry.

"To find this exact point of top matching speeds takes many, many practices." He took Terry by the arm, and pointed to all of us, saying, "Terry...*or you the receiver...* must not be accelerating beyond the ability of Wendell to reach out and place the baton securely in Terry's hand." Betts grabbed Wendell's extended arm and stretched the baton to touch Terry's hand. "Terry's top job...or you the receiver...is to blast out when Wendell hits the 'go mark'. Now watch..." Coach urged us, and the demonstration started. Betts backed Wendell up eight yards. "Let's walk this in slow motion." Wendell started to walk.

"Everybody look: See how Terry spots Wendell at the go-mark, and now turns to accelerate," Betts waived Terry to turn. "Now, after the six or seven strides, they match up. At first, Terry looks only straight ahead. No looking back and slowing down! Now, Wendell sees Terry stick his *left* hand down and arm backwards to wait for the baton snap. Terry's left arm and elbow is straight. And it is steady. Terry's left hand points down, his palm faces backwards. His thumb is open and apart from his fingers, and his hand forms an upside down V."

Betts led Wendell up to Terry within passing distance. Then Betts hand-guided the next two steps between the two sprinters, to demonstrate the pass, and explained, "Now, Wendell is right-handed, so he runs with the baton in his accurate, steadiest right hand. With Terry's left hand down and steady, *Wendell's top job is to sight the baton up the gap between Terry's thumb and fingers.* Wendell reaches across his own chest with his right hand, and snaps the baton up into Terry's secure left grip." At this point, Betts took Wendell's hand and snapped the baton up into Terry's hand three times to demonstrate.

Betts stopped the show, and stood like a Prophet. He raised his right hand and pointed high in the air, then called out, "Terry does not slow down, does not look back, and does not waver-around, and risk being disqualified by stepping outside the lane.

Terry has only one easy job: clamp his hand shut on the baton when he feels it. And take off like a scalded rabbit." Coach paused for all this to sink in, and then went on,

"*Now, listen up, this next question is big.* What if Wendell...or you the passer...miss the first snap?" Betts waited for that scary chill to settle down on us all. We stared at Coach Betts. We were as clueless as Thumper the rabbit. With his finger high in the air, Betts said, "Uh-huh. Well, it's easy." A bright smile swam across his face. Betts demonstrated a missed snap, "Terry changes nothing! Just glance quickly back, and see if Wendell has a stumble or a gap. *If yes, Terry slows slightly to let Wendell catch up and try again, and continues to reach back with his open hand.* Wendell simply snaps it *again,* into Terry's hand." Betts snapped Wendell's hand and baton successfully into Terry's grip.

"So, remember. Terry...or you the receiver...*do not panic.* Just be patient, and keep running until there is a firm snap into your open downward hand. You will get to perfect this adjustment to a missed first snap, in practice. Show 'em again, a little faster."

Wendell and Terry executed it perfectly, this time running at a fair pace.

"Now, show 'em at top speed."

This time, Terry out-ran Wendell a little on the first snap, but got it on the second snap. Betts waived us all in together.

"You see? The method itself is perfect. *Everybody,* has to practice this, leading up to top speed. Practice eliminates panic and errors. Questions?"

We were stunned by Coach's brilliance, and the details. We could see it now. Only one question came, from Gary.

"Why is the pass made across the chest of the passer? Why can't he pass it to Terry's better right hand, if Terry is also right handed?"

"It is an option. But remember, that way has a real risk of a runner in the next right hand lane bumping into these same-side passes. In most cases, a cross-chest pass from the passer's dominant hand minimizes the risk of another team's interference and is safer."

Betts gathered us around in a circle, with friendly waves. He actually smiled and put his arms around some of us, and said, "Boys, this is a big reason why we are the best in the business. It is one reason why we win State championships. Be patient. If you pay the price, and do the practices, then all the records, and any team you face will fall in your dust. *It is your choice.* Tomorrow we'll watch some films of great relay passing teams. You guys split up now, and do some practicing. We'll be around to see you all."

Mastering the brotherhood of the baton was like learning magic. The state indoor and regular season was five weeks away.

* * *

None of us could explain it then. Not Gary, or Wendell, or country philosopher Louis. I would tell my sons, ages later in campfire discussions, why all this baton-passing and torture of running mattered. It wasn't about the crazy batons.

It was all about replacing *fear* with *hope*.

You see, we spent much of our days stunned by the chilling fear that we would die in a jungle far from home in a year or two. The great meat grinder of Vietnam chewed at you every day. It could grind you down into a selfish animal. The kind that thinks only "go for the girl" or "why not more drugs and beer?" We were next to die, and our friends, and then our younger brothers, in the only war ever planned to have no end.

Hovering above this was the greatest fear: *the death*, which stared at our entire generation and the whole world itself, from the Minuteman nuclear missiles being placed around Concordia. These missiles here and in the USSR were the *real* devils of the *real* Armageddon. We could drive our Chevys and Plymouths past these sleeping demons in the nights on our dark country roads.

These were the blackest fears that could ever smother young lives, descending on us at our time of dreams, hungers and innocence. To speak of the fears seemed pointless. How are you supposed to live today, when there is no tomorrow?

We had no answers. But in track, we found this: *Our lives might mean something. We wouldn't be just sardines trapped in a net, our lives snuffed out with no memory or meaning. We knew who we could be, in track.* We felt this in our bones, much more than we could put words to it: we might vanish, but in track our names could still be writ in stone, and we could run into life with joy, and pay back those who came before us.

Terry, Coach Betts, and the perfect brotherhood of the baton, *all gave us hope.* Sure, we'd run our hearts out. Like blowing on embers of a fire in a terrible storm, the love of track and the brotherhood of the baton kept the flame of life in us alive. We had the *mastery* of the baton, with Terry in the lead.

Laying Low for Awhile...

Roger had been layin' low for a couple months, hoping to keep the confusion going among authorities and students alike. He hoped to fog up how much he, or Brady, or other suspects, had been to blame for any of the rising revolts against the "rules" and the prevalent oppressors and secret abusers. The heat was on, in all directions, in the bigger social war between the insurgent rebels vs the old ways, and the Administration. The at-home war was staked out in the various rebellions of the swinging dummy of Kramer, the dunking of Betts in his suit in the pool, the rebellions of Zorro, the inflamed female resistance to Kramer's sexist-pig policies, and in the building wave of counter attacks to the tortures and dominance of bullies. *The revolution* was underway on many subtle and stark fronts. Roger just didn't want to be anybody's scapegoat for all this serious mischief. So layin' low and obfuscation was his game. *But it sure was getting boring...*

That weirdly warm afternoon, Roger was "rolling east" down Eleventh Street east near the tennis courts in the '57 Chevy, glad to escape the confines of classes at the last bell.

"Let's head to A & W and snag some onion rings," Tim Brady suggested, bringing some purpose to their post-school cruising, as he rode along in the passenger front seat side of Roger's Chevy.

"Damn straight," Rog tossed back, "that'll get my mind off that oily tuna casserole they forked out at us as an excuse for a school lunch. And maybe a beer from your dad's back-room stocks might be waiting for us, after?"

"I guess. I'll have to keep him diverted..." Tim replied, scratching his head.

Rog flipped on the under-the-dash switch for the CB radio he had installed, which he used as the youngest member of the civil defense disaster and tornado-spotting crew in the north counties. It was easy for all town-folk to identify Roger because both our '49 Plymouth and Rogers '57 Chevy had nine foot long whip antennae sprouting out of their backsides. The Chevy's whip antenna was topped-off with a small, triangular red flag, with a white CHS and black Panther blazed on it, and a gold and white streamer beneath which was so small that you had to really squint to make out the small print logo, *Miller High Life* .

Rog grabbed the CB mike, and clicked it on. "Let's see if any of the 'eagle eye brothers' are out there," he grinned. "Breaker, breaker. This is civil defense MX 81 Fast Daddy. Anybody alive out there?

A few seconds passed.

"*Jesus H. Christ...*" Tim cried in panic, pointing straight ahead. "What's with that shit-head? He's taking his half out of the middle of the road! Damn it... he's, he's..."

"...Aiming right at us? Yup. Relax, bozo," Rog replied. "That ain't no shithead, really. It's just my Dad."

"*Just your dad?* What the hell are you doing?" Tim screeched, his voice shaking, as Roger gunned the motor, and veered into the center of the road. Roger straddled the yellow line, and aimed straight toward the on-coming Valiant station wagon. Tim watched in mortal panic, his head swimming in disbelief that neither driver veered away. Both cars sped on at each other like hormone-crazed bisons out for blood.

"Bozo..." Roger piped from the side of his mouth "you ain't got nothing to fear. We do this all the time."

Tim took to wheezing like a ruptured steam engine. He rocked back and forth, grunting "*agh...agh...agh...*" Tim blinked and shook his head in shock, as he watched the two vehicles rock their wheels from side to side a little, faking the other guy, and still they madly drove head-on.

"Now, watch this, sports fans!" Roger leered at Tim, and wiggled his eyebrows. The cars sped on to only fifteen feet apart. At the last second both drivers partially braked, and spun their wheels in carefully executed turns. With precise distance and space calculations, both drivers turned slowly aside, skidded gracefully around....*and smacked into their right vs left front headlights and fenders with a deafening crash of metal and glass.*

"Maniacs!" Tim raged, shaking his fist to the silence. The puzzled drivers stared blankly at each other across open windows.

"Uh...Daaad...you forgot...*it was last time we both turned left. This time you were supposed to turn right!* "

After a second, Tim heard a double "Awww, hell..."

Tim was wheezing again. After a couple big wheezes, Tim felt a warm, steady hand on his shoulder,

"Not to worry, Kimosabe, we'll just make a visit to the Emerald City Garage."

* * *

That night after dusk, Dad and Roger were a little late to supper, but it was good and dark. They drove both cars home, up the steep driveway between the two grand blue spruces, and veered to park the cars on the side driveway.

"Mom'll never see 'em..." Dad whispered, as they headed in the back door for mom's goulash. The damaged fenders slept in silence, facing the north, away from the house windows. At two in the morning, Roger snuck carefully down the second floor stairs, and met up with Dad in the breezeway. The cars backed silently down the long drive to the street. Quietly they were roll-and-clutch started by coasting down the street. No grinding electric starters at two AM. They puttered silently down the city avenues with no headlights on, and drove downtown to the Hamilton laundromat. In the back of the long building, Dad maintained an auto body shop from the old Dodge dealership that Grandpa Tom ran until the late 1950s.

A few hours later, both vehicles stood flawless, and without guilt to the rising dawn. In the seasoned Catholic way, many moons passed before confessions arose and mom's laughter and absolution came down.

Velvet Curtains and Tiny Lights

After practice and a hot shower in the cold, gray dressing room, I tripped up the stairs, past the ever-whispering class track record board. My path weaved down the twisting narrow hall that led out to the marbled and chandeliered entrance hall which opened to the big auditorium and stage. I passed the old, large, oak and lighted glass trophy case, which had been built as original into the building walls in 1929. If you spare the time, you can count all the way back to the 1890s, year after year, and decade after decade, the astonishing number of ancient silver and gold track championship trophies. I passed it again, as most do, barely feeling the whispers of the dim but shining stories coming down the generations.

I spun to the back stage door and entered quietly into the front row seats. The cast of "Our Town" was in the last minutes of rehearsal. Soon they dispersed into the night, the stage emptied, and I waited silently as a church mouse until Audrey's head and shoulders peeked out around the north red velvet curtains.

I whistled.

"Yay. You came!"

I leaned forward from the brown velvet and leather seat,

"Yes, ma'am. I caught a few minutes of the lines."

"Stick around, I'll be back. Stay quiet, and don't be afraid of the dark. I'll get a light on."

She popped out of sight, and scurried around to the backstage stairs, going down to one of the green rooms. In a few minutes, the stage lights were out. A couple minutes more, and the spotlight booth lights flipped off above the third story balcony seats. *Possibly that was Louis, up there, leaving for home. If he makes it back from the Iron Man runs, he steps in to be a backup light and sound guy for the play.*

The keys of the great Baldwin Grand on the stage seem to dimly shine in the dark. Not supposed to do that...must be my imagination. The glass panes high above in the circular windows creaked from puffs of the balmy southwest winds outside. A low moaning whistle arose from the winds.

"Okay, Trackman..." the whisper carried across the auditorium in luciously low alto tones from the north edge of the stage. A tiny clear yellow Christmas tree size-bulb snapped on, at the back of the north side wall of the stage.

I could hear my heartbeat race up, as I skidded out the row of seats, and up the front stair steps to the north side of the stage, the stairs and oak planks creaking a bit. I stepped around the velvet curtains drawn to the side of the stage. In making the turn in the dark, cool arms and curtains wrapped around me in a spin of velvet and White Shoulders perfume.

"So, Trackman...are you all spent?"

"Uh, no."

"Betts didn't wear you out?"

"No tortures in running today, thank God. Just baton-passing drills."

"Hmm. How good can you pass your baton?"

"Uh...I'm okay at it..." I gulped. *Oh yes, her always brilliant double and triple meanings.* My heart raced again, and I felt hers race too. Her raspberry lipstick, searching kiss, our racing hearts, and the musty smell of velvet curtains made up a swirl that whisked our hearts and souls into a new, little universe. We felt the two of us distinct, and yet one.

"You know what they say about making love standing up..." Audrey breathed.

"Uh, yeaahh. I do know the joke...it's about Baptists."

"Well, we're not Baptists."

A little spark from our futures flashed the tiniest light into our dream, and into my head. I paused.

"Audrey...let's be in these curtains for awhile...but we should talk over some things too."

Under my ear, she breathed in slowly, richly and deeply.

"You're right, Trackman... we don't want to move too fast..." The tiny, brave light of the futures we were trying to liberate from the stifling grip of the unreasoning order and abusers of our time, shone just brightly *enough* into us that some restraint still held sway in us. Her gorgeous auburn hair and the raspberry kiss came swirling again, and a delicate universe came alive inside red velvet curtains.

Feminine Dissuasions

Early in the mornings, at about seven a.m., the Skyliner Restaurant attached to the Skyliner Motel was filling with the usual mix of motel customers, and a decent crowd of '40s-to-'60s middle age, rotund, business-dressed males. If you were one of the rotund ones, in Kansas lingo you're a town "honcho". In the South you'd be "running with the big dogs." This morning, a different, most unusual gathering of souls took the table nearest to the counter with the classy Cain's coffee urn. As they entered the restaurant, they drew a few side glances and raised eyebrows from the "honchos", who rapidly recognized the status of the peculiar ones, and turned nervous shoulders ever-so slightly away from the table as the group gathered.

As the Cain's coffees and cream-cheese danish were ordered, two obviously Alpha figures emerged, leading the hush-hush conversation. Mr. Wilson, seated at the bar counter next to the lesser-status Hills Brother's coffee urn, was the closest "honcho" positioned to strain an ear to catch the conversations of the group. One of the waitresses, hawk-eying the doings, caught the shifting eye and leaning ear of Herr Wilson. And so alerted, she occasionally popped by to do a check run on the blender that made "orange juilus", just to spite the eavesdropper.

One Alpha figure sported a nifty, wide-brim cranberry color hat dressed with a purple silk ribbon, and silvery-white sparkled snowmen. Her auburn-frizzy hair sprouted out sideways under the brim. This was Mrs. Abigail West, whose family was in the toy and health equipment business. The object of her affection, and distended, protecting cat claws was her sixth grade daughter, Carla, who tagged along today. Carla had her mother's color of hair, but to her mother's chagrin, Carla's hair was stringy and thin. Except in a straight downpour, her hair would splay out in bizarre ways due to static electricity.

Mrs. West's heart pounded like a lioness for her daughter's prodigious abilities in math. During Christmas break, Carla had devoured her older brother's sophomore-level algebra textbook, in her latest spurt of math prodigy. She wrote out the answers to exercise questions at the back of each chapter, in late night stints, while holding a flashlight under her bed sheets. Her brother Palmer, a science geek himself, had discovered her scribbled answers in the back of the chapters by New Years day. Carla now sat uncomfortably at the table, fidgeting like a cat zapped by a hot copper wire.

"We all know why we're here..." Mrs. West spoke in low tones to the assembled group, with her cat-claw finger extended and pointing low across the table. They were munching the danish pastries and sipping coffee. A loud burst of "Hmmmphs" and irritated coughs zipped out in all directions from the ladies, carrying the sting of rock salt bird-shot fired from a sawed-off Remington shotgun.

"Last night's school board meeting was tense. We managed to handle the issue with a compromise procedure of a secret ballot vote. We're lucky we had two members on the board, since the secret ballot procedure was approved by a one vote majority show of hands." This voice rang out in high nasal tones through the steel-cable blue knitted wool scarf that Mrs. Constance Norwest was slowly unwinding from the neck cuff of her Polish grey wool long coat. A widowed Catholic mother who hailed from somewhere "back east", she had moved into Concordia a decade before, her daughter in tow, to take a catalogue librarian position that opened in the city library. Her daughter Ruth now was a CHS sophomore, who had played flute since she was five years old. Ruth had almost gleaming silk-black hair, black as the deep-bottom of Mammoth Cave, and narrow fingers that flew like lightning over the keys of the flute.

For three years, Mrs. Norwest had tossed coins in a jar, and had returned discarded pop bottles she gathered from ditches and parks to get nickel rebates from the Coke and Nehi soft drink delivery truck drivers who serviced the bowling alleys, bars and gas stations. With this money, she dreamed to buy Ruth a refurbished classic silver Selmer-Louis Lot flute made decades ago in Boston, which she had located in a Kansas City music store. Her lay-away down payment was a costly $50 for a librarian's meager wages. The miracle of the purchase came from the Kansas City store owner, a fellow-Catholic and Knight of Columbus, who took sympathy to stow away the flute and cut the price for Mrs. Norwest when he heard her blurt "Holy Mary, Mother of God" when he first quoted her the flute's much-higher market price over the phone. Ruth hoped to play this fabulous flute to record her Interlochen audition tape, using the new Ampex reel-to-reel recorder in the high school band room. Ruth hoped to follow in Evelyn's footsteps, and send her tape to Interlochen the following winter, praying many rosaries that her classic flute might be her winning edge for a scholarship to the famous summer music school. As for Evelyn before her, perhaps the east-coast music gods would smile.

"Of course, we don't know the final result of the secret ballot vote of the school board." Mrs. Norwest's nasal east-coast twang resonated above the raised coffee cups,

"But we do know how to count the winks and raised eyebrows on certain male board members..." Mrs. West tried to continue the sentence, only to be interrupted by Mrs. Norwest.

"...Who share certain yellow-metal bands with sister-members of our committee here..." with Mrs. West then interrupting.

"...Whom we thank, for the sake of our daughters, for exercising certain feminine means of dissuasion."

"Blackmail, dear..." Mrs. Norwest clarified.

"Well, it is about the issue of our daughters' desecration at the hands of this, this fanatic, troglodyte Assistant Principal ..." a frustrated group member yelled out, pounding the table. This outburst triggered a widespread and stifled jerking of the necks among the "honchos", who glanced around to catch an identifying glimpse of the apoplectic woman.

The cat-claw extended upward again, across the table, gathering silence. Mrs. West took a sip of Cain's, put her cup down, and spoke in hushed tones,

"All we can be is hopeful. The executive board will announce the vote count and any recommendations at a meeting they will call in the next night or two. If there is action, we'll hear about it."

* * *

Five days later, at one-fourteen p.m., Miss Beasley, the spinster high school secretary of twenty six years, heard a rap on the front counter of the school office. She looked up, and stepped to the counter to glimpse the retreating grey-jacket figure from the U.S. Post Office, and gather the letters he laid in the inbox in the counter. She slid them into staff mail boxes. At one-seventeen p.m. Assistant Principal Kramer spun through the double doors after lunch room duty. He passed the mail boxes and pulled out the batch under his name. He shut his door, lit up his pipe, and thumbed through the letters. He stopped at the fourth letter. It carried a minimal return address of G. Ganstrom, USD 333 School Board.

At one-eighteen p.m. Miss Beasley heard the strangest *whomp* and tinkling of glass from inside and half-way up the east wall of the Assistant Principal's office. By August, all the bits of glass, pipes, tobacco and personal effects were finally swept out.

On February 23, one-thirty-six p.m., Coach Betts strode down the hall toward the American Government classroom, in the upper northwest corner of Concordia High School. His black wingtips skipped up the stairs quickly. Reaching the classroom door, he knocked, pulled it open, and scanned the room. Eyeballing the teenager he hunted, Coach Betts raised his eyebrows, pointed directly at the teen with his right index finger which flipped over to give two quick snaps of "come hither". All heads turned to watch the youth sidestep up the narrow rows, and scoot over to the door.

Stepping a bit outside the half-shut classroom door, Betts paused and handed the teen a letter. Coach whispered a bit too loudly, "You'll have to get used to this news..." The paper unfolded.

A few nauseating seconds ticked past.

"Hell yeeessss!" split the silence. The chalk snapped on the blackboard in the government teacher's fingers.

The youth skipped back from Betts, strode into class, folded the paper and stuck it in his shirt pocket, with all eyes staring. Terry just looked to the ceiling, shook his fist joyously to the heavens, and quietly sat down.

The state track indoor was just two days away. And our eagle was now in the lead.

Late January, 1967

Chapter 15
AD ASTRA

Charlie Tidwell's Flickering Shadow

We had the gift of one more day. It was almost as warm as yesterday, and the new asphalt track was dry. And there were things to stretch the heart.

A metal whistle blew three blasts in the dressing room, cutting off conversations, and triggering a little jerking of necks.

Betts' throaty chuckles and voice rang out, "Okay men, gather in here. Important stuff today." The coughs, laughs and conversations dwindled as guys gathered in around the jacuzzi tank. Betts was getting ready to unleash another of his secrets.

"All-right, you distance-guy jaybirds back there, Smith, Hattan and Rivers, put a clamp on it. Unless you want to chatter while you do stairs after you get back from whatever Coach Smith does to you." Chatter quickly ceased. Betts beamed. You could tell he was warming up. "*Sprinters and relay men.* The Great Spirit above has given us a good day to learn better one big thing you will need at the indoor, and all season long. You head first into the shop, and into the drafting arts room. We got a special for you there. After that, head out to the track, north side. Stay off the grass and mud. *Weight-men.* Obviously, it's too muddy to throw outside. But Coach Frohardt and I have a new little belated Christmas present for you." He reached into the red and white sports bag, and held it up. "No, it's not an orange from the Florida Orange Bowl. Here, Bauer, catch..." He tossed it three feet out to Steve. Steve lurched, fumbled it as it fell, and caught it at his ankles. A few test squeezes later, Steve raised his eyebrows. "Cool."

"It's the latest. Thank you, USC and Dallas Long. It's a silicone thick-coated shot-put. You can throw it indoors. You boys hit the weights, and then go with Coach Forbach up to the old gym, where you can practice your tosses. See what your season starting distances are. Iron Men, you're off to Smith's tortures..." he chuckled, with a Cheshire cat smile, "...no pain, no gain. Let's get poppin."

* * *

We gathered in the drafting arts room. The top sprinters plopped down in the front seats, we freshmen in the second rows. Betts strode in, and, without words, pointed Coach Frohardt to the middle of the room. Betts flipped off the front classroom lights, pulled down a silver screen in front of the blackboard, spun around and sat on the teacher's desk. He eyed us back and forth.

"Well, we ain't got popcorn. Maybe next time. Better than that, though. We got Robert Lee Hayes, and Charlie Tidwell." A few puzzled looks spread among us.

"Robert Lee is..." Betts started "...Bob Hayes, Olympic Gold '64," Wendell finished the sentence.

"Exactly, Mr. Ganstrom," Betts replied. "Bob Hayes, possibly the fastest human who will ever live.[3] You got the film jiggered up yet, Coach Frohardt?"

"Ready to fire."

"Okay, hit it."

The film flickered in, with a scan of the Bell Tower on the great hill at the University of Kansas, and then panned to white letters, "KU Athletics, Track and Field Training" with Allen Fieldhouse in the background. Betts's KU connections. The film then panned to "Sprints and Relays" in white letters, and then to "NCAA and Olympics Finals, Robert Hayes."

"Dial the machine on pause, Coach Frohardt." Betts continued, "In a few seconds, you'll be watching Bob Hayes' starts and gold medals at the 1963 NCAA collegiate 100 yard championships, and also the 1964 Olympic 100 meter gold medal finals. Mr. Hayes here ran a 6.4 high school 60 yard dash and the first sub-6 second 60 yard dash in 5.9 seconds after college, a world record. Terry here can probably run 6.4 if he wants, at the indoor, which would tie the high school national record as Bob Hayes ran it. That's if he wants too..." Terry sat inscrutably smiling, as the rest of us exchanged raised eyebrows. Betts went on,

"Now Mr. Bob Hayes set the world record 100 yard dash in 1963 at 9.1 seconds..." at that, whistles flew through the room..."which is two tenths of a second faster than the NAIA and AAU national youth record of 9.3 which Hayes set just *after* high school. Mr. Terry here is taking aim at that record, too." There was electricity in the air, and some shuffling in the room, at this. Betts continued, "Later in '63 Hayes tied the world 220 yard record with a 20.6 and set the world 200 meter record in 20.5 which really is a slight bit slower than the 220 pace. Not shabby for times all on the old, slower cinder tracks.

Now here on film is the NCAA 1963 100 yard finals. The point is: Watch Bob Hayes start, both here, and at the Olympics. Roll the film slowly, Coach Frohardt."

In a few seconds, the 1963 NCAA championship 100 yard dash came on screen. The sprinters moved slowly out of their blocks at the gun fire.

"Stop the film. Note that Hayes is the last guy out of the blocks. He does a lot of things wrong. That's why you're watching it. Crazy Hayes, if he had been coached or at least learned things right, he could have bettered any time he ever ran by two tenths of a second, and that's almost two more yards of a lead. Coach Frohardt, run the start over and over again, please."

The film ran the start repeatedly. Betts explained each mistake,

"His feet are set in the blocks too close to the front to get a good forward thrust. He strains his neck looking ahead, which puts his whole body muscles in a strained condition, unable to respond quickly and automatically. He stands almost straight up at the gun, or at least too high, so a lot of his energy goes up, not down the track.

He clenches his fists and lumbers out from the blocks in wavering strides, which puts energy and wastes time in going back and forth, not straight ahead. *He's just lost two yards at the start.* And you can see the other sprinters are ahead by just that much, due to their better starts and habits. Despite this, Crazy Bob wins hands down, due to his unmatchable pure speed down the stretch. Too bad he doesn't know how to run, huh?"

"If you run like this, we will un-teach you," Betts proclaimed.

Frohardt let the film run on through to the 1964 Olympics 100 meter. Betts commented again on the Hayes' mistakes,

"He broke the 100 meter record with his 10.0 on a chewed up, crappy cinder track with a bad borrowed shoe. Now think what he could have done with a real start, and a real track. Hayes loses the same two yards or two tenths of a second, in every race from his bad starts. Too bad. Now, Coach Frohardt, put on the Charlie Tidwell film." Coach complied.

Meanwhile, Betts explained, "Charlie Tidwell was KU's greatest 1950s collegiate sprinter. He was talented yes, but not more than several of you. However, Charlie Tidwell was Mr. Start..."

Frohardt repeatedly played the old films of Tidwell doing starts.

"Stop the film every four seconds as we go, please, Coach," Betts explained, "and you boys get down what Charlie Tidwell does right." The projector rolled slowly, snap-crackling like a popcorn machine. Betts eyes gleamed in the dark, like a Prophet addressing his disciples.

"Number One. In the blocks, Tidwell's feet are back, and placed about a foot-length or more apart, with the left leg in front. This gives him forward thrust, from his strongest leg. *Two.* At the call 'on your mark' Charlie leans forward only a little to transfer considerable weight to his arms. Stop the film. See here: his head is down and relaxed, so his mind can focus only to hear the gun, and so *Three,* his loose muscles can react in the fastest unclenched response time. *Four.* He leans forward, fingers arched, with little weight on his legs. Now this lets his left leg thrust the body weight forward, and not straight up. *Because of all this, at the gun he is the first out of the blocks...see?* Now run the film very slow, and watch. *Five. Look:* Charlie snaps his right arm up at the gun which naturally helps coordinate his left leg response in balance with his right arm weight. Why? *So he's not wasting energy wavering down the track to catch his balance like Hayes did. Six.* He digs out in small, very fast, and low strides that reach straight ahead down the track, and *Seven.* he pumps his arms in close and fast to actually help speed up his legs. *Stop the film. See? After six strides he is out a full two or three yards ahead of everybody else..."*

Frohardt and Betts repeated this film run of Charlie Tidwell four more times, in silence. Betts then killed the film and flipped on the lights.

We sat spellbound, as if we'd seen our first sunrise.

Betts strode slowly and patiently around in a circle. He eyeballed us back and forth, and then slowly spoke, "Do you want to beat everybody else by two and three yards? Then you learn Charlie Tidwell's seven secrets. Gentlemen, we will un-teach you to not be Bob Hayes with bad starts. Learn the seven secrets, and you will be winners. But there's just one thing. *You have to want it. It's your choice.*"

* * *

Minutes later, we were gathering at the dry north end of the asphalt track, thriving in Mother Nature's warm gift day, and mindful of the seven secrets. Our hearts were stirring to climb those distant mountains we all glimpsed a month ago when we passed through the all-connecting glass tunnel.

Once more, the terror of the creeping Storm of the war, the great maw that could swallow us all, fled into the shadows against our brightening hope that we might be something, together. From a dark, unlocked storage, the coaches and the seniors rounded the curve, with Terry in the lead. They were carrying to us new silver starting blocks.

Out of Anglican Shadows

The rounded arch oak door to the Anglican Episcopal meeting hall is graced with a stained glass mini-doorway at head-height. The arch and walls of the building are cream yellow limestone boulders, cantaloupe-size. At ten minutes after nine o'clock Wednesday night, the burnt-out street light allowed the stained-glass of the thick-grained door to radiate happy, warm lights of blue, burgundy and gold back to the darkness. The stained glass glowed forth a promise of tranquility which grew as I strode down the brownstone path in the storm, to the hall. I was late. Finishing up after the first showing of *The Graduate* at eight-thirty at night had me creaking the oak door open a good forty minutes after Father Long had started the panel and group discussion about the film among the willing town clergy and teen youth group members. I pulled the door open slowly. Sure enough, it squeaked.

Some high energy here, nobody even sees me coming in, I guessed. *Uh, correct that...* I shivered, as a certain pair of deep-pool, blue-green feminine eyes sparked across the room into mine. With no place to sit, I stood with my back to the round-stone wall near the door. Soft steps carried the deep-pool eyes around the room, to me.

"So, there are two seductions of the young mind being shown, don't you think? The seduction of youth with sex by the older neighbor lady, and the seduction of life toward greed by capitalism, symbolized by the after-graduation party when Dustin Hoffman hears 'plastic, plastic' as a sort of siren call to 'success' and 'the good life'.

Of course, this was sagacious Jack going at it again.

"Yes, and it has a double meaning, 'plastic' does..." replied Father Long, trying to catch up with Jack. "It means both the call to, and the false-god of success and money are plastic, or artificial."

"All the churches would agree on that," said Father Hotaling, the Anglican brave-heart priest. He'd joined in league with the heretic Catholics to promote this ecumenical gathering.

A hand popped up in the crowd and Father Long called on a young lady. Blue-eyed, and face radiating, she stood quickly and her voice rang in firm tones:

> *"It is better to hear a rebuke of the wise, than for men to hear the song of fools. Ecclesiastes 7:5."*

A warm moist hand gently gripped mine, and a firm, clear voice whispered in my ear, "Oh man, here it comes...gimme that ol' time religion." Tension and fear rippled the room like wolves howling beyond the fire at the edge of a winter's camp. A culture war cloud enveloped the room. The nordic warrior-lass Evangelist continued.

"You people need to understand, this is all simple, black and white. 'For the wages of sin is death'. That's all you need to know. This movie pumps temptation at you. It's not a thinking thing. We don't need to be here, any of us. Just stay away from porno and movies like this."

Audrey clenched my hand and stepped out from the shadows at the oak door, her blue-green eyes glittering. She spoke in melodious, clear and gentle tones.

"Well, that's a terrific knee-jerk response, isn't it...everything's a sin. Thinking's a sin. So you read your bible, do you? Hand it to me, if you don't mind." Audrey strode into the crowd and took the bible from the Nordic lass and backed away a bit. Audrey flipped back and forth through pages. A minute ticked past, the tension thickened.

"Yup, found it. You know your bible. So then, you know the bible says this:

> *"And the LORD God said, Behold, the man has become as one of us, to know good and evil.' Genesis 3."*

"To know good and evil it says," Audrey continued, "Uh-huh. Do you suppose this just might mean we are to *know*, and to *think* about what is good versus evil? That we're supposed to use our brain that God gave us? Hmm. Maybe some of you still doubt. Maybe I need to be even more clear." Audrey flipped pages again for thirty-something seconds, and sang out, "Yeah. Here 'tis... Thank you, Father Hotaling, for all those bible studies."

> *"And I gave my heart to seek, and to search out by wisdom concerning all things that are under heaven: this sore travail hath God given to the sons of man to be exercised." Ecclesiastes 1:13*

Audrey snapped the bible shut with a pop, and whispering sweetly, passed it to a guy sitting next to her.

"She'll want this back..." Audrey straightened her shoulders, looked around the room, and said, "Hmm...to seek, search, and exercise wisdom. *Darn.* So, it *is* a thinking thing. Well, let's get back to using our thinkers, shall we?" She beamed. You could swear the crowd parted to let her stride back into the dimmer shadows by the oak doors, to stand again by me.

Father Long cleared his throat.

In a split second, the cheery, kindly voice of Jack Kasl sang out like a meadow-lark: "You know, there's a third and fourth seduction..."

"Really?" Father Hotaling raised his voice and blinked a couple times, "Please go on."

Jack smiled, "Well, look at the symbols. There's the cross. And also the 'pot' or marijuana that the wild-man English professor, Donald Sutherland, passes out to students in his house. The pot strikes a challenge to the status quo. But more important, the golden cross Dustin Hoffman takes up looks like a sword to me, to fend off the church members, family, and minister. His cross-as-a-sword represents Truth, the truth of real love over 'country-club arrangements' and church ceremony. Dustin holds the cross, the truth of Jesus, which is love... and he's swinging it against the dogma of the church, or any doctrines that tell people 'get more money', or 'marry for profit and social status'. Too-often that stuff worms its way into the church, if you ask me. You know, 'pass the plate' and 'business is business' all week, except maybe for Sunday when sacraments, or 'believe' is what supposedly saves you. That bull, and the rich, elaborate, loveless marriage for money in the church is what Dustin is saving both his woman and himself from. He's beatin' back the blasphemy, if you ask me."

The Anglican candles burned brighter in the room. Our heads were spinning fast, trying to keep up with Jack. Winter winds whistled through the arch door, but the candles burned on. Good Father Hotaling sniffed twice. And Father Long, the Jesuit-Paris trained theologian, interlaced his fingers under his nose. His eyes were a-sparkle.

* * *

Three nights later, at six in the evening, our doorbell rang.

"Mom, you get that?" I called from the bathroom, shaving with a Wilkinson sword single blade shaver, and Burma Shave. I smiled, remembering the Burma Shave road-signs newly planted on Highway 9 going out to Louis' farm nine miles west of town.

When Super-shaved
Remember, pard
You'll still get slapped
But not so hard

Stupid fire-plug red beard sprouts fast these days, I fussed. *Still, I don't have to shave twice down the neck on both sides, like Bruce Johnston.* Steps clicked down the hall, the oak boards creaking.

"You certainly are a lady-killer, there, Mr. Louis..." Mom's voice floated stronger coming down the hall. Louis chuckled at the open bathroom doorway, flushing a little splotchy-red on his cheeks,

"I'm not sure of that...but thanks for the compliment, Mrs. Hamilton. You ready, hambone?" Louis called from the bathroom door. Dressed out in a black pin-stripe suit, with a pink carnation, and the only black-polished wingtips at the school on a teenager, Louis was armed for bear.

Tonight was the concert. Carol Orrf's towering *Carmina Burana,* our eighty-voice choir, and our dueling genius pianists. Mr. Miller, we hoped, would don his Italian, sparkling gold silk tie, and his deep-burgundy suit. Practices at the various churches, and the incredible story and recording of the London-bombed War Time Whitehall Choir had pressed a sense of reverence, and mission into us. The Kansas in us, the "Ad Astra" had called us out, the challenge thrown down by the wizard choral director.

"Well, you're not bleeding," Louis offered. "Shouldn't you really try the electric razors these days?"

"I don't know, this has just got...a feel to it, I guess." I turned to look at him, wingtips and all.

"Tonight we answer the call," Louis whispered in low tones, striding through the door and up to me. His slightly moist hand strongly gripped mine. Louis was self-consciously a frontier knight, partly haunted by severe expectations from being surrounded by three sisters.

"But, I got a joke for you, about tonight," Louis winked.

"Okay, shoot..."

"I say Carmeena, You say Car-my-na,
I say Bur-ahna, You say Bur-aye-na.
Let's *Carl* the whole thing *Orff...*"

"Ah, sheesh," I groaned. *Surely, he didn't just invent that...*

Two minutes later, we hopped out into his '51 Chevy pickup, the White Ghost, and slowly backed down the snowy-but cleared steep driveway. Mom and Dad would come over for the concert, at the CHS auditorium. We spun down Eleventh Street, as the snow-drifts sparkled from the passing headlights of the old '51 Chevy. The heater grumbled and whirred like an unbalanced mixer, as it pumped out surprising amounts of hot air. We pulled into a south parking slot, silent in anticipation as we shut the pickup's old creaking doors. We couldn't help but glance at the crystal pure night sky, the Milky Way etched above in luminescent wisps, punctuated by crackling-bright stars against black silk. Unspoken, we always wondered who or what stares back at us across that unsettling, glittering infinity.

Twenty minutes later, the thundering *Carmina* was resurrected. It shook the chandeliers of the great auditorium as it shook the souls of the mortals, and seeped out of the cracks of the high windows, to speak back to that infinity.

Ad Astra, on Roads Less Taken

Mr. Miller sat quiet as a church mouse at his desk in the choral room, after the concert. He looked down at the special metal box he had ordered from Hume's Music Supply in Topeka. Not a publicly emotional man, he was happy for the refuge of his office from the teeming crowd which had finally trickled out the front doors of the high school. The last of the choir members had hung up their robes and skipped out, carrying on like jaybirds.

His hands trembled a little as he wiped his eyes. *You have to wait awhile, for your time.* The brilliant discordant echoes from the great *Carmina* lit up his mind like deep-summer heat lightning. He heard once more the main themes of the high tenors and sopranos...*They sang like silver trumpets in a mountain river gorge. Crazy damn kids...* His greatest bolt of amazement came in his flash-backs of the syncopated dueling grand pianos ... *Maybe I imagined them...*

His eyes re-focused on the metal box on his desk. In a Buddha-like stillness, his fingers seemed to work separate from his body, as he dated and signed the small label, and placed the high grade metal oxide reel to reel tape into the box. He clicked the clasp shut. A small stir of air wisped in the room behind him. He glanced back over his shoulder: Marlene, his wife of seven years.

"They're gone, honey. You shoulda heard 'em." Her voice rang with the "Chi-cagah" twang, which roped his attention at the K-State department of music where they met.

"I couldn't stay out there."

"I know."

"At the beginning, well, I wondered if all this was going..." he started,

"...to crash like the Wright brothers' first flight," she finished his sentence.

"It was...a thing of hope," he said to himself.

She nodded winsomely, *Yes, absolutely yes.*

* * *

After the concert, Mrs. Freeburne drove the four miles east of town to their farm in the old Ford pickup, with Evelyn beside her.

"I thought maybe three years old was a little early for you to start piano..." her Mom stated. Evelyn held in her reaction. Her only give-away was a slight rising of her head.

"But surely that was something tonight, dear."

"The rest of the family wasn't there."

"Well. Maybe they just will be, next time," came the insipid reply. *I never knew entirely what to say to her.*

The pickup lumbered through the snow pack and frozen ice chunks on the crushed limestone road, wavering like an old bloodhound that lost the scent that leads back home. Evelyn glanced at the east horizon, out the pickup window. A cold-silver moon rose so gigantic above the bare elm trees that it caught her breath. *Good Lord, you can see the crater rims up there on his face.*

"See that, Mom?"

"Yeah. He's a giant, isn't he. What's that next to it, to the right above the moon?" The two squinted for several seconds. Evelyn narrowed her eye lids to focus crisply.

"It's... a second, tiny *crescent moon!*" Her mom's voice shook, "How can that be?"

"Good grief. The only thing that big is Venus. So it's a *crescent Venus*...I think."

"I could never ever imagine such a thing. Such a display going on tonight."

The pickup bounced down the path to their farmhouse, its leaf springs wheezing a rusty complaint. Through the screen and kitchen door, and into the kitchen they fled, to quickly greet the warming wood stove.

"You got some mail today, sweetheart. It's a different looking envelope, over there on the counter," said Evelyn's mom."Had to sign for it. Never had to do that be-fore..."

Evelyn stepped to the counter and lifted the large manila envelope. Her eyes scanned quickly, *Certified letter. Ann Arbor, Michigan.*

Evelyn's heart raced, and spots spun around her eyes. She fumbled in tearing the seal, and pulled out the letter. *Feels like starched linen...* Eyes wide, she searched the page.

Evelyn gasped, turned slightly pale, set the letter on the kitchen table, and fled to her room. Her mother raised the letter from the floor, her hand shaking, and read,

"..international competition...based on your audition tape, the University of Michigan Department of Music and Interlochen Music Camp staff hereby award to you one of three full scholarships... all expenses paid for both sessions of the young piano masters workshops this coming summer..."

February 25, 1967. The State Indoor High School Track Champion-ships. Kansas State University

Since we were freshmen relay guys, Gary, I and Don Liedtke were allowed to ride the team bus with the upperclassmen. We stepped off the bus at the K-State indoor fieldhouse, an hour and a half before the State indoor meet was to start.

"We could go wandering around the Aggieville sports bars and shops..." I sug-gested.

"Nah." Gary replied. "They're not open now. Anyway, the program says the doors open about now. Let's go in cruise around, check the place out." We agreed, entered the arena, and milled around inside the musty fieldhouse, buying cokes and hotdogs, and eyeing the facilities. Our interests were at a peak fever, as this track season had a great buildup in the area papers as "the year of Kansas high school track."

Conversations with Gary, who followed the newspapers like a medieval scholar, had us hearing the glittering names of athletes, across five grades or sizes of high schools in Kansas, who were coming to the Indoor track championship meet.

"Papers say the Kansas outdoor and indoor relays are among six of the biggest high school track events in the nation. And of course, we got the KU Relays too," said Gary. "Betts says in Kansas, there are several near-4 minute high school milers, one of them is Jim Niehouse from Salina Sacred Heart. Terry's gotta run against him in the 440 yard dash here. Betts talked him into it. And there are speedballs from all over we don't hear about: several unbelievable hurdlers out of Wichita, a black guy from a tiny Kansas town and school called Bogue, name of Dale Alexander, Jr. He could break all records in the 440. Not just Terry is out there."

The day spun forward like it was normal, but abnormal things were in the making. We sat in the nosebleed section for quite awhile, watching the various types, comparing the indoor State and national records to the competitors, across sizes or classes of schools. Field events competitors were so-so. No state or national records were under threat from this year's crop of weight-men. But things got interesting when the distance running events came up. The half milers Bob Barrati and Jim Niehouse, from big vs small schools, ran separately but both could run within a few seconds of Jim Ryun's national indoor record.

Coach Frohardt was sitting with us, and he pointed out that several of the nation's leading hurdlers were here, entering as sprinters in their class AA 60 yard and 440 yard races, since hurdles weren't held at this indoor meet. These included Bob Bornkessel of Shawnee Mission North/Kansas City, Maurice King and Marcus Walker both from Wichita East, and Preston Carrington of Topeka High. We could compare Terry's times with these guys, to take their measure of running talent.

The big unknown was marked up in the lights that day. We overheard a little of Betts and Terry talking in the trainer's room after practice three days before. It was the showdown that Betts had arranged, by pitting Terry up against the incredible half miler Jim Niehouse from Salina, in the one race which hit them both in the middle of their talents: the 440 yard dash. Wendell had recounted to us the nervous full conversation between Betts and Terry, several days before: "Man, Coach. I'm a sprinter, not a distance guy!"

"The 440 isn't distance, Terry. It is just the longest sprint. The human body is really capable of an almost all-out sprint in the 440. You also have endurance, and you can work strategy...and you'll take him." Betts was playing to one of Terry's internal strengths: He was quiet, but absolutely fearless. Betts had explained, "Niehouse has almost got the endurance of Dotson, plus the speed of a decent sprinter. He'll be good at the longer 440 dash. Last year he cut about a 22.6 outdoor in the 220, not a bad time. But Terry, he cannot maintain that speed in two tight laps indoor. And you are much faster than that. It's just not a race long enough to wear you down. You just run a pace that will push him on the first two curves, so he has to strain to keep up with you, but slow enough so you can save up energy. Don't burn yourself out going after him on the first two curves. And then blast him off the track on the last two straightaways. You'll cook him when it hurts him most, and he won't have the speed to be able to do a thing about it."

Terry shrugged nonchalantly, "Okay, Coach."

* * *

It's surprising how fast the indoor 440/400 dash is over with.

Down the first straightaway and into the first curve, Terry slipped a bit on the track as he tore a bit too strongly into the curve. He fell about six yards behind Niehouse and two others, but recovering quickly, Terry passed the second two in the pack on the second straight away. But Niehouse had the luck of being in the lead on the inside track, and he had been well-coached, and he knew he simply had to turn it on from the start to even hope to win against Terry. Terry hung and crept ever-closer behind him in the third turn, burning energy. He tore into Jim on the too-short straight-aways, gaining yards. He gained on Jim like a jackrabbit in the last straight away, but it was not quite enough to catch him at the tape. Second place in his first competition 440.

"You were eating his lunch, Terry," said quiet Charlie Switzer, when Terry strode back up to our "encampment". Charlie was one of the few two-minute half milers in the state who could give Niehouse a bit of competition.

"Yeah, but I slipped on the first turn, and didn't burn fast enough on the remaining turns," answered Terry.

"There won't be a next time like that, I'll say," said Gary. We weren't sure Terry heard that. He just smiled, sat down and dug out his favorite, bananas, and asked, "Anybody got sunflower seeds?" Wendell, always loaded, obliged.

The 60 Yard Dash Preliminaries

An hour later, the 60 yard dash prelims were up. We hustled down from the nose-bleed section where freshmen had retreated, back to the CHS group down midway, at the end of the straightaway. From there, we broke out the binoculars, and watched John Riggins[4] from tiny Centralia, Kansas run a 6.7 prelim for fastest time in his BB class, and the amazing Bornkessel from Kansas City run a 6.6 prelim to top the other big name hurdlers in the class AA 60 yard dash. They were just a few tenths off Bob Hayes' national record. It was, of course, an old dirt track.

Then Ganstrom and Collins ran 6.7s in the Class A prelims, and we knew we were *there*. Not just Terry, but two more of our guys from no-where Concordia had just lit up the 60 yards/55 meters almost as fast as the amazing hurdler Bornkessel from the giant Kansas City Shawnee Mission North. Then came Terry.

His first heat. Certain parts of the crowd, mainly runners from other towns and cities, stood up. The eerie quiet settled in which always precedes the starts in running events. "Guns up!" shouted Betts. Betts stood like Ezekiel, watch in hand, as a dozen of us popped up with watches too. A mysterious tension shivered in the air.

173

A split second after a starting gun fires, some people blink. Those who blinked missed the crowd of fairly accelerating sprinters dig out from the blocks. Those who stared hard saw red silk disappear from the starting blocks and become an instant three yard lead. Terry's acceleration took your breath away.

Terry hit the tape at 6.4. On a dirt track. It was Bob Hayes' record, all over again. The Red Silk Streak from "no-where" had given the "big boys" notice.

Years later people still go quiet, and struggle really hard to find words to describe what they saw. Most say Terry ran so smoothly you could place a champaign glass on his head and maybe it wouldn't fall off. Any sprinter knows that every sprinter *always* tears up the track with some kind of excruciating effort, or strain, or at least a grim face. *Not Terry. He ran like he was in another world. Serene. Untouchable.*

Coach Betts told the papers it was "simply unbelievable, his acceleration."

Terry ran the 6.4 again in the Finals.

He was showing us something all-right. I talked this over with Gary. We were trying to gather it in and make sense of it.

From then, the crowds just got bigger and strangely more quiet.

Chapter 16
A TIME FOR EVERY PURPOSE

In all of 1967, bizarre winds swept into, and pounded the nation.

The nation was deeply torn and suffering waves of urban riots, conflicts and violence over race issues, the war, the sexual revolution, the escalating nuclear arms race, and now women's rights. *February:* Fierce fighting broke out between the Viet Cong versus the US/South Vietnam forces in Operation Cedar Crest. U.S. forces increase to nearly 500,000 and the annual spending for the war reaches $80 billion inflation adjusted 1967 dollars per year[5] (or $ 388 billion in 2008 annual dollars). *March:* Martin Luther King, Jr. publicly states his opposition to the war. Muhammad Ali is stripped of his world boxing titles, and imprisoned due to his refusal to enter military service because of his religious beliefs. *July:* In Seattle, white feminist Gloria Martin organizes radical women and publishes the "Radical Women's Manifesto". *September:* The sensational African-American actress Nichelle Nichols (as Uhuru, in Star Trek) carves out new roads to opportunities for minority women. Together these two feminists ignite heated debates over women's rights. The battle explodes in bedrooms, boardrooms, in high schools, at family meals, in work places, and on campuses. The battles against "the system" were significantly boosted by the scorching comic genius of the spectacularly popular and controversial Smothers Brothers Comedy Hour on CBS. **Fall 1967:** The most intensive bombing attacks in world history were unleashed on North Vietnam, with terrible power but incomplete success. Since before Christmas 1967, Paul Simon's top song "Silent Night/7 o'clock News" sent chills down spines throughout the world as it bitterly chronicled these spiraling terrors.

In Kansas, these bitter winds, revolutions, and other amazing rarities played out in ways rarely seen before or since. Of course, from the coasts, these storms and wonders blowing into Kansas were out of sight, not "on record"...

Solomon's Advice? February, 1967

"That's all he said?" I asked sister Sue. "Hard to believe," I lamely offered. I was trying to fix my mind on what she told me the school "counsellor", Mr. Enoch Twuertweiller, had said. Sue and I had finished washing the dishes and were sitting at the kitchen table after supper. Mom had gone downstairs to do laundry.

Mr. Twuertweiller had been one of two school advisement counselors, and he had been at CHS since the late 1940s. He was short. When he stood on his toes, his Lenin-looking cap would barely pass Sue's nose.

Ol' Twuert was definitely a distracting kinda guy. One distraction was the left-front gold incisor tooth in his smile, which some British dentist had installed during

World War II, so he said, after an alleged bar-fight with Her Majesty's Sailors. We had doubts about his story, given his size. Another distraction he radiated was his habit of crunching and gulping down raw garlic, and trying to cover it up with Listerine gargle and Black Jack gum. (Some folks said Ol' Twuert was from somewhere east of east Germany, maybe even Romania, where people thought garlic was great for staving-off pneumonia, colds, and the shingles). Another distracting thing about him, if he forgot his cap that day, was you could spot him in a crowd, especially outside in the sunlight, his bald knob gleaming like the polished hood of a silver Edsell. But the darndest and most distracting thing about Twuert wasn't any of these quirks. It was what my sister Sue, the Amazon-woman who rode with bikers, had told me that Ol' Tweurt and the main school counsellor, Mr. Van Kotten were giving out as career advice to "girls".

"It was creepy-enough, going in there," Sue said. "You know, the garlic, the gold-tooth, the whole nine yards. But February is 'career-advisement time' for girls, like Betts said over the intercom. And the sign-up sheets were a lot more filled-up for Mr. Van Kotten. So, I said to myself," Sue continued, "What the hell ? Twuert can't be any more weird than Grandpa Tom who used to blow blue cigar smoke at me and threaten to show me his pickled pigs' feet in Mason jars in their basement, every Sunday when Mom sent you and me over to visit him and Grandma Bessie."

"Uh-huh. I remember..." I croaked out.

Sue continued, "I got in there, and he asked me...'Hey kiddo, you want some gum?' "

" 'No, I'm here for some ideas about college, and some jobs' " I said.

"You related to *Roger* Hamilton?"

" 'Yeah.' " I said.

"He has an interesting future..."

" 'Yeah, I want one too...' I told him. So I tried to tell him what I wanted with advice." Sue continued, "I'd like to live in Colorado. I've got three brothers, so I've grown up pretty much having to stick up for myself, to keep up with them. I can take care of myself. I don't know what I want exactly, but maybe something outdoors, some work with a challenge. What do you suggest?' I figured I had laid it out pretty good to him. But you know what that crap-head said?" Sue leaned across the table to me. I could see that yellow-blaze in her dark brown eyes, which we all got from Mom.

"Well, you got three choices, sweetheart. You can be a school teacher, a nurse, or a secretary. College could help you with that, or vo-tech school. It's stuff you can go back to, after you raise your kids."

"That's it. That's all he said. He sat there, chewing gum like a stupid cow chomping on a cud. I told him, 'Hey. My Mom is assistant personnel director at the hospital. She says there's even college degrees for jobs like that. I want to see what the colleges have to offer me.' Then that snot-ball asked, 'What's your GPA?' I told him, 'It's good enough. And I want to see those books you got on the colleges up there on your shelf.' "

"He said, 'Okay. You can look them over, out in the lobby here. But a lot of the college programs are kinda hard on women. Like I said, your best shots, given your GPA, the college programs, and the jobs out there for women, are school teacher, nurse or secretary'."

"So I asked him, 'What if I want to be a something else, a dentist, or a police officer?' That crap-head said, 'There aren't many women with the moxie or the brains for that, sweetheart. It's a guy's world out there. But I guess you could give it a *try*. You still got a few years, so you're not wasting time yet.' "

Sue gave a long sigh. "He's lucky I said, 'Excuse me', and grabbed those college book catalogues off his shelf, and got out of there before that gold tooth of his got me to re-locate it somewhere down his throat. *Sonofabitch.*' "

Pretty much, it came to me then. I figured I should stare harder at the way the house rules were stacked.

"I am Woman" February, 1967, 1122 Willow

"You guys are going to have to step up. I'm not the only one breathing around here." Dad bobbed his head back and forth, raised his eyebrows, and didn't commit much to say to Mom. Dad was religious about two things in the way of household work: he cooked up bacon and scrambled eggs on Sunday mornings, while Mom and us got ready for Mass, and he drove the old Dodge flatbed, carrying the fifty gallon trash can of ashes and burnt-out cans to the dump south of town just west of Fahring's farm, on a regular once a month basis. Roger, for his part, sometimes came along with Dad and me, but when we got to the city dump, Rog snuck off to shoot rats with his carefully hidden .22 pistol.

"Mom'll skin you, if she ever comes across that pistol," I warned Roger. He just shrugged, and dodged off to leave the throwing of the trash into the dump to me and Dad. I was right, about Mom. Mom saw gun-owners and hunters as "Bambi Killers," and she had generally banned guns from our house. Her new streak of swearing recently made for some stark impressions. Over washing the dishes these days you'd hear her say, "I *am* gonna shoot that sonafabitch Lyndon, for startin' this crazy Asian war," or "If I wasn't a patient, God fearing-Catholic woman, I'd plug a hole in the backside of that swindler lawyer Jackie Welch right in the middle of Mass as he swaggers down the aisle like Napoleon, toting that Knight of Columbus sword of his."

"Something has gotten into Mom," sister Sue said a couple times, obviously worried.

"If I'm out making money at the hospital," Mom carried on, "putting up with those squirrely nuns, the least you can do is keep up with the chores." She taped a typed list on the kitchen blackboard. We stared like confused rabbits at the blackboard list. "And you, Ryland..." she gave Dad that whip–your-head around look, "You can pick up a bit on doing the general laundry, seeing as how you *do* know how to run washing machines, or..." she finished, "I'll be 'a-cutting your water off at the spout'."

It was a few years before Sue and I could smile at what she meant by that, all those years ago.

"I'll be earning two dollars and seventy five cents an hour up there..." She slapped the goulash on the table. "And typing faster with my left hand than three of those dang nuns and the Major that runs the place put together." We had few doubts about that. She steamed on, "Not like the old days. This time, there are laws about paying us women, and keeping us on." She shifted gears, "Anyway, Chris, you're to pick up on the sweeping, and the mowing come spring." She scowled at Dad sideways about this. His idea of lawn care had been "spray paint the weeds green, the neighbors will never tell the difference." Mom went on, "Chris, you do your own laundry downstairs, and fill the pets bowls in the mornings. Sue will get her assignments when she gets back tonight from running the theatre concession."

Mom sat down with a plop and sighed. Silence spread while she recited the Catholic prayer before meals. When she finished, we started passing food around the table. Mom looked straight at me.

"It's okay, you know, it's good that women go to work. We did in the war. We've got to have a little more, to help Roger cover college expenses in the next years at K-State." She paused. "He told me yesterday he was looking into the National Guard. I guess that's a better way to avoid Lyndon's meat-grinder, if Roger's draft number comes up. If he gets drafted, I'm afraid he'll be blown to pieces in Lyndon's war, or get himself shot in the head during training by some rabid red-neck Missouri Master Sergeant, if he shoots his mouth off. The National Guard and Army training base is somewhere deep in the swamplands in southern Missouri. God knows, people disappear down there, and you never see a hair of 'em again. I can see it coming. Either shot-dead by a deranged Sergeant for mouthing off at him, or eaten alive by a Missouri wild boar, or strung up by those Missouri good ol' boys who are still fighting the Kansas Border and Civil Wars."

Mom was a class-A worrier, for sure. Outside, the temperature was dropping, as a fierce blizzard from the Canadian northlands buried us for the next three weeks in three feet of snow and sub-zero conditions. She would worry about the baby rabbits getting cold at night, as the blizzard hit. I puzzled it out in spurts, to guess why she'd become so good at worries. I read on a brass plaque in the CHS Halls that some brothers in her class of '39 named Bonebrake had been roasted alive in the submarine Arizona in the Pearl Harbor attack. Uncle Norm told sometimes how he almost froze solid in fifteen minutes on deck in the World War II north Atlantic arctic boat supply runs. And there was Uncle Billy Green talking quietly over Thanksgiving dinners about what it was like to drive a jeep for General George Patton, into the Nazi death camps. Slowly, these pieces pulled together in my head. I scoffed a bit at mom's worries at the table that day, but only for some months more.

Our Winters in the Undiscovered Country

In the central plains, these times of February, March and some weeks into April are marked by bizarre climate contrasts. Temperatures may drop to minus twenty or thirty degrees in minutes, and blizzards hit the far west and northern counties. They can pile up drifts that cover twenty foot tall barns, or dump eighteen inches of ice and bring power outages that last several months.

The beauty in these acts of nature is as stunning to the eye and soul as staring out to the galaxies from a space suit. Icicles hang in jagged, surreal formations from wires, trees and houses. Bright sparkling snow drifts shoot tiny rainbows into your eyes as you climb these mounds as tall as sand dunes in the great deserts. You top the crest of the drifts to breathlessly survey an ice-world cousin of the polar caps, a dazzling crystal vista ruled by lone circling hawks.

Stranded state politicians and cattle both freeze solid, and folks do wonder about them, for days or weeks, until they are found frozen harder than the meatballs in your freezer. Never mind that one week before, in the same counties, the thermometers topped out in the seventies.

* * *

Out here, the greatest experience is when the months of winter through the spring help teach us the deepest lessons, by the passage from the frozen bitters of winter to the spring's promise of life renewed, from seeming death to life. In Terry's exile from school, his return, and extraordinary track performances we would learn the lessons of renewal in this cycle of life, in the winter and spring of 1967. However, the same parallel months of the following two years would present this cycle to us with the great lessons agonizingly reversed. As the revolution, assassinations and the growing war bore viciously down on us, it seemed we saw the greatest of promise fade into the devouring dark. And yet a light would shine for us onto a path back...

...One Year Later, 1968

January 20, 1968, Concordia, Just East of Town

Sleet and snow drove hard at the front door at forty miles per hour, making it difficult for Terry to pull the door open easily. The door slammed hard behind him, as he stared from the doorway, stamping his shoes clear of the ice and snow on the drenched rubber mat. It was break time at DJ's dance hall, east of town. The hanging red, blue and white lamps cast enough light that Terry could scan the bar tables spread out to the left, which led up to the bar. It was lit up with a Hamm's "The Land of Sky Blue Waters" neon sign, with flowing waterfalls pouring into a Minnesota lake so clear you could see down deep into the waters, even from across the room.

A friendly hand waved at Terry, as a whistle floated across the room,
"Over here."

Terry trotted over, having spotted a few guys he recognized in a small group at a table. The hand that waived belonged to John Luecke.

"Pull up a chair, man," John piped. "Guys, this is Terry Householter."

Several guys introduced themselves. They were from out-of-town, but now were students at the newly opened Junior College.

"Hey, man. That's the real thing," Terry said in low tones, pointing to one guy in uniform. The uniformed guy smiled back. His bright red hair, cropped close in a buzz, distracted Terry a bit from the U.S. Marine uniform.

"Yeah. Sign up and the beginnings of induction for me were pretty recent," the Marine replied. "Surprised that I got a leave for Christmas break, or rather, New Years."

"When do you have to go back?"

"I'm out on the bus in two days. Down to the airbase in Salina, and back out to Camp Pendleton."

"You know, I remember you. Aren't you from Beloit, and didn't you run track?"

"Yup. I was one of your so-called 'competition' in the 100 yard dash. I was running against you the day you buried the state record, and the rest of us by fifteen yards..." Terry just shrugged, smiling. He studied the Marine's uniform, while the other guys asked the Marine a few questions.

"So what's it like?" Terry asked, putting his question to the Marine during a lull in the conversation.

The Beloit guy pulled a long suck on a twenty ounce Coors draft, in the quiet before he answered. The glass smacked down hard on the table, making some long seconds of distraction. The guys around the table leaned in to hear the Marine's answer, trading nervous side-glances.

"You know, there's some real killers out there in the bootcamp Sergeants. They want you to get it that when you set butt down in 'Nam, being shot at is gonna happen to you."

"Jesus..." replied several guys.

"Well, it's a long haul from anything about Jesus."

"How do you *feel* about it?" asked Terry.

"Well, it's a long ways from Kansas. But it's the right thing, and somebody has to have the balls to do it."

"Hi, Terry." A waitress stopped at the table, interrupting the conversation. "Can I get you something?"

"Yeah. You got any Coors?"

"Yessir, be right back."

The "Foosball" crowd in the bar erupted. The juke box ground to silence after finishing the song "Mrs. Brown" by Herman's Hermits.

Floor's a little sticky. Maybe a cig... thought Terry.

"Would you like a Lucky Strike?" Terry offered the Marine from Beloit.

"Sure. But I can't be on these too heavy. They'll run my ass when I get back," cracked the Marine.

"Surely not worse than track practices did, huh?"

The Marine paused long, and shifted his eyes back and forth between pondering Terry's question and ogling the waitress delivering Terry's Coors, as she bent over to give back change and flash some heart-pounding cleavage directly in front of both guys' eyes.

"Might be jail bait..." John Luecke teased.

"Huh. I'll leave that to you," the Marine drawled. "Actually, no."

"No what?" Terry asked.

"No, our track practices were just as bad-ass as the Marine Corp in running your butt off, to tell you the truth, Terry. It helped me adjust. The Marine drew another long pull of the Coors, and slowly set his glass down.

"You're about to tear up the track and kick some national-ass out there at Fort Hays State, aren't you, Terry?" Luecke asked, changing the subject, referring to Terry's track scholarship.

"I, yeah," Terry stammered. An awkward pause followed. "I want to run, for sure. But I'm saying school's not for me. In fact, the college thing, it's not doing it for me. I'm thinking about maybe enlisting."

"You're kidding," replied John, as widening eyes spread around the table from Terry's statement.

"No."

"Terry, you're the fastest nineteen year-old in the world. Olympic gold, man, I can smell it on you," the Marine himself said in disbelief at this news.

"Yeah."

"And you, you're sure about this?" asked John, exchanging a worried glance with Terry and the Beloit Marine.

"I can always run. It's only a year over there, and you're back. True? I can be back in a year or so, stronger than ever on that count. It's really more what you said... it's right, and somebody's got to have the balls to do it."

The seconds stretched out long and sobering as a flat tire in a blizzard. John rubbed a pain in the back of his neck with his left hand. The juke box kicked in with a tune that carried an ache.

"Gary Lewis and the Playboys, This Diamond Ring," said Terry, breaking the silence.

The Marine nodded. *Man, that feels like a long time back.*

The silence grew as the group listened to the famous song, each harboring nervous thoughts about the drift of the conversation. They drained two more rounds of beers and Terry plugged a couple more dimes in to ring up another Gary Lewis tune, and "A Hard Day's Night" by the Beatles.

"Okay. So. What branch do you think?" Terry asked the Marine, as the Beatles song rolled on.

"Well obviously, I'm a Marine."

"So they're the best, except for maybe, Green Berets, Navy Seals...?"

"Some say. But we don't do deep-sea around here, do we? There are no brothers like the Marines. And besides, they don't lose," the Marine continued, "and if you don't mind me saying so, that's you all over."

Ringo's riveting, fabulously timed, kick-ass drums behind "Hard Day's Night" drove the sentiment of the age deep into their hearts, to echo down the years. A blast of wind blew spinning snowflakes into the bar, as a shaded figure in a long coat stepped through, wearing shiny black boots. The dark figure took a step back, and shoved the door back against the snow and wind. His red-brown hair became visible under a hanging lamp.

"Hey, John," Terry cried out, "It's Ken Campbell..." Terry stood to catch Ken's attention and to waive him over to join the table. The jukebox spun into quiet.

"I'll be thinking it over," Terry said quietly to the Marine from Beloit, as Ken strode over.

"I'm so glad to see you, Ken. Been taking care of yourself?" Terry asked. He and John rose, taking the lead to extend a handshake and back-pounding hugs to the snow-blown Ken.

"Good to see you, man..." replied Ken. They swapped more hugs, smiling deep at each other. Ken seemed to glow a bit in his new uniform.

"Hey, we got guys to introduce to you here around the table," Terry called out, "This guy's from Beloit, and you can see he's in your line of work..." The two United States Marines now stood shaking hands, as a hush spread lightly over the bar-crowd. In the silence, the outside wind rose, and whistled fiercely through the cracks of the door.

* * *

By late January 1968, U.S. Forces in Vietnam and politicians in Washington D.C. were reeling from the combined effects of the infamous Tet Offensive when North Vietnamese forces attacked the US Embassy in Saigon, and took an invasion into the South. Five hundred students protested at Dow Chemical headquarters, the maker of the highly toxic defoliant Agent Orange. February: Eugene McCarthy, the peace candidate in the New Hampshire primary, nearly defeated the politically plummeting incumbent President Lyndon Johnson who was staggered by the immense North Vietnamese invasion and the rising racial and anti-war protests and conflicts in American cities. By March, a broken-hearted LBJ announced he would not run for re-election as President. April 5: Martin Luther King Jr. was assassinated by racist bigots in Memphis. June 8: Robert Kennedy too was gunned down a few seconds after his California presidential primary victory speech. After all this, hope died in the hearts of very many Americans for more than a generation.

In a cold November, Richard Nixon barely won the Presidency. The winds of the Storm rose higher, year after year. Terry and the rest of us were sucked into this dizzying maelstrom of hell vs hope...

Late February 1968, U.S. Marine Recruiting Office, Salina, Ks

Terry drove to Salina through an ice storm. He pulled the borrowed Chevy slowly into the strip mall, trying not to skid. Firm thoughts swirled in his mind, wordless, but deep... *time to step up...might as well be us...* His Lucky Strike burnt strong and bright against the steely cold north winds. A few minutes later, in the temporary warmth of the office, the recruiter asked in a sugary Georgia drawl, "Well kid, ya want a week or two play in your fly-out date? Or you want to kick-ass and go now?"

"Can it be early April? I got a few things to set straight the next six weeks," Terry asked. *I gotta clean out my stuff from Ft. Hays State. Take some things down to John. Talk to Mom a couple times, break her in on it so they all don't freak. Run a couple bar trips with Skip and John.*

The recruiter sat for awhile, lifting his eyebrows and squinting, chewing a plug of Red Man, thinking if there were loopholes he could work out for this kid to give him this much time.

"Okay, kid. We'll ink this down as two weeks from now, and that'll maybe give you what you want. Don't get yourself married or a DUI in the meantime, and don't leave the territory. No guarantees. You'll get a friendly letter from the Corps at your home address. Watch for it. You got a thirteen month tour. You can re-up. Sign right here. Leave me your phone, in case I forget something, or they come up with something new."

April 1968, Salina, Kansas

"To everything there is a season..."

Ecclesiastes c. 3 King James Bible version

The door to the Marine recruitment office in Salina squeaked, closing behind him. It was his last time here now. It was Terry's time of bizarre contrasts. The keys to the borrowed Chevy tinkled, coming out of his Wrangler jeans pocket in the early-April winds. Thin, wispy clouds strung out like stretched cotton candy across the cobalt sky. The smells of mown-clover and early lilac bushes came to tickle his nose. Terry breathed in these scents of April, the sweet, familiar traces of Kansas, which calmed the strange electric panic in his throat. *The panic you get,* he reflected, *when your back wheels slide left in a rain. That battery acid taste rises up your throat, and your head spins, and you have a second to turn the steering wheel left to halt the spin,* he imagined, *and maybe you'll miss that truck barreling at you from the fog ahead. Oh yeah, all this feels weird, all-right.* Terry shook his head to balance his realities. *The ink is drying in there, on those last minute Marine Corps forms...*

His thoughts raced across the strange, opposing visions: *It's track season, I can smell it. Wendell, Pete, Gary, they're blazing it out on the asphalt back home. I bet they're chasing down Collins. Clover, lilacs...they always trigger the track season in you...*

He flipped the keys of John Luecke's '57 to his left hand, and stared at his right hand. *This hand signed all those Marine forms...school's all gone...the real deal is at hand.* He chuckled nervously at this unintended pun. He drew in another breath of lilac and clover. *Ken's over there...we'll meet up...somebody's gotta take care of this business, and it might as well be us...*

Terry stood silent as a church mouse next to the Chevy for a few minutes, the keys in his left hand, staring at his right hand. He drew in more breaths of lilac and clover to still his dizzied mind. He flipped the keys back to his right hand, and took a last deep breath. *Okay. Time to go see Mom now, five minutes across town.*

In mid-April 1968, Terry flew out to Parris Island, Camp Pendleton, near Oceanside California, for ten weeks basic training. As Ken and others told him, it was a whole different, brutal world. The Drill Instructors were near-killers. Right after landing, the Corps was out to erase the new recruits' past, their identity, their world. Shaved, slapped around, and screamed at was the friendly starting point. Up before twilight, in shorts and t-shirts for drills, running and push-ups, it all came to much worse in the live-action training. Beaten, shot at with live fire, things were just different then from today. The only starting similarity between then and now are the four rows and fifteen sets of yellow footprints with heels painted together at a forty-five degree angle where new grunts just off the planes are ordered to stand silent at attention, while being introduced to the Uniform Code of Military Justice. The wide, flat fields, the bowling alley, the flat, grim wooden benches, the ever-present palm trees, the two and three-story white washed, non-air-conditioned barracks of Pendleton in those days, live starkly in every Marine's memory. But they are not as searing as the memory of their Drill Instructors who haunted their dreams almost as much as 'Nam itself, then and now. None of us who weren't there can pretend to know what it was like, nor what it was leading to.

Chapter 17
RED SILK RISING, APRIL 1967

Chapman Relays, March 31, 1967

Our silver bus carried the upperclassmen, and a yellow International Harvester 1960 school bus filled with us freshmen and sophomores, pulled into the stadium at Chapman High School. It was a warm, partly cloudy day, with highs in the lower seventies. The spirits of Kansas were blasting the field with gusts up to sixty miles per hour, spreading a cloud of dust, and throwing down the gauntlet to sprinters and hurdlers. The races would be run from the north going into the teeth of the vicious south wind, which threatened to hurt our times in the events.

Gary shouted, "Asphalt boys, asphalt!" as we stepped off the bus.

Back home, we were benefitting from the new asphalt track at CHS. Asphalt was not as fast as rubber tracks. But there were no rubber based surface tracks in the entire state. Even KU was still using pressed cinder. The fastest current tracks were asphalt. Ours, and the new one being laid down in Salina, and the brand new one at Chapman where we were to run today, were the only ones in the state. "Finally, we can burn times here like we can do at home, if the winds allow," muttered Gary to Wendell.

At several relays, like Chapman, our freshmen relay teams were allowed to compete in separate relays, to earn points for the team. Our half mile and mile teams, anchored by Gary, were determined to wipe out class records and spin times as fast as some of our varsity team's competitors. We'd get to run right before the varsity relays, toward the end of the meet. We were pumped.

Betts had the trainers unveil a box-like Army tent, low to the ground, five feet high, fifteen feet deep inside, and twenty feet wide. It had a back wall and an open front, but no floor. Our money was bet that Charlie Blosser coughed it up for nothing from his trove of World War I and II tents. The trainers staked this combination new home, medicine lodge, and meditation temple out beneath the big elm trees at the southwest end of the stadium, where afternoon shade and winds could waft away any concentrations of heat.

The Chapman invitational relay was quite an operation. Eight schools were represented, some from big towns like Topeka and Salina. Gary and I wouldn't do much for most of the afternoon, waiting for the relays. We wandered over to the concessions, bought some chili dogs, and ran into Alan Luecke and Louis.

"What you up to?" I asked the two Iron Men.

"Not stoking up on goodies that, if we were running, we'd just throw up later. Must be nice to be a sprinter," joked Louis.

"We're going to watch the drama," Alan remarked.

"The drama?" asked Gary, between bites of chili dog.

"The two mile run, boys," Alan clarified. "A new event this year in track. It brings out the best in the distance guys, Jerry, Lyle and Ron Smith."

"They're running in the shadow of Bill Dotson," Louis ventured. "The story around Jamestown, where Bill and I come from, is that Bill the legend starting serious running when his dad's pickup kept breaking down at their farm. Bill found it easier to run miles across the vast hills to round up the cattle on foot. Just run 'em down! Can you imagine? Jerry's cut from the same stuff. Can't stop running."

"I got dad's Navy binoculars," I said, changing the subject. "We can watch the guys from up in the stadium."

Weaving through the crowd, Alan pointed and said, "Let's get up high...Come on." He waved Louis to join him and they led us up the stadium stairs to the nosebleed section. Up there we could whip out the binoculars and watch the spectacles unfold before us.

Across the center field, we could see the small teams of two milers doing stretches and warm-ups. "Okay boys, check out the south end," Alan said, looking through the binoculars. "Spot the red silk, you know. One of them has a white t-shirt." He thrust the binoculars at Gary.

Gary took a long look, and smiled, "Yeah."

"What's up?" I asked.

"Look for yourself." I took the glasses.

"Uh-huh. *10:05.* Jerry's still wearing the T-shirt from cross-country days," explained Alan. "Hoping to crack that two-mile time."

We sat at the top, downing chili dogs and drinking up cokes and lemonades, and watched our way through the Iron Men's magic moment. It was the beginning of demonstrating the results of their long road of pain. Jones and Smith won first and second in the two-mile run that afternoon, burying the competition in 10:45 and 10:51. Not fabulous times, but respectable this early in the season.

An eye-popping moment came when Salina's Jim Niehouse, the state's distance star set a new Chapman field mile record in 4:30.5. Like Dotson, he lapped the slowest runners, with Red Silk CHS Lyle Pounds and Doug Rivers pacing third and fourth, some twenty-five yards behind.

"You don't see milers get lapped every day. Niehouse is chasing Dotson's records for sure," blurted Gary. Incomparable Bill had run 4:20.2 nine years before, warming up to even better times. Gary hand-timed the mile run. We all imagined the shadow of slender Bill at the 4:20 mark, some ten yards ahead of the blazing and fierce Niehouse, who was fighting with all his might the vicious, gusting winds in his face at the final turn.

"I couldn't possibly do what these guys do, Gary," I confessed, nodding toward our own Iron Men. "Their sacrifice is astonishing."

"They are alien, aren't they...". We just sat, holding our heads. Alan and Louis beamed back at us.

By mid-afternoon, the capricious and heartless south-wind was still raging. At unannounced moments a sky-scraping, rumbling roar could be heard descending on the track. In breathtaking gusts of wind and sand, the hurdles would shift or blow around on the track, with several of the lighter ones blown over. Trainers and volunteers ran out to put sandbags on the base of the hurdles, to hold them in place as the warm-ups for the 120 yard (110 meter) hurdle races were setting up.

"The point count isn't great," we overheard Coach Betts say to Coach Smith, outside our low-sitting Army tent. It had its back slanted and staked with huge spikes, against the south wind. Several of us had taken refuge in the tent for a break from the winds, after cruising to observe the pole vault, shot put and discus events underway. Our freshmen relay might actually be important for points. We strained to overhear Betts, whose top half was cut-off from view by the low hang of our tent.

"The Iron Men so far have saved our butts. Jones and Smith, Pounds and Rivers turned in second and third places in the two- mile, and the mile against that machine Niehouse out there. But in this effort, they burned out, so we fell to a flat fifth place in the two- mile relay. I didn't expect that," Betts exclaimed. "But eagle-man Charlie Switzer came close to pushing Niehouse in the half-mile. Charlie took second place. They were running like demons against the wind, pushing right at two minutes. God, it takes guts to do that. I can hardly believe the courage of these kids."

A brief blast of howling wind slapped us, strong enough to steal conversation away from the coaches for a couple seconds. Catching his breath, Betts continued, "No team is dominating out there. We're just not pulling points in the field events. Hell, only wild man Pete Foster pulled out fourth place in the javelin, barely out-tossing Swaggart. Son-of-a-gun Pete hasn't thrown that damn thing even six times in his life, and he's just a dang sophomore. Hurdles, javelin, high jump, pole vault, he does it all. If he was a year older, I'd give him two names, Jesus and Moses, and enter him as twins and we'd win damn near everything," Betts joked. "For the moment, we're in third place, thanks to the Iron Men and spear-chucker Pete."

"The hurdles and relays have got to come through," Coach Smith worried out loud, "because the distance men and sprints can't make all of the point spread up against the better teams, like Salina, and Topeka Washburn."

The tent rattled and popped like rifle shots in the winds. One of those deep-toned, freight-train groans descended on the field at the edge of a huge downdraft, and hit like a sledgehammer on the field. It spewed dust like a sandstorm, and splattered birds northward, helpless and tumbling across the sky. It was an ominous, deterring scream thrown down upon all of us from Mother Nature.

* * *

187

The hurdlers fought seriously against the vicious winds, slowed by a good second of time. The winds momentarily faded, as the preparations for the sprints, and sprints relays, took shape in the lengthening hours.

The gusts were intermittent in the late afternoon as the 100 yard dash men drifted into the starts areas. Our relay team guys, plus Luecke and Louis, returned to the top and middle part of the stands, next to the main runway to watch the sprints. Coach Smith joined us. We stood witness with five stopwatches and a few binoculars. We watched Terry sit out in the middle of the field, doing only a few stretches, just wiggling his legs. It seemed like nearly two dozen guys, in different uniforms, drifted past and stopped to talk with Terry. After a couple minutes, they'd lean backward and laugh, and maybe give Terry a high five. All the time, Collins and Ganstrom were down near the starting blocks, stretching and running a bit, and placing their starting blocks. The asphalt track would allow no slippage of the blocks, from loose dirt. This would help shave parts of seconds off the race times. However, the gusting winds would beat down any advantage there.

Minutes passed. House still sat in the field, greeting lots of folks, popping up to stretch a little, and looking like he didn't have a care in the world. The announcer belted out the advent of the 100 yard dash, and only then did House grab his bag and stroll over to the starting blocks. Sprinters were readying the last second adjustments of their blocks, jumping to stay loose, or backing into their blocks. Terry loosely jumped and shifted back and forth in front of his blocks.

"Now that the race is about to start, he says nothing, to no-one down there," spied Gary, with my binoculars in hand.

"Check out the dark glasses." Luecke pointed.

"No kidding," replied Gary.

House was wearing prescription, black nylon, dark-lens glasses on, and he was staring straight ahead.

"Black Panther glasses," I ventured. We wondered silently what it would be like, to line up against him in his Red Silk and Black Panther glasses.[6]

"They're probably peeing in their pants down there," said Pete, in what had to be the observation of the season.

Terry's red-shocked hair blew wildly in the winds. He was the last to lower down into the blocks.

"He's not always perfect in his starts. But, man, he's drilling at it and getting better," said Gary, still hogging the binoculars.

The sprinters rose up and we looked for the gun-puff, as the gusting winds rose a bit, flapping and popping Old Glory on the silver pole near the starting line, like a whip in the wind.

House was out low and fast against the gale, like a screeching Chinese bottle rocket. "Seven secrets perfect", he was five yards ahead at eight yards into the race. accelerating like a motorcycle, his Red Silk uniform whipped wildly against the wind. He sailed like a silk arrow down the track, suspended in a timeless nirvana, loose and free.

We stared as two other Red Silks emerged from the pack at the thirty-yard mark, putting distance between themselves and the rest of the multicolored pack. They ran with a similar silky smoothness, in the tailwinds of Terry. By the eighty-yard mark, Terry led by seven yards over Wendell and Steve Collins, who led yet again by four yards over the straining, buffeted pack.

The winds tore at the Red Silk sprinters with a cruel revenge. Terry took the ribbon, leaning smoothly. A meet record of 10.1. Respectable, yet he was held back by three, or maybe four-tenths of a second by the winds, which still rocketed in forty-mile-per-hour gusts. First, second, and third places, 10.3 for the junior Collins, 10.6 for Wendell. The red silk gauntlet had been thrown into the snarling winds.

A needed rest for the sprinters came in the sprint and distance medley relays, where we had entered our second-best team of runners. They took first and second in those relays. Then the 220 was up. The Red Silk Trio of sprinters lined up on the far side of the track. They had the wind to their backs for about twenty yards of the start, but then came the tight unbanked curve, and then the long 100 yard home stretch. Against the stifling winds again.

So much yardage to run against vicious winds in the 200 meter, or 400 hundred meters, is draining to the body and spirit, and is exhausting well beyond the bounds usually trained-for. Half a second and more can be mercilessly sucked right out of your time. Midway down the track, in the strain, your arms and legs seem to mutate into pain-filled, un-moveable rubber stumps. Oxygen literally drops away from your brain as you struggle to maintain concentration and pace against the wind-boosted energy drain. A few athletes usually drop out, especially in the 400, woozy from the oxygen-drain from the brain.

Facing the competing athletes and the exhausting winds, the two Red Silks, Collins and Terry, backed into their blocks. Seeing across the field through the binoculars, Gary said, "The Black Panther glasses are on again." This was the first heat. Two heats would be run, with no finals, just the best times sorted for the final rankings. Niehouse was in the first heat. He was Salina's best shot at the sprints. The second heat would pit Wendell against, no doubt, the first heat's best times, as well as his second heat competitors.

The crowd rose to watch in silence. Multiple stopwatch holders stared intensely for the gun-puff. Terry soared again against the winds, as his greatest competitor. He broke the tape at 21.8 seconds (21.6 secs 200 meters), leading the second place Niehouse by an amazing seventeen yards (23.2), with Collins in third (23.5) and the rest of the pack ten yards further behind. Terry had won against the remaining normal human competitors by an astounding thirty meters. The brutalizing south wind which tore at him for the last 110 yards, beat him back by a half a second.

In the second heat, startling sophomore Wendell won the heat, tying for second place with Niehouse himself of the first heat (at 23.2). For the first time, Wendell out-zipped the pace of Steve Collins, edging himself into the top rank of state sprinters.

Then the bell tolled for us. We freshmen were up. Our second team of relay speedsters earned four points in second place in the mile relay. The torch now passed to Gary and us, in the half mile 4 X 200 relay. We barely came out first in 1:46.1, for five more points, with Sacred Heart second,

Then came the relay with all the chips on the table: the half mile 4 X 200 varsity relay. Collins, Ganstrom, Switzer and House were arrayed against the vicious wind. They came in at 1:32.6 (1:32.2 m), a pretty decent meet record, a second and a half faster than the old mark. House anchored at a blistering and incredible 21.5 (21.2), considering the winds. All that Coach Smith would say over the stopwatches was, "We'll have to check the record books on this kid..."[7]

Fifteen minutes later, as we were packing up for the bus, word came that the last event, the long jump, was almost over. Betts ambled over to the tent, as we were helping pull up the stakes.

"Terry long-jumped like a dang sail-plane over there. He's out past twenty one feet," Betts broadcast. He then hopped back to the long jump pit, to catch the final jumps.

"Christ," replied Coach Frohardt, who was helping pull up the stakes. "He's only five-foot and eight inches tall. But the kid tops out at twenty-seven, or twenty-eight miles per hour. No wonder he flies forward pretty decent."

On the way home, as the buses lurched perilously in the gusting winds, in the middle of a game of black jack in the back of our bus, Wendell cried out a victorious "21". He scooped in the winning pile of mini-Snickers bars. In the last scoop into his sports bag, he casually put his opinion to us:

"I'll bet there is *no-one* like Terry."

Clay Center, April 6

"Dirt and cinder, but *more* dirt than cinder," Gary commented, as we stepped down from the bus.

"With narrow track lanes and tight turns," I replied. The Clay Center track begged for a make-over. The weather scowled cold and drizzly above us.

"Sure enough. Mushy half-way through the lane," whispered Gary, as we and the upperclassmen sprinters spread around, testing out the weak spots around the track. The day was mostly cloudy, in the low '50s with a chilling north wind. Times and distances were slowed down by a bad combination of the too-wet track, the slight drizzle, and the general chill. Terry turned in a 10.2 which tied the meet's record, but he struggled with the spongy track from start to finish. The Red Silk Comet cranked out a meet record 22.1 seconds 220 (21.8 200 meter) dash that buried Wendell and Steve by a dozen yards, and the rest of the struggling, hypothermic mortals by a dozen yards more. On a slippery, bone-cold dirt track, Terry's time tied last year's State Meet best.

These days were just the beginning. One of the most fantastic performances in state history would be unleashed by Terry the following week, at Abilene.

Mercury Unleashed. Abilene Relays, April 14

190

It was a warm day, seventy degrees, with a very slow south wind, and crystal blue clear skies. Rain had pounded the track and field the day before. Track conditions were no better than the last meet, maybe worse.

Abilene had an old, concrete-poured stadium, with tall elm trees shading the west side, both north and south, at the edge of the stadium. The stadium side straightaway had a set-back starting area of forty some yards. This made a straightaway long enough for the 120 yard high hurdles, without forcing that race to end or start in a curve.

The upper classmen were meeting with Betts in the silver bus. We were the first advance scouts, assigned to report on the track conditions. One word applied: miserable.

"How can we run on this?" Gary asked the rest of us freshmen relay sprinters. We toed the track. "Big cinders. Some of this must be burn-out chunks from a coal fired electric plant, or else it's..."

"...Lava chunks...", I finished Gary's sentence, "And mushy like the devil, more wet dirt than cinder." Gary kept up the micro-analysis, as our group of five tested the track, going north from the fifty yard mark, toward the starting blocks.

There were sodden piles of hay dumped on the sides of the track. Obviously, the Abilene team and coaches had spread the hay to soak up the wetness in the lanes. A little hope to dry the mud came from the overhead sun which shined cheerfully, granting its share of help to firm up the top crust of the track.

"It'll dry some. Might be okay," prophesied Liedtke, a gallant optimist. By mid-afternoon, the elms would put the starting lanes back in the shade, just in time for the hurdles and sprints.

Our field report was given to Betts. He was not happy, nor were the first rank hurdlers and sprinters. The upperclassmen hurdlers and sprinters buzzed around the starts, some grousing, others looking grim. In contrast, the Iron Men stretched their legs out in a few slow laps around the track, somewhat oblivious to the dark pessimism that hovered over the speedsters.

We crossed mid-field, on our way on orders from Betts to help set up our Army tent in mid-field. Out there, the drain-off was better and the clover and grass were dry.

Gary tossed a question to Lyle and the distance men as they loped by, warming up:

"What do you guys think about this place?"

"Thank God we're not getting our butts blown off the field today," Lyle replied. A different perspective they had, for sure.

The meet picked up fast. The stadium filled with a majority of "Abilene Cowboys" fans, lots of them sporting cowboy hats. To our surprise, the Abilene cheerleaders, not usually something you see at track meets, arrived in their cowgirl get ups, short skirts, fringed sleeves on the blouses, and cute little cowgirl hats.

"Definitely an Abilene secret weapon, a hormonal distraction of the strongest kind," opined Alan, in his Sherlock Holmes mode. "New girls for us outsiders to ogle. No doubt they are more ho-hum to the home front boys. Absolutely a devious strategy. This will distract pole vaulters, field men, and speedsters... but we distance guys won't get distracted, we run in too much pain!" We were persuaded his creative imaginings were right, and we steeled ourselves against hormonal distractions.

The Iron Men hummed into action like a well-drilled team of Navy Seals. Salina's distance terror Jim Niehouse laid down notice again that he would eat his state competition alive, by taking out Bill Dotson's league mile record of 4:20 with a state-leading mile of 4:17.2 This indeed was a gauntlet thrown. Unsettled, but not brow beaten, the Iron Men chased him down the track for third, fourth, and fifth places, trumping Jim's point total in the mile. Niehouse replied in a vengeance with a blazing 1:56.6 half mile (1:56.0 800 m) for the state's fastest half-mile so far that year, and for as long as anyone could remember. Eagle man Switzer nobly chased Jim at almost 2:00 minutes flat, for second place. Smith and Jones laid down third and fifth for some points in the two-mile. This kept us in the race for top total points against the little army of distance men put forth by Salina Sacred Heart, led by the near-invincible Knight Niehouse.

Other bright spots dawned. In the broad-jump, House sailed over twenty-one feet for first again, Collins won the high jump, Big Mick, the pride of CHS and your best ally in a bar-fight, snagged second place in the discus, and mild-mannered Greg Tracy copped fifth in the shot-put. This stirred Betts to say around the tent, "Boys, we're not so down on points at this stage. We're showing some life in the field events." And then the 100 yard dash was up.

The soft wind rustled the elm and cottonwood leaves in a sighing song, as the sprinters gathered under the now-growing shade, in the starting blocks areas. Betts and the sprinter crowd had mulled over what to do about the mushy track in the 100 yard dash. Coach Frohardt had been sent off to the local farm coop, to hunt down extra long barn spike nails. The plan was to spike-nail our aluminum starting blocks through their spike hole, with a much, much longer nail. The hope was to compensate, a little, for the speed-stealing and balance-robbing mushiness of the track lanes. At least we lucked out with House getting lane three, which was less soft than lanes four or five, the outside lanes. Wendell, and Collins had bad lanes two and five respectively. Wendell drew the worst one.

House prowled around the outskirts of the starting area near the north goal posts where it was drier, doing his occasional stretches, chatting at ease with folks, and arriving a bit late again. Others worried themselves over blocks placement and track conditions.

From a distance, in mid field at the forty yard line and outside our tent, we younger runners gathered, sprinkled in with hurdler Ron, the Fosters, and a few of the Iron Men. Our plan was to watch the course of the race and sprint along to watch the mid-part of the race, and the finish. Betts had parked himself up a few rows in the stadium, at the 60 yard line, and had planted assistant coaches at the end, all with watches. Something we hadn't seen before, a sort of stand of stairs was parked on wheels at the finish line, with officials looking down, holding stopwatches. We didn't have a stopwatch among us.

Then it happened.
The thing that lies in genetic deep sleep across
several generations, and then returns.

From the side of the field, we couldn't see the start very well through the crowd. The puff of the starting gun came, with the delayed pop of the travelling sound. It all seemed normal, with the rustling of the leaves, and the crowd quieting. The first indication to us on the field was the silent rising of people in the stadium.

We stared through the gaps in the crowd on the field, and caught a glimpse of Terry. What we saw made us feel like children watching an approaching comet.

At forty yards, House was already ten yards ahead of Steve and Wendell. "Holy Christ" arose from somewhere. House sailed at fifty yards with the smoothness of a glass of wine. In the vast silence past fifty yards, Betts roared "Loose! Loose!" In us, the call triggered an electric shock, a skipping of heartbeats. But the call was not needed for Terry. As he sped past midfield, Terry's face shone like he lived in another world.

Gary, the Fosters, and I exchanged blood-drained looks. We took out like Air Force F 4 chase planes pursuing a plummeting satellite, to try to follow along and watch Terry. At seventy yards, Terry was *still accelerating*. The gap to Steve and Wendell expanded to twelve meters, with the stragglers twenty and more behind.

Terry burst the tape. The stadium crowd was stunned into momentary silence, but we team mates screamed our lungs dry. A second and more later, first Steve, then Wendell hit the finish, and then the others straggled through.

Bedlam swamped the officials. We stared in disbelief as one official grabbed Steve and declared him the winner!

In outrage, the CHS coaches and Betts descended on officialdom like winged Valkyres. The idiot official had actually missed Terry, he was so far ahead! Steve, all 190 pounds of him, practically strangled the official on the spot, but barely held himself in check, spurting colorful phrases of denial. All sprinters on the track gathered in a circle around Terry and silently pointed to him, to make clear he was the winner. The erring and flustered stopwatch official was dismissed. The crowd erupted in chaos and astonishment.

Then the stop watch battle began full-blast. The officials on the stand wildly waved watches and arms at each other. An equal number brandished watches with 9.4 seconds as did 9.6. A minority few had 9.5. Betts and company landed on the spot, with four stopwatches, showing 9.4s and 9.5.

The tempest raged for fifteen minutes. Terry just skipped out and retired back to the tent. Gary, the Fosters, and the rest of us crawled into the tent and sat, just watching Terry sit down and unlace his shoes, to put on flats. Steve and Wendell tore in and sat down next to him.

"Do you realize what you have just done?" Steve asked, simply and quietly. Terry only shrugged a little, raised his eyebrows and smiled. Gary and the rest of us couldn't breathe, and even the Fosters, Green, and Wendell could say nothing. They just sat or stood still in a crowd around him. The bedlam beyond at the track buzzed on like a giant, angry hornets' nest.

Suddenly, Terry hopped up and disappeared with coins in hand.

"Well, dudes," he cheerfully cried, "I'm getting some Pepsi, and sunflower seeds."

We sat clueless. Betts finally returned to the tent. He was flushed, and his voice shook.

"Boys," he said, his face flushed and his voice shaking, "The argument over there about Terry, after getting rid of the poor idiot who thought Steve had won the race, was settled on a 9.5, but they rounded it up to a 9.6.[8] That's what they do, they round up a tenth of a second from the average of the watches, if there's a dispute among the watches. More people than our four watches had him closer to 9.4 or 9.45, almost the national record, on this crappy old track. It doesn't matter, 9.6 is the all-time state best. Just so you know..."

Before the day was over, Terry also tied the class A state record in the 220 on the same sloppy track, in 21.6 (21.4), the state's best time. At least this time all the officials were "bright-eyed and bushy-tailed" at the finish line, buttressed by four of the CHS coaches' watches. They all were on the same page with the recorded times. Even though he had to run on a mushy track, Terry was closing in on the state and nation all-time bests.

On the buses home that night, conversations were hushed. What we had seen was still hard to believe. It hung before our eyes, shining.

Concordia Relays, April 18

The April track days spun by us quickly. Training was grueling, four days a week. By April, we would run start drills for a day, followed the next day by relay baton passing drills. Hurdlers would drill hurdles every day. To reach peak conditioning, Mondays and Wednesdays would end with sprinters and hurdlers running "ladders", all at approximately three-fourths speed, in moderately respectable times. A "ladder" is run in timed 100 yards, two 220s, three 330s, four 440s, and is topped off with a 660 yard run. A three minute rest break was granted. And then the "ladder" is run "back down" at slower speeds, tapering off to a single 100. Often, several of us dropped off the ladder in nausea. When you finished relieving yourself on the grass, you got back on the ladder. The severe training paid big benefits by the end of the month.

By April 18th at the Concordia Invitational Relays, on our new home asphalt track, records would fall like leaves in October. At this single meet three state class A, all-time best relay marks would fall to the Red Silk: the mile relay (3:25.8 Switzer, the Fosters, and Terry), the half mile 4 X 200 class A record (at 1:31.0 with Collins, Wendell, Switzer, and Terry) and the all-time 440/400 relay (at 44.0 seconds in yards or 43.7 seconds in meters).

The most dizzying moment dawned on us unexpectedly that day. A pack of state newspaper photographers caught Terry's electrifying 48.0 440 yards (47.7 400 m) anchor leg, faster than the all-school, all-time state best, and equal to fourth in the nation at the time. *Terry had only run two competition 440 yards in his life.* His pace was *more than 20 yards* ahead of the time of the first 440 he ran at the state indoor where he barely lost to Niehouse, who looked on this time, shaking his head. The indoor was the last time Terry would lose. Terry ran a 9.7 in the 100 prelim. He was now the fastest sprinter in the state in all three races, and was closing fast on the top four times in all races in the nation.

Niehouse for his part, ran a blazing 1:57.1 half mile and an equally blazing 4:17.2 mile, which set him atop all middle distance runners in the state. "It was a decent day," Betts told the papers. Multiple state records were reeled in, plus the first three places in the 100, and three in the top four in the 220. The Iron Men in their valiant chase of Niehouse came through with multiple seconds, thirds and fourths in the two mile, the mile, and the 880 yard half mile.

The following week loomed like Mt. Everest. The KU Relays, one of the jewels in the national crown of top Olympic, NCAA, AAU and high school meets, was calling. Thirty thousand spectators and national press coverage were waiting.

Rock Chalk Jayhawk. The KU Relays, April 22 – 23, 1967

The KU Relays is a major track event, one of the top six in the nation. Annual, world, NCAA and national high school records fall each year there, by the half-dozen. The competitors through time read like an alphabetical list of world and Olympic record holders. High school events draw competitors from the mid-regions of the country, sometimes from the coasts. Betts took aim at the best competition from the bigger schools in the state, and from multiple states in the U.S.

At practice Tuesday April 19, Betts explained, "Many greats have started their run there, even out of high school. Many return, year after year. Glenn Cunningham, Wes Santee, Al Oerter, Bill Dotson, Jim Ryun, Billy Mills, Charlie Tidwell. We'll take our shot, this year. Some of these big city teams, they got a lot of fast guys for their relays. Some of their times are better than ours, I'm not gonna lie to you. But you guys are good. Really good. You got a shot. And none of them have Terry." Betts continued, "KU is *Big Time.* The van is taking you guys who have qualifying times and marks. It leaves Wednesday afternoon, at 1 p.m., outside the Shop. If you're going, you're on the list we post after practice today outside the shower room wall. The rest of you will train here, under senior leadership this week."

KU Memorial Stadium is the oldest collegiate stadium west of the Mississippi, finished in 1921 to honor KU students who were World War I veterans. It stands through time, refurbished occasionally, never abandoned. It rests at the bottom of great hills, beneath an over-powering skyline of grand buildings. It is graced by the great voice of the Veterans Bell Tower at the top of the hill, also erected after World War I. You cannot stand in the stadium and hear the great deep bells from above and not feel history, including the defense of the campus in 1863 against pro-slavery Missouri invaders who massacred two hundred men and boys in Lawrence, then set fire to the city, and turned battle onto the campus. The real beginning of the Civil War looms here with the border raids of the late 1850s. A great spirit lives here.

* * *

The small CHS school bus, an International Harvester van, pulled into Lawrence late Thursday afternoon. Rooms were taken at the Eldridge Hotel downtown. It is within walking distance of the campus. Betts told the boys before they stepped out of the van, "This is the best list of talent in the high school division that I've ever seen. It'll be tough on you guys tomorrow, but this is your chance to show 'em. You guys are free to roam around downtown or walk up to the campus after supper," Betts announced, "but curfew and room checks will be made at 9:00 p.m. Don't come up AWOL."

After supper most of the guys roamed around the inviting stores, snack shops and bars along Massachusetts Street. Terry made connections with an old high school friend, who had an apartment up on the big hills near the campus and above Memorial Stadium. These were the days of the growing counter-culture, and KU was a hotbed regional center of all this radicalism and more. Two days later, Wendell winked at Gary and I, saying, "Terry made curfew, with a smile on his face. Terry spent an hour or so being introduced to campus friends, a little beer, and brownies spiced with a certain native plant common along Kansas rivers and fields.""He was a free spirit," John Luecke always said.

The meet picked up speed Friday morning, a cloudless day with meaningless, small, westerly gusts. Relays records fell during the preliminaries at the university and college divisions to a stellar field of athletes capped by one of the two "fastest men in the world", Jim Hines from Texas Southern. He ran in the 100 yard dash and 440 relays. Hines ran a 9.6, but that only equaled Terry's official fastest time on the sodden Abilene track a week before. The KU track at least was a decent, pressed cinder track in good condition. The program of athletes was remarkable.[9]

The 100 yard high school dash preliminary was scheduled for one-thirty-five in the afternoon. The first event up was the 880 relay prelims at ten-thirty a.m., pretty early. The all-time state record was around 1:29 (1:28.4 400 m). "And I think you guys will sometime hit that mark," Betts said on the way to the stadium. "You can push the big boys from Shawnee Mission East, and Wichita East, because Terry can whip both Bornkessel and Walker, their anchormen. The rest is up to you."

Wendell explained to us freshmen two days later after the van had arrived home, with Gary and us waiting outside CHS, "We were spread-out in mid-field, doing stretches and warm up runs when it happened. Steve came running over and cried, 'Come now, Terry's been hurt.' My heart jumped through my throat. A crowd gathered around Terry at the northwest corner of the infield. Trainers were examining Terry's foot. Betts looked like he'd swallowed a frog."

Mercury Wounded: The Legend of the Spiked Foot and the '67 KU Relays

The amazing events involving Terry were the lead headline stories in the big newspapers.

"I was just standing on the infield watching a race when some distance guy with spikes on came by and stepped on my foot," Terry told the regional and AP newspaper reporters, who pushed their way through the crowd gathered around him. He showed the reporters where the blood had come through the side of his shoe. "The three-quarter inch spikes went clear through the outside edge of my foot."

A quick pow-wow was held between Betts and the Relays officials, off to the side, for ten minutes. Betts came back saying, "We're keeping you on ice, Terry, and we've got an hour and a half to get you a tetanus shot before the 880 relays prelims. How do you feel?"

"At this point, all of us were on the verge of throwing up. I thought it was the end of everything," Wendell later told us. "But Terry just looked up, and said, 'This thing ain't bad, coach. Let's get this shot deal over with. I wanna get back here.' " Wendell explained, "We were really scared. We were whispering 'what about the 880 relay, without Terry, when Terry must have overheard us. He just looked over at us and said, 'You guys aint' got a dang thing to worry about. I'll be right back. You'll see. It's no biggy.' Coach Betts didn't say a word after that. The coaches rushed Terry off to get a tetanus shot at the university hospital, and rushed him back, icing his foot all the time, and giving him aspirin. Betts said Terry just joked around with the nurses. He came back to our stadium spot and sat with his foot on ice. The officials shuffled a few things, and they set back the 880 relay for an hour." Wendell continued, "And they did something else unreal. Before taking off for the hospital, Betts came up and told Terry, 'The meet officials have re-scheduled the 100 yard dash prelim to be the last event of the day, so you can maybe re-cover. I told them you are rarin' to go. They owe you a chance.' "

* * *

As the team waited for Terry's return, up the stadium stairs skipped spear-chucker Brett Swaggart. "Marcus Walker and the black power Wichita dudes are strutting around out there, gloating about Terry," said Brett. "I just walked past 'em. I'd kick their ass if there were a few more of me." Muffled grunts of agreement were the replies.

About noon, and forty minutes before the re-scheduled 880 relay showdown between the big Kansas high schools and us, Terry went down to the field to join in with his relay team of Steve Collins, Wendell, and Eagle-man Charlie Switzer. Betts had discovered that Charlie could run sprints in very fast times in practice, so he was thrown in as a newly discovered ace on the relay team.

Up to this point, these other three Red Silk sprinters could turn in 22.4 to 22.6 second 220 yard legs in the relay. Against the biggest Kansas City and Wichita metropolitan schools, these times would be one or two-tenths of a second slower than several of the competitor runners. Famed Wichita East had the two senior hurdlers, Maurice King and Marcus Walker (as anchor); KC area Shawnee Mission North had the incredible junior hurdler Bob Bornkessel as their anchor; and gigantic and palatial Topeka High (famous for its Gothic Tower architecture, in the 1940s the largest high school building in America) had ace hurdler Presston Carrington.

Wendell recounted later how Betts described this competition at the hotel Thursday night when they were waiting for Terry to arrive at supper: "You boys deserve to understand. House will be up against four of the six fastest high school anchor men-hurdlers in the U.S. all in the same race. It's amazing what the Relays have stacked against him. But you guys run the race of your life, and you may surprise 'em. When Charlie gives the baton to Terry, stand back and watch. If those Black Power boys are not more than ten yards ahead of Terry, and he can run despite his injury, they will be wondering about the Second Coming in a whole new way..."[10]

"Frankly," Wendell said, giving us his patented pause and laser-beam, leaning-at-ya stare, "We were worried sick about Terry and his spiked foot."

The Prelims and the Finals: the 880 Relays and 100 Yard Dash

The CHS hopes for the 880 relays were bruised in the preliminaries. KC Shawnee Mission East turned in a blazing 1:29.6, with Bornkessel cranking. The next three places out of six teams were grouped tightly, with just a few yards between them.

"We got fourth in the prelims," Wendell gloomily reported to us that Saturday night. "I guess we first three relay runners were rattled some in the prelim on Friday. We'd run almost two seconds faster before in meets, that's twenty yards better than we ran in our prelim time of 1:32.2. Maybe Terry was nursing his foot for the final, who knows. But in the Final on Saturday, we closed the gap. We hit 1:31.3. That's an eleven yard gain. We were just a few yards behind the winners, led by Bornkessel. And House, despite his foot, gained about eight yards even against him! Another five yards and Terry would have cooked him. Maybe his foot hurt him some. It was still a little swollen. He went back to ice his foot, and take more aspirin, and get ready for the 100 yard dash Finals. He didn't say a thing about his foot."

On Friday, in the University and Open 100 yard dash, the world-record challenger and sprint legend Jim Hines running for Texas Southern, laid down his 9.6 finals time on the cinder track. Again this was not faster, and probably not as fast as Terry's 100 at Abilene one week before. Hines was a contender-for-fastest man in the world. Terry sat in the stands with his Black Panther glasses on, watched the older Hines win his university 100, and downed aspirins to help the pain in his heavily iced foot, as he waited for his own high school 100 yard preliminary. "There was considerable talk in the general stadium crowd about Terry being as fast as Hines," said Wendell.

At the end of Friday afternoon, the ice came off, and Terry tried some warm-ups and stretches in the center field, testing his foot. At the announcement of the coming 100 yard preliminaries, Terry ambled down toward the delayed high school 100 yard dash starting line, at the north end of KU Memorial Stadium. A baker's dozen photographers swarmed at the finish of the race, setting up cameras. The prelim "competition" included the later famous John Riggins, of Centralia[11], and others from the big urban schools. The KU Relays prep record (on the antiquated cinder track) was

9.8, four tenths or about four meters behind the national prep record of 9.4 (shared by several, including Hayes and Hines).

"The cameras clicked like firecrackers at the finish," Wendell reported. In the media interviews Friday, Terry said, "I like competing against the biggest schools, the competition is better. I had ice packs on my foot the whole afternoon. The swelling has gone down some. It didn't hurt too much. I didn't figure the competition would press me as close as they did in the preliminary. I arrived, and the starting blocks were set too close to the line. But I was late, so I didn't mess with them because I didn't think the race would be that close." With spike wounds clear through a pained and swollen foot, Terry was the headline, lead photo, and lead story in the papers.

Terry in the Red Silk sailed through the tape, with Riggins and the "competition" in desperate yards behind. The sorely wounded Silk speedster had tied the KU Relays 100 yard prep record at 9.8 in the prelims.

On the next day, Saturday, incredible individual high school times and relays marks were chalked up. In many cases, the high school times were equal to or better than those ran at the University or "open-Olympics" levels. Barrati vs Niehouse continued their middle distance gunfight, both of them finishing the mile at near record-tying times 4:18.7, 4:19.6. Walker tied the Relays 120 yard/110 meter hurdles record (14.3), with King and Carrington breathing down his neck every inch of the race. Bornkessel erased the Relays record in the 330 yard hurdles (38.2). Carrington stole the high jump. All of them were top national leaders with these marks.

On Saturday at the 100 yard high school Finals, Tidwell's ghost surely smiled over the starting blocks. Against a stiff south wind, John Riggins, and the miracle hurdler Bornkessel, and the rest of the competition ate Terry's cinders right from the starting blocks. "Seven Secrets" perfect and injured, Terry was still untouchable. He took first, matching the record. Even with blood on his shoe.

* * *

After the van arrived home Saturday night, Gary and I followed the entourage into the locker rooms, hearing bits and pieces of the story. We had read what we could in the Blade Empire. Outside the locker room, Wendell stood with us under the light of an old incandescent lamp and the glittering stars above, and told the tale, and showed us the Lawrence and big city papers. When he drove away in his *Carmen Ghia*, we fairly sprinted home. We stopped at Gary's place first, but neither his dad nor mom were at home. "She's probably at the Methodist Women's meeting, and it is Dad's night to work at the store late," Gary guessed.

"Well, let's head up to our place. Surely Mom's got something cooked up, and we'll give them the news first." We fairly flew up the hill over Tyler's yard, and past our budding three cherry trees. Spring had burst forth in the last day with such entrancing beauty. The air was rich with perfumes, and the evening star Venus hung bright as a Queen's diamond against a deepening azure sky. In the far distance, to the southwest, a thin, jagged, blue-black line of clouds was laced with lightning. It didn't seem to be coming. All was right as we burst through the back door.

"Mom, have we got something to tell you!"

"You won't believe it, Mrs. Hamilton," Gary continued, "but Terry Householter today…"

Mom dropped the wooden spoon into the big, shiny steel pot where she was making up creamy potato and bacon soup. She listened with glistening eyes at Gary's breathless story.

He spun the story exactly as Wendell told it. Mom sat quietly at the table, her fingers laced together on the tabletop. She listened with the soul of a poet. Her green eyes were wide and never blinked. When Gary finished, she took a deep breath and let it out slowly. She rose in silence and stepped out the back door through the breezeway into the back yard. We followed into the quiet. The crickets' harmonies sang and the regal perfumes of her rows of lilac and purple iris rose in rich waves. As Kansans do, we took gaze on the glittering vaults of stars.

"I've seen that boy run everywhere since he was maybe ten years old when his grandparents took him in," Mom told us quietly. "Poor as church mice. They haven't got a dime to their name. But I've never seen a bigger smile on a boy's face in my life. One day he ran into Paul's IGA grocery, ran right past me to grab some grapes, and ran to the cash register, and ran out with 'em. No doubt he was on an errand for his grandma. Smiling the whole time. I believe the Good Lord made him to run so he'd be happy, and the rest of us would have something to think on."

Gary and I carried on many nights, trying to make our teenage brains think through how Terry could have cheerfully run with the spiked foot, to match the KU Relays high school sprinter record. Here was a big, puzzling chunk of amazement, and a subtle challenge to us. Wendell reminded us, "Terry just sat there, calm as a cat, telling us 'this was no biggy'."

Years later, when my family faced tragedy in my older son's terrible car wreck, and when I watched my aunt succumb to the awful mind-gobbling demon of Alzheimers, I could somehow draw a little calmness to me, to help myself and my family cope. Terry's astonishing calm and cheer in times of trials helped me remember how to endure when things turn dark.

We sat at the table that night, eating mom's creamy potato-bacon soup laced with Ritz crackers and parsley. We felt like princes. We were near the middle of finishing off slices of her cherry pie, and Mom was going through the mail when she screamed.

She ran to the phone, repeating to herself, "He's got to be at work," and dialing frantically. Gary and I stared at each other, our hearts racing, feeling like we'd been stabbed with an icicle. Our hearts hung on mom's every word.

"Roger, Roger...we've got a letter here. It says...they want a verification of your address, and things..." Mom's voice dropped to a slight wheeze, "It's from Kansas City." She couldn't seem to get the words out. I looked at Gary. I slid over to the countertop to search the opened envelopes, with Gary following. Gas bill, electric bill, Our Lady of Perpetual Help contributions envelope. Nothing there.

We looked over. Mom was holding it, still talking to Roger on the phone. "You did? You're sure...last week. Thank God. I'll talk to you when you get back to the house." She came back to the table, and sat down, shaking. She slapped the letter and envelope on the table.

"Chris, take that thing before I burn it. Hide it somewhere, away from me. When Roger gets home, give it to him." The address was upside down, but we could read it: United States Government. Selective Service.

"They won't get him after graduation. He signed into the National Guard last week, he says."

Our soup was growing cold on the table. In the distance, we could hear a little thunder, and the evening bells of the Cathedral.

...Two Years Later... April 1969, Vietnam

Chapter 18
FIRE AND RAIN

First days of April, An Hua Marine Regiment Base Camp
Near Que Son Mountains, and Da Nang City.
Company Mike, 3rd Battalion, 5th Marine Regiment, 1st Marine Division

A Bad Moon Rising

Several Marines of Mike Company, the "Mighty Mike", were playing a card game of "spades" in the squad tent as nightfall approached. A new "grunt" or Marine recruit had choppered into the An Hua Base that morning, a "cherry". The new grunt looked down from the helicopter that morning to see almost millions of small, perfectly round ponds. On the ground it was clear, "they weren't ponds, they were bomb and shell craters." A first sign of so many new dangers to discover. A "cherry" was not somebody to cozy up to. You didn't know if he would be dangerously stupid, or live more than a couple days, or not. Now as evening crept in, the "cherry" sat in the tent, staring at his hands, getting no questions. He was about as alone as a man can get, in a crowd.

The card game ended, and the veteran Marines grabbed their weapons and walked off, with no words to the new grunt. They were heading out to man bunkers for the night. The NVA, the North Vietnam regular army and their VC buddies were showing signs of infiltrating in large numbers into this mountainous region, near the South China Sea coast. An Hua Regiment base, on the flat plains near the mountains, was not twenty "klicks" or kilometers from Vietnam's fourth largest, coastal city of Da Nang. Everybody was skittish in Mike Company, and in the entire battalion for that matter. They'd lost some good guys recently, in Operation Taylor.

As darkness fell, the night sky lit up like the fourth of July, in huge, booming explosions, with shrapnel, and whizzing bullets sputtering everywhere. Desperate Marines dove into sandbagged, underground bunkers, and screams split the night. A Sergeant grabbed the new grunt, who was diving for a bunker, handed him a measly Smith and Wesson .38 and screamed, "Shoot the bastards, they're in the wire!" The Sergeant sped off like a madman, to organize counter-attacks.

The VC had set off the base camp ammo dump. It was wildly spewing bullets, and flames, and exploding huge amounts of ordnance in demonic blasts. A short watch tower near the Mike Company tents was engulfed in a firefight, and it caught ordnance and burst into fire at the base. To the horror of the entire base camp, the watchtower on the edge of the ammo dump slowly toppled into the flaming, sizzling maw of the ammo dump's hellish explosions. Screams of rage, fear, and frustration of the doomed Marines in the watchtower seared into the night, as the entire Regiment helplessly watched the slow-motion death of their comrades.

The rage of the Marines tore the night, and revenge like a volcano drove them up and out of bunkers into seething counterattacks of infinite fury. Base camp weapons fire screamed through the cordons of wire, into the night, shredding as many retreating VC as could be hunted down by our guys in hot pursuit.

Clumps of Marines gathered in their patrol tents, and underground bunkers, raging and sorting through their stories for hours, as security was beefed up on the perimeters. The month before, the Regiment had lost over a hundred guys, in tough action in a sweeping operation called Taylor. It was the second big thrust in the area to reduce the infiltration of NVA and VC forces. Mike Company was already mourning the loss of several dead. And now this.

The new grunt, and any new ones to come, were just going to be resented more, as reminders to Marines that they were replacing dear, fallen friends. It wouldn't be a "cake walk" for the cherries. And there would be no more relatively quiet sweeps or night bunker watch patrols. Things were dangerous in these spring months.

Such deadly clashes between the Marines, and the ever-building NVA army and VC support had been increasing in the Que Son valleys since 1967. Over the next two years, the Corps battalions would conduct operations to run the NVA and VC forces out of the valley. But the enemy would bide its time, and re-inforce its ranks, only to be again decisively defeated by hard-charging Marine platoons and companies. Over time though, the NVA was to target Da Nang itself, and thrust major forces into the valley. The pressures on Marine forces gradually increased, and the horrors of being badly outnumbered tested their mettle, but they never lost a battle. Artillery and air support built up, but so did the strain on the Marines.

* * *

The reality of Vietnam, and the real greeting awaiting a new Marine were unimaginable. After the attack, Grady Rainbow, the new grunt from Oklahoma City, retreated to sit stunned in the squad tent. Mike Company guys, either shell-shocked, or chattering like anxiety-ridden robots, stumped into the tent. *Not so much as a glance. Like I'm not even here*, thought Grady, completely depressed by the shunning. *The Staff Sergeant was right on the money...*

That afternoon, as Grady trudged into the Regiment command areas, the day of this fateful assault, the company Staff Sergeant who was to "orient" him, had told him this:

"These days everybody will get Purple Hearts in this unit. You're a cherry, no one wants to know your name or be friends just yet. Odds are you won't make it past the first few days alive, you'll get blown away....*If* you make it past the first month, then you might have a chance. Until then, keep your mouth shut, and don't fuck with the guys in this company. You're just a warm body replacing friends they lost on this last Op. Your only worry is if you live through it...So put anything you think out of your mind, and learn from the Marines in your unit".

"Orientation" to the area was supposed to be five days. Usually it was a few hours. The real "Indoc" orientation training at your first base site had you lay down behind a stack of sandbags, "...and after being told to not raise up under any circumstances, the NCO in charge began firing several different weapons over our heads...to listen to the different sounds the weapons made. Each makes a unique sound as it passes over your head...after awhile in the bush, you can learn to tell the difference." A difference you needed to know, to stay alive.

* * *

Grady Rainbow is the son of a Marine, in an unbroken string of other branch military officers, back to the Civil War. Tall, black-haired, strong, honest and polite but straight-talking, Grady quietly distilled the essence of duty and penetrating intelligence into his trim frame.

A short, eerily confident, wiry tough-looking Marine with nylon black glasses strode last into the tent after this night's attack. He leaned against a brace, panting, took off his helmet, shook his head, and looked down at the floor. Grady noticed he didn't join in immediately, in the raucous chatter. He eye-balled around the tent, catching bits of the animated talk. He spotted Grady, eye-to-eye. Grady just looked down at the wood floor. A few seconds later, a hand poked him in the shoulder. Grady looked up.

"Well, pal. Nice home-coming for ya, huh. A real introduction. So welcome to Mighty Mike, and scenic An Hua basin. I'm Terry Householter. I've been radioman, sometimes. Other times, well, it's all fun and games."

"Thanks."

"The shit hit the fan out there. Third squad is going ape, still hunting down the last of those bastards. An hour of that, and we were sent back to help re-secure the base, do any last controls on the fire..." His voice trailed off. They both knew what the other was thinking, about the guys in the tower, roasted.

The veteran and the cherry sat side by side, suffering their weird, semi-separate worlds of grief, after-shock, and rage. Terry's hands shook and reaching to cover his eyes, he sat on the cot with Grady, who suffered bewilderment, and dread.

In a little while, Grady looked down, barely registering the growling voices around the tent, and saw a gritty hand poke in front of his eyes, holding something. It was Terry again.

"Want a cigarette? All we got is off-brands."

"Hey, thanks man," Grady smiled, reaching for the cigarette Terry stuck out to him.

"I'm from Kansas. You?"

"Oklahoma City."

"No shit. 'KOMA the 50,000 watt voice of the heartland, broadcasting rock around the globe from Okla-homa Cit-ayyy.'" Terry shouted, pumping his fist in the air.

A deepening smile spread across Grady's face, watching this display of enthusiasm. House spun around in a little dance, singing "Glo-ri-a, G. L. O. R. I. A..." A little bit of the world is still here, Grady mused, and this guy-ain't half-bad.

"Hell's bells, we can sometimes pull in KOMA here...damn, Oklahoma City, huh."

"Yes, sir."

Terry sat back down on the cot, pulling on his cigarette. "Don't mind these cats here, Grady. They're a pretty decent lot, really. They don't know Oklahoma, back home, not yet. They'll warm up to you, 'Oklahoma.' This place will fry your ass, if you're not careful. I'll slip ya some clues on staying alive around here. Keep your chin up..."

Terry would become Grady's best friend, and vice versa.

The very next day, Grady had to suffer out some inquiries about his rifle kicking on automatic fire during a patrol, the stupid trigger safety not working right. It took a bunch of yelling, and half-assed accusations by the Captain until he did his own firing of Grady's rifle, which proved Grady's claim of the trigger malfunction. That night, neither Terry, nor Grady had to pull listening post, or outpost bunker duty. In the shadow of skittishness in the squad, about Grady, after the automatic fire episode, Terry sat with Grady inside the tent as the darkness of night fell, and one of those crappy, incessant drizzles set in.

"Okay, Oklahoma," Terry said, lighting up a cigarette and offering Grady one, "let's go over a few things that'll keep you alive in these weird-ass parts." The cigarettes glowed cheerily.

"We gotta talk low. With this drizzle, Charlie can't see our cigs or lighters. I swear this damn rain is the one thing above all that can drive you out of your gourd." They drew on their cigarettes quietly. Fire was two things...the oily, towering flames of napalm, the devil incarnate; or a cheerful spark of a cigarette glowing in a dark night, a memory of campfires, back home.

"Rain here kills you," Terry said, starkly. "It goes 'on and on and on and on', for days and weeks. It'll make your skin peel off in big patches of white wrinkles. If you get any cut or scrapes out here, you can get the jungle rot spreading on you in a couple hours. You can rot to the bone, fast, so you better treat it fast. Thank the damn rain and humidity for the bizarre germs, fungus, and bugs they got here."

Grady pulled on the cigarette, registering every word.

"I better stop bitchin' and get to first things first, Grady. Look. Like you learned today, no reckless gunfire. Make no noises at night. Black your face and arms up. For God's sake, don't wear any rings, or jewelry or nothing shiny. Charlie out there will try to spot something shiny. Shiny isn't the junge, day or at night. Shiny is a stupid, soon to be dead American, maybe you. Another thing about this. The Academy boys, you know, officer training schools, etc, show up with their cool big silver rings. But if they turn out to be snots and dangerous wise-asses....some guys might hold back on the 'don't wear shiny stuff at night' advice... just to have Charlie get rid of those guys. This is a weird place, Grady. We're not in Kansas and Oklahoma anymore..."

The silence of the rain bore on.

"Terry, what the hell is the smell around here?"

"Well, it's not Dorothy's fields of poppies. It ain't gonna put you to sleep. Rice paddies. The locals use any kind of waste, water buffalo, their own shit, you name it. For fertilizer. Works great. No big corporation getting the money. You get used to it ..."

Terry drew heavily on the cigarette again. "Okay. I'm coming at ya now on more stuff, that if you don't get it right away, you're dead meat. How fast a learner are you? Didn't the orientation Sergeant warn you on any of this?"

"Just a few things. He sure woke me up."

"Well, he's damn straight about it. Here's the next thing. We got unfriendly animals here. You gotta watch out like a rabbit, to stay alive. You got your cobras, wild pigs, water buffalo, monkeys, bamboo vipers, fruit bats, rock apes, even elephants and tigers. The bamboo viper snakes are maybe the worst, hell of a lot more dangerous than our rattlesnakes back home. You get bit, you'll start quick into convulsions. Soon you can't breathe. Your heart starts to quit. But you're not a goner until after you enjoy going blind first. We got anti-venom, but it's worthless crap. It has to be refrigerated. Do you see any portable refrigerators that we carry on our backs? Any dry ice anywhere? Too many dumb bastards in command." Terry drew on his cigarette, and continued, "I'll also show you how to spot the bamboo vipers, they're sneaky little monsters. You won't miss noticing the cobras though. King Cobras. They get up to twelve, maybe fifteen feet long. They're about a dozen inches around. The venom milk from one of them can fill a coffee cup And that's just one bite. The Doc says that one bite is enough to kill several elephants. And get this. If you kill one, then you've really stepped in it. Because they travel in mated pairs. Kill one, and the other comes after you."

Grady's eyes were glazing over, and rolling around at hearing all this.

"No place like home, huh," he croaked out.

"The last first thing. You got your leeches. We didn't have no frickin' leeches in Kansas. How about Oklahoma?"

"Well. Maybe the hippies, the lawyers' sons, or the country club Republicans. All of them work to get out of the draft. Equal opportunity leeches. At least, the hippies work from what they call their principles."

"Huh. Anyway... About your leeches. If you go in the water, you must get the damn leeches off. You got your two basic types: long bright green ones from the rivers and paddies, and the small black ones from the jungles. We get constantly eaten alive by these bloodsuckers. You get them off by sprinkling salt packets from our C-Rations on them, and it makes them burst and shrink. Then we pick the heads off each other. If we got no salt, we use the issue bug repellent 'bug-juice'. Using a cigarette to get 'em off might work, but you'll generally get burned."

Terry paused to snuff out his cigarette.

"I can tell you're a good listener. That's good. Shows you want to stay alive."

"Well. This place will get your attention. But thanks," Grady replied.

Terry went on, "Now, standing watch at night, or going on sweep patrols, or both in the same day is what we do. We get no real sleep. At best, it's four hours a night. I think standing watch at nights is maybe the worst. You gotta rotate in sleep. You got to listen like a maniac, sense for anything different, Charlie creeping up on you. He'll blow you sky high in a second, like you learned tonight. If it's raining on watch, hey you get to buddy up with rats, and bugs in the rain, and you do not want your helmet on. You gotta learn to hear past the rain, for Charlie sneaking around. On watch, you gotta signal "OK" to regiment every now and then by clicking your radio on and off. Charlie can't hear that. But. You'll be dead on the first night, if the fruit bats dive at you when you click. You gotta watch immediately for them, because the radio signal click can confuse the radar of the bats, and cause them to dive bomb you in massive numbers. This tells Charlie exactly where to blow you up."

Grady coughed, trying to soak this all in.

"And during the days, drink only camp water. If you don't drink and carry enough water, you'll hump yourself to death into dehydration in half a day, out there. If you drink that crap water in the streams, the parasites will eat your gut in less than ten minutes, and you'll get the runs and cramps so bad, you'll wish you were dead."

"Christ. No wonder people die out here." Grady swooned. "I'm not sure I can take in any more right off. How much more does a guy need to survive tomorrow?"

"Be leery of the villagers, and idiot new commanders. But we'll cover that more, later. So hey, let's get off this shit for a bit," Terry sighed. "Too depressing. We are making it out of here, you know. Back to the world. So let me ask you about Oklahoma..."

The two heartland boys found common ground, talking about sunsets, and farmers' daughters, and Coors beer. They discovered they both ran track, a topic that kept their minds and spirits alive when doom crept too close. Terry was liked and admired in Mike Company, for his cheer, level-headedness, practicality and wit. He was one to "adopt" and advise cherries, being a friend in a very unfriendly place.

* * *

Terry didn't let on to Grady about everything. The treacherous risks in the region were unimaginable enough, and getting worse, and some supports for the Marines were less than standard. Mike Company Marine letters home were usually devoid of any such descriptions, as guys simply didn't want to terrify their family and loved ones with the facts of Spring 1969:

Patrols of the outlying regions and villages, to spot potential VC, were increasingly taking place under sniper fire, or mortar shelling.

Patrols in the jungle canopy were especially dangerous, because retaliation was difficult. The canopies were so thick that "even the heavy air strikes couldn't damage it, the bombs...piercing only two or three layers of branches and mulch". The danger in the canopies was they could extend fifty feet or more above ground, and you wouldn't realize it while walking on it. A perfect place for the enemy to hide and spot you from below. To increase the fun, the Army, and Navy filtered the worse equipment to the Marines:

"...Our field gear was World War II issue, —1947 packs and web gear. We were told to 'shitcan' the stuff all the time. If you can't use it, dump it. Find something real...

...The first thing any grunt hoped to do was waste an NVA or 'VC gook', and then capture his pack, as theirs were much better than ours....

...The flak jackets were heavy, hot and were Korean War gear. The flak jacket was designed to stop very small pieces of hand grenade shrapnel; they didn't stop bullets or anything (we used to joke they couldn't even stop the damn bugs from biting through)...

...The Army had more up to date gear, and we stole anything that wasn't nailed down when they were around. Most Marines took a perverse pride in this...we were "Hard Corps"...and the rest of the others (in any other service) were all candy-asses. Here we were, the finest fighting organization in the world, and we had to wage war on shoestrings, treated as disposable..."[12]

* * *

An Hua Regimental base camp was on fairly flat terrain. Small villages with huts, are in all directions, along rivers and streams. Rice paddies are everywhere. The mountains, covered with the impenetrable "canopy", are some dozen miles distant. A bit further is the big coastal city of Da Nang.

The Mike Company tents at the base were canvas, with wood floors, unbearably hot in the day. At least they were a little shelter from rain at nights. Most of the time the majority of the Mike Company Third Squad Marines would not sleep in the compound's tents, but were assigned at nights to a dug-out defensive bunker, or to a listening post bunker at night.

At the listening post bunkers, careful listening could detect infiltration and troop movements at night. Later, electronic aid listening devices could sometimes help detect the enemy encroaching. Most of the detection relied on "a sixth sense", some guys had it, others not so much. Changes in the night-sounds of birds or insects, dim shuffling or thumping, or just a sense of imminent danger raising hairs on the arm were the signs of enemy encroachments.

The armed bunkers, spread around the camp and dug in deep, were both defense and targets. More dangerous was the camp's high observation post, manned at nights upon a hill outside of the camp. It was armed with machine guns, surrounded by an actual moat, and it was further made unreachable by a drawbridge.

The armed patrols, and fire fights seem to go on endlessly. The treks were long, totally exhausting, often under fire. Most guys used M-16s, or the older, more reliable

M-14s, which were less prone to jams, mud, etc. The enemy "Charlie" was hated, yet respected for stealth, inventiveness, stubbornness, brutality, deception, sniper fire, and mortar attacks. "He was especially good at explosions."

Certain activities could help relieve the strain, boredom, or exhaustion, when the squads were in camp: Cards, listening to the radio at nights for their favorite rock stations, cigarettes. "Sometimes we can actually pull in Radio from all over the U.S.", Terry relayed in letters to home. Marines could get only one or two makes of cigarettes, not quality brands.

In the compound tent of Terry's squad, the guys developed an "understanding" with one particular rat, on a boundary issue which kept the corpsmen and the rat on good terms. Other rats would die quick deaths, by squad knives, usually not ammo. But the smart rat would penetrate at night to hunt for food, and eventually the squad taught the rat by knife stabs, to not cross a certain line on the ground, or table. When the rat stopped before the lines, he could make noises and get crumbs and little offerings thrown in his direction, and he was expected to leave thereafter. The knife fate had been demonstrated again and again to the rat-intern; he learned to behave himself and not invade personal or food stuffs, in trade for his life.

Such black humor kept you sane: "Against regulations, we decorated our helmets and flak jackets with popular stuff like peace symbols, state flags, and bulls-eyes (gallows humor ran high). Sayings were words like "Short-Timer", "Shoot Here", nicknames, state terms (like Jayhawks or Tar Heels), or ethnic slang..." wrote Grady.

"Once this spring, Terry called down to me from the watchtower to see something strange after a defensive, short firefight with the enemy," said corpsman Rainbow. Terry, in the observation and defense fire tower, pointed his friend's attention to a large white rabbit, who had taken up a position of relative safety, in the compound's middle, away from the more concentrated fire around bunkers. "That rabbit became our favorite for awhile."

The psychology of the warriors, under the severe pressures, was mercurial, sometimes incendiary. Guys had many reasons to enlist, and fight. But usually the strain of protecting yourself and your buddies was so over-powering, that the motivations to fight and kill reduced down to the protection of oneself and friends, or revenge. Dead buddies, sneaky attacks, tragic or senseless deaths from accident, or clandestine VC forces among villagers were other common reasons to fight and kill fiercely. These otherwise normal teenagers would instantly "flame on" into cold-eyed warriors, fighting furiously. "We didn't fight really, for gung-ho patriotism," Grady said. "And we didn't talk much about family, or personal history, or religious matters, unless we sensed that 'our time had come'."

"Hope came from remembering what it was like 'back in the world', eg, back home. During the tough times, or relaxation, we'd get ourselves together by remembering what it was like back in 'the world'. We'd dream, and promise beer, parties, and foods. Different memories of 'back in the world' is what kept our sanity going," explained Terry's letters, and his buddies.

Rest and recreation was very infrequent, and was sometimes granted by the Company brass, after a severely stressful action, or after a long-term period of patrols.

R & R was either a short time off, or a longer five day trip to an R & R base camp. For many it was all about eating, to gain back strength and weight, and then came beer, women, radio and music, or maybe a movie.

Aside from physical restoration, it was a time to revisit the sometimes private struggles, or mysteries of the soul and psyche which were held inside, even from best buddies. Terry's best friends from home and letters made allusion to Terry becoming a Buddhist by sentiment, maybe an extension of his great admiration of philosophies in Beatles songs. Terry visited village kids with packets of Kool-Aid and sugar. A mysteriousness seemed to feed his cheer, his willingness to "flame on" as a warrior to protect buddies, his caution, and kindnesses.

In all this, it's good to remember that the majority of new Marine recruits were just eighteen to twenty years old. Things were about to get a lot worse.

* * *

April 28, 1969

Lance Corporal Terry Householter, and the rest of the corpsmen of 2nd squad of Mike Company staggered back into An Hua base camp, after two days and nights on a sweep patrol of the nearby villages. The main aftermaths of this relatively lucky outing were a minor shrapnel wound to one squad member, deafness from an exploded mortar, and weariness from cross-and-return fire that scattered and killed some VC, plus leeches, dehydration, dizzying exhaustion and blisters.

Terry, Grady Rainbow, and Waterbull gulped down some water, and too tired to eat, slumped into the squad tent, and flopped stone-cold into instant sleep on the musty cots. Clouds and a mist held down the heat, as the sunlight faded. If there were a firefight, or storm tonight, the squad might sleep through most, or all of it, oblivious to any visiting bugs, rats, or short bursts of weapons fire.

The Marines under stress, had fitful dreams. Some dreams were of food, beer, approachable and comely women. Others were of surreal re-winds of explosions, VC dismembered by machine and semi-automatic fire, exaggerated huge, blood-sucking green leeches, or napalm bombs that spewed flaming streams and colored blossoms of arcing jellied gasoline across the skies, blazing over and engulfing parts of villages.

Like so many nights, Terry fitfully dreamed again of back home, and what got him here, over the last year...

...Cooley's Bar, Concordia, July 9, 1968

...screen door opens with that weird spring sound, the Hamm's Beer sign over the bar bubbles out "Land of Sky Blue Waters". Sour beer smell, nobody recognizes me, think I'll see if Ike has any Coors... Terry's mind raced, in a world of reflections and feelings about his

dizzying experiences the last four months. It was strange that the real-world conversations seemed to go on in a separate compartment in his mind.

"Hey, Terry, dad-gum, you're back."

"Hi, Ike."

"Marines, right? You back for awhile?"

"Oh yeah. I got leave 'till the end of August."

"Hey, guys, Terry Householter's back...looking pretty fit and tan. What can I get you?"

"How about a Coors?"

"Yeah, right up..."

...huh?...hand on my shoulder,"Hi, Terry"...dang if it's not Big Mick...

"How're ya doing?"

"Could be worse." *...wish I was better, wish I could stay longer...*

"How's it been for you? What's it like? Ya look pretty wiry and tough." Mick offered.

"I'm Okay. It does take a lot out of you, pushes you in new ways." *...man, whaddya say, none of these guys, not Big Mick, would believe what the Drill Instructors push at you, firing tracers over your head, beating guys up, Vietnam couldn't be worse...*

"Yeah. So, do you like it?" Mick asked.

"Well. I'm ready as anybody could be, I think." *...I'm ready to kill, I guess, but how I got onto this...*

"Did they spell out what Vietnam is really like, the Cong, all that?" Mick asked.

"I guess." *...little kids with bombs, snipers, poison punji sticks everywhere, scorching napalm...*

"What did you learn most?" Mick pushed on.

"Lotsa things can kill you over there, and the Marines make you ready for it," Terry explained. "Marines, Mick, they're like brothers. The drill instructors are assholes. Assholes. But, Uncle Sam has some damn cool weapons, though, you wouldn't believe the chopper they call the Huey, and the AC-47 and the machine guns it carries..."

"Here's your Coors, Terry. On the house," Ike said, cheerfully planting a huge twenty ounce clear glass of the "Rocky Mountain Spring Water" brew, at Terry's elbow.

"Man, you didn't have to do that..." Terry complained.

"Well, why not this once..."

"Thanks, man. Anyway, Mick," Terry continued, "The AC-47 has a 7.62 mm gatling gun they call 'Puff the Magic Dragon', and when they unleash that monster, well, it's like the finger of the devil himself. Six thousand rounds per minute per gun, sometimes three guns blazing. You can't imagine what that does, looks and sounds like. That thing can rip down forests like a giant razor. I suppose we'll see them over there...and napalm, good God..."

...geez, it's sooo weird, the Marine world, this world, home, Kansas...

"What about fried chicken?" Terry suddenly asked.

"You what ?" Mick replied.

"After the beer, here, you wanna go get some fried chicken at Ray's Café?" Terry asked, on a sudden impulse. *...no taste like home, no taste like home...not sure when I will get some, again...*

"Uh, yeah. Sure. Any day, every day, you know. But...how about I whup you at pool, first?" Mick challenged.

"You're on, man." Terry lifted the Coors, and found his way back to the pool table, ribbing Mick on the way, living the moments at home as much as he could live them...

...but Terry's dream fitfully shifted to another memory...

...August 10, 1968. Belleville County Fair

"Glad you talked me into this thing, Ted," Terry said.

"Hey, what's more fun than the rides, cotton candy, roasted peanuts, dirt track racing? We're just glad you came along!" Ted Easter replied.

The air sang with incredible smells, onion-garlic fried hamburgers, corn dogs with chili, deep fried onion rings, new strewn alfalfa hay to walk on. Every now and then, the air would be split with the growl of a dirt track car engine, pumped and racing, popping out small explosions, from dirt track stock car circuit, always big at the Belleville County Fair.

Terry bummed around the grounds, following Ted, as they were joined up by Ted's younger sister, Jenice. A few years younger, she clearly had an admiration for Terry.

"Let's do rides for awhile, then I want one of them Big Mother sloppy hamburgers," announced Terry.

"...with red onions, and tomatoes, and bacon, and mayonaise..." teased Ted.

"I don't think anything in the whole damn world can smell better than county fair, onion-garlic fried hamburgers," Terry proclaimed.

"The carnies have got the magic down, for sure," Ted replied.

The carnies in the West are a wild lot, a special breed, like the old cowboys, or the still-roaming gypsies. When the carnies, or the travelling circuses came to towns, magic boiled out from them.

The trio spun through the fair, caught up in all the magic: the high Ferris wheel, the bumper cars and the ozone electric spark smell, the Whirlybird Mixer, the spinning drum where the bottom drops out and you are plastered by centrifugal force against the wall, and you try to raise your leg straight out against the force.

After the spinning drum, Ted teasingly asked, "Hey, how about checking out the bearded, naked lady?" Jenice giggled.

"Agh, you serious?" Terry smiled. "It could be weird in there..."

"Roger Hamilton and Tim Brady ragged on me about it, when they and I ran into each other last night here. They say it's worth a gander..." Ted pressed on.

...that's them, that's not me right now...

"Nah. Not now. I'm starving. Let's grab some burgers," Terry dodged the question.

Ted relented, his sister tugging at his sleeve, begging "Yes, food. We humans are starving."

Late that night, after the dirt track race, and the "Eve of Destruction" old car smashup race, Ted, Terry and Jenice met up with Ted's dad, for the drive back home.

Terry rolled down the window of the '57 Chevy, as it growled smoothly down Highway 81, fifteen miles south back to Concordia.

...smell that alfalfa. Stars couldn't be brighter. Milky Way really is milky. Wonder what that big, blinking blue star to the West is. Man, the crickets sing...wonder if there's crickets over in Vietnam...I guess it's innocent enough, Jenice sitting back here, what the hell, she's a good Kansas kid to sit by. I'm missing Kansas even now...

"Thanks Easters, for asking me along. Those burgers really are killers, huh?" Terry spoke up.

"Couldn't be more right, dude," Ted replied.

...But Ted strangely seemed to drift away, as the dream shifted again...

...August 25, 1968

He pulled hard against the wind, as the glass and shiny aluminum new door resisted coming open. That smell hit Terry, stirring a million, zipping memories. *...Wax floor polish, musty smell of marble, drippy caramel and cinnamon rolls, many subtle, slight perfumes...*

Terry strode through the doorways of CHS, and turning to the right down the hall, his arm was grabbed by a familiar girl.

"Terry, gosh, it's so nice to see you. You look so terrific, in the uniform."

"...Hi, Mary," Terry replied. *...Mary Emory...so many people...*

"I guess you're going, right?"

"Three days. Going to see Mom, tomorrow, in Salina."

"Good luck, Terry. Don't forget us." Other "Hi, Terrys" echoed down the hall, as friends passed. Terry threaded his way to the front office, rumors of his visit spread fast.

...gotta say bye to Coach...

Terry wasn't at CHS long. Long enough to say thanks, and get good wishes from Coach Betts, and more hellos! and startled looks from many. *...sure glad I did that, when I come back it'll look different to me probably, I'll miss this place for awhile...*

His dreams and sleep slipped away to the dawn in Vietnam, with the light and the screech of the monkeys.

* * *

Sept 1, 1968

Terry shipped out the first of September, through the Kansas City Airport, and on to California, then Okinawa. On Okinawa, Marine recruits were subjected to endless paper checks. After hours of this, they were flown on to the Da Nang airport. September was hot, unbearably muggy. Still, the Marines got donuts and coffee, and were choppered out to their bases. Terry flew on to An Hua. Strangely, the new arrivals were stripped down of their equipment, given a couple hours of brutal "orientation", given their squad assignments, and literally dumped at squad tent camps, enjoying the isolated life of a "cherry" for at least a few weeks.

There wasn't a lot of communication back to home from Terry in his first weeks, and months. The shock of the difference between Vietnam and Kansas, and even the Marine boot camps, descended on new grunts like Terry. Endless hazards, the fight for survival in missions, the unannounced, vicious firefights and mortar assaults, took awhile to adjust to. By December, letters from Terry started to arrive home. He wrote Coach Betts Dec 2, 1968:

"I got over here the last of August, and believe me it was HOT. Thirty two miles south of Da Nang. I think Vietnam sucks. I'll sure be glad to get out of here Started my 4th month over here the 1st of December. I've seen some action, can't say I like it. I've been written up for the Navy Commendation Medal. I hear I got it, but don't know for certain."

Through the fall of 1968 and into 1969, Terry would become one of the most liked and admired men of Mike Company. He was one of the most careful, savvy, and helpful, especially to the new "cherries". As Mike Company, and An Hua base, came under increasing enemy assaults, back home, the social and political battles also raged and escalated, the center of which was the War itself:

January 21, 1968. The horrendous Battle of Khe San between U.S. Marines and the NVA regular army raged until April 8. The powerful Tet Offensive re-shifted the politics and the fate of the War itself. *By March 9,* General Westmoreland asked Congress and the Administration for 206,000 more troops. Within two months, he was fired and replaced. *Feb. 29,* the legendary Defense Secretary Robert McNamara resigned in the aftermath of the Tet Offensive. *March 16,* the great massacre of civilians by U.S. troops at Mai Lai killed over 500 villagers; courageous individual soldiers eventually broke through the higher Brass cover-up to tell the world, but it would take eighteen months. *By the end of March,* President Johnson himself had announced his refusal to run for office again. *April 4th,* Martin Luther King was assassinated. *In April,* huge university student demonstrations broke at Columbia University. They spread across the nation, and overseas to France, where protests of ten million threatened to bring down the government. *June 5,* the nation was rocked even more by the assassination of Robert Kennedy. *By November,* Richard Nixon was elected President, and the Beatles White Album was released.

The bell was tolling. *The Storm's* full fury had come.

...*Two Years Back...May in Kansas, 1967...*

Chapter 19
MIRACLES IN MAY

The time of nature's transcendent display in New England is October, when the blaze of primary colors of the hardwoods light up the narrow village streets and the mountain sides. In the South, perhaps the glory visits best in March and April, when the honeysuckle, dogwoods and redbuds delight all with their heavenly smells and pastels.

October also reigns in the Rockies, the High Sierra Madres, and the northwest Cascades, when the silver and gold aspen leaves flash in the winds against the brilliant sun and neon sapphire sky, as the song of the ancestors rings to you from the great peaks and lodge pole pines.

The Great Plains, however, are twice blessed by glory. In October, the Flint Hills in Kansas, and the great prairies and dazzling buttes that stretch up up to Canada, are dressed with the tall native grasses, maples and sumac, all painted in an autumn rainbow of colors as stunning as the supernal hues in the grand canyons of Arizona and Utah. The native grasses shimmer in their fall colors against golden-pink sunsets, in color phantasms that shift in the winds before your eyes. It is sad, that too few have seen this October miracle.

The second blessing of glory to Kansas is mid April and May. These weeks bring the illimitable scents and colors of the lilacs and iris, a twin symphony of scents and pastels like no others on earth. These traces of providence spring from the thawing earth. Their perfumes lace magically in the bracing winds with the deep smell of black fallow earth, a scent that hungers for life, like the sturdy peoples who hug the land. Reigning above everything is the controlled burning of the great prairies in the Flint Hills every spring.

From these fires, we see life itself is revitalized on the prairie.

The vast prairie fires are the very spirit of the West. Their eerie-orange, towering tongues of flame can be seen from a hundred miles. At sundown, their wavering, luminous glows blend with technicolor sunsets, to thrust soaring pillars of lighted smoke high into the heavens. These twisting night beacons which rise against the neon twilight are the only rivals to the Great Northern lights, for queen of the skies. If you witness the Flint Hills prairie fires at sunset, its winsome beauty will attend you all your life.[13]

By the end of May, the great thunderstorms, which tower up to fifty thousand feet, bring electric fire, ice, downpours, and tornados to the early summers. All of this crowns May as the great teacher of our place in the circle of creation.

* * *

We were conscious of these glories of May, as we raced through the month, caught up in the suffering joys of track.

It was Thursday May 4, the night before the North Central Kansas League Track championship meet. The screen door slammed behind Gary, smacking Skipper on the nose. We were carrying cots and sleeping bags up from the basement to sleep out in the breezeway once more. *We're getting older. Probably won't be doing this much more again,* I was thinking.

This year the league meet was to be held across the street, at the CHS stadium, down the hill from our house. Betts had the new asphalt spiffed up with newly painted white lines on the six lanes. The asphalt was hand-swept to be rid of gravel, or dirt.

"All-right, we got the basics here," I said. We had the benefit of the screens in the breezeway between the house and the garage, to keep out bugs, and give us a view down onto the streets and part of the field and stadium below. It was one of those soft, fragrant evenings of early May when the colored lights of sunset play on the new green grass.

"We need some snacks, drinks, cards maybe," Gary offered.

"Yeah. You go down to your place and bring up some stuff. I'll scrounge around here in mom's kitchen. We'll meet back up here in fifteen, twenty minutes," I proposed.

We scattered, to get the stuff. Sundown was almost over, dusk was settling in. The incandescent bulb street light at the intersection of Eleventh and Willow Streets, near Gary's house, would pop on any time now. I fished around in mom's food shelves and came up with Jif peanut butter, the new whole wheat bread that Mom discovered, and Knotts Berry Farm blackberry jam. *Better get a flyswatter for any wasps and the red kerosene lamp.*

In a few minutes, we gathered again in the breezeway, with our various contributions.

"I got corn chips, and French onion dip," said Gary. "And I brought a D.C. comic magazine, The Green Lantern, and the Sports Illustrated issue about the up-coming NCAA outdoor track championship, with speed-demons Juan Carlos, Charlie Greene and other great runners. And a transistor radio to pull in KMOA from Oklahoma City."

"Good deal. And I snuck down Roger's short wave radio, so we can try again to pull in overseas broadcasts later in the evening, when reception gets better."

"Cool. Hey, Chris, I noticed a cloud bank coming in from the north-northwest. It's just a single thunderhead but, man, it is tall, and topped out with an anvil.

The sun is still lighting up the top of it even though sundown has passed. Come, let's go look."

We zipped out the breezeway door, and headed a bit north, over to mom's cherry trees and the top of the hill that slanted down into Tyler's yard.

"Sure enough," I said. The cloud bank was slowly approaching. The very top of the anvil was still pink-orange tinged with the last traces of sunlight fading fast. Bolts of blue-white, green-white, and purple-white lightning zipped around inside the giant cloud, illuminating the three-dimensional interior of it from different angles, so it seemed to shift its shape every split second. The lightning raced with crackles spreading out at different angles.

After a few minutes of staring in dead silence at the mesmerizing display of providential power, Gary said, "Funny thing. No rain under that thing that I can see."

"Yeah. You're right," I whispered low.

"And the thunder is more like a continuous rumble rather than any big earth-shakers."

"Yeah."

"And it isn't moving too fast. And more strange, have you seen any bolts come down to the earth?"

"Uh., no. Now that you mention it, no."

Minutes passed as we scanned this creeping giant of the sky. Darkness stole in on us, and the outline of the thunderhead faded, with the electric fireworks ruling the sky. Off to the west and southwest, the stars brightly twinkled against a black velvet sky, a crazy contrast that made us wonder if nature was playing a colossal tease on us. I pointed out this weird contrast to Gary. He shook his head, saying, "Uh..didn't you think the cloud bank looked like Lyndon Johnson there for awhile?"

"Yeah. Strange."

Five more minutes passed. Our neighbor's Great Dane had stopped barking at us, and he was taken indoors. The air vibrated with the grumble of thunder and of droning neighborhood air conditioners. The special tang of ozone from the great stabs of lightning wafted through our nostrils.

"That thing's not getting here fast. It'll be awhile. Let's go back," I suggested.

In the breezeway, we cranked up Gary's AM radio and checked out KOMA, but there was too much static from the storm to pull in the station. Surrounded by the song of crickets, the flashes of lightning and muffled thunder, and the tang of ozone, we played cards, and read over the Sports Illustrated article on Carlos and Greene, and scarfed down some chips and dip. We were able to pull in about ten minutes of Radio Moscow.

"It's been a while since I've been able to get those guys," I said. "Wonder what Assistant Principal Dick Kramer would say about us catching the commies on radio?"

"He's gonna be outta here, Betts told my Dad," Gary reported. "He crossed too many women in this town, being such a hard-ass on their girls. He hasn't got much say about things any more. Anyway, it's just funny to hear what Radio Moscow's got to say. We're hardly commies."

"So, speedball," I started in, "now that you're running with the big boys on the relays sometimes, what do you think? How're we going to do tomorrow at the league championship?"

"Ten years in a row, league champions since 1957. Three state championships. Terry is getting faster and faster, and so is Chuck Switzer, really. Salina's pretty good, but Betts doesn't seem worried, so I'm not worried."

"Is Betts gonna place you or Wendell in there tomorrow, on the 880 relay?"

"Probably Wendell. I'm pushing him. He's pushing me. But he's in the class ahead, even though we were born about two weeks apart. We're about the same talent really, I think. Sometimes I think we're gaining on Collins in training runs. But we're not catching Chuck Switzer. He just gets better. I don't see how he runs the 880, and the sprints. Betts told us that Terry's 9.6 at Abilene is the second fastest in the nation this year...and, well, you know what that really was..."

"Man, that storm's almost on us. And still no rain. And listen to that thunder," I said, noticing a change.

The cloud of thunder and lightning was a rolling monster in the sky now, as the thunderhead passed above. We stepped out of the breezeway, onto the driveway, and sat down at the top of the downturn slope on the concrete, to watch the fireworks above.

"*Still* nothing is coming to the ground. How *weird* is that?" Gary exclaimed.

After a few minutes, as we gazed at the startling display, it seemed to speed up. The lightning raced around inside more frantically, in blue, green, yellow and blinding white bolts.

"Holy Mother of God, Gary, see those?" I pointed, my eyes bugging out. Above the great anvil, it shot forth dazzling red sprites, and blue jets[14]. A part of it seemed to swell up for a second. We exchanged glances, wondering like three year olds what was unfolding before our eyes. Suddenly, just north of the stadium, in the very middle of Eleventh Street, a sizzling ball of blue-white light at least five feet tall, simply materialized below the mother cloud.

"*Jeeesus*, check that thing out...What is that?" Gary shouted.

"Uh. Christ..." I ran to the front window of our house, and pounded on the glass, trying to get Mom and Dad to come to the window. When they did, I pointed toward Eleventh Street, and ran back to Gary.

The blue-white ball *pulsed* on the ground in the middle of the street. It grew larger and began wandering around. It set-off sizzling sparks and waving, noodle-like, streams of light. It spat and jerked itself over toward a car near the curb, and leaped on top of it. It spun around on the car, burning swaths of paint and vinyl right off the roof, then slid down to the front hood, to eat more.

"Ball lightning!" I shouted. A thing of legend it is, on the sea and out here on the high prairie. Mom and Dad ran from the front door, and over to us on the driveway, with Skipper trailing and weirdly wailing in the night.

"It looks like...the electric arc light... in the big projector at the movie theatre," I said. We all had trouble looking directly at it; it was so bright, like a fourth of July sparkler.

A car drifted up the street. As if it sensed a victim coming, the electric demon ball whipped itself off the hood of the parked car, and zig-zagged on the ground, and went for the on-coming car, a huge 1965 Mercury four door. The Mercury itself was a monster. The driver wavered and slowed, but the demon ball kept coming.

The zillion-volt devil jumped on the Merc's hood and went straight to burning off large, wiggling widths of paint, and finished by sizzling up the car's antenna and sitting there, throbbing in the night. The driver bailed out of the vehicle, and fled down the street, gurgling like a madman, and looking back like a tiger was after him. He vanished into the night.

The Merc just sat there, with the big ball throbbing like an outer space invader pondering its next move. Cars piled up on either side of the street, watching, waiting. Skipper wailed like a banshee, firing up neighbor dogs all around the block. In a split second, the lightning ball zipped off the antenna and fled to the other side of the street. It zipped and zagged insanely toward a steel cable wire attached to a pole across from Gary's house, at the top of which was a big electric transformer. The demon sizzled up the cable.

"Shit-fire!" shouted Pop, pounding Gary on the back, "It's going for the big one!" Dad's brain was overloaded with endless, colorful phrases, which spilled out like sneezes at unpredictable moments.

The devil-ball plowed itself into the transformer and blew like a comet in the sky, scattering flaming bits and multi-colored pieces for a hundred yards. The doting "mother cloud" sizzled its merry and colored way across the horizon to the east, no doubt planning to plant its next "egg" in the town of Clyde, fifteen miles to the east.

It took the whole neighborhood, and the dogs, a while to calm down. The big Merc got hitched and towed off by Babe Houser's Chevrolet, Oldsmobile and Cadillac tow truck. The Merc's driver never returned.

We relaxed in the cots that night, munched on peanut butter sandwiches, drank Coke, and wondered what-all this was supposed to mean. I guess it's the wondering that really counts. We plain forgot all about Roger's short wave radio.

May 5, 1967, NCKL Track Championship

By noon the next day, the sky had cleared off to a crystal blue. Gary and I were dressing up in the Red Silks in the locker room, and headed over to the track, before the start of the NCKL League championship. Slowly, the buses crept into the stadium's gravel parking areas, or parked against the curbs outside of the fenced stadium. In came the Chapman Irish in their green silks, the old-enemy rival Marysville Bulldogs in their ominous black, and the good-Catholic Sacred Heart Knights of Salina, in their more placid burgundy and whites, led by middle distance wizard Jim "Bony" Niehouse. Then the untiring Clay Center Tigers arrived in their orange and whites, and the Abilene Cowboys, with their nerve-rattling Cowgirl cheerleaders in short fringe skirts. The whiffs of corn dogs and cotton candy, reminiscent of football season, wafted out from the west-side limestone concessions building, manned by the C-Club athletes of other sports, and the booster club.

Our tent was set up at the northeast corner of the field, near the high jump.

"I want you boys away from the crowd, the girls' perfumes, and those dang Abilene cheerleaders. Keep your mind on business," Betts lectured us, as we underclassmen helped Ted Easter and trainers lug the tent equipment out to the field.

This was a fresh day, high in the upper seventies, with little wind.

A terrific assault on the mile and half mile records was waged by Jim Niehouse who, this time, chased past Bill Dotson's league mile record, to run a blazing 4:17.2 Like Bill Dotson ten years before, Jim lapped his competition. This tied his own state's best mile mark for a whole two hours. But word came the next day that his distant, big-city nemesis, Bob Barratti of famed Wichita North, had turned up the heat on Jim with a faster 4:16 mile, the quickest in the nation. This battle of distance titans would see another day.

CHS Iron Men earned some pay-back in Lyle Pounds, who grabbed second in the mile, and Doug Rivers who grabbed fourth, equaling Niehouse's point total. "Sweet mother justice!" crowed Lyle. But a little later, Niehouse flashed a terrific 1:57.1 half mile, second only to his 1:56.6 state best, two weeks before. Even Barrati still chased that mark. Sacred Heart then delivered some payback when Jerry Jones and Ron Smith came in third and fourth behind Sacred Heart's first and second.

"Well, we're gonna have to kick some tail now," Collins groaned in front of the tent.

Luecke and I sat at the front of the team tent, all dressed up, with no place to run. We were window-dressing.

"Gary broke into the big time," Alan reported to me. "Betts has put him on the medley relay, a freshman with seniors,"

"Man," I shook my head in wonder.

"Terry, though," Al continued, "Betts has him in the 880 relay, but not the broad-jump. He's aiming Terry at big time individual records, three events, the 100, 220, and 440. I tell you, nobody is the national leader in *three* sprints. Jesse Owens didn't do that. Bob Hayes didn't do that. It's the barrier thing: a human is not made for super speed across that kind of spectrum of demands on the body. Either you are a short sprints specialist, or a 440 specialist. Either, or. Likewise, you are either a middle distance man up to two miles or you are a marathon man. Middle distance aces don't win marathons, and 440 or 880 speed merchants never have the speed necessary to win the short sprints. But Terry, my friend, is a genetic wonder. In the words of Mr. Spock, Terry 'does not compute'. The Great Spirit above either gives a person fast-twitch muscles and not much endurance, or endurance but not the fast-twitch muscles. No one gets both."

"But Terry..." I ventured.

"...has both," concluded Al. "Terry could probably run a 1:48.0 half mile on his first try. He is a new marvel of DNA." Scientifically speaking, Alan was usually right.

"Were you at the track after practice, last Thursday?" Al asked.

"No...but I heard about it..." I replied sheepishly. I had been up at the ring, throwing the shot put late into dusk, and missed what Alan was alluding to. At that moment, Gary sidled in, carrying something.

"Hey, sports fans, you want some bananas?"

"No man, we're not running in the medley relay, you are..."Alan replied.

"Yeah." Gary plopped down next to us, and began unpeeling a banana. Bananas and sunflower seeds and *Gatorade*. These made up what we called Householter fuel.

The House ran on this crafty combination, he just somehow knew it was right. The rest of us were picking up his habit. The combination is easy to digest and keeps your performance up. Bananas stop cramps from heavy exertion, excessive heat or loss of fluids. The new Gator-aide restores fluids and electrolytes to regain quick muscle reaction. Sunflower seeds are perfect for staying power.

"Big Al here was just explaining about Terry and last Thursday," I told Gary.

"Excuse my French, but hell yes," the soft-spoken Gary replied. "He was timed in practice...at 9.4 in the 100," Gary and Alan's voices overlapped.

"That's the same as Bob Hayes and Jim Hines national high school record," Gary wheezed, taking over the conversation. "I saw it from across the field. It was kind of a quick challenge thing, right after practice. Louis, Malcolm Morgan, and a few others were watching at the finish line with the coaches. They had him timed with multiple watches. Coach Frohardt told us the time. But it can't be counted, it's not a meet," Gary continued. "It's not official."

"Yeah, well, who's surprised?" Alan shrugged.

"...after Abilene and the half-mud track at 9.5/9.6..." I replied.

"Well, today we get to see what happens. He'll try to set record times in the very different three sprints," Alan concluded. "It's *the man* against *the barrier.*"

* * *

Betts had reasons enough to be pleased that day. And the Roman god of speed above, Mercury, once more had his reasons to be nervous. Terry ran 9.7 in the 100 prelims, 49.2 in the 440, and 22.2 in the 220. The 9.7 was second in the state only to his official 9.6. The 49.2 tied Terry with the stellar specialist Dale Alexander in the 440 for the state's best time. And the 22.2 was a league record and very good. Normally, it would win state. But it was not close to Terry's nation-leading 21.6 that he ran on the curve at Abilene's infamous mushy track two weeks before. Terry was just warming up that day. We would see that in spades.

The thing that stills the mind, and steals the breath came again.

In the 880 relay.

The time earned that day in the 880 relay, in print, anyway was: 1:31.2 But it tells *nothing* of what happened on the last anchor leg.

The last few weeks there had been talk of being able to wipe out the all-time state best 880 relay record of 1:28.4 After all, the team of Steve, Wendell, Eagle Man

223

Switzer, and House had put up a very good 1:31.0 earlier, and they were chopping off half a second or so every time they ran, closing in on the all time mark.

Terry had already run 9.7 that day. So things were intriguing...

All of us freshmen relay guys took to the stands with the Fosters, the coaches, and the Iron Men, as the 880 relay was called out. There were a dozen watches in the crew, taking it down.

The new track asphalt was a saving grace. House and Company blew like the wind into a fifteen yard lead over, of course, Marysville. The passes were spectacularly smooth and fast. With more than a fifteen yard lead, Eagle Man Chuck Switzer was approaching the last hand-off to Terry at the far, northeast corner. This was a cinch.

"They're gonna push below 1:30 with House cruising," Betts called out to the bunch of us. We all were hawk-eyeing the baton-pass.

Terry was out too fast, we could see it. Eagle Man pushed himself to the limit to get it into Terry's back-reaching hand, but Chuck was maybe an inch or two short. *The baton dropped.* It bounced and slid forward, but it stayed in the lane: *No disqualification.* House, who had torn ahead, had to launch his air brakes and turn around. He was speeding back. Marysville passed him, and then Abilene, and Chapman. House was still heading backwards, as the league sped the other way. In the sciences of the sprints, this is impossible to fix. It is truly the bridge too far, the ocean dive too deep.

The scene was agonizing and surreal. Terry reached the baton, and he stretched to get it in an effort to regain a couple of inches of hope. He stretched too far and fumbled it again. He lurched back and grabbed it the second time. By now there was a gap of twenty-five yards and expanding between Terry and the league crowd of anchor-men rounding the top of the curve.

From a standing start, against what had to be a little *more* than the actual 220 yards coming out of the first quarter of the hand-off lane, *House let it loose.* It was over twenty-five yards from Terry to the Marysville leader.

The crowd rose in dead silence.

"I swear, you could see the asphalt bits kick back from his cleats," Gary would later say of Terry.

The Fosters and Betts kept spouting, "Sweet Jeezuss..."

Every stride of Terry accelerated; smoothness took second place.

When the Marysville anchor-man made the next forty yards to the 100 yard straight-away, Terry had eaten the huge gap down to twelve yards, passing Chapman and Abilene even before the curve was complete.

Except for silence, Betts could find no other words than "Jeezus." That day, we all saw a Terry no one had ever seen.

The Marysville anchor ran desperately, straight-backed, white as a sheet, straining and splaying his feet out, leaning too far forward. He fled like he was about to be eaten alive by a beast of prey.

Terry leaned forward, into the straightaway, and lowered his head. Instead of running in his special ecstasy of silky speed, you could see him lazer on Marysville like a Falcon diving from the skies.

Terry *ate* the twelve yard lead at the mid field mark. Whoever Marysville was that day, he lost his heart and staggered when Terry buzzed past him.

Still kicking asphalt, Terry assaulted the tape with his right hand like a mother Tiger in revenge, swatting a snake from her cub. I wondered, what could drive him on like that? You could see it in his face: he wasn't out-speeding the world just for the joy of it this time. Something else was going on in his head.

Eight watches: From a standing start, in 20.4 or 20.5 seconds (20.2 or 20.3 200 meters), Terry had covered a little more than 220 yards (202 meters). *A twenty-plus yard lead* had melted into a *six yard loss.* This time was five-tenths of a second better than Henry Weibe's 1955 all time Kansas best. It was three-tenths of a second faster than Mel Gray's best on a straight-away rubber track that year, out in California. It was as good as Olympic stars Juan Carlos, and Charlie Greene's times that year. And it was three to four-tenths of a second off the *world record.*

Of course, the "official" time was 1:31.2 But the *real time* was so different. We had a chilling sense that nothing quite like this had been seen before.[15]

We reflected on this for days and nights. Wendell, Gary and I talked about it in a partial fog. It couldn't be just about him wanting glory or winning the race. He did that every day. It had to run deeper than that. Something had clicked inside Terry. It was a puzzle that took me a long time to decipher. But I got a clue to it, in the next several days.

* * *

The final season team meeting was held on Thursday, May 18. This was a couple of days before the Concordia High School senior graduation, and the day before the looming State Meet. We met on the track after school, in performance Red Silks. We were going to get the big wrap-up by Betts just before the State Meet, we thought.

Gary and I strode along, eyeballing the groups on the field. Some were in the middle of the field, lounging and stretching. Another group was at the far south end, watching and trying pole vaults and broad jumps.

"We've never tried the long jump. Let's go. We got speed. Surely we can jump a distance..." said Gary, so we took off down there. Byron Beauchere and House were long-jumping, having fun, "Wishing for the 'old days' when I used to whup 'em in long jumps, too," Terry quipped.

A crowd traded turns, trying the long-jump, seeing what we were worth. We were milling around the sand pit, checking our marks, when a ruckus broke out by the nearby south goal posts. We looked over at the rising voices. A shoving match was heating up, not a good one, between Swaggart, and Foster, and quite a few others.

"Oh, God," I said to the group. "Tangling with Pete ain't a wise idea, I can tell you from Catholic School." The crowd was starting to drift over there.

"Let's go see about this," Gary said gamely. Our group followed him over. We were all scared. You know, when your ears ring, and you get dizzy from fear. Worse, I felt that cold ghost again rising up my spine. A bad feeling was spreading fast.

Before we got there, we saw a slight figure, red-headed, maybe Jones, cut into the middle of the group. Things were obscured to us. The ruckus died down as we approached, and guys drifted apart.

We bumped into Jerry, coming out of the crowd.

"What were you up to there? What was happening?" Alan and I pelted Jerry with questions. The soft hand and quiet voice of Jerry reached out to us younger guys. He was always that way.

"It wasn't just me going in there. It's okay, guys, really. I think it's been worked through," Jerry assured us.

"Yeah? How so? It looked like some guys were aiming to carve a chunk out of Swaggart, if you ask me," I said, still simmering. *Son of a bitch can only understand one thing,* the ghost whispered to me in its frosty, raspy voice. Gary glanced hard at me and saw what was going on inside me. He knew what was ticking, and he spoke in his quiet, calming way. "Let's just hear out what Jerry says..." Jerry was solid gold, in my book.

"Oh. There were words," Jerry explained. "It was a group of hot-heads. Brett said something nasty to somebody. It turned into sort of a group shoving match. I was pushing in there, to see, maybe help put a stop to what was going on. Terry just walked in there too, cool as a cucumber, and said quietly, 'Hey, guys, we're all a team here. We're together.' Terry had that mile-wide grin going. Brett looked back and forth for awhile, like he was thinking. Then Brett said, 'Terry, you're right, man. You're so doggone right.' Brett turned and walked out of there, and the whole thing broke up. It was over. It's all over, now," Jerry repeated. He slapped us on the back and strode off toward center field, where the crowd was drifting in to Betts' whistle. Gary and I looked at each other. We turned to follow Jerry. In fact, we all did.

Salina, Kansas. State Track Meet, 1967 May 19 and 20

The Kansas state-wide high school track meet is one of the largest, most elaborate of its kind in the nation. 1967 looked to be one of its greatest years. The Regional championship meet at Shawnee Heights High School in Topeka proved uneventful, as it was miserably cold, rainy, and on a muddy cinder track.

Salina High School, the site of the meet, had a newly pressed asphalt track This was historic. It would be the *first* time the State Meet was not held on the slower cinder tracks. Asphalt was not quite as fast as the fancy rubber and banked tracks, which mainly appeared on the East and West coasts, at the biggest universities. Not even KU had asphalt, much less rubber.

This meant a lot to us. Here, we could show what the Iron Men, and the relays teams, and our sprinters, could really do. The East and West Coast newspaper darlings like Mel Gray and others to come, had their chance on a modern track almost every day, certainly at every big meet. But out here in Kansas, this was our *one* chance. It was Terry's *one* chance to step into history, on a virtually modern track, against something like real competition.

At the team meeting Betts put it well to us on Thursday, as he slowly clenched and raised his fist, "Men, let's go and *show 'em*."

Friday, May 19, the Preliminaries

It was partly cloudy, in the low seventies, with a light, gusting wind from the west and south. Most races started from the north, so the shorter races were either not in a wind at all due to a west-side stadium blocking the southwest wind, or the runners raced *against* erratic, small gusts.

We settled in up high in the stands on the east side of the stadium. From there we could spot the races especially well with binoculars, and see complete races from the start to the finish. If we sat in the west side stadium where the races were actually run, we'd be closer to the runners, but the starts and finishes of races would be partly obscured from view by the west side stands.

Some three thousand athletes, from hundreds of schools, were arranged in four class sizes from the smallest to the biggest schools (classes BB, B, A, AA). Schools competed only with their same-sized schools. Class BB, the smallest schools, had well under 100 students. The class AAs were the biggest mega-urban schools like Wichita East, or monster Topeka High, which had over two thousand and five hundred students. Concordia was Class A, with less than five hundred students. Sadly, there has never been head-to-head competition between individual great athletes or relay teams from the different sized schools or classes. Even so, all eyes were still on the fastest times and best marks, regardless of school "class". The stadium was packed with five to six thousand people, including dozens of newspaper photographers.

Sitting in the middle of the Red Silk of CHS team members was Josephine Duffey-Householter, Terry's mother, and his older brother Skip. He was the former state high school pole vault champion for Salina High. Terry's family was a blended, re-married group. Mrs. Duffy-Householter was a two-time widow, and she had much younger kids to watch after school in Salina. That was one reason Terry lived with his grandparents in Concordia, to ease the care burden on his Mom. Because of these circumstances, this was the first and only track meet Terry's Mom had ever been able to attend to watch her son. She sat with her first son, among the CHS Red Silks, quiet and proud as a Mother Hawk, perched high in the stands. She had numerous binoculars within her reach, and we all knew what this meant to the family.

But no one fully knew what beat in Terry's heart, those two days.

Because of the newspaper buildup, all eyes and attention were on certain events and athletes, who were going after some of the fastest marks in the nation. The 120 yard hurdles in the big AA schools was a hurdler's and sports reporter's dream: *Four of the six fastest men in the nation were from Kansas schools* and *were competing in the same races. In effect, these hurdles races were the high school national championships.* And indirectly, these athletes, running in relays, would be pitting their best times against Terry and Company, a repeat of the KU relays.

There was tremendous attention to Terry himself, as the fastest sprinter in all classes and all sprint races in the state. He was ranked among the top three sprinters in the nation.[1619] Then, there were the un-competing wizards of distance, Niehouse from Salina in our league, and Bob Baratti from big school Wichita North. They could battle out the time for the state or nation's fastest mile, but only on the electronic boards, not head-to-head like they did at the KU Relays.

The prelims started about ten in the morning, it was still fairly cool in the upper sixties. Individual heats in the 120 yard high hurdles (110 meters) tantalized the crowd, as all four top national hurdlers easily wiped out their heat competitors by a dazzling eight or more yards, and buried the old state record (the best was 14.1 secs Marcus Walker, Wichita East). Only two-tenths of a second separated all stellar hurdlers, Preston Carrington of Topeka High, Marcus Walker and Maurice King from Wichita East, and Bob Bornkessel from Kansas City's Shawnee Mission North. They all had murdered the old 1955 record by sprint/hurdle legend Henry Wiebe. This had left the crowd buzzing and hungry for Saturday's monumental hurdlers show-down. As if this wasn't enough glory, the very same thing repeated itself, as all hurdlers blazed away at murdering the state record in the 180 yard lows (best 18.8 seconds, by Walker again and Bornkessel).

Rarely, in the history of any State Meet in the nation, would so many great prep hurdlers and sprinters run so fast against each other. The atmosphere at the State Meet was electric.

The relays events were also unparalleled, since they featured the same stellar runners. Big Schools Wichita East, Topeka High, and Shawnee Mission North (KC) ran preliminary heats that morning with their same super-athletes, turning in fabulous 1:29 seconds marks in the half-mile relay. Again, the relays finals the next day tantalized the entire stadium.

When it came time for the class A half mile relays, high tension filled the stadium. House and Company fully intended to wipe out the fabulous half mile relay times of the Class AA schools, and set the all-time fastest mark, and stake our claim after the KU Relays, as the best sprint squad in Kansas, or maybe anywhere. Betts loaded up the 880 relay with Collins, Wendell, Chuck Switzer, and Terry. And our mile relay contained the two Fosters, Wendell, and Eagle Man Chuck Switzer, as the sub for Terry, who was limited to four events. The big schools' athletes also laid down very good times in the 220 (21.6), 440 (49.3) and a new state record in the mile relays preliminaries too (3:19.0 Wyandotte). So things were primed. The gauntlet of times had been thrown down by the big schools. They were nervously very much aware of "little Concordia" and Terry, as challengers to their fame and glory. House and the boys were chomping at the bit to take down the big schools.

Back up in the stands, we had dad's navy binoculars.

Shoes of Gold

"Did you guys hear about Terry's *new track shoes?*" asked Gary.

"Some things," Liedtke piped up, "tell us the whole deal."

"Betts made the rounds downtown, at Ray's Café, at the banks, the shoe stores, and out to the Skyliner Restaurant, where Terry works," Gary explained, "Local businessmen offered Betts enough money to buy Terry the best sprint shoes in the world: *Adidas Olympic Golds.* They're over one hundred dollars. You can't imagine. Each shoe is the weight of only a dozen pencils. They're a little thin for the hardness of asphalt. Everybody chipped in. Betts gave Terry the shoes Thursday night. Terry hunted me down, to show them to me before he boarded the bus this morning, before we all drove down here. Nobody, *nobody* has these shoes in this state." We were silenced by this.

The Class A hurdles races were due up next, now that the Class AA schools hurdles prelims were done. Then the 100, and later the 220, and then 440, and finally the 880 and mile relays preliminaries were coming, where we had guys entered. Tomorrow, the Iron Men would get their one run at the finals, because they had no prelims. The stadium crowd and army of reporters simply waited, in a quiet buzz, for the Class A sprints and relays to come up, to see House & Company

We had the binoculars out, hunting for Red Silk, for Steve Collins, and for Terry himself, when the 100 yard preliminary heats were announced. I spotted Steve in the first heat. He blazed out a 10.1, to win the first heat. The second heat was up. I passed the binocs around.

"Hot damn, I've got him," Louis called out low. "I've got those gold shoes spotted on the black asphalt." Cries of "Don't hog 'em, Louis!" and "Everybody gets twenty seconds" spun out, as friends grabbed for the binoculars and spotted Terry. He was looking loose and flashing the shining gold Adidas.

They went down into the blocks. Terry was the last man down, showing he was serious. The stadium went silent, the cameras readied, and the gun-smoke set off a thousand stopwatches. Terry out from the blocks was two yards ahead, seven secrets perfect.

In the passing of simple seconds, beneath the Kansas blue, the crowd rose in waves, like wheat, to see the Red Silk rocket flash down the track, as smooth as cream. Terry stretched the gap every second to five or six yards by the fifty yard mark, and sailed effortlessly away down the stretch.

Terry's Mom and brother stood with us at first in silence.

"Good God Almighty," her voice finally trembled, "He runs like the wind."

Terry snipped the tape and the watches around us showed 9.7, the fastest time laid down at the meet.

"He's saving up for tomorrow. He's got a lot to run through today in short order," Coach Frohardt called out from behind us.

"And that's saving up?" asked Liedtke.

We found our way down to concessions, Louis and I. The experiences today were fracturing our sense of normalcy. We needed a break. Besides, we were usually the first ones to eat, so we had to keep up appearances. "Got a dang hollow leg," Louis quipped. We gathered up the chili dogs and Cokes.

"How are we going to explain this someday?" Louis asked, as we headed back to the stands. In this question, he had hit the spot. *I have no answer*. I just raised my eyebrows in reply. We ascended the stairs back into the brighter lights.

By the time we got up to the CHS stakeout in the stands with the chili dogs, Gary and Alan waved us in, saying, "Dudes, the 880 relay's up."

"Too many of those, Mr. Hanson, and we may have to migrate for cleaner air pretty soon..." quipped Coach Frohardt. A wave of smirks spread among us for a couple seconds.

Frohardt leaned over to talk seriously to us. He had been our coach for the freshman football team. A compassionate social scientist with a Masters degree, he was more like a trusted older brother than a whip-cracking sports coach to us. He had our attentions.

"Look, you guys. Coach Betts has put all his cards on the table with this half-mile relay team. He loves these guys. And he's betting that their fanatical...do you mind if I say fanatical... devotion to sprints training, and the science of baton-passing, will put them into the record books, by one or two seconds under the Class A state record, and better than the all-time best. And God knows, they've got Terry. So. Hold tight to your shorts on this one."

At the gun, it was clear in seconds. Steve Collins took the lead at the curve, cutting ahead by three yards. The baton-passing was exquisite,

"See, see?" Diebel called out to us. "If you follow the baton with your finger, and the baton does not slow down when it is passed, you got a team that knows what they hell they are doing, and that team is going to win." By the second baton pass Wendell had put four more yards of space between himself and the nearest team, and in Wendell's flawless second pass to Chuck Switzer, we instantly gained two more yards.

"It's a science, man, it's a science!" I yelled, whomping Luecke on the shoulder. With his mile-wide, and girl-swooning grin, he pounded my shoulder back, "Damn straight, damn straight!"

When Terry took the baton, smooth as a greyhound he doubled the lead, and split the tape. A new state class record, 1:30.6 for 880 yards. Just a few tenths short of the State Meet best, just set by dynastic big school Wichita East, fueled by their wonder-hurdlers, King and Walker. We gladly waited to match our times with theirs in the Finals.

This chalked up state record number two for the House. A few athletes had won quadruple gold in State Meet history.

"Just to let you know," Frohardt said, bending over us again, "we could find only one athlete, not even Bill Kimble, who has chalked up both four golds and four all-time or State Meet records in the same State Meet, and he was Jim Ryun. And House is now on track even for this."

To get past the tension and a huge batch of events, we had to down a few more Cokes, wander around ogling girls, and twiddling our thumbs, before we got to see House's next challenge: The 220 preliminaries.

We knew, from Betts and from the walking encyclopedia named Diebel, that Kansas had a long list of great 220 yard/200 meter men down through the decades, especially from the 1930s to the 1960s. The names of Charlie Tidwell, Henry Wiebe, Duane McIntyre, Bill Kimble, and Wallace Hulse, always came up in conversations. We knew Terry was like them, a breed apart. Kimble himself, the year before in 1966, had a fantastic, national-record class 21.1 second wind-aided 220 in the Finals of the State Meet. This couldn't stay on the books as the official all-time State Meet record, Betts had told us, because of a disqualifying stiff back wind. The question stuck, unspoken in us: what would Terry show 'em?

The Afternoon

The Class A 220, the tension-filled 880 Relay, the Mile Relay, and the grueling 440 were next up in order.

Just after noon, Wendell dropped in from the field for a visit to us, just after noon. The 220 was scheduled for about 1 p.m.

"How's it look down there, studly?" I asked, as he plopped down.

"Hey. Give me a sip of that thing." He grabbed Louis's Coke for a quick slurp.

"Yeah. Dish out the news from down there," Gary prodded Wendell, as he slurped down the cola.

"We're loose down there. We're ready. Switzer looks a little pale, but Betts tells him 'Charlie, if I didn't think you could tear up the anchor in the mile relay in place of Terry, and get that baton to that red rocket in the 880 relay, I wouldn't put you in both relays. Nobody can do this like you. And Terry is limited to four events.' Charlie got all his color back after that, and the glint in his eye." Wendell was great at reconnaissance reports.

"We're primed," Wendell remarked. "And House, he's cool as a cucumber again. But he's not talking today. So something big is going down."

Terry's Mom turned around, overhearing Wendell. She reached out and touched his arm, "Wendell," she asked in a quiet voice, "today's going to be good, don't you think? It feels good."

"Yes, ma'am. Today is gonna be better than good."

She smiled a winsome smile and reached out to hold Skip's arm.

"I'm heading back, gents. Going to sit watch at the finish line," Wendell announced. He was down the stairs in a flash.

The announcer blared out the coming of the 220 yard Class A preliminaries and gave introductions as to who was who in which lane. Terry was in the first heat.

Gary grabbed the binocs. "Let me check something. He looks good. They're getting into the blocks. But something *is* different."

That got our attentions.

"He's first down into the blocks..." Gary put down the binocs, "...and he *never* does that."

The crowd hushed again. The first seconds seemed normal, people staring, waiting.

Then came that mystifying time that felt so outside of ordinary time...

The gun puff hit. It was Abilene again.

"It was like he was shot out of a cannon," Niehouse said to the state newspapers.

Terry was three yards ahead at six yards out, and his smoothness, like silk, held up. The flashes of his gold shoes seemed faster than ever. He moved like one of those NASA test rockets on rails, on the flats of the Great Salt Lake.

At forty yards, the crowd could see this was going to be different, and stood quickly. The gap behind Terry was eight yards and growing. The competitors looked like struggling middle schoolers, straining and aghast at what they saw streaking away from them down the track. An electric chill went up my spine.

"Jesus, God. He's still *accelerating*," Gary cried out, at eight yards. Gary's eyes bulged in disbelief. Nobody accelerates through the 200 meters. *Nobody.*

"A hundred yards at 10 flat, and he's got twelve yards on them!" Frohardt cried out, his voice breaking.

Terry's Mom stepped up on the stadium seat. She shook her spring hat in the air, and cried out with a mother's voice for the ages, *"Go Terry, go !!..."*

We shook like flowers in a spring thunderstorm.

At one hundred-fifty yards, the gap was an incredible *twenty yards*, and still Terry bore down and the gap lengthened.

Oh, this was different. He was truly flying. Smoothness and picture perfect ecstasy. But this time there was a fierce back-kick at the end of every stride.

Terry unleashed every trick in the book. Trained to see it, we watched, transfixed. He drove his hands and elbow speed faster, pulled his arms in a little, and lifted his knees. From this he picked up a last notch of speed in automatic response. He was not leaning until the last split second. Sprinters face a great temptation to lean at the tape too soon, which only slows you down. Not Terry. His head lifted slightly to the skies, as his iron will tore him through the perfectly timed lean at the tape.

He led the field by an impossible thirty yards.

There was a primal scream from both sides of the stands. It was downright unearthly. The stands boomed from people pounding their feet. The booming stretched into long seconds with a roar like the giant drums of Japan. Terry's Mom burst into happy sobs, hugging Skip. Some people danced berserk in the aisles.

After several minutes, the announcer clicked on the big speakers: "Ladies and gentlemen. You have just seen Terry Householter run the 220 yard dash in...21.3

seconds (21.1 meters). This appears to match the all time State Meet record, is a Class A new record by far, and...it is the fastest time in the nation so far this year, in our records here."

Gary and I sat in the stands, holding our heads in our hands and watching the crowd boil, for a moment that has never really stopped for any one of us. Terry's other preliminary races that day were similarly spectacular: four events, four state records. His prelim of 9.7 seconds in the 100 was the best of the meet, he broke the 440 yard record at 48.9 seconds, and ran a blistering 20.7 leg in the 880 relay, which set a new class A state record at 1:30.6 The Red Silks appeared set for greater things in the Finals the following day.

That Friday night, Terry celebrated with his Mom and family, at her home in Salina. At breakfast the next day at the Skyliner Restaurant back home in Concordia, Gary and I were downing some eggs and hash browns. My Dad was going to drive us back to Salina to see the Finals. Dad came back to the table after tracking down a refill of coffee, and plopped a newspaper down before us. It was the Saturday May 20 Topeka Daily Capitol, the official State Meet newspaper of record. On page 18 it had all the times and marks of yesterday's preliminaries, and articles about the athletes. Gary and I poured over this page like hungry rabbits. Still, there were the Finals today...

...Thirty seven years later...

I pulled out this old newspaper from my dusty collection, to look it over with Lyle Pounds. The old Topeka Daily Capitol, May 20, 1967. Suddenly we noticed on page 17 of the paper was a stunning photograph. It was a big feature photo of the fastest man in the world, Nebraska's Charlie Greene at the finish line of the 220 yard dash in the Big 8 university championship meet on Friday May 19, 1967, up in Lincoln, Nebraska. Charlie Green, the fastest man in the world in 1967 and 1968, and a Gold and Bronze medalist at the famous Mexico City 1968 Olympics, had hit the tape in 21.5 seconds. Of course, the photo of Charlie Greene was from *May 19, 1967, the day before, at the Big 8 University championships.*

But on the next page 18, was Terry Householter's same race report, also *from May 19, 1967, the same day, at the Kansas* high school *state track meet.*

We simply didn't realize for thirty-seven years: on the same afternoon, one hour later, eighteen-year-old Terry Householter had run his 220 yard preliminary *two-tenths of a second faster* than Charlie Greene, the fastest man in the world.

Chapter 20
DAYS OF BLOOD AND GOLD

The Finals of the great meet sprang into action on a day of slight, gusty winds from the west. Ambling puffy clouds sought to wander somewhere east by north, in a sky of robin's egg blue.

Early that morning, the trainers Rick Radcliffe, Steve Thompson and Ted Easter bandaged and re-taped the bottom of Terry's right heel tightly enough that the skin wouldn't shift, but not tight enough to pressure the wounds. Only a few knew: During yesterday's blazing runs, Terry's right heel suffered splits in the skin, and a blister. This was due to the thin soles of his Olympic grade shoes. They were designed more for the new, softer rubber tracks than for rock-hard asphalt. Still, Terry wore his shoes today, and what happened is not forgotten.

* * *

The spirit was bracing, and amazing high drama abounded in all corners of the meet. Newspapers had trumpeted Terry as the fastest sprinter in the state and a national contender. Terry faced the Finals in the 100, 220, 440 and the 880 relay, with the prospect of four gold medals, and state and even national year's best times. The four remarkable hurdlers from Wichita, Topeka, and KC were anticipated by all to battle it out in inches, in a "super show-down" that also threatened to erase state records, or national year's best times in the two hurdles events. Not to be outshone were the two iron-willed, invincible distance machines, Niehouse and Barrati, from the smaller Catholic school vs the Big City Wichita East track dynasty. They had re-captured the intense fervor that surrounded the world phenomena of Kansan Jim Ryun just a few years back at the same legendary Wichita East High School. They would fiercely drive themselves into the ground to beat each other's time, since they couldn't race head to head. The Iron Men of the state suffered high anxiety over this fierce duel. Eyes were on "little Concordia" and its sprinters and Iron Men, who had won three years of State Class A team championships. We were symbolically challenging giant Wichita East which also had won three years as AA Champs.

One more very unusual element laced the air. It was the time of "Black Power" in the streets of America, and one public arena of protest and statement was the world of track. The big schools of Wichita especially were blessed with the fantastic talents of the young black prodigy hurdlers. There was a slight air of race tensions and rivalry, given the indomitable talents and irrepressible cheer of Terry "from nowhere", the nation's fastest prep sprinter, and the blazing kid prodigy of Bob Bornkessel, one of the nation's fastest hurdlers. Both happened to be white superstars competing in the same galaxy of African American super-talent in Kansas.

This "who's the greatest" rivalry would play out in a one-time amazing event, scheduled in Wichita one week later, called "The Meet of Champions". This "super meet" was created by a group of big school coaches. The State Association had approved this one-time only high school meet, which would finally pit against each other the great individual athletes and relays State Champions from all the schools, to see who could outrun whom. The "super meet" has never been held again. This hoped-for showdown energized everyone at the State Meet. It was obvious "who" was going to compete with "whom" today, and at the Meet of Champions. The anticipations were high.

We Red Silks settled into the same stands on the east side, with binoculars again, in much the same groups as the day before, including Terry's Mom and brother. Gary and I had ridden up with Dad. Louis, Al and the others came separately.

We watched Bob Barrati set the day off with fireworks, taking the two mile in a brief rain shower, running a soaring all-time best Kansas record of 9:18.3 The Class AA school high jump all-time record was shattered at an amazing 6' feet and 8.75 inches by the incredible Presston Carrington of Topeka High School, using the old roll method. He now lay in wait to ambush the hurdles events.

Diebel and I were jittery and shuffling our feet, as we watched with binoculars, the lining up of the nation's greatest teen hurdlers, across the field in the long-anticipated finals of the Class AA 120 yard hurdles.

As with House, the crowd rose in silence, mesmerized. The start was blazing. The clearing of hurdles and the "quick snap down" of the hurdlers legs over the 120 yard high hurdles, were lightning fast. The stable of great athletes ran in a deadlock heat. Only a few inches separated the top four, Marcus Walker, Presston Carrington, Maurice King, and Bob Bornkessel. They soared and sprinted, faster and faster, desperate to gain an edge, hurdle, after hurdle. It was a spectacle of desperate grit, speed, and perfect forms.

In hurdles, the most complex of all track and field events, usually several athletes make a mistake. Some unfortunate clips a hurdle, or clears a hurdle too high, or has a slow recovery to sprint, or messes up their pacing between hurdles. Someone, at least, wavers a little bit off balance. Not these guys. *They ran a perfect race, in the one event where Perfection never visits.*

In the last four yards, Marcus Walker, the pace-setter in the prelims was holding a three inch lead, but Presston Carrington was gaining. At the tape in a photo finish, they were *all* clocked at 13.9...two yards, and two-tenths of a second better than Walker's all-time state mark he set only yesterday at the prelims. It was the fastest mark in the nation at the time.

The crowd went totally berserk. The officials swarmed over themselves for long minutes. *It was a tie for the ages*; not even a photograph would definitively sort out who was first, second or third. Marcus Walker was eventually awarded the gold, and Presston was awarded the silver, with King dropping to third.

"First time I ever took down either of the boys from Wichita East," Presston Carrington told the state newspapers. "But I've been working out some kinks and secrets all year long. I was determined to take them, and they were a bit surprised."

In truth, *nobody* could really tell who got third or fourth, or maybe even second. Yet Maurice King was granted third, with the one-year younger Bornkessel given fourth.

"I can't believe that isn't 'seniority', or maybe Wichita officials kicking in over there," said Gary. "I thought Bornkessel had caught them all with his blazing speed at the last sprint. I had him at third anyway." We guessed half the stadium thought the same. Only the guardian angels knew.

Next up were the distance events of the Iron Men. We breathed heavily, watching Barrati turn in a terrific 4:19.2 mile. We sighed in relief at the tape. So far only Bill Dotson, San Romani Jr, and miracle Jim Ryun had run mile times better. The very next mile race was Class A Jim "Bony" Niehouse's to run, chasing the records of the former champions, and now his nemesis Barrati.

We knew Jim was in high gear when he lapped a competitor on the third lap. At the bell for the fourth lap, Jim cut loose, kicking in his considerable speed. The CHS Iron Men were on their feet, screaming their lungs out and pumping their fists. They were joined quickly by the rest of us.

"He's on track, he's on track...he's not that far from a flat 4 minutes!" yelled Coach Smith.

Fabulous Jim, the distance pride of the Class A, and a Catholic school kid, must have said his Hail Marys for sure. He split the tape at 4:13.7, the fastest time in Kansas. Six seconds or fifty yards the better of Barrati, and twenty yards better of Dotson's shadow. We swooned to watch him return in only fifty minutes to break the 880 state Class A half mile record at 1:55.1 This was just short of the new Class AA prodigy Clardy Vinson's 1:53.7 run only five minutes before, a State Meet all-time best.

So far, the Iron Men and the astounding hurdlers ruled this great day of days in State Meet annals.

Finally, Terry's turn came. Terry took first in the finals 100 in 9.8, and the 220 in 21.6. Both of them were the fastest sprints of the day in all classes. He topped out at 49.0 in the quarter, a yard slower than his prelim record 48.9 yesterday. Terry now held three gold medals and three State Meet records, with the promise of four waiting in the finals of the 880 relay. But something seemed suspicious. He should have clipped two, maybe three-tenths of a second, or more from these times, given his blazing performances yesterday. Quickly the question found an answer.

"Binocs don't lie," Gary said, after watching the 220 finals. "Terry's down. *He's down!*" Terry was sitting on the field. Easter, Radcliffe and Thompson were working on his injured heel for a long fifteen minutes. Jerry sped down to get a report.

"Can't tell for sure," Jerry said. "They got him re-wrapped pretty good by the time I got there. He was joking with Easter, telling him he could borrow a little of his speed for the taping, if Ted needed it. All I could get Ted to say was that Terry's heel had some slits in it."

The 880 relay was looming. The big show down, with all of Betts's marbles in play.

The Class AAs were first up. We sat stunned to watch Presston Carrington of Topeka...again... close in on Wichita East's Marcus Walker on the anchor leg 220. At the finish, Walker obviously could sense Presston gaining on him down the stretch. Presston out-leaned him at the tape. Sweet revenge this time. Fabulous Topeka High took the 880 relays finals at 1:28.6 We were wondering if House, patched up, and Chuck Switzer and the boys could increase their afterburners to make up this much. We were a little skittish, because our mile relay had taken second to Buhler, when we thought the combined assault of the Fosters, Wendell and Chuck would have taken them. The 880 Relay was now big stakes.

Gary looked at us, as the class A 880 relays teams took their lanes. He spoke to everybody around, in his quiet way, "You guys, you need to remember something. Terry ran that 20.4 seconds 220 leg at the Concordia Relays, making up about thirty yards when the baton was dropped. Remember the 9.4 at practice, and the 9.6 at Abilene? Do you remember how Terry handled the spiked foot at the KU Relays?"

We all sat kind of dumbfounded, afraid to believe in one corner of our hearts, but knowing what burned in Terry...

The gun was off and the stop watches were running. Betts was on the field, but coaches Frohardt and Copple were behind us clocking it, along with Gary's watch. Collins passed the baton smoothly to Wendell, with a five yard lead. "22.0 seconds!" Frohardt cried out. It was Steve's fastest time ever. Wendell took the baton and burst forth. You could see his laser-like will pushing him on in every stride, widening the gap yard after yard to nearly a dozen yards at the pass to Eagle Man Switzer.

"Relentless," I wheezed out. Louis and Gary nodded their heads. Wendell pushed the afterburners,

"22.0!" shouted Frohardt. This was unbelievable. With a perfect pass, Switzer soared forth like a scorched antelope. Approaching the pass to House, Frohardt cried out "They're over two seconds faster than their own state record! If House gets it, we'll blow away the all-time state best for damn sure!" We held our breath.

Somehow, on the last up-take of the baton as Charlie was to reach out to Terry, the baton hit something, and it bobbled down into the lane. *It was a nightmare. It was the Concordia Relays all over again.* We watched the baton scoot down the track. It was impossible: the twenty yard lead vanished as House had to hit the brakes. He scrambled back, getting passed by Marysville. Miracle of miracles, the baton may have stayed in the lane...because *Terry picked it up*! *And he was out like a Nike missile!*

"God Almighty, with Terry there's a chance!" yelled Gary. Terry's Mom hopped up and down. The crowd went berserk, all over again. The stands thundered. *If the baton had stayed in the lane, nothing was impossible for Terry.*

The Marysville runner glanced back twice, something nobody does, in total panic. He no doubt remembered what happened to him at the Concordia Relays. *The earthly god Mercury was coming for him again,* and the poor devil knew it. Terry bore down on him like a cheetah, eating yards every second, honing in like a Hawk on a field mouse.

It was simply insane. The dropped baton again. The impossible dream, a 20.5 or 20.4 second 220 from a standing start, was being unreeled again by Terry, this time with a wounded foot. Like the idea of a moon landing, this couldn't be possible, but here it was.

Terry torched the staggering, tortured Marysville guy again at the tape. The stadium lit up like a Saturn 5 moon launch. Terry's Mom was coughing, finding it hard to breathe.

We couldn't have been more blown flat in disbelief if a Vulcan Mother Ship had landed in front of the White House, on TV.

In a minute, the wavering voice of the announcer clobbered us with the news that *Marysville* had won. The baton was ruled to have bounced out of the lane, despite protests by Chuck, and Terry and Betts. The stadium groaned like a wounded lion. But this black cloud had a silver lining that shines on. In spite of not being able to take down the all-time record, which had almost been matched by smirking Wichita East, and in spite of losing the fourth gold, even the official record shows that Marysville's winning time of 1:31.6 was ten yards, or a full second behind the new class A state record set by Concordia the day before in the prelims: In the official program of the following year 1968 State Meet, the picture and Company on the page for the class A best 880 relay team in 1967 was that of Terry and the boys after their state record in the prelims, not the Marysville finals winner. Perhaps this was a gift of the officials to Terry and the boys.

Ad Astra Per Aspera

"Yes, my foot really hurt in that 220 finals run, (21.6). It didn't get better by the 440, and the 880 relay," Terry told the newspapers after the Meet. The truth came out. One newspaper article summarized what happened:

"Friday he suffered some tears on the outer layer of skin and then, during the quarter-mile preliminaries (48.9, new state record), there was *a deeper break, nearly to the bone.* Saturday (at the finals) he ran with the wound bandaged, *but it oozed blood through the shoe,* and he had to change the bandage after each race."

You will never shake the image from your mind: With the skin split on his heel nearly to the bone and bleeding through his shoe, Terry ran the fastest 100, and 220, and 440 and the incredible 880 relay leg in 20.6 that day, in record times, and by the clock he out-raced some of the greatest all-time high school speedsters at the meet. In one hundred years, no single State Meet sprints champion in Kansas has ever run all three races in faster times.

Yet these things are not what we took with us into our lives. What mattered to us were not his records or wins, nor even his spectacular runs. It is what he showed us…the blood on the gold…that taught us something much greater. Yet the biggest trials for Terry and for us were still to come. Peace of the soul for the lot of us was a long way off.

...Two years later, May and June, 1969, Vietnam

Chapter 21
DAYS OF BLOOD AND BRONZE

An Hua Basin and Mountains near the South China Sea.

The port city of Da Nang and surrounding An Hua regions before the war was famously dreamy and picturesque, with its quaint food markets, French quarters, pristine port, and slow pace of life. The rich, green surroundings in the hills outside the city led off to mountains. The intrusive arrival of vast military forces after 1965, both American and the NVA, starkly altered this paradise.

Throughout late 1968 and into1969, the North Vietnamese command was undertaking a slow build-up of forces in the Que Son mountains and An Hua Basin, preparing for major battles that began in the summer and carried through the fall of 1969. The An Hua Marines Base was a main staging area for Marines of the 5th Regiment, to support the 1st Marine Division in its mission to decimate these forces. Heavy, torturous night and day battles built up through the winter and intensified in the spring. The villages were becoming more infested with VC supporters who took pot-shot, mostly night attacks, on Marine patrols and the bases, using buried explosives, mortar assaults, and sniper fire. The NVA plan was to eventually launch a full-scale assault to take the nearby key port city of Da Nang by the fall. Marine commanders decided to block this by wiping out NVA and VC forces in the regions, after the winter "clearing" operations had not run off the NVA. The basin areas below the mountains, including rivers, fields of grass, and rice paddies were dotted with many villages increasingly associated with VC forces. Another center of enemy power was an island stronghold in the middle of the Ky Lam River, known as Goi Noi Island.

The job of Mike Company, from late May until late June, was to help other companies surround the island and block escape routes, while seven full Marine battalions plus air power were to pound the island fortification into decimation. The outlying Marine companies would attempt to stop and kill escaping forces, sweep villages to round up or kill VC attackers who constantly ambushed the Marines at night, and chase down any NVA forces that might escape to the nearby Que Son mountains. Mike Company, with its three squads, was given those very three assignments. From late May until July, the company was involved in increasing battles, losses and casualties.

The 5th Marine Regiment/First Marine Division/ 3rd Battalion / Mike Company

"...The Fifth Marine Regiment (5th Marines) is one of the most highly decorated regiments in the world. Among its' many honors are seventeen Presidential Unit Citations, service in every major campaign and war since Vera Cruz Mexico in 1914, and the Croix de Guerre with Palms, gold and silver stars from the French Government. Members of this regiment wear a fouraguere, (a twisted rope in the colors of the Croix de Guerre), while serving with the unit. Marines who have served with the "5th" are always proud of that service, and tend to think they have been among the best in the Corps. This is not a slam to any other unit in the Corps, or any unit of military anywhere, it just serves as an example of the Esprit de Corps that molds a fine fighting unit. This was a pride in the history and honors of the regiment that was bought with the blood and sacrifice of those who went before..."[16]

The Marines of Mike Company, Spring and Summer of 1969

Terry was the new Second squad leader. Lance Corporal.

Frago, known as "Flower Child". A hippie at Haight Ashbury in San Francisco before being drafted. He was always joking, had a great sense of humor, and was the best man with a rocket launcher anywhere.

"Waterbull". A giant of a man, he got his nickname by carrying at least six to eight canteens at all times.

Maxwell: A tall well-built black Marine in weapons as a machine gunner. He always carried the gun with a belt of close to one hundred rounds loaded and ready, and he damn sure knew how to shoot it.

Michael "Dutch" Lennehan was a big crazy Dutchman from Pennsylvania, a little town called Sugar Notch. A terrific storyteller.

Paul O'Connell: A tough street kid from Boston, the squad leader for First Squad, and a year-long friend of Terry's. Paul always wore a boonie-hat curled up at both front and back like an "Old Corps" Marine would wear a campaign cover. Cocky and self-assured, he seemed to relish combat. Paul was recommended for a Bronze Star Medal for capturing three VC single-handed, in March.

The Company Corporals: Corporal Westfall from the weapons platoon; good-looking, quiet, sturdy. Corporals Main and Weitzel of weapons were the kind you could depend on. Corporal Boren was a dark-haired tanned Marine, with a no-nonsense attitude about him. If you ticked Boren off, or he caught you screwing up, he had no problem with decking you.

Ronny Smith. A machine gunner, likeable and dependable.

242

Grady Rainbow: Tough, reliable sharpshooter, with keen senses for survival. Oklahoma bred, wiry and swarthy, from a long military family.
Staff Sergeant Wagner was the Platoon Sergeant. He was reserved and rarely let his guard down. He played poker, but wasn't a buddy."
Lieutenant Thomas Mahlum was the Platoon Commander, known as "Mike 1 Actual". Young, and rash, he knew how to lead this group of wild kids. He made it a point to always look out for them, even obtaining beer.

* * *

The night attacks, and the day-time village sweeps throughout May, left the Mike Company squads increasingly traumatized. Most men were psychologically frayed, and boiling in anger at losses of friends, a few subject to self-injury and suicide, and all men physically exhausted to human limits:

"The heat was unbearable and the humidity (would) sap the very life out of you... Unlike our forefathers in other wars, we didn't go into the lines for a campaign, and then withdraw to re-supply and refit for the next battle. We arrived 'on the lines', were either under attack, on operations, or standing patrols to watch for attacks from the first day until you left country (thirteen months)...do this all day and stand watch at night, it took its toll quickly. Sleep became a rare jewel to be prized, we probably got four hours a night."

By mid-May, Mike Company Marines would fall asleep while on march, even when under threat of attack. Making all this worse, the Mike Company Marines had developed an underlying streak of desperate fury at the company command, regiment captains and officers, since the late days of Operation Taylor in March. On March 3, simply unbelievable orders from above forced the squads of Mike Company to withdraw from a most intense battle when they were desperately fighting, trying to rescue and bring home the bodies of comrades killed on the field near Fire Support Base Tomahawk.

Three Marines bodies became the battlefield for two days, forcing the loss of even more Marines. The North Vietnamese Army had viciously made their bodies a killing field, knowing the Marines would go to the ends of the earth to bring the bodies home. The rage, fury, and dishonor forced upon them by the Company Commander, who subsequently left, knew no bounds in the hearts of the Mike Company warriors.

"The bodies of three comrades were left, unrecovered. This was a bitter pill for the men to swallow, Marines don't leave their dead or wounded, but Mike Company had done so: friends left to rot in the jungle, alone."

Three weeks later, under a new battalion Commander of Force Recon, the company officers involved in transmitting the order to abandon the Marines killed in battle, were personally ordered to return and retrieve the pathetic remains. But the damage was done. It haunted the men like a black demonic force through May and June.

243

This outrage and betrayal by the former commanders made worse the pressures of battle in May and June. Together these pressures would drive individual men into incredible acts of despair, psychological break, fantastic battle heroics and, as the end approached, unbelievable fighting fury, as June wore on.

The cat-and-mouse game of the Marines defeating the NVA and VC in sweeps over the last year, only to see them creep back in to the region, led the Division Command to devise a severe solution.

"Major General Ormond R. Simpson was tired of this bullshit..and had a plan: Operation Pipestone Canyon, nothing less than the total destruction of the enemy in the An Hua basin region, and it's retreat stronghold, Goi Noi Island on the Son Ky Lam River."

The operation slated to start by the first days of June was incredible: the 1st Marine Regiment of the Division, reinforced by no less than seven Battalions, including two Battalions of the fearless and merciless "Rock Soldiers" of the South Korean Marines of the Blue Dragon Brigade, were to turn the entire region into a vast, barren desert. Two Marine Battalions were to attack from two directions, driving the enemy into the Goi Noi Island and immediate areas, while the greater forces remained disguised behind the initial attacks. Additional Battalions would be hidden as blocking forces behind the Island and areas beyond, so that no retreat of the enemy could take place going south or east. When the enemy was driven to the Island, all our disguised forces, the great mass of power, would enter from behind the original two attacking Battalions, and drive east onto the Island in the river, and decimate the NVA and VC forces. Certain Marine Companies, including the "Mighty Mike", were left relatively free to seek, chase and destroy any fleeing forces, and also to "sweep clear" any villages that might harbor remaining VC.

"Sweeping" these villages meant something rather extreme, in these conditions. Here's what the Mike Company Marines had to deal with, during patrols of the areas in late May, and just as Operation Pipestone Canyon commenced on June 3:

"...we'd lost a Marine, and then a Navy Corpsman (medic) who both sacrificed themselves by jumping on grenades to save the rest of us (from these booby-traps everywhere). There was no doubt ...the villagers...in the Goi Noi Island region were either VC or VC sympathizers. So to defend ourselves, one of the local women was 'drafted' to lead our way into the village. As she moved, she often side-stepped the devices set to maim and kill us, as she wasn't game to commit suicide for her political beliefs...The Marines of Mike Company had lost so many friends to death and wounds around all these villages, the anger, the desire to 'Get Some' in revenge for the bloodshed rose high. They found no men in the villages (another sign they were totally owned by the enemy), just women and children. These valiant warriors were 'not the Army', nor were they unthinking killing machines. Other units under this pressure had cracked that year, notably the Army's Division at My Lai. But the Mike Company Marines, as young as they were, were professionals. They checked their anger and rage, and pushed back the urge to just start killing for revenge, and they swept (the villages) for signs of enemy support and weapons, and no more." (Grady Rainbow Memoirs).

Even so, two days later, on May 28th, booby-trapped explosives claimed the life of Navy Corpsman Medic Doc Pyle, and a missing new Marine engineer. In the bottom of an old bomb crater, the squad members found the medic's body, mutilated, and cut up, with multiple body wounds designed to generate pain and a slow death. He had been captured alive, brought to the crater for questions, and savaged.

"Our squad members (themselves teenagers) were horrified. Morale lunged to new lows in these days," wrote Grady. In the middle of all this hell, one day several bomb casings dropped down on the Marines from friendly aircraft. It was ice cream. Surprise was hardly the word.

It was under these bizarre mind and soul-strangling conditions, the Mike Company was ordered on June 3rd to support the long battle of Pipestone Canyon, to "pursue and destroy" any escaping enemy forces, and "sweep villages" in a new way:

"Sweep through the villages, and upon any attack, burn the village, kill all the livestock, but round up the villagers for re-location, and interrogation...There was a report of a child killed by stray fire during a fire fight between a different patrol and the NVA. No one in the company felt any sorrow. The effects of the previous losses suffered were beginning to take their toll. We were losing our humanity...our ability to care about anything but survival..."

To make things crazier, if that was possible, Mike Company Second squad was unable to assist Mike Company First squad, led by Corporal Stuart H. Tyson, who was trying to block the escape of enemy forces. Corporal Tyson and his Marines were desperately fighting to not be overrun and slaughtered. Terry's Second squad watched the battle helplessly, for two days, unable to assist, and under orders to not fight through to help.

"Our squad could see the NVA pour down the back side of the berm and run over and past the First squad Marine lines for cover...they looked like a stream of black ants in the distance. I watched Marines cry in frustration, we couldn't fire because we might have been firing directly into our own lines and surely killed or wounded Marines..."

Tyson's men fought fiercely, driving back the first assault, and the Corporal raced under fire to rescue two of his Marines. In the second assault, Corporal Tyson stood exposed to horrendous firepower, and threw his hand grenades into the face of the rushing enemy infantry, killing two NVA and breaking temporarily breaking the back of the charge. On the third assault, the NVA overran his position, killing him and half the squad, as the enemy raced into the distance to escape.

Mike Company Second squad never felt so helpless in all their lives.

Over the next ten days, Operation Pipestone decimated the NVA and VC on the Island. On June 20, the three "search and destroy" companies of the 5th Marines, Mike, Lima and Kilo Companies were ordered to turn and chase the fleeing remnants of the escaped enemy, and destroy them in the distant, high jungles of the Que Son Mountains.

The enemy was fleeing to the difficult, high mountain jungle canopies, as they would provide best turf to kill Marines, and escape to fight another day.

The "search, destroy, and sweep" missions died down a little after June 7. Terry, the Second squad leader, had left on June 16th for three days in-country R & R. Terry wrote in letters:

(April 5, to Coach Betts) "Yes, I did 'lose a race' with malaria, but the bugs over here out number you ten million to one...Concordia is continuing to dominate track. I knew of course they would...I am still planning on visiting you, when I do finally get back to the world. I am planning on going back to school on the G.I Bill, but I also want to run, I hope Coach Francis would like me to go back to Ft. Hays (State University)..."

(May 18, to Coach Betts)...I also got a letter from Doc Berner. He told me he saw you at the Regional. He told me he timed Pete in 9.9 in the 100. I remember once he timed me in 9.4...Yes, I am more serious than ever to go back to college. I have really missed being out of school, and I miss Fort Hays an awful lot...I will still go out for track, naturally, and with even more desire to win than I've ever had before. Ken left for the world two days ago..."

(June 18, to John Luecke) "Just getting off R & R...ate eggs, steak, drank some beer...gained ten pounds. I should be out by early July, and home before September."

Terry never bothered people with a word about the hell that the boys were living through.

On the morning of June 20, Mike Company Second squad with Terry as the leader, and the other two squads, were ordered to "saddle up" and hump their way into the Que Son Mountains to search out the enemy, to pin point where to bring in the final fight in this high mountain, jungle battle hell.

To Find A Passage Back. Que Son Mountains, June 21 - 23

The Mike Company squads humped like mad over to the base of the mountains. Spotting a gully that provided something of a pass up the side of the mountains and through the wall-thick jungle vegetation, Grady Rainbow was chosen to move second squad up the mountains. Squads one and three would go along as well, the entire Company. The goal was to track and find the location of any concentration of enemy forces, and report it back to Regiment forces. The strategy on the map was to skirt around the mountain, watching for encampments, staying clear of firefight engagements and detection to the degree possible. Then clear themselves from the area, so that air power, helicopters gunships, napalm and bombs could devastate the areas of troop concentrations, leaving nothing alive.

"The mission was simple: search and destroy. Look for any signs of enemy activity, shoot any lone renegades, get to the top, set in for the night then climb down the other side the next morning and link up with the Battalion. Piece of cake."

The passage back from this assignment became more difficult than anyone ever imagined.

During the ascent up the mountain, the Marines encountered a smelly, light oil covering everything. It was the toxic defoliant, Agent Orange. The climb up and around the mountain led by Grady Rainbow was at first, too slow for unit command-ers. They ordered Second squad to increase the pace. A few hours into the trek, the point men suddenly came into a clearing, with a thick canopy above. They pushed through a hedge of vegetation, into a cleared area, and came across a big encampment, and several NVA laughing and cooking. Mutually spotting each other, the NVA fled into the "bush", which was a thick wall of nearly vertical, un-cleared vegetation and canopies. The NVA had placed the camp, but dispersed into the jungle, presumably to eventually organize multi-angled sniper fire and firefights with Marine forces, which might appear. The abandoned enemy camp area was so large that the squads broke into two groups, to cover the perimeter borders. But the edges of the camp halted at vertical walls of vegetation and canopy.

Regiment orders were to not fully engage the enemy, but rather report on their positions for a later combined assault. This was a little difficult now that elements of the NVA army, which had sought deep cover in the virtually impassible jungle and terrain, had spotted the Marines. Yet Mike Company's orders didn't change, with the changed circumstances.

The orders were easier said by commanders, than done on the mountain. Attacks on Mike Company throughout the first night were sporadic. After dawn, Third squad had the lead to go up, around and down the mountain, but fire broke out on the Ma-rines, as they were winding down the trail. They'd been spied, and were now under withering, sporadic attack.

"Word filtered down, the point squad had run into a well-placed ambush, some of the squad members were wounded, the point man was dead. Sporadic fire ripped through the camp keeping us pinned down; the Skipper called for air support, Cobra gunships. We began to see small clearings in various spots around the perimeter; we had missed these in the darkness of the previous late afternoon. Units of NVA were just the other side of each of these natural fields of fire and we returned their attack burst for burst, but ammunition was becoming a critical issue."

Cobra gunships flew in and zapped the canopy with six thousand rounds per minute machine gun fire. Still the surrounding canopy ripped with enemy cross fire. Down below, on the trail that wound like a "twisting snake", the enemy forces had gathered where clearings popped out. That's where the point man and three other Ma-rines of the Third squad were chopped up. Any recon group or squad heading down the trail would walk into a ten meter clearing and get blown to bits.

Over a pitch-black night, the men prepared. Come dawn on the second day, every group sent down was picked off again, and again the next day. Three days of steady, in-evitable losses ensued, but still Battalion headquarters refused to allow the Company to reverse field and go back around the mountain, for safety. That alternative would allow massive firepower bombs and napalm to be applied below. Instead, the insane radio calls from headquarters continuously called out, "Where are you? Attack, come down the mountain."

Air delivery of supplies, including dwindling ammunition and food, were promised and flown in and dropped in small clearings, only to be viciously fought over by Mike Company and the hidden NVA snipers and forces.

"Hungry Cobras laced the landing drop zone with rocket and mini-gun fire. A massive firefight ensued, neither side giving an inch. I crawled forward to the cover of a pile of rocks joined by Terry; we could see Paul O'Connell directing his Marines to give cover fire. One attempt to recover the supplies had failed, and second and third attacks were launched, to little success. Some ammunition was dragged into the perimeter, but the majority was still raked with fire from both sides and the light on this second day of combat was failing. The food, cases of C-Rations, was out of reach of any friendly hands, as were the cans of water. We weren't going to recover anymore before dark. The Skipper called up Corporal Frago, "Flower Child" and his 3.5 rocket launcher. Repeated rounds were fired into the boxes of ammunition and supplies. Flames exploded over the wooden crates setting off secondary explosions. If we couldn't get the supplies we were damned if Charlie would."

The third day of battle, June 22 dawned. Sporadic firefights, and attacks at the clearing below still steadily picked off Marines ordered to go down the mountain trail. Battalion leaders still screamed for the company to come down the mountain, a sure death sentence for them all. Water and food had run short, as well as ammunition. The men took to drinking mountain spring water, and swallowing dried rice from the abandoned NVA camp. Rotation for a point group to find an escape through the clearing below, for the third time resulted in dead pointmen and Marines. Another supply drop brought food and ammunition.

The fourth day of being surrounded and picked off, with men sent to their death below, was approaching. Mike Company squad leaders and Lt. Mahlum were convinced the NVA forces below were at least of Regiment strength. This was suicide for all of them to try to cut through such a superior force which was not being precisely targeted by air attacks.

The fourth day would be Second squad's turn to lead men down the mountain, to virtually certain deaths. Grady Rainbow and Terry couldn't sleep the night before. Terry thought they might not make it out of there and asked Grady if he would "talk to his Mom". They agreed to do this for each other.

The fourth morning, June 23, dawned with some clearing of the skies. Terry reported "good news" to Second squad: Staff Sergeant Wagner and Lt. Mahlum had shifted the "point duty" to lead the Company down the mountain to press for a breakthrough to First squad. Second squad members felt a moment of relief. Soon, however, shouting broke out. The Staff Sergeant had found the First squad leader, Paul O'Connell, holed up in a cave. He refused to lead his men down to certain death. The pressures had finally gotten to him, a tough guy from the Boston area. He condemned the senseless orders, and all of Vietnam itself, saying "I'm done with Vietnam," again and again, refusing to lead his men to death. The squads seemed on the verge of mental, and organized collapse, as well as certain death.

The raging battle went on between Staff Sergeant Wagner and the uncompromising Paul O'Connell.

With Terry distracted by sporadic fire and the distant raging shouts, the Lieutenant and Staff Sergeant called for him. He ran over and back.

"Terry walked toward me. I didn't need to hear the verdict; the second squad now had point. I told Terry that I would walk the point personally. He laid out the plan for today. Two M-60 machine gun teams would flank me as a point man. We planned to prep fire damned near every inch of the trail down. I was to walk with the M-14 on auto, no planned shots today. The word passed that as we cleared the camp, a detail would cut open and spread the CS over the entire place, denying the use of the facility for at least six months."

Grady was sure of his own remarkable sixth sense to detect danger and where it lay hidden. It had worked repeatedly so many times before in battles, it should serve them well. He was worried that Terry, so recently back from R & R, wouldn't have this kind of sixth sense tuned up as high as Grady naturally had it going that day. And Grady knew that Terry was less than two weeks away from going home. Grady jumped into action without too much discussion, to get the lead going and over with, and get Terry off the line of fire as squad leader. After readying to go, the squad hit the trail, with Grady and the radioman in front, the Corpsman medic, the Lieutenant and Terry, and several squad Marines. Part way down the trail, sniper fire zipped the air, and cut into Grady's mouth, drawing blood, and lodging an AK-47 bullet in Grady's jaw.

Instantly, Terry rushed to check his fallen friend and call in the Corpsman medic. Grady, not terribly wounded, was bandaged up and left with an assistant medical Corpsman and the Lieutenant. Terry jumped into the place of his friend, and took up the point lead.

Down the mountain they went. Maxwell and Ronnie, the two machine gunners, were alongside and right behind the point this time. With the radioman in front, and Terry beside him as point man, the Corpsman medic and support gunners slowly explored the edges of the clearing down the trail below. The radioman carefully crept over a hump, just before the clearing, to see dead Marines spread out in the open field before him. NVA rifle fire split the air, the radio man went down. Terry went instantly over the hump, and grabbed for the radio to call up the trail for help. He had the location and enemy sightings before him. The Company machine gunners were seconds behind them, readying to pour fire onto the enemy snipers. Over the hump, and to the radio, the "baton" had been dropped, and picked up by Terry again...Up the trail, the sniper and machine gunner fire exchanges could be heard. A minute or two passed, and then up the trail tore the Navy medical Corpsman:

"I recognized the Doc as the figure sliding over the knoll to me," Grady wrote. He and other squad members up the trail were rushing down to the firefight scene. "Over his shoulder was Terry, his eyes looking at me in pain."

"Hey man it's okay," said Grady to Terry. "The Doc will take care of you."

The Corpsman bent to his work...

Semper Fidelis

The battle raged that day. The rest of the squad on the trail poured down the mountain and onto the clearing, and let loose everything they had. Ronnie Howard's and Maxwell's machine guns were blazing away, along with Waterbull, giving back the NVA a bigger taste of their own treatment. Master sharp-shooter Grady un-shouldered his M - 14 and precisely cut down a sniper on the far edge of the clearing.

The radio handset lay on the ground shattered. The Sergeant barreled in from the trail, looked around and pointed at Grady, shouting, "This wouldn't have happened if you had done your job." Dazed, Grady slowly raised his M - 14 and leveled it at the head of the Sergeant. For long minutes, Grady refused to waiver, as Company men pleaded with him, "Grady, man. He wasn't here. He just doesn't know. Lieutenant Mahlum will explain it all. Just lower the weapon."

After awhile, on his own time, Grady lowered the rifle. Battalion was called again about the location. The Staff Sergeant and Lieutenant had words, and nothing was said to Grady. And airpower came, first the new Hueys and their bone-rattling guns, then the bomb strikes, then the napalm devil itself. Revenge came, but it was not sweet. The retreating NVA Regiment would not return this time to fight another day.

They had their last encounter with Terry and the Marines of the "Mighty Mike"... those who suffered death burning close, but fought on and carried Hope.

Chapter 22
THE SUNSETS BEYOND

The doorbell rang, Skipper whooped. I stepped to the door, and was glad to see the pearly white, dazzling smile of Gary.

"Come on in, man," I greeted. "Shoot. You get better looking every day. What's your secret?"

"Aw, pshaw... spinach helps, though," Gary joked.

"Come on, let's get some ice tea."

We strode into the kitchen where Mom was grinding ham to make her tasty ham salad, with eggs, mayo, red onions, and a little parsley.

"Where do you get all those muscles, boy?" Mom teased Gary. "Why don't you come over here and grind this grinder, for awhile, use some of those Greek biceps of yours. I'm tiring out."

"Oookay," Gary said with a sheepish grin, but he stepped right up to grind away for awhile.

"So. Terry's back, right I'll bet that's why you're here. You guys want to go down to see him."

"Yes, Ma'am. We sure do," Gary replied.

"How about taking your, uh..." I started to say, when Gary finished the thought, "...ocean blue 1969 The Judge." He knew I drooled over his car.

"...Guess you can figure out what I'm *'driving at'*, huh..." I replied with a smirk.

"Does he ever quit this, Mrs. Hamilton...?"

"Not really. He repeats the puns too..." Mom replied with a smile.

"I just bet Terry could be pleased to see that new Pontiac Judge of yours," I offered.

"Yeah. I'm sure." Gary replied. "He always appreciated anything fast..."

"Let's head out pretty soon..." I said. "There might be a crowd."

July 5. A little south of Oberlin, Kansas

The vibrant, bull-dog jawed man with the soft eyes, and steady voice was working in the granary. The wind scooted across the landscape at better than forty miles per hour, an average day. An average wind. His attractive brunette wife, active in the Methodist church as the head of the usually progressive Methodist Women, answered the phone. She traded news for awhile, and walked slowly out the back screen door, toward the granary. *Darn wind*, she thought, *and this god-awful drought.* It was hard to steady herself in its gusting force. It was so strong it was a little hard to draw breath. The Storm last night, with its terrible thunder and meager rain had not been able to heal the cracks in the ground which widened beneath their feet over the last year or so from the drought.

She entered softly, through the granary entrance, into the dusky interior. The stolid but soulful farmer couldn't see her face, just her silhouette black against the light at the door.

"What's the matter ?" he asked, as he reached her side and turned into the light to see her face. "Well, it's such big news, I don't know if I can tell you," was all she could say. Odd, she kept thinking about the stubborn, widening cracks in the earth, despite the rain. From the information she shared with him, he replied, "I just got a letter from him, a few days back. I've still got all his letters in my drawer in the office. I just love that kid. He's just like a son." Herschel Betts told his wife they had to make this visit, especially for this return. "The farm will get along by itself for a day or so."

June 28. Salina

The ten year old girl's mom was ironing clothes. It was really hot out, but there was a stiff wind, which helped dry the clothes on the line out back of the house at 316 South Connecticut. Her sisters were outside, playing in the yard. Her brother was down at the creek, fishing. The girl sat looking out the window, waiting for her older siblings to come back inside. They had promised to take her fishing, too. Out through the front window, she could see a blue flash in the drive way.

Outside, her sister ran up to the car and stared at the strange men, three of them, in amazingly beautiful blue uniforms. One of them carried a bible, and being fourteen years old, she knew. She tried to run to the front door before the men got to the bell, but she couldn't quite get there.

Inside, her younger sister whispered, "Mom, someone's here." Her mother walked to the door and opened it. She began to scream, and scream, "You ain't coming in my house, you son of a bitch..." One of the men carried a telegram.

June 25. Concordia

Up on the high hill, two blocks west of Highway 81, going east on Eleventh Street, the grass and weeds were getting mowed down fast. I was finishing mowing the steep side hill near the street on the outside of the fence of McKinley Grade School. I planned to mow next into the playground area, and cut the grass on its periphery, about twenty feet inside the fence.

Pushing the mower into the sun, I saw a bright yellow flash. Shading my eyes, I spotted a car parking out front. A tall thin, speeding form slammed the door, and moved like a cat toward the fence opening. A little closer, and I could tell. *Hey, Man, its good old Ted Easter.* He and I had paddled ourselves silly up in Canada a few years before, on the Explorer Post Canoe Trip. *Wild man Ted. Fastest sports trainer in the West.*

Ted and I shared the job of mowing all the schoolyards and practice fields of the grade schools, junior high, and high school. We had great fun, gunning the motor of the 1958 Cub Cadet, the first model of the International Harvester small tractor mowers ever put out. It still buzzed around really well.

As Ted came closer, and out of the sun, something seemed weird. Ted wasn't grinning. I cut the mower.

"What's up studly? Is the harem still following you around?" I joked with him.

"Chris," Ted grabbed my arm. He paused longer than I'd ever seen him.

"It's Terry. He's been killed in Vietnam. They're sending the body home. There's gonna be a funeral, at the high school." Ted couldn't talk any longer.

My eyes rolled into the back of my head. My ears rang and heart pounded like a sledge hammer. I couldn't think or speak. And some damn burning thing rose up my throat.

Ted watched me grab the lawn mower in my right hand, spin around two times, and fling the thing twenty feet in the air. It gracefully flipped around twice, before it bounced into the fence. I slid onto the ground, crushed. Good old Ted came over, and we just sat on the green clover and sobbed.

July 1, and 2

At 6:13 p.m.. on July 1, Terry arrived in California on a flight originally out of Saigon. On July 2, he was flown from California on TWA flight 270. It left at 4:30 p.m. Pacific time, and arrived in Kansas City at 6:15 p.m.. On that same day, a letter from a big Marine Corps General arrived at 316 S. Connecticut. It told Terry's Mom that in addition to the deep regrets of President Nixon, the Marine Corp honored Terry's heroism.

Terry would receive the Bronze Star. He had previously been recommended for the Navy Commendation Medal.

July 5. Concordia High School

Terry's funeral was attended by two thousand people, in our town of six thousand. The Mayor Rex Gerard proclaimed July 5 a citywide day of mourning, and requested all flags be flown at half staff. All town businesses closed for the funeral. It was held in the High School auditorium.

The eulogy was said by Father John Long. It was so hot in that auditorium. But that day everybody loved everybody, and nobody cared about the closeness, or the heat, or the adversity. We are, after all, sons and daughters of the pioneers and the Native Americans. Wendell, and other friends and family were the pall-bearers, out to Pleasant Hill Cemetery south of town, on the high west hill, above the newly constructed Community College.

Gary and I attended the High School service, and midway through Father Long's eulogy, I told Gary and other friends that I had to leave. Like many others, I couldn't stop the grieving, but that wasn't why I left. I had to figure out how to keep the spirit of Terry still alive in me in some way, and still say goodbye. I had to be alone for that. But it took more than a few days.

That night after the funeral, and into the next day as Gary and I camped out on the cots in our breezeway for the last time that I ever remember, we talked over the last years: the war, the loss, and the fear. The *Carmina* and what Mr. Miller was teaching us with that. When Terry picked up the baton at the League meet and raced his 220 leg beyond all ability for his age, not far off the world record. Why he blasted the State 220 prelim for the fastest time in the nation, and why he kept quiet about his bleeding heel all the way through the State Meet finals, and laughed off the spiked foot at the KU relays. Gary asked, "And how about that time when he went running out west with us younger guys instead of taking off with the seniors, what was all that?" Reflecting on Terry's life and death took us nearly forty years.

Postscript…The Light that shined for us onto the path back…

The effects of Terry's life and death are deep and long-lasting, echoing down the years, and taking many variations among our people. Everyone sorted out the lessons from this over the decades, and no one can fully recount the impacts. It was hard enough for us younger friends, yet we knew it was so much worse for Terry's classmates, best friends, Marine buddies, family, and Coach Betts. Some were enraged, and joined the military services, seeking patriotic recompense, or maybe revenge. So many suffered depression, and some of us turned for incomplete solace to that long road of habits that can numb the pain. All of us harbor the scar in one way or another, and make something from the scar. For some, Terry's death is the indescribable loss of war. So many wonderful people, and much great promise were lost. I think for most of us though, Terry and those like him helped us remember to reach for the better. The great loss of promise, paradoxically, was re-born. Many of us were powerfully stirred to live our lives "running like Terry", partly for him, and partly for our children. The lessons learned from sacrifice are many, and many persons will tell of them.

Grady Rainbow said what other Marine friends like Paul O'Connell wrote and said, "He was my best friend, the best you can have."

Wendell said, "The hard thing for me as a young man was the sound of the clicking of the bolt action rifles of the Marine Guard, before they fired the salute to Terry. It sounded like a certain-death trigger, for him and many of us. Eventually this was made easier by putting into action some things Terry had taught me. I learned to question things, in a searching way. This led me to be a teacher. I try not to preach my views to students but to stir up their interest to ask important questions and seek truth. The government had lied to us about this war, and learning to see past lies is important; that's one thing that Terry's sacrifice gave me. The other thing he left with me was his fearless, cheerful heart, free spirit, and devotion to friends. War is a waste. He was an inspiration to us all and his death a terrible loss. Yet we grew better, thanks to him."

Gary says, "Terry had a huge heart. It was so unusual for a senior to be such a friend to younger guys. He cared what happened to us. He treated me like his kid brother. He encouraged me to believe I could be as fast as him, and when later I was seriously injured I just didn't want to let him down...He was probably more misunderstood by some in the community because he didn't have an ideal life growing up, but he excelled in a way very few ever get a chance. He truly had a God-given talent so few share."

It is striking how the many dozens of friends, coaches, competitors, and family members when speaking of Terry will take a deep breath, and say the same things: "He was no choir-boy, but he was a friend...always cheerful, the first to greet others... more interested in their stories than talking about himself...he never put himself above others...a regular guy with a charismatic way who never put himself forward as a big deal... Carefree, a free spirit, unpredictable, filled with life...but...when Terry was angered at an injustice, or an injury to a friend...or called upon to help Marines on the battlefield...or as a competitor on the track...he'd 'flame on' with a fierceness and fire that took your breath away..."

I would tell my sons years later that it took me, and maybe most of us, a long time to make any sense of these things, and become stronger and better because of them. We didn't have all the parts of the puzzle either: we did not hear from Terry's Marine buddies until nearly forty years after Vietnam, about what happened in that very deadly place, when terrible odds were against Terry and the Company Mike Marines. Back home, they didn't explain things to people in those days, those silent Marine Guards at the funerals. I guess you can't rush some things. But forty years was a bit too long to wait.

The times to speak truths sneak up on us on quiet wings. If you are not careful, your moment passes, and you cannot go back and say what you need to set things right. Terry's amazing gift, and quiet, cheerful ways I believe helped us understand the value and power of working to *be* a friend, to say a kind word, to make the most of your blessings, even when the demons and the impossible are before you. It took a long time to sift through some of what he showed us about sacrifice, and the beauty of that thing called Hope. We can see more now, and we remember.

Not bad, Terry. Not so bad, after all...

* * *

A year after Terry's death, Grady Rainbow came to Kansas. He had served a second tour in Vietnam. "Tell my Mom" was Terry's request. Grady is a man of honor, among the Mike Company men of honor. He visited Terry's mother, and brought her to Concordia. There Grady visited a few friends at CHS, and took a letter to a younger friend that Terry had written. They visited Terry's grave, out on the high hill, where the clover grows forever and the sunsets never cease.

Epilogue:
2008 KU RELAYS. MEMORIAL
STADIUM, UNIVERSITY OF KANSAS,

Lawrence, Kansas

Mike Keegan and I hurried up from the concessions, with chili dogs, to watch the 2008 Kansas Relays. We deserved a break. Mike patiently survives, with wit and care, the days of a social studies teacher in a special high school for "troubled boys at risk". I needed a turn away from life's problems. Each year, I pilgrimage to the Kansas Relays at KU, and to the State High School Championship Meet in Wichita. It's a thing of the soul. It helps renew hope.

"Mike, the spectacle of the KU Relays will amaze you. To the relays come some of the world's fastest and best professional and Olympic tracksters, remarkable university and college teams, some crazy older dudes like us in Masters competition, and the most amazing high schoolers from many states around." Mike wasn't a hard sell. We bled KU blue anyway.

Along the toll road, covering the twenty miles from Topeka, I let Mike in on the story. The story of the spiked shoe, and Terry, and the 1967 KU Relays.

Mike, a native of Connecticut who "married the Angel he heard singing in the campus Mennonite Choir" at K-State, had fallen to the charms of the various beauties from the Flint Hills prairies in more ways than one. "Maybe it's a good thing folks from the coasts don't much come out here," Mike said. "The place would get ruined by all the 'get me some' attitude, the investment bankers, and SUVs."

"I'm sure the Dorothy stuff, and the tornado stories keep them out," I replied. In fact, chance of death by homicide or car wreck is far, far above the chance of death by tornado. I don't know of anybody actually killed by tornadoes. They mostly eat open fields.

The more I told Mike the stories of the 1967 KU Relays and the 1967 State Meet, the more he became intrigued. We sat in the east stands, chowing down on chili dogs, and pouring over the Meet guidebook for events and athlete summaries.

The day seemed to fly by, as we saw some of this year's best national marks set in the pole vault, and long jump, the open women's hurdles, and women's 100 meters. Things had changed drastically since the 1967 KU Relays...*the women and high school girls ruled track and field in equal measure to any of the men and boys.* Oh, things are different now.

Achieving basic equal opportunities for girls and women was a part of the struggle in 1967. How were these athlete-daughters of today to understand the restraints their mothers faced back then? Girls track started in 1967 at Concordia High School, with the girlfriends of the boys track team. Since then, under valiant coaches, especially Bob Baumann, the Red Silk girls have become a growing powerhouse of individual

State champs for girls track, with two team state championships. The CHS boys still rule the roost in track teams in the state.[17]

Teaching university students has led me at times to wonder if many young athletes and adults today don't know, or care, how the opportunities they enjoy were won not long ago in long, painful struggles in the times of their mothers and fathers. A few today, like Terry, just live to run. Fewer know the history of track, and run like they mean to carry hope forward to the next ones coming. Imagine today: forcing any teenage girl, much less a star female athlete to *kneel* before an Assistant Principal so he can check the length of her skirt? Any protest and she's tossed out of school, with no recourse? Throwing the fastest kid in America out of school because he smoked a cigarette, and asked questions of the Coach? In contrast, Mike sitting next to me, has to have an unlisted number, in order to avoid personal attacks by renegade former students or their gangs.

Things have changed, all-right.

We aging baby-boomers, Mike and I, carried on this discussion about these two vastly different times. Unlike the Vietnam war, there is no universal draft now for the Iraq war. Today, the vast majority of young men don't have to desperately live in the imminent, looming shadow of their own likely death in a jungle, or by global atomic destruction. How would today's athletes understand the feelings about track and running when you knew probably it was your last chance to run?

The Vietnam war killed untold numbers of Vietnamese, and twenty times or more the current worst weekly count of young Americans in the "war on terror". One cannot grasp the dilemmas and horrors they faced. The U.S. Veterans were all young friends, the dead coming home in body bags, their stories not told, their lives and memory lost to history. Our old Coaches both Betts and Baumann frankly told me, "You almost can't find a way to motivate the youth today, and you sure can't discipline them or you'll get tossed out on your can by a whining parent, or a spineless school administrator." We would not want to wish a universal draft on young people today, to provide them discipline and motivation to study and stay in school. Yet we marvel at how different these motivational habits and circumstances are today.

"There's an upside, like equality for women, and a downside today like this other stuff, that comes out of our revolution back then, I guess. Here we are, chastened revolutionaries," Mike quipped, "forty years later, worrying about the youth, just like Coach Betts and George Ganstrom did at Ray's Café those many years ago." We laughed at ourselves. To everything, there *is* a season.

Inevitably, our conversation changed when the sprints and relays started up.

I urged Mike to follow me down to the track edge. I intended to explain to the poor guy, the science of baton passing, and the advantages of modern tracks and automatic timing. He was going to hear and see a blow-by-blow account of hurdles form, and starts in the sprints. He heard how track is most like mountain climbing...the beauty is in the suffering and the will to go on, and the devotion to teammates, and how track is a metaphor and training ground for life and death, and how mistakes can have monumental consequences. An amateur sports philosopher, I was.

But Mike was surprisingly intrigued by this drama, and I felt like a story-teller from ancient times transported to today.

At the end of the day, I checked the various times and marks recorded by the athletes in sprint and relay events. I did my meters to yards conversions. I carry those formulas in my head. As we were approaching the end of the events, and picking up to leave, I told him, "Mike, it's like this every year. I come here and go to the State Meet. The years that I can't, I check the papers. It never changes. The times of these high school athletes almost never equal or surpass Terry's times. Not at the KU Relays in 1967, but especially not at that State Meet. Oh, once in awhile, one guy spins past Terry in the 100, maybe. Or the 400, maybe. They do have rubber tracks these days. But never on the same day do several athletes, much less a single guy, spin out the three sprints equal to Terry's three times at the State Meet in 1967. Terry remains, every year, the fastest all-time State Meet performer in the three sprints in a hundred years. And the question forces itself: What about the split in the bottom of the heel, bleeding at the State Meet? Or the spiked foot? How would these challenges be faced today?"

We shook our heads at these questions, and at the conversions on the sheet. It is the same, every year.

* * *

On the way home, KU disappeared in our rear view mirror. We could see in the distance, beyond Topeka, *one of those sunsets*. Spiraling towers of glowing smoke and tongues of flame licked the horizon. It was late April. The Flint Hills were burning against the back-drop of a western sunset.

Mike pointed. "Drive out there, Chris. We're going out there."

We drove to mile marker 343 on Interstate 70, west of Topeka, the exact spot where cultural geographers mark the true beginnings of the Far West.

This is where the trees end, and the first giant cattle ranch appears on the south side. The vast Flint Hills prairies rise up before your eyes, and the soul of the West in the sky and the buttes stand before you in ageless, wordless splendor.

We drove to the top of one of the great hills on a gravel road, and watched the evolution of colors that stands no rival on this third rock from a star. The illuminated, twisting smoke-pillars of many colors, and tongues of prairie fire reached to the emerging stars, through the vast rainbow-hued sunset.

Here, where the sky rules the world, I told Mike the final story of Terry, at the one-time only "Super Meet of Champions" in Wichita, one week after the 1967 State Meet. Here all the Wichita coaches of the big Wichita schools combined their best athletes to be "their high school team" of 880 relay runners. This was possibly the fastest half-mile relay high school team in America, an All-Wichita team rigged up from different schools. Of course, there were the other single school, true Class champion teams, too. But obviously, our Class A team of House and Company was a target. There were many possible, unspoken reasons: big school jealousy, the Black Power times, the legacy of Wichita track schools, politics. Who knows?

"Our team almost scratched at the last, to protest the 'stacked deck', but after heated discussions, we decided to take on the All-Wichita team," reports Eagle Man Charlie Switzer.

I told Mike of *the two photographs*. One of them says "photo by Jim Ryun", who was the free-lance photographer of the Wichita Eagle-Beacon, on May 27. *The* Jim Ryun. The photos show in the 880 Relay at the "super meet", that the All-Wichita team baton was passed by Maurice King of Wichita East (the third fastest prep hurdler in America) to Marcus Walker of Wichita East, the team anchor, the fastest 120 yard prep hurdler in America. At the baton pass, the All-Wichita super-team was only two yards ahead of the CHS Red Silks, from "little Concordia." The moment of fate had come, and House was out to cook them. (See photos).

The photos show Eagle Man Chuck Switzer trying desperately to pass the baton to House. The problem was that Maurice King after his pass on the straight-away to Marcus Walker, somehow "fell" *and* rolled sideways across the lane, directly in front of Chuck, interfering with the pass to Terry. Rules dictate that another team interfering with a pass is automatically disqualified. The photos show King splayed out in front of Chuck, and Chuck trying to hurdle him. Of course, no disqualification of the Wichita team was forthcoming.

So Again. For a third time in the year, the impossible was thrown at Terry and Chuck. Chuck had to slow down to hurdle King, and was raked across his leg by Kings 3/4 inch cleats. Even so, Eagle Man Chuck was not to be thwarted this time. *He held on to the baton*, stumbling but continuing. *Again*, House slowed down and turned back to securely pick up the baton, and then he turned...*And took-off.*

Walker now was a dozen yards ahead. Walker, the fastest high school hurdler in America.

"Something important happened in those two crazy times..." I told Mike, "When Terry in Vietnam, under fire, led the last point team down the mountain, went to pick up the fallen phone and call for help, only to fall to sniper fire. When in his last race two years before, Terry fought the impossible and gained on Walker, like a greyhound on a rabbit. Terry was still closing on him at the tape, only to fall a yard short. Mike, for almost forty years, we hardly knew anything about what happened to Terry over there. And over there, they didn't know much about Terry over here. Two worlds apart, and Terry was facing down the impossible."

Mike was quiet, for a long time. We watched the miracle in the sky before us. When the skies turned past purple, and the stars to glittering silver, he replied, "You get to where you can see pretty far, out here."

PHOTOS

Yearbook photo Terry

Terry Householter Sprinting, 1967

880 Relay Team 1967

1967 Championship Track Team

TRACK TEAM BACK ROW: T. Easter, A. Logan, L. Nelson, R. Goodwin, D. Truedell, R. Blochlinger, M. Campbell, G. Betts, S. Thompson, R. Radcliff, J. Tyler. 4TH ROW: M. Gillan, B. Dutton, L. Hanson, M. Hepperly, B. Johnston, E. Yarnell, J. Strait, G. Hattan, D. Vignery, J. Minard, Coach Farber. 3RD ROW: J. Bauer, J. Hotaling, J. Gould, D. Swiercinsky, D. Holechek, S. Wilson, D. Winters, K. Liedtke, C. Hamilton, A. Luecke, G. Diebel. 2ND ROW: D. Burt, S. Townsend, B. J. O'Brien, S. Clark, R. Green, D. Johnson, W. Ganstrom, P. Foster, B. McDaniel, D. Rivers, Coach Frohardt. 1ST ROW: R. Reeves, B. Snyder, C. Foster, G. Tracy, L. Pounds, R. Smith, T. Clark, C. Switzer, S. Collins, P. Pickard, J. Jones, Coach Betts.

1967 CHS Complete Track Team

Bill Dotson, 1958 CHS Senior

Coach Herschel Betts 1967

Wichita's Maurice King slides along track after exchange of baton with Marcus Walker.

Wichita Super Meet 880 Relay 1967,
Photo Wichita Eagle-Beacon, May 27

Wichita's Maurice King fell after handing
off the baton in the 880 relay as Terry
Householter (left) grabbed the baton for
Concordia. Wichita won the race anyway.

Wichita Super Meet 880 Relay photo two

268

Terry, Marine Bootcamp 1968

MAJOR CHARACTERS, REAL AND FICTIONAL.

Herschel Betts in 1969 left Coaching and became Principal, and later the School Superintendent of Oberlin, Kansas Public Schools. He farms near Oberlin today with his wife Jody.

Byron Beauchere is a composite fictional character.

Charlie Blosser was a World War I flying ace, and Concordia businessman.

Mario Brichalli is a regional manager for State Farm Insurance.

Tim Brady is for-real, living proudly in Clyde, Kansas. He is a United States Marine veteran of Vietnam, and a businessman.

Greg Bryant is a community college professor of English literatures.

Grant McCoy is a fictional character.

Steve Collins was a state meet 100 yd sprint champion in 1968 and a state meet 880 relays champ in 1966, '67 and '68. He is a successful contractor.

Ken Campbell was a state meet 880 relays champion in 1966, and is a United States Marine Vietnam veteran.

Tom Clark is a college instructor and business consultant in Texas.

Gary Dieble was a state meet 880 relays team champion in 1968. He is a successful business man with a career in railroads and real estate.

Charles Dixon was a medal winning tennis champion, and is a prominent Methodist Minister in Hutchison, Kansas.

Bill Dotson was inducted into the KU Sports Hall of Fame in 2008. He held national, NCAA and world records in middle distances and distance relays. He holds more University of Kansas men's best track performance marks than any athlete in KU track history, except for Jim Ryun. See Appendix A.

Coach Farber is a fictional character.

Evelyn Freeburne is a fictional character.

Coach Lou Frohardt was government teacher and track coach at CHS, and also at Cloud County Community College, where he is social sciences department chair.

Peter Foster was a record-setting state meet 180 yd hurdles champion in 1969, one of the fastest five in Kansas history. He is a prominent financial advisor.

George Ganstrom was a lifelong banker and Scout leader in Concordia, and passed away in 2007. Mrs. Louise Ganstrom still graces our lives in Concordia.

Wendell Ganstrom was a record-setting state meet 880 relays champion in 1967 and 1969 and is a community college professor and advisor.

Ron Green was a state meet champion in the 120 yd (110 m) hurdles in 1969 and is an attorney in Kansas.

Mrs. Isabelle Hamilton was a short story writer, and personnel administrator, and feminist before her time. Husband Ryland is a Navy Veteran welder, residing in Concordia and Topeka.

Roger Hamilton is a third generation Chrysler salesman in Manhattan, Kansas.

Sue Hamilton is a deputy sheriff for the Boulder County Sheriff's department in Colorado.

Louis Hanson is a prominent general practice osteopathic physician in Maine.

The Hanson twins, Rachel and Rebecca, respectively became a Lutheran priest, and a college professor.

Father Hotaling is a retired Anglican priest.

Skip Householter is retired, and lives in Texas.

"Hondo" Douglas Johnson is the chief ranch manager for the billionaire Ted Turner and his gigantic wilderness ranch in New Mexico.

Jerry Jones was a state meet medal winning relays star in 1968, and works as a sports broadcaster in Kansas.

Jack Kasl was a reasonably decent spear-chucker, and became a prominent Clinical Psychologist (Ph.D.), residing in Minnesota.

Assistant Principal Dick Kramer is a fictional character.

Don Liedtke is an executive accounting manager for a major corporate U.S. hospital chain in Tennessee.

Father Melvin Long is a Catholic priest in California.

Alan Luecke has multiple graduate degrees in jazz and rock history (BA, MA, ABD), owns a house painting company and a boat building business and plays in jazz and funk banks in Kansas City.

John Luecke lives happily on the grand prairies east of Concordia.

Bick Mick is a composite fictional character.

Everett Miller since 1968 is the choral music professor and director at Cloud County Community College.

Mrs. Norwest and West are fictional characters, based on real mothers.

Lyle Pounds coached cross country for 27 years at Concordia High School, where he still teaches.

Grady Rainbow is a United States Marine Vietnam War Veteran and lives in his beloved Oklahoma.

Brett Swaggart and his buddy Axel are fictional characters.

Charles "Eagle Man" Switzer was a record setting state meet 880 relays champion in 1966 and 1967, and works for the City of Salina, Kansas.

Enoch Twuertweiller is a fictional character.

Audrey Zimmerman was the youthful girl of my dreams, but a fictional character.

Zorro was never identified, but some suspected Miss Fletcher the English teacher.

Appendix A
KANSAS MISSING? THE INCREDIBLE SAGA OF BILL DOTSON AND ARCHIE SAN ROMANI JR.

A classic example of Kansas overdue to get balanced and fair notice comes in the spectacular story of Bill Dotson and Archie San Romani, Jr. The U.S. Track and Field News "annual reports" always list the greatest athletic feats and times each year, in track. The nation was riveted in the '50s and '60s by the quest to break the 4 minute mile barrier. No high school athlete had ever come close to this mark.

In 1958, *two of the top five fastest high school milers in the nation were from Kansas,* and all were closing in on the 4-minute barrier: Bill Dotson and Archie San Romani, Jr.

Bill Dotson was a farm kid from tiny Jamestown who ran and graduated from nearby small town Concordia High School. Bill started running as a kid, when his dad's pickup broke down, and so he herded cattle from field to field by running over the vast plains!

Archie San Romani Jr, was the son of 1936 Olympics great and world mile record holder Archie San Romani Sr. Archie Jr. ran out of big-city Wichita, and the famous Wichita East High School track program, the same high school his father ran for twenty five years before.

Archie's father was Kansas' Glen Cunningham's great rival in taking turns breaking the world mile record in the 1930s, and Archie Sr. won fourth in the 1936 Olympic mile. So in 1958 the San Romani name and the novelty of the "father-son" legacy, both from the same big-city high school, caught some national media attention. Out of this, the Archie Jr vs Bill Dotson rivalry became the modern "big city vs farm boy" drama, and a dramatic re-visit to the Archie Sr vs Cunningham epic battles in the 1930s, all over again.

The in-state newspapers and the national media chronicled the career-long rivalry of the early stages of the two national stars. But the "national" media was not so attentive when Bill, and Archie later dominated university and AAU meets. The 1958 US Track and Field News dutifully reported their top ranked times in their annual "high school bests" list. But it ran no story in its magazine on the great rivalry when the two Kansas boys counted for 2 of 5 of the years' top high school milers. Like Illinois Bill Cornell and Tom O'Hara, Bill Dotson and Archie Jr. from Kansas all became national High School, AAU, NCAA, U.S. and world record holders, and Pan American and Olympic greats. But these mid-west superstars were served with much less national attention compared to the press coverage lavished on their west coast rivals, the Oregon duo of Dyrol Burleson and the older Jim Beatty. Why the neglect of these greats? Perhaps Big Coast bias?

Bill was a year older than Archie. In high school, the storied rivalry played out in only two show-downs between the two youth superstars. In cross country, sophomore Archie won the 2 mile against Bill at the 1956 State meet, but then Bill won the revenge match by 30 yards in 1957. Then at the stellar KU Relays in April 1958, at age 17 years, Bill Dotson was the first to break the 28 year old Kansas and former national high school mile record of Glen Cunningham (4:24.7) with Bill's new state and KU Relays record of 4:20.2.Archie Jr. answered back to Bill in June, when at the Junior National Olympics in Wichita, Archie ran 4:18.2, but absent his great Concordia rival. Bill had also run 4:18.2 but missed this showdown with Archie in the National Junior Olympics, because Bill could not get his parent's permission to leave the family farm's harvest work in June, or find a ride to Wichita to take on Archie again. The re-match would have to wait.

A year later, Archie broke Bill's KU Relays high school mile record (not running against Dotson) by one tenth of a second. And after high school, Archie unofficially lowered the national high school mark to 4:08.9 at the Junior Olympics again in June. Dotson himself, had gone off to KU on a track scholarship, but then Archie in 1959 chose Oregon over KU. So the great rivalry deepened, as they became members of the top two rival distance track programs in the nation, Kansas vs Oregon.

Archie returned on his own to the KU Relays in 1961 to fire up a final showdown, only to lose to Bill in a spectacular photo finish in the mile. Bill dueled Dyrol Burleson twice in inches for the NCAA championship mile in 1961 (4:02.4) and in '62, both pushing the 4 minute mark. Burleson hit 3:59.8 in '62 with Bill inches behind in 4:00.6 But a week later, Bill returned the compliment to top Burleson's time, and also topped the rivalry with Romani when Bill became the first Kansan and Big 8 athlete and only the 6th man in the world to run a sub-4 minute mile, at a great 3:59.0 at the 1962 AAU national open championships. Bill was the only collegian fast enough to place that week amidst the greatest Olympian milers in the world in the so-called "super meet" of milers. Bill placed 4th, basically in the world, in his 3:59.0 mile, in a tight group just barely behind the winner, the older Beatty at 3:57.9 Archie didn't try for the meet.

In 1963 at the March Chicago Daily News meet, Bill became the third man in the world (a month after Beatty and Chicago's Tom O'Hara) to run the extremely difficult sub-4-minute *indoor* mile, a feat that is rare even today. Bill ran it on a difficult 11 lap indoor track. (Today, indoor tracks are easier at 8 laps per mile/1500 meters). This remarkable feat, Archie never matched. Archie became the second Kansas miler to hit a sub-4 minute mile later in June of 1964, a year after college, in his terrific best time of 3:57.6

In the 45 years since 1964, Archie still ranks 3rd fastest and Bill still ranks 5th fastest of all the thirteen Kansas born milers who have run under 4 minutes.

Amazingly, Bill's KU records still burn very high and bright: Almost 50 years later, Bill still ranks second of all KU track men athletes with 7 individual and relay records listed on

KUs All Time Men's Best Outdoor and Indoor Performance Charts (_Jim Ryun has 16_). Bill still holds the second fastest KU outdoor mile, the second fastest outdoor 1500 meters, the second fastest indoor mile, and the ninth fastest indoor 1000 meters records, all of which were run on the old, slower dirt tracks. His four relays team records were American national records, and are still among the very top KU best times. Bill's fastest half mile 880 yards (800 meters) was a blistering 1:46.5 (1:45.29) on an 880 anchor leg of the KU two-mile relay team at the 1962 AAU national Modesto, California meet. When compared to official best KU outdoor 800 m race times, this relay leg would be second only to Jim Ryun's best (1:43.69) and is still faster than today's Big 12 record (1:47.12), the KU Relays record (1:48.22) and the KU Memorial Stadium record (1:47.79).

Both world-class milers became half forgotten when Jim Ryun arrived at KU in 1964. One wonders what Bill's and Archie's marks would have been if they too could have ran on the faster asphalt or rubber tracks like all those who came later, for Bill and Archie ran only in cinder and dirt.

For health reasons, Bill retired in 1964 after placing fourth in the Pan American Games 800 meters final (in a spectacular recovery from having been bumped to the back of the pack by a Venezuelan who was disqualified). That slender Kansas farm boy Bill and his rival Archie _could run._

In 1967, ten years later, the spectacular high school sprint achievements of Terry Householter were also less noticed by the track national establishments, focused and located on the coasts.

APPENDIX B

The True Fastest Sprint/Hurdles Times at the Kansas High School Outdoor State Track Meet since 1909 (Gold Medals Finals or Prelim State Meet Records)

Conversions +.24 hand time added after 1969 rubber tracks to events 200 m or less +.14 to times to events over 200 m. **y** yards **w** wind-aided disallowed **vp** verified prelim **st** state meet class record. **stb** state meet best **atkb** alltime kansas best   by Prof. Chris Hamilton, Washburn University, Topeka Ks.

<u>Multiple Individual Gold Medal Winners of Multiple Sprint Events (Eras)</u>: Last year of Cinder tracks 1966; asphalt 1967-1969; rubber 1970 and after).

BY YEAR and EVENTS:		200 Meter/220 Yds Conversions:	100 Meters/100 Yds Conversions:	400 Meters/440 Yds Conversions:	110m/120yz	180yd	300m
1938	Dick Overfield	Independ.	21.1m 21.3y st	10.7m 9.8y st	—	—	
1940	Wallace Hulse	Wich. East	21.0m 21.2y	10.9m 10.0y 51.5m 51.8y	—	—	
1950	Dick McGlinn	Immaculata	21.1m 21.3y	11.1m 10.2y		—	
1955	Duane McIntire	Gardner	21.0m 21.2y	—		—	
1955	Charlie Tidwell	Independence	20.9m 21.1y	10.7m 9.8y			18.5 st
1962	Henry Wiebe	Newton	20.8m 21.0y stb	—		—	
1962	Bob Hanson	Wichita East	21.2m 21.4y			—	
1965	Bill Kimble	Hoisington	20.9m w 21.1yw	10.5m 9.6y			19.5 180 y
1967	Terry Householter	Concordia	21.1m 21.3y vpst	10.7m 9.8y	48.6m 48.9y vp st		
1969	Frank Johnson	Wyandotte	21.3m 21.5y	10.5m 9.6y	—		
1969	Mike Larrimore	Wellington	21.3m 21.5y		47.7m 48.0y vp st		
1969	Anthony Glenn	Sumner	21.3m 21.5y	10.5m 9.6y	—		
1970	James Carter	Wich. S.East	—	10.1m / 10.44 cm vp st	9.3y / 9.54 c **	—	

– 1980 conversion to meters –

			200 Meter/220 Yds	100 Meters/100 Yds	400 Meters/440 Yds	110m/120yz	180yd	300m
1983	Doug Hedrick	S.Mission.E.	21.4m 21.6y-		48.2m 48.5y			38.2 st
1991	Wendell Gaskin	KC-Wash.	21.29m 21.49y	10.59m 9.69y	46.76m 47.06y stb atkb	13. 90 110m st		
1996	Mario Ponds	Wichita S.East	21.4m 21.6y	10.36 m vps st 9.46 y				
2004/05	Jarred Huske	Highland Park		10.7 m 9.8 y		13. 91 110 m		
2006	Terrance Thomas	SM East		10.4m 9.5y				37.7 st

APPENDIX B

Approximate Fastest Kansas High School State Track Meet Multiple Individual Gold Medal Winners

Year	Name	School	200 Meter/220 Yds	100 Meters/100 Yds	400 Meters/440 Yds	110m/120y	180yd	300m
First - Rank Overall Fastest Athletes:								
1955	Henry Wiebe	Newton	20.8m 21.0y atb	—	—	14.5		
1965	Bill Kimble	Hoisington	20.9m 21.1y w	10.5m 9.6y st			19.5	
1967	Terry Householter	Concordia	21.1m 21.3y vp st	10.7m 9.8y	48.6m 48.9y vp st			
1991	Wendell Gaskin	KC–Washington	21.29m 21.49y	10.59m 9.7y	46.76m 47.06 y atb st			
1955	Charlie Tidwell	Independence	20.9m 21.1y	10.7m 9.8y			18.5 st	
1969	Frank Johnson	Wyandotte	21.1m 21.3y	10.5m 9.6y	—			
1955	Duane McIntire	Gardner	21.0m 21.2y	10.8m 9.8y				
1969	Mike Larrimore	Wellington	21.3m 21.5y	—	47.7m 48.0y vp st			
1968	Bob Bornkessel	* Sh. Miss. No.	21.5m 21.7y	—		13. 8m/14.0 ystb	18.1 atkb	
1969	Anthony Glenn	Sumner	21.3m 21.5y	10.5m 9.6y				
1938	Dick Overfield	Independence	21.1m 21.3y	10.7m 9.8y st		—		
1940	Wallace Hulse	Wichita East	21.0m 21.2y	10.9m 10.0y	51.5m 51.8y			
1983	Doug Hedrick	S.Mission.East	21.4m 21.6y		48.2m 48.5y	13. 90 m		38.2 st
2004/05	Jarred Huske	Highland Park	—	10.7 m 9.8 y	—	13. 91 m		37.7 st
Second - Rank Overall Fastest Athletes:								
1950	Dick McGlinn	Immaculata	21.1m 21.3y	11.1m 10.2y				
1967	Bob Bornkessel	S.Miss..No.	21.3m w 21.5y w	—				
1962	Bob Hanson	Wichita East	21.2m 21.4y	—		—	18.8 st	
1996	Mario Ponds	Wichita S.East	21.4m 21.6y	10.36 m vp st 9.46 y		—		
1970	James Carter	Wichita S.East		10.1 m / 10.44 cm vp st	9.3 y / 9.54 y **	—		
2006	Terrance Thomas	*SM East		10.4m 9.5y		—		

Other State champion medal or record times at the State are slower than these above.   * Bornkessel held the National High School record 400 meter hurdles of 49.8 seconds from 1968 until 2002. 1970 and after are rubber tracks, so hand-timing gaps are added to performances on rubber tracks from 1970 until FAT arrived.   Many of these athletes set state class or state meet records in Relays, in addition to multiple individual gold medals.

APPENDIX C

Fastest U.S. High School Sprinters, 1967
Best clocked times, 1967 (Multiple watches at practices, or
relay legs at meets, or other such as AAU off-season).*
*Best individual performance at official league or sanctioned
meet times only, 1967*

ALL THREE EVENTS

	100	220	440	Other
Jim Greene				
Eminence, Ky	9.4*	20.6 st*	47.2	
	9.4	*21.2*	*47.2*	
Terry Householter				
Concordia, Ks	9.4*	20.4*	48.0*	
	9.55	*21.3*	*48.9*	
Jimmy White				
Houston, Tex	9.5*	20.8 w*	47.6*	
	9.5	*21.2*	*47.6*	

TWO EVENTS

	100	220	440	Other
Mel Gray				
Santa Rosa, CA	*9.4*	*20.7*	--	
Larry Harbaugh				
Indianapolis, Ind	*9.2 w*	*20.5 st*	--	
Don Schneider				
Plainfield, NJ	--	*20.5 st*	--	
Bill Gaines				
Mull Hill, NC	9.3	20.6 st w*	100 meters 10.2*	
	9.3	*21.1w / 21.3*		
Dan Moore				
L.A.CA	*9.5*	*21.1 st*	--	
Johnny Gentry				
Odessa, Texas	*9.5*	*21.3*	--	
Aaron Thompson				
Opelousas, La.	*9.5*	--	*47.6*	
Juan Franceschi				
Ponce, Virginia	--	--	*46.8*	

Sources: DyeStat.com and/or newspaper records, coaches interviews.

END NOTES

1. See Appendix A.
2. In 1990, the Oasis was immortalized by Garth Brooks, in his song "Friends in Low Places", with the phrase "head on down to the Oasis", as one of Garth's drummers was from Concordia, and the Oasis lived for decades as a famous blues/country/rock bar in the old, 19th century Baron's Hotel. The Baron's was torn down in 1988.
3. Bob Hayes is still probably the fastest man in world history. He was clocked at an astounding 8.7 seconds in a hundred yard leg of a 4 x 100 yard relay, which converts to a 9.6 100 meters, which possibly was faster than Usain Bolt's 2008 astounding 9.69 100 meter world record at the 2008 Olympics.
4. John Riggins later broke the legendary Gayle Sayers University of Kansas football rushing records, and was an NFL great running back.
5. The $1 trillion inflation adjusted total costs of the Vietnam War divided by 12 years adjusted to 1967 dollars is $80 billion annual cost, which in 2008 is equivalent to $388 billion annual cost. The annual costs of the Viet Nam war versus the on-going Iraq war are about the same per year in inflation adjusted dollars.
6. The Black Panthers, of course, were the embodiment of radical strength and machismo, in the world of African- American political revolutionaries. For a white kid to wear them was not a subtle statement of courage and power.
7. The practice, in those days, before "automatic timing" emerged in the late 1970s, was to take the average time, and ROUND UP to the nearest tenth of a second. The advocates and rules of today's electronic timing which call for the addition of the hand-timing "gap" for comparisons of old marks versus new do not conveniently recall or take into account this old code of practice, in comparing the great runners of old vs today. On this day, a track in truly pathetic conditions scientifically stole at least two tenths of a second from the times of all contestants including Terry, compared to a rubberized track. The terrible track conditions neutralize any argument for further "hand timing" deductions. A reasonable average estimate is that Terry ran a legitimate 9.4 or 9.45 (10.2 100 m) *on this slower track,* despite the official "rounded-up" 9.6. This was .2 better than the all-state best time, and virtually equal to the national best mark. With modern blocks on a rubberized track, it is anyone's guess how fast Terry would have run this 100 yards, but 9.4 or 9.3 (10.2 or 10.1 meters) is not an unreasonable estimate. "Modernists" who yet still recognize how fast Bob Hayes and Jim Ryun ran in the face of the similar track limitations of this older era, should be reasonable enough to grant the same recognition for high school and college era greats of these times and not simply "retire" the old times. Instead, efforts should be made to post the

older times next to the new ones, with rough equivalent conversions, as is done by the State of Michigan high school coaches association. See Appendix B.

8. This tied the all-time state of Kansas best mark, at that time, and probably surpassed it. See footnote 7.

9. The individual records set by *high schoolers* at the 1967 KU Relays tied, exceeded, or came very close to the best university and Olympic open athletes times at the 1967 Relays in the following events: 100 yard dash (Householter); the 120 yard/110 meter hurdles (Walker, King); the high jump (Carrington), and the mile (Barrati, Niehouse). Never before, or since, even in the days of Jim Ryun, was there a comparable prep year at the KU Relays. Later NCAA champions and leaders would come from this prep list, including the incomparable hurdler Bob Bornkessel of Shawnee Mission North (who held the US 400 m prep record of 49.8 seconds until 2002), and his close competitors Marcus Walker, and Maurice King of Wichita East, and Presston Carrington of Topeka. These account for 4 of the top 5 1967 United States prep hurdlers, and 4 of the top 5 all-time fastest Kansas high school hurdlers, all competing in a single year. Bob Barrati and Jim Niehouse were NCAA middle distance stars in college, as was Dale Alexander of Bogue who tied Terry Householter for state 440 times. Dale later was the fastest Big 8 400 meter man over several decades time. Terry's story continues...

10. Truly, these were the fastest hurdlers in the nation, all in one race as relay anchormen. In fact, Marcus Walker had the second fastest 120 yard hurdle (110 meter) time in the nation that year at 13.7 (13.6m), and his team mate Maurice King was third in the nation at 13.8 (13.7m). Bornkessel who was just a junior in 1967, was second in the nation at the 180 yard hurdles, and as a senior Bornkessel set and held the US National 400 meter prep record of 49.8 seconds, which was unmatched for *thirty four years*, from 1968 to 2002. Carrington ran 14.3s consistently. See Dye stat records online at: http://www.dyestatcal.com/ATHLETICS/TRACK/TFN/1967tfn.htm

11. The famed fullback John Riggins of the NFL, and of the 1969 KU Orange Bowl team.

12. The accounts and quotes here are based on four main sources: the memoirs of Grady Rainbow which comprise his History of the Marines of Company M, 3rd Battalion, 5th Marine Regiment, 1st Division, (copyright, unpublished); from Grady's gracious taped interviews conducted by this author in the spring of 2007; and from information in the public realm online of the memories of Mike Company members at various websites; and from Terry's letters to home. http://www.stripes.com/photoday/gonoi/index.html Operation Pipestone Canyon photos http://www.securenet.net/3rdbn5th/mike35/oconnell.htm Paul O'Connell online. http://www.combatwife.net/mmrainbow.htm Grady Rainbow memoirs, online http://www.khesanhvets.org/Section 5/section 5.htm summary of Pipestone Canyon operations OPERATIONS OF U.S. MARINE FORCES, VIETNAM (0073 pages) [01 June 1969] Item Number: 1201002036 http://www.virtualarchive.vietnam.ttu.edu

13. This incomparable beauty has been captured recently by National Geographic. What took them so long. *See the photos:* http://ngm.nationalgeographic. com/2007/04/tallgrass-prairie/richardson-photography.

14. These events in the sky, and other experiences in natural settings, stimulate creativity, socially cohesive values and intelligence in children. Current science is examining whether a host of behavioral disorders in current urban young generations are due to insufficient exposure to nature and the outdoors. See the New York Times Bestseller: The Last Child in the Woods: Saving Our Children from Nature-Deficit Disorder, Richard Louv, April 2008. Long before the 1990s when atmospheric scientists "discovered" these startling color displays called red sprites and blue jets over high plains thunderstorms, the native Americans and we high plains euro-immigrants have been mesmerized by them for untold generations. These are among those "little gifts" out here which remain less known on the Coasts.

15. Three verified times in 200 meters have been faster in the official national high school records. See: dyestat.com But the 220 is longer than the 200 meters, and the -.2 second conversion would leave Terry's 220 relay leg at about the same time, from a standing start. Of course, this can never be legitimately compared to the verified times, partly due to handtiming inaccuracies, and the uncertainties of a timed relay leg. But then, Houston McTear's reported informal times of 5.8 seconds in the 60 yards in 1972 makes printed due notice as a matter of interest, and so should this. As at the earlier KU Relays, tremendous athletes competed in the 1967 Kansas State Meet, among the best in Kansas and the nation's prep history. Four of the six nation's fastest high school hurdlers in 1967 were from Kansas high schools, competing in the State Meet. One of them, Bob Bornkessel, is generally regarded as the fastest U.S. high school hurdler in history. Bornkessel ran an unbelievable 49.8 seconds in the 400 meter in 1968, a national high school record for 34 years, not broken until 2002 when it was deliberately assaulted under the best of conditions. Another of these hurdlers, and long-jumper, Preston Carrington of Topeka High, won fifth place in the long jump in the 1972 Olympics. John Riggins, a sprinter, was the leading fullback of the 1969 Orange Bowl KU Football team and one of the greatest fullbacks in NFL history. Jim Niehouse and Bob Barratti, dueling wizards of middle distance, were among the top seven fastest prep kids in the mile, half mile and two-mile in the nation in 1967, and were NCAA stars in their college years. Dale Alexander was, for many years, the Big 8 and Big 12 record holder in the 400 meter for Kansas State; in high school he traded and tied Terry Householter for 440 Kansas best times. See Appendix C. Terry's best times were among the nation's top three fastest sprinters in all three sprints considered (the 100, 220 and 440) in 1967, vying with the also incredible Jim Greene of Eminence, Kentucky, and Jim White of Houston, Tex. Close to these three leaders of three events were several two-event stars: Bill Gaines (N.J.), Aaron Thompson (Louisianna), and Mel Gray & Dan Moore (Calif). In 100 years of Kansas State Track Meet champions, Terry and Wendell Gaskin

are the fastest State Meet champions in marks in all three sprint categories at the State Meet (100, 220/200, 440/400. See Appendix C). The other great State high school meets in the nation include Texas, California, Illinois, New York, and Michigan. Terry's preliminary time of 21.3 (21.1 200 meters) remains one of the top three fastest times in State Meet history, in preliminaries and finals. His State Meet final the next day of 21.6 was run under great adversity (see Epilogue), and was judged to be wind-aided. This was not true of the preliminaries, see Topeka Daily Capitol, pg. 17, May 20, 1967. See Appendix C.

16. Quotations herein are from Grady Rainbow's unpublished History and Memoirs of Company M, 3rd Battallion, 5th Marines, First Marine Division, Vietnam, and his oral accounts. The battle information is from these accounts, and on-line military histories of Operation Pipestone Canyon. See References in footnote 14.

17. Since 1960, at the State Meet in their class 4 (formerly class A before 1978) the Concordia High School boys track team owns more championships and runner-up placements than any school in the state. They own 39 times in the top 20 finishing teams, 20 times in the top 5, and 13 state team championships. "The Wall" at CHS lists many dozens of individual state champions. Individual champions have been numerous especially in the sprints, the pole vault, the javelin, and relay teams, but also in the hurdles, shot put and discus. Only the Liberal, Kansas class 5 boys track team owns about as many championships, the two dominant historic track dynasties of the state. See: Yeas for 1960 to 1979 added to Tom Brosius, "Comparison of Kansas State Track and Field Results, 1979 to 2005"; contact: tbrosius@cox.net

4265974

Made in the USA
Lexington, KY
09 January 2010